TERROR MAN
1

Written by: Dongwoo Han
Art by: Jinho Ko

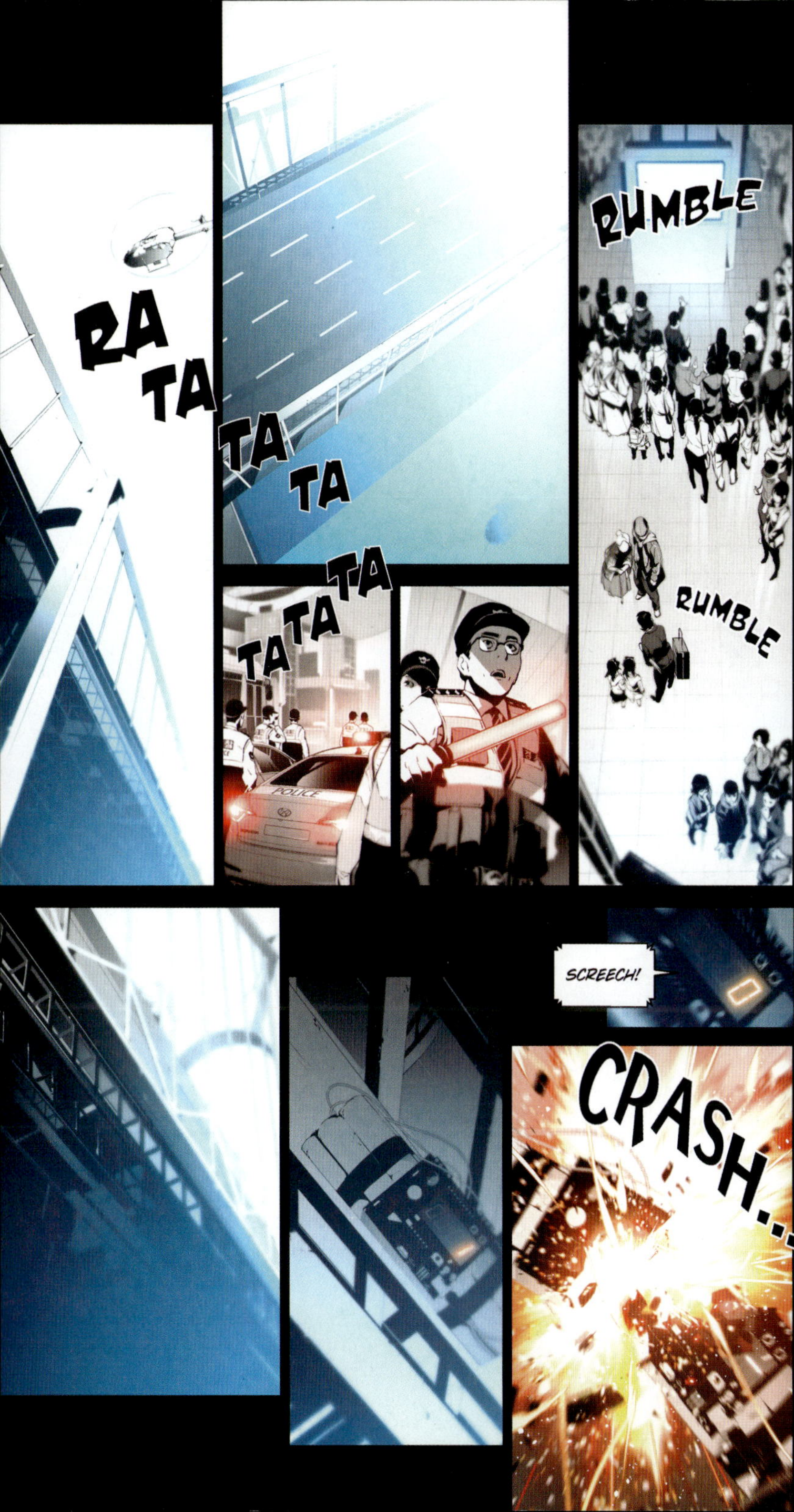
RA
TA
TA
TA
TA
TA
TA
POLICE
RUMBLE
RUMBLE
SCREECH!
CRASH...

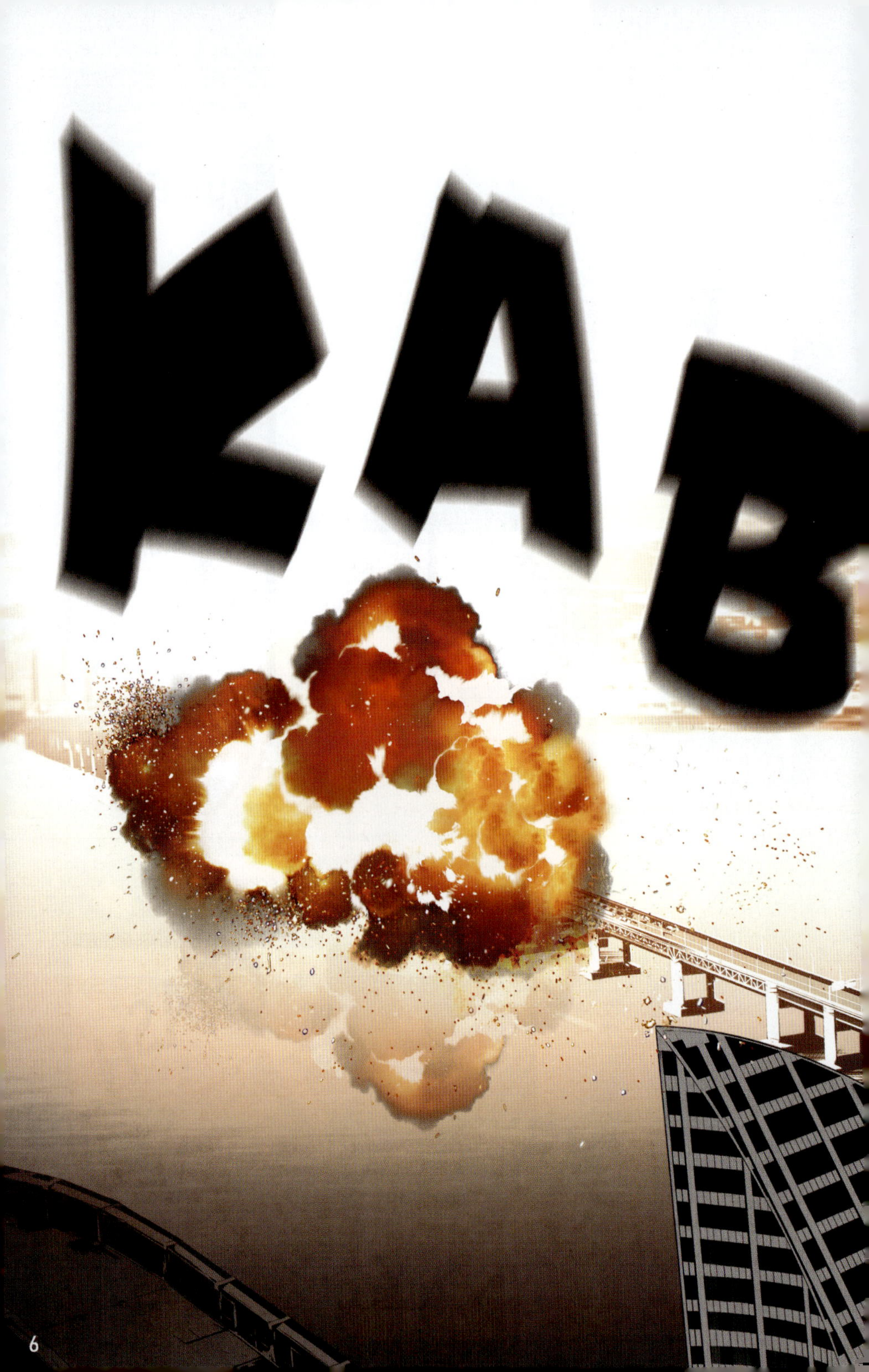
KAB

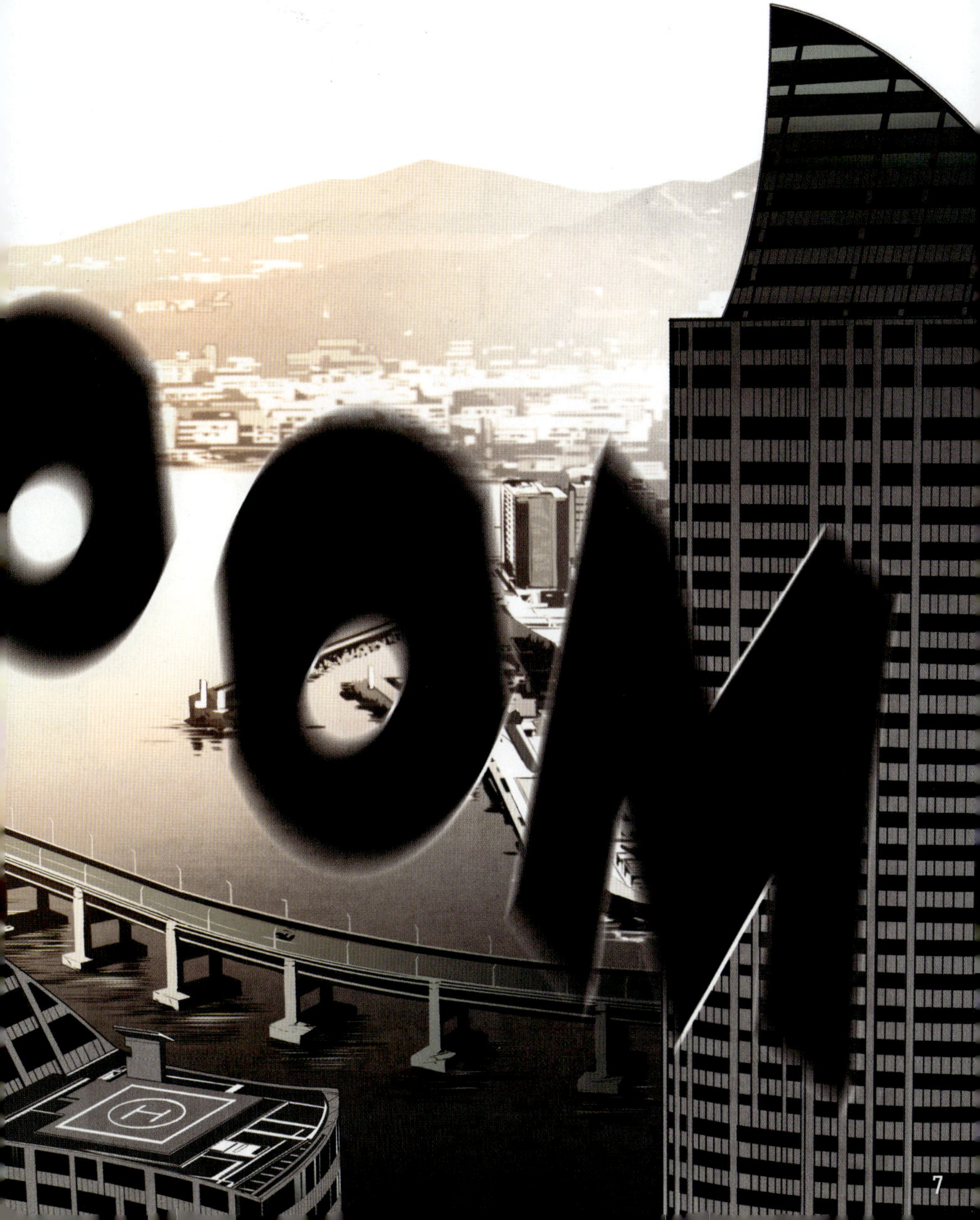
OOM

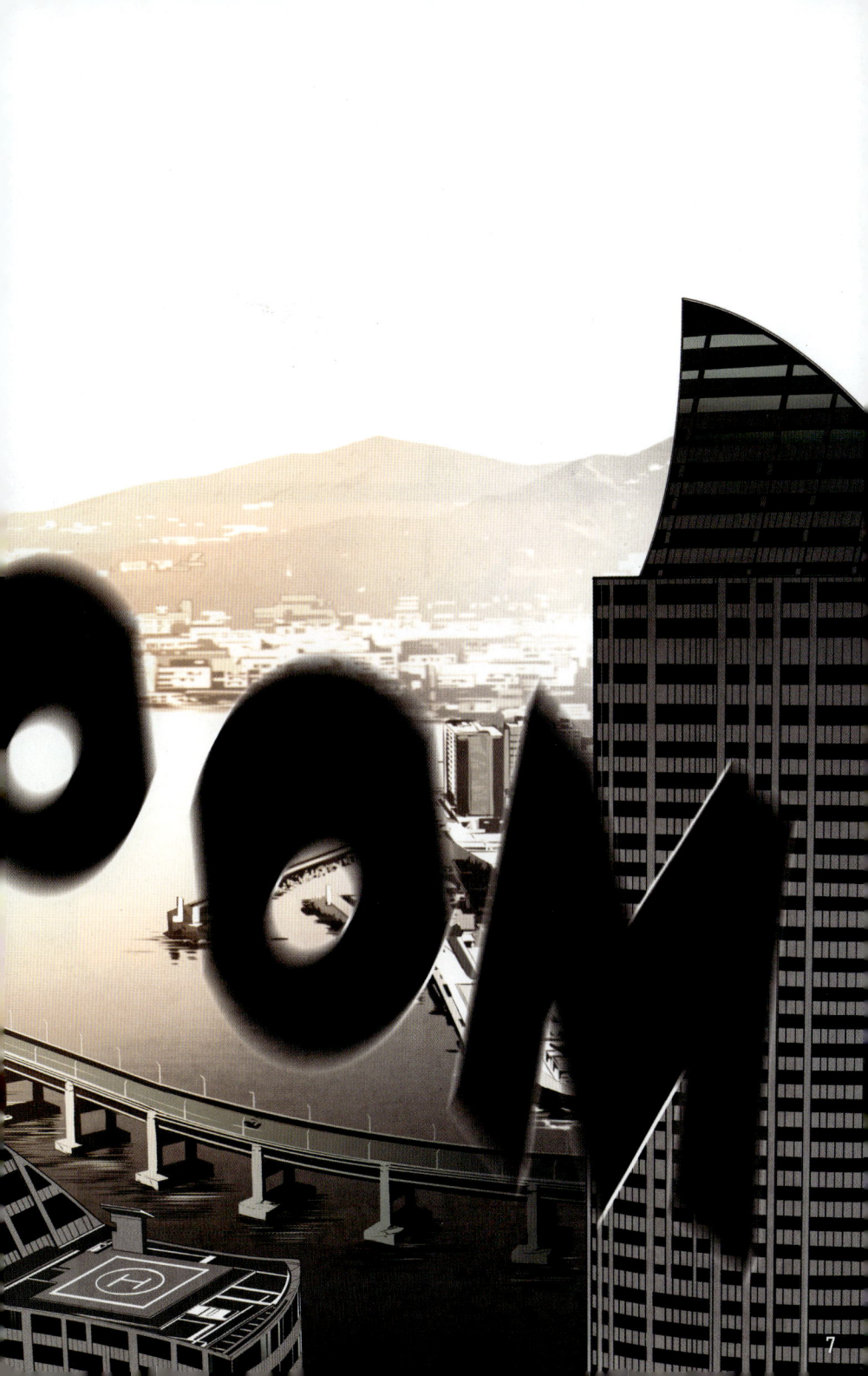

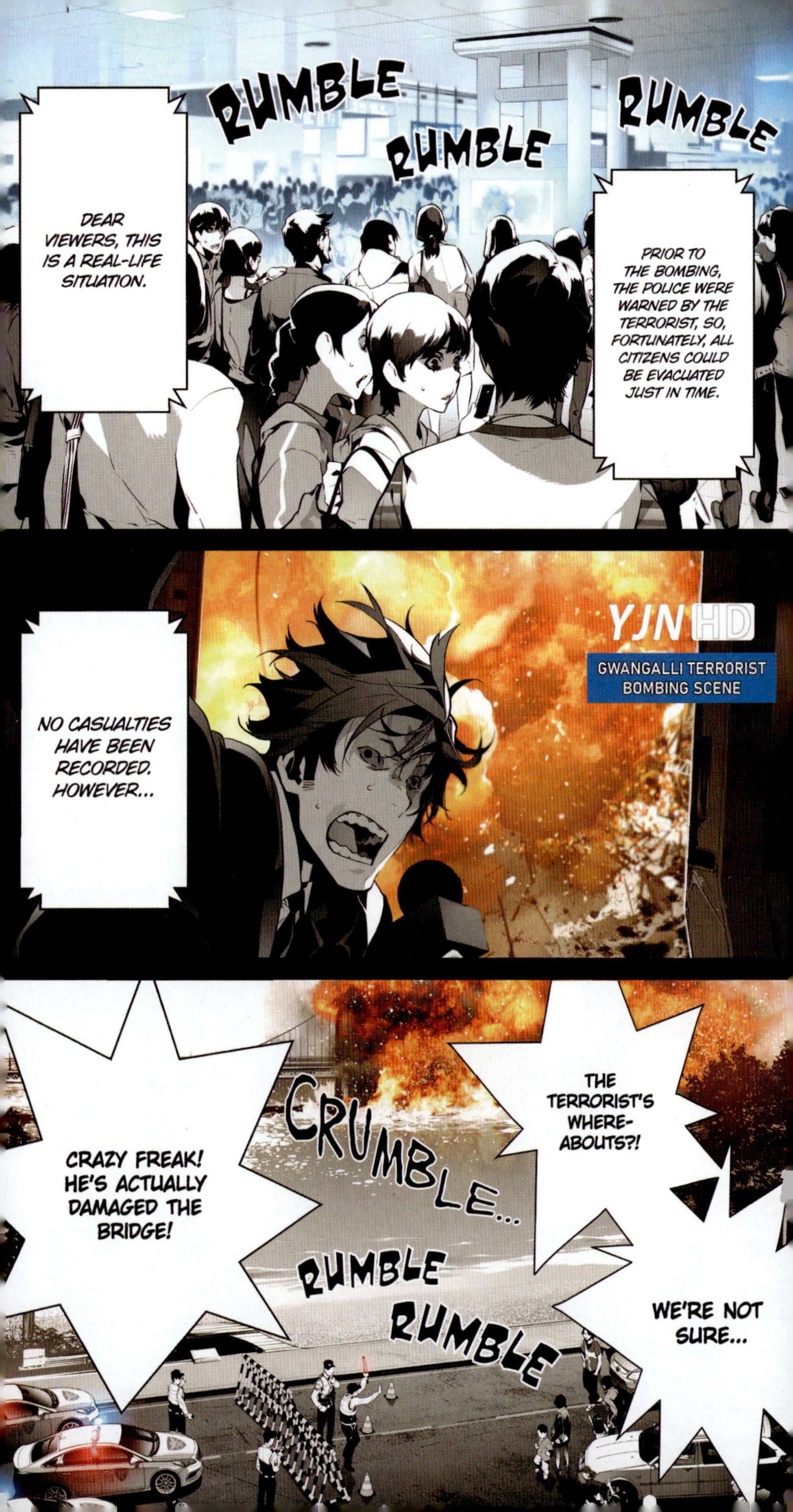

DEAR VIEWERS, THIS IS A REAL-LIFE SITUATION.
RUMBLE
RUMBLE
RUMBLE
PRIOR TO THE BOMBING, THE POLICE WERE WARNED BY THE TERRORIST, SO, FORTUNATELY, ALL CITIZENS COULD BE EVACUATED JUST IN TIME.
NO CASUALTIES HAVE BEEN RECORDED. HOWEVER...
YJN HD
GWANGALLI TERRORIST BOMBING SCENE
CRAZY FREAK! HE'S ACTUALLY DAMAGED THE BRIDGE!
CRUMBLE...
THE TERRORIST'S WHERE-ABOUTS?!
RUMBLE
RUMBLE
WE'RE NOT SURE...

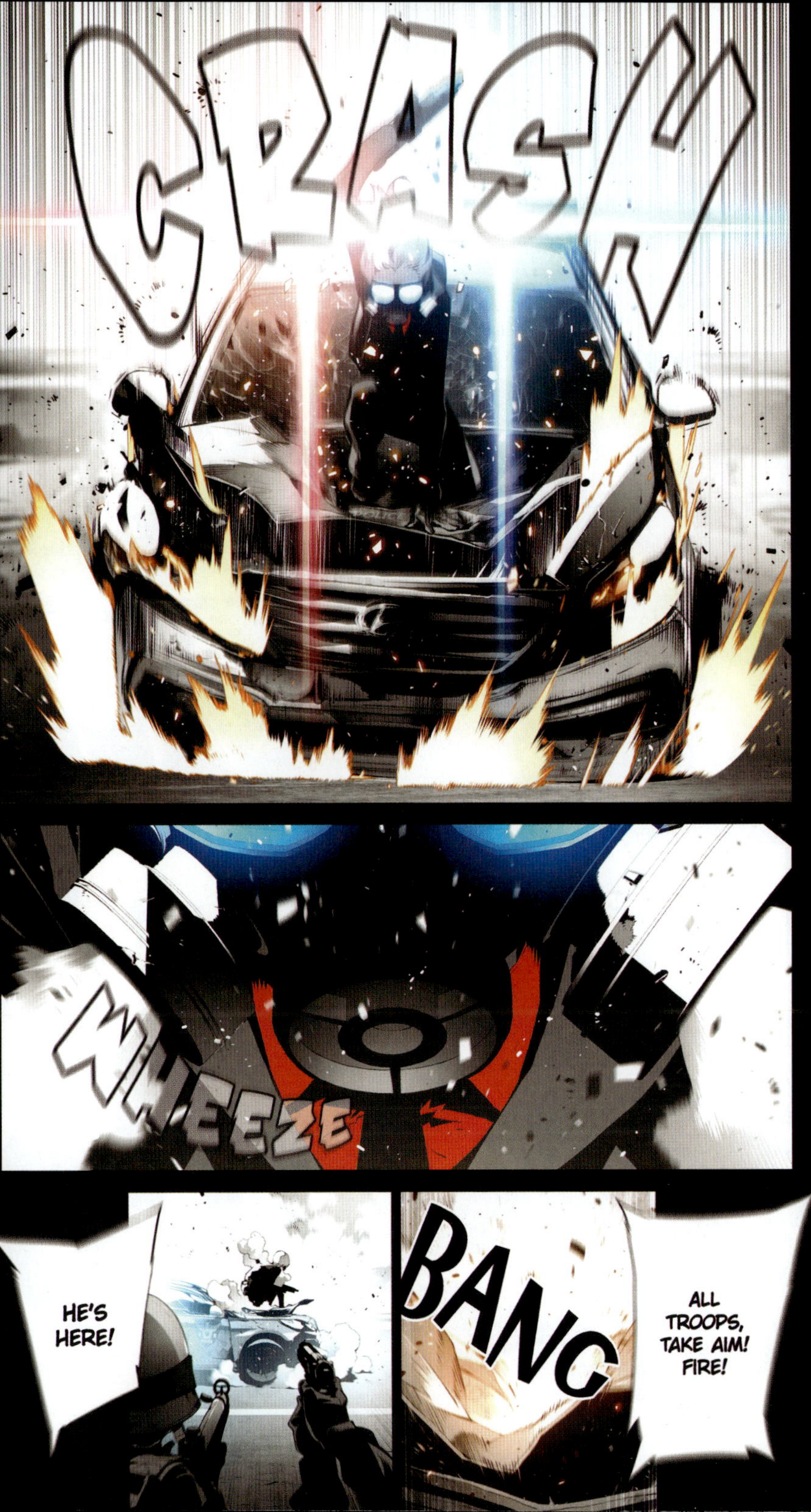
CRASH
WHEEZE
HE'S HERE!
BANG
ALL TROOPS, TAKE AIM! FIRE!

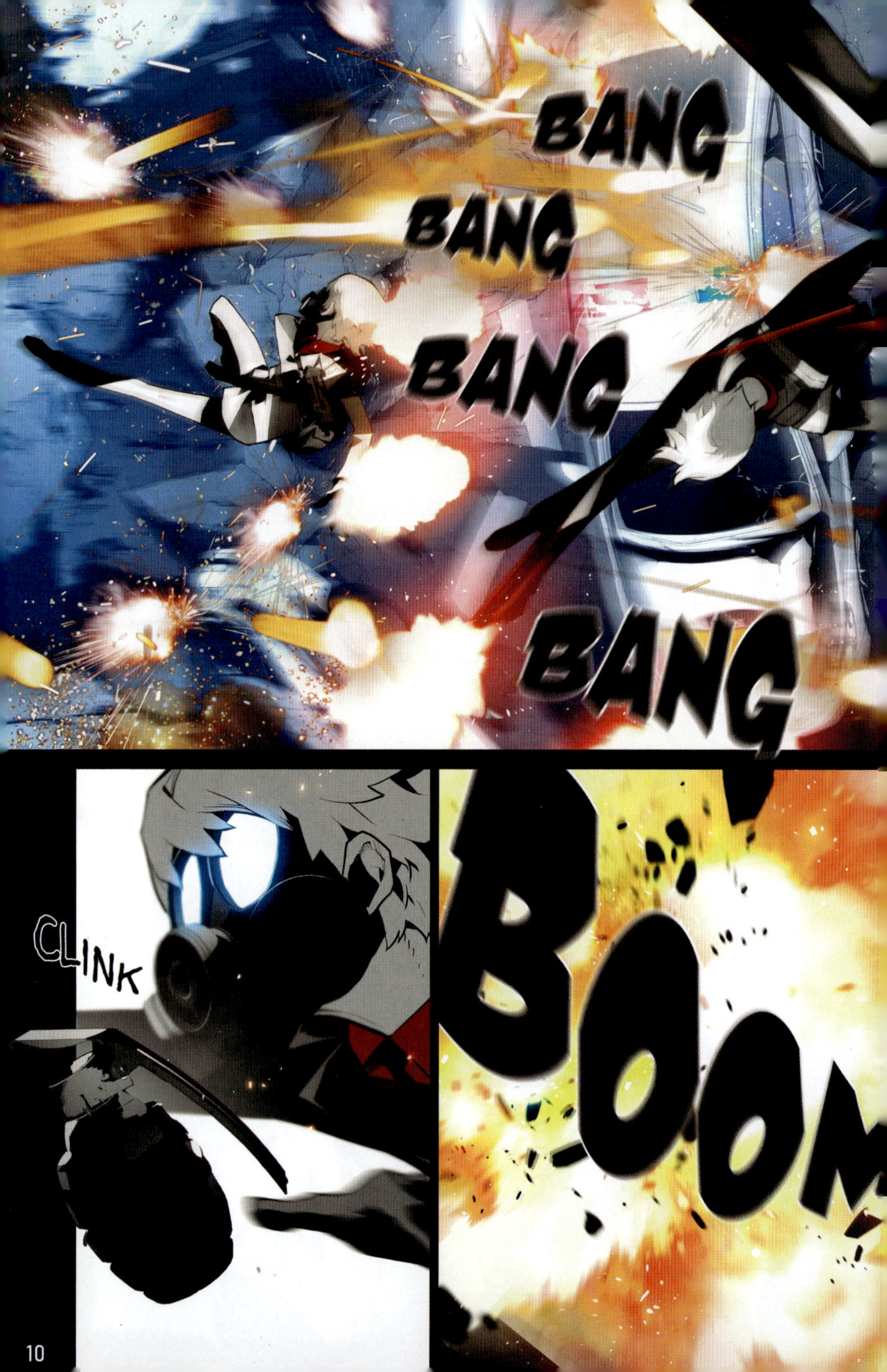
BANG
BANG
BANG
BANG
CLINK
BOOM

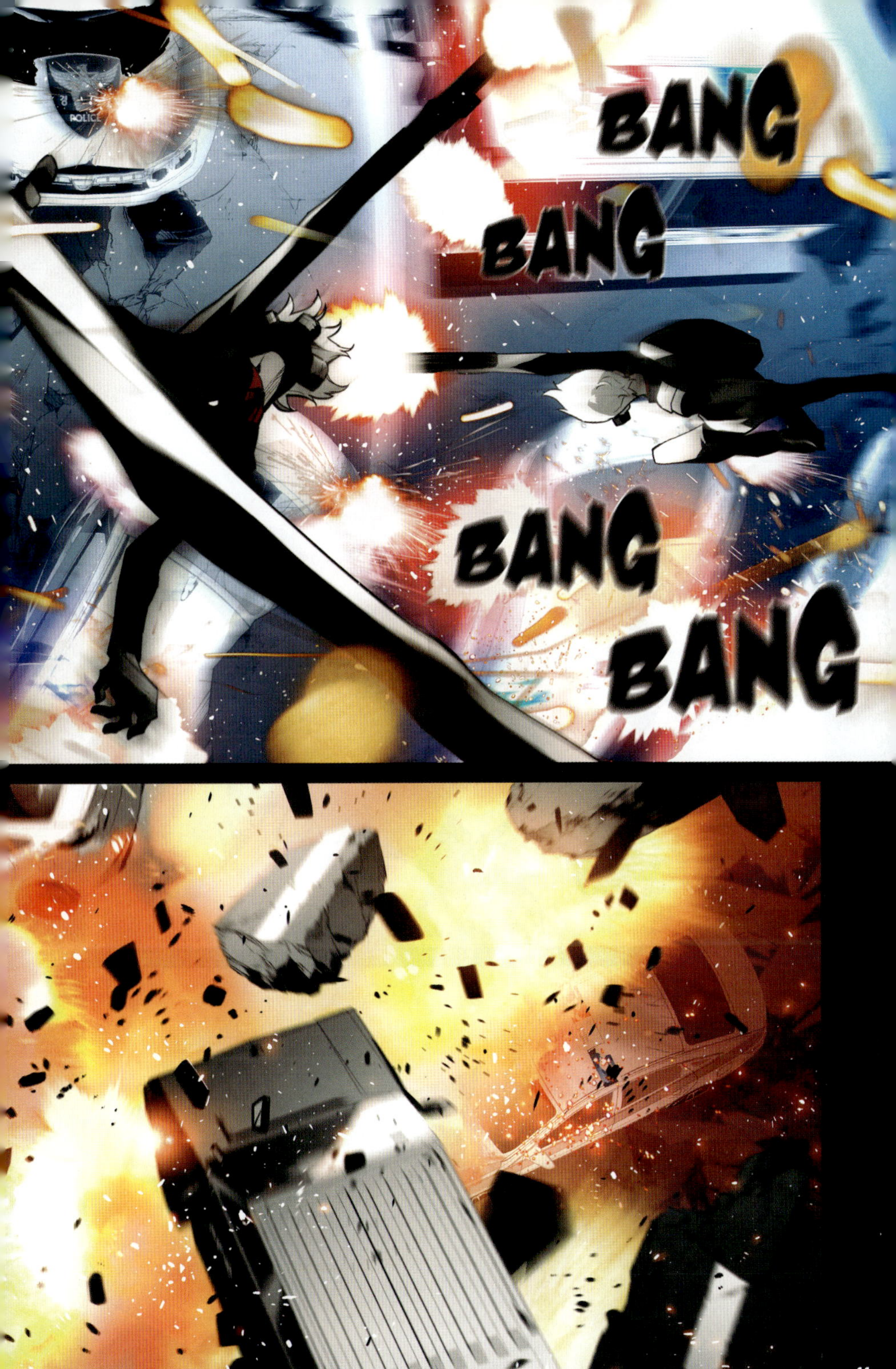
BANG
BANG
BANG
BANG

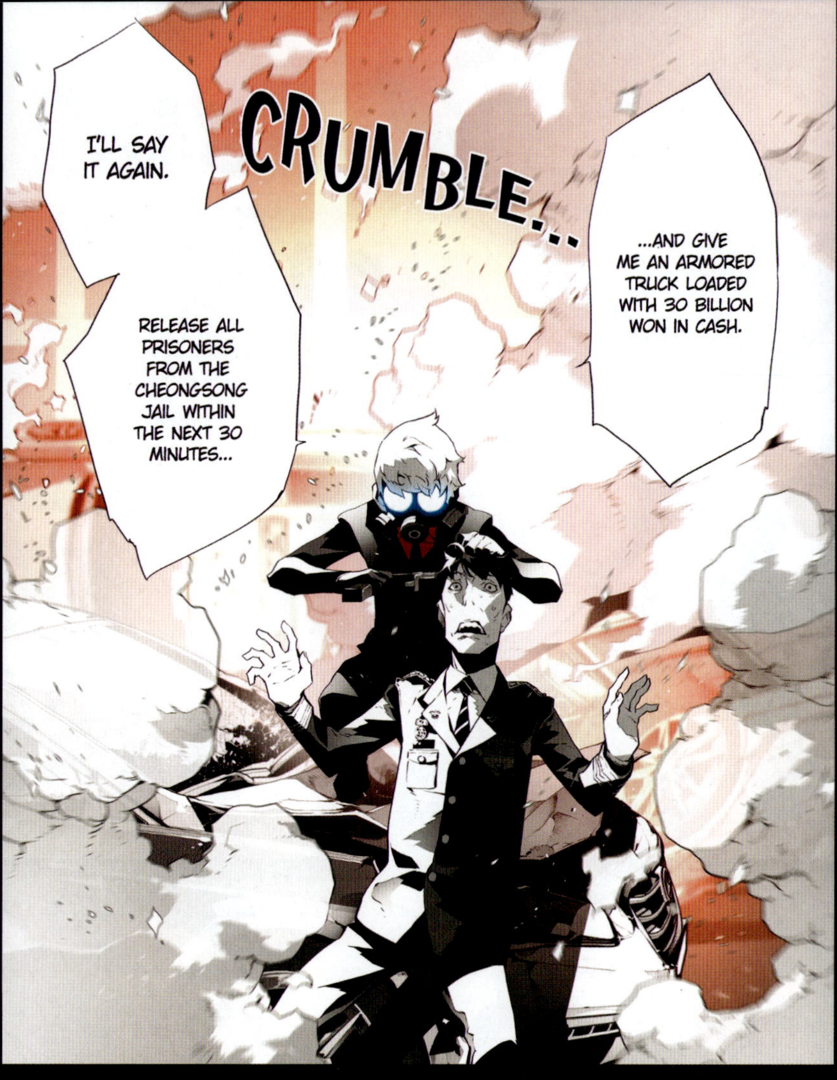
CRUMBLE...
I'LL SAY IT AGAIN.
RELEASE ALL PRISONERS FROM THE CHEONGSONG JAIL WITHIN THE NEXT 30 MINUTES...
...AND GIVE ME AN ARMORED TRUCK LOADED WITH 30 BILLION WON IN CASH.

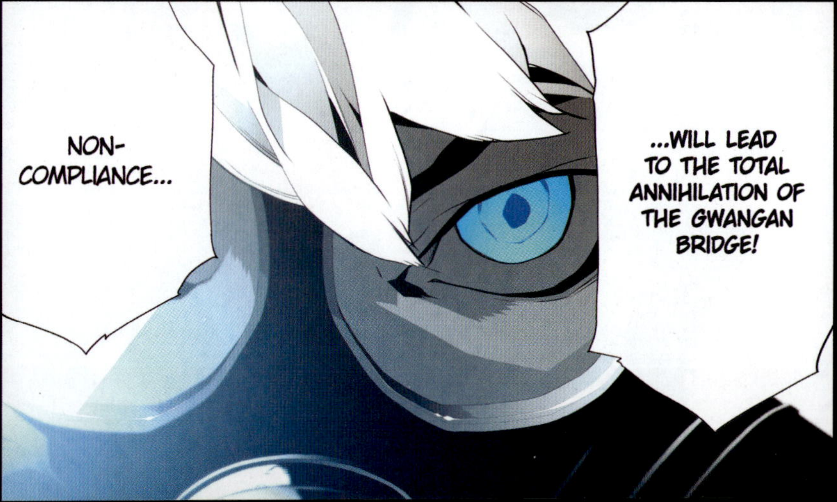
NON-COMPLIANCE...
...WILL LEAD TO THE TOTAL ANNIHILATION OF THE GWANGAN BRIDGE!

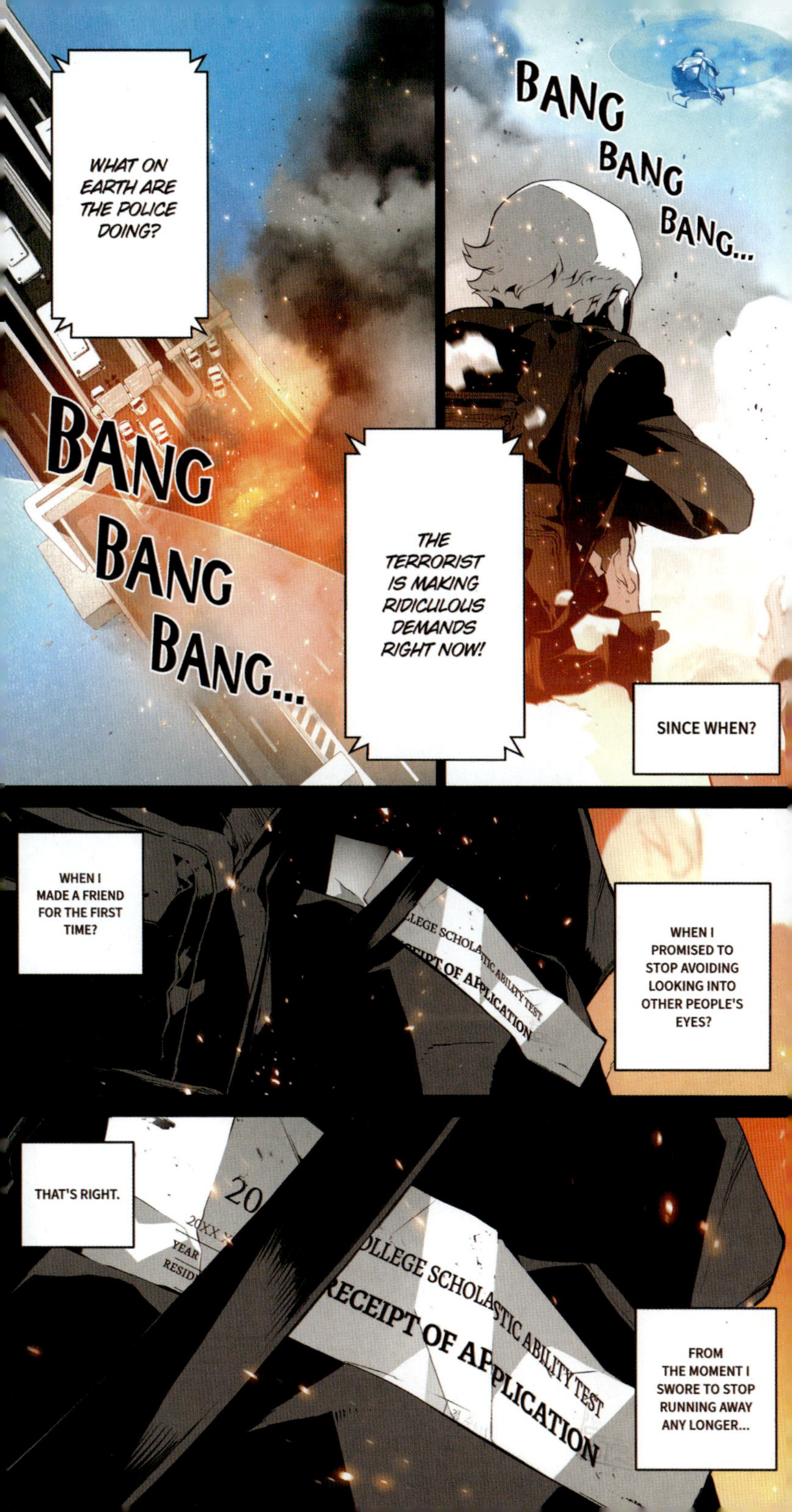
WHAT ON EARTH ARE THE POLICE DOING?
BANG BANG BANG...
THE TERRORIST IS MAKING RIDICULOUS DEMANDS RIGHT NOW!
BANG BANG BANG...
SINCE WHEN?
WHEN I MADE A FRIEND FOR THE FIRST TIME?
WHEN I PROMISED TO STOP AVOIDING LOOKING INTO OTHER PEOPLE'S EYES?
LLEGE SCHOLASTIC ABILITY TEST
RECEIPT OF APPLICATION
THAT'S RIGHT.
OLLEGE SCHOLASTIC ABILITY TEST
RECEIPT OF APPLICATION
FROM THE MOMENT I SWORE TO STOP RUNNING AWAY ANY LONGER...

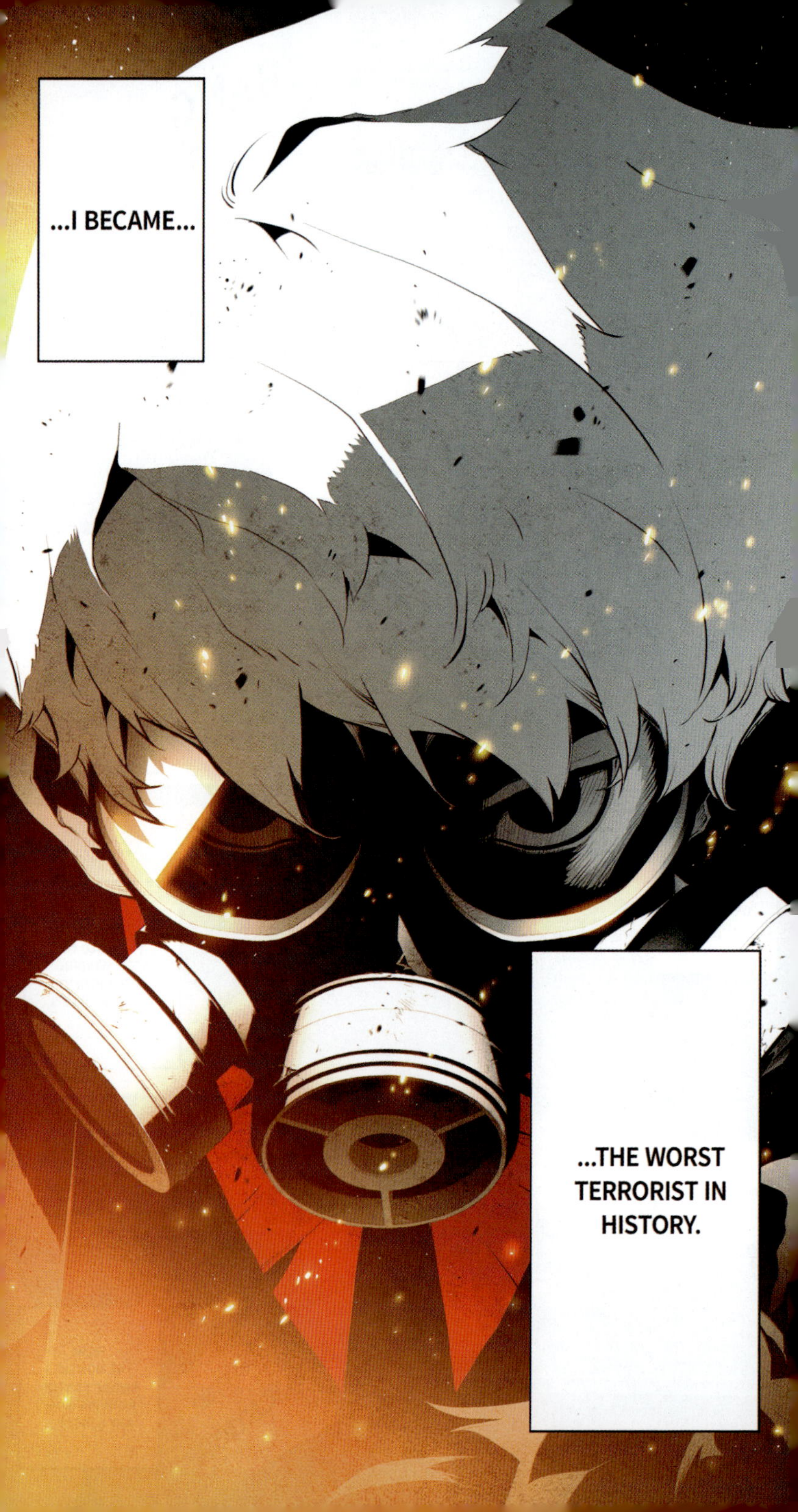
...I BECAME...
...THE WORST TERRORIST IN HISTORY.

TERROR MAN

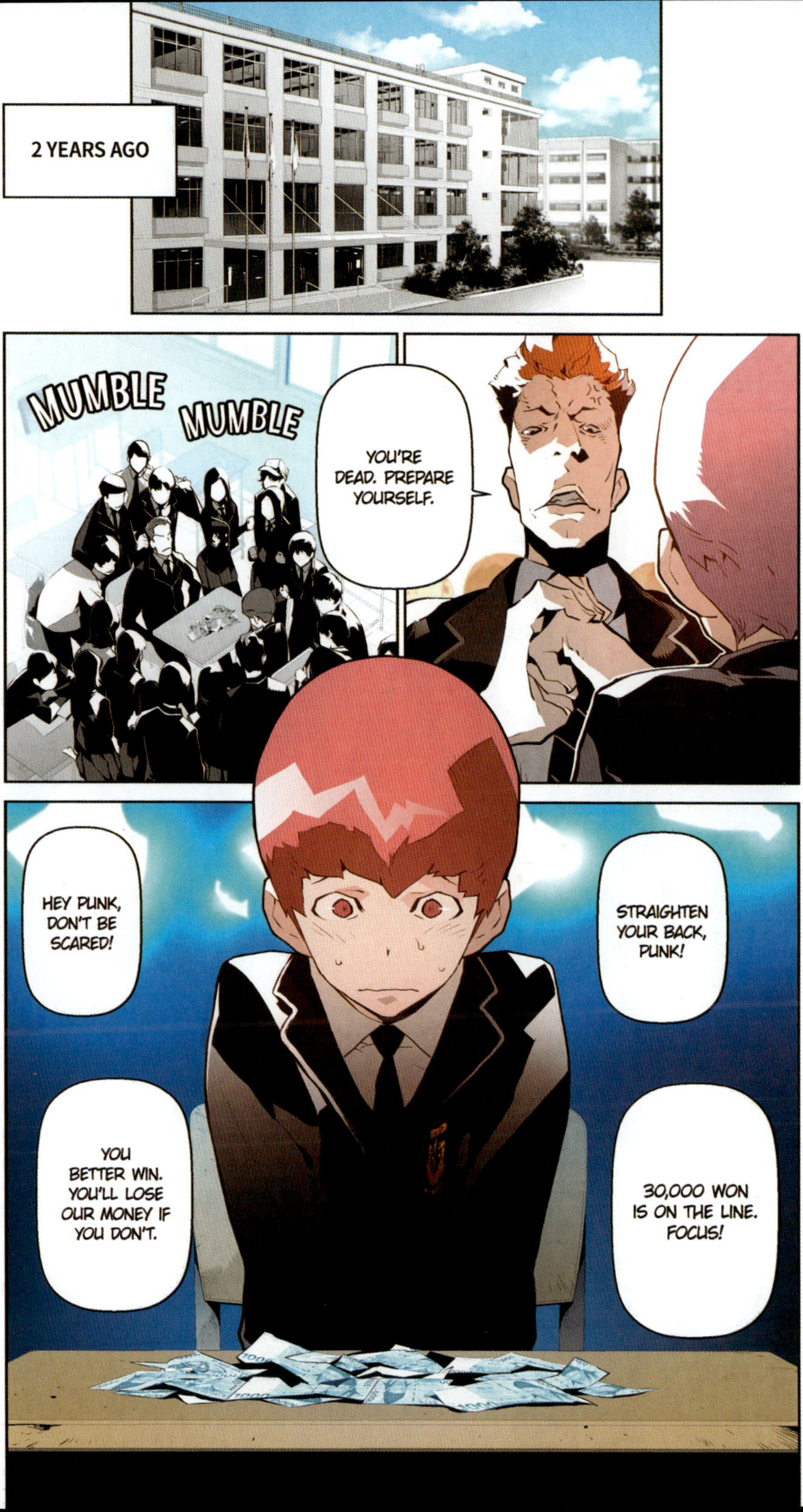
2 YEARS AGO
MUMBLE
MUMBLE
YOU'RE DEAD. PREPARE YOURSELF.
HEY PUNK, DON'T BE SCARED!
STRAIGHTEN YOUR BACK, PUNK!
YOU BETTER WIN. YOU'LL LOSE OUR MONEY IF YOU DON'T.
30,000 WON IS ON THE LINE. FOCUS!

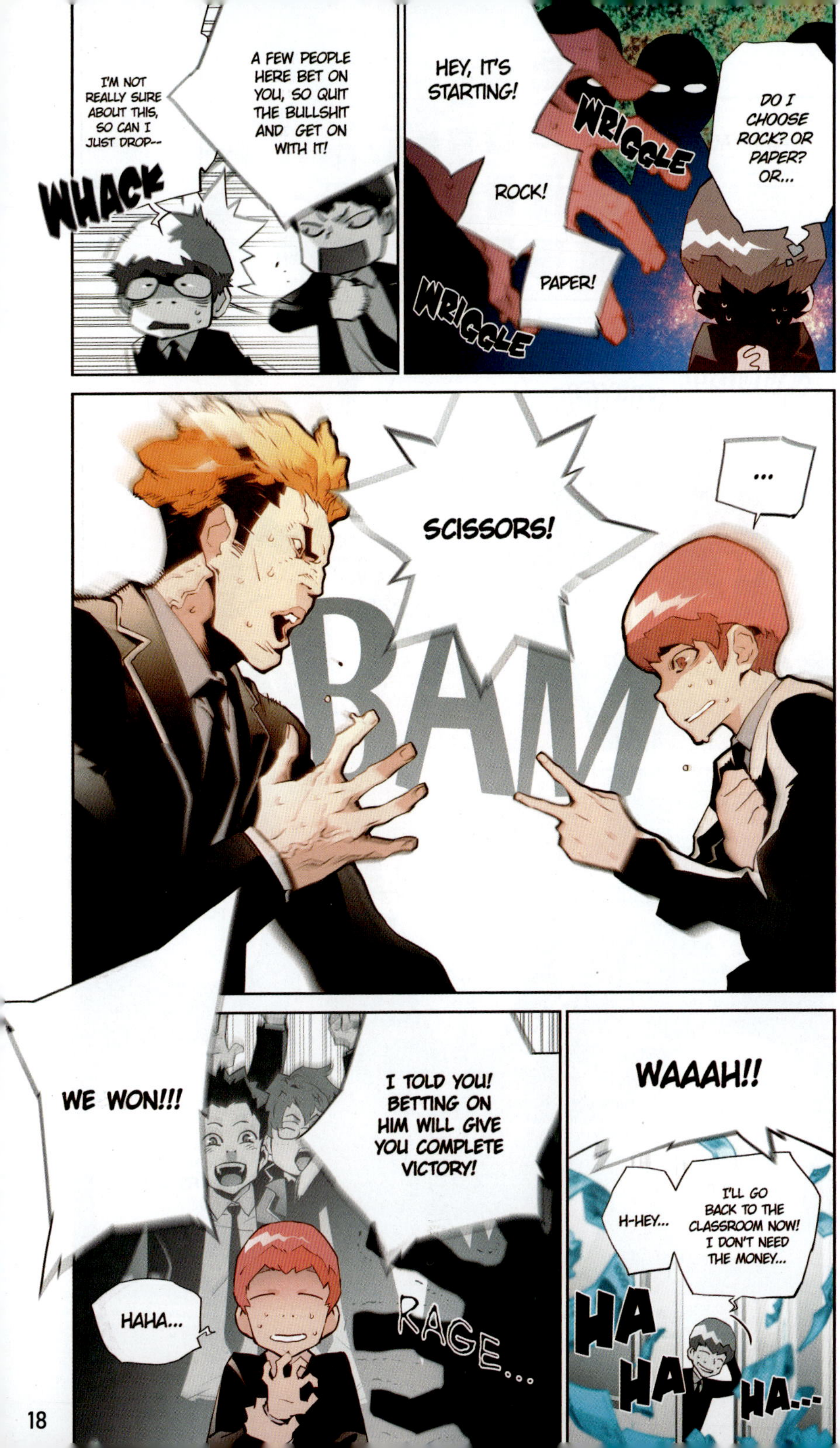
I'M NOT REALLY SURE ABOUT THIS, SO CAN I JUST DROP--
A FEW PEOPLE HERE BET ON YOU, SO QUIT THE BULLSHIT AND GET ON WITH IT!
WHACK
HEY, IT'S STARTING!
WRIGGLE
DO I CHOOSE ROCK? OR PAPER? OR...
ROCK!
PAPER!
WRIGGLE
SCISSORS!
...
BAM
WE WON!!!
I TOLD YOU! BETTING ON HIM WILL GIVE YOU COMPLETE VICTORY!
HAHA...
RAGE...
WAAAH!!
H-HEY...
I'LL GO BACK TO THE CLASSROOM NOW! I DON'T NEED THE MONEY...
HA HA HA...

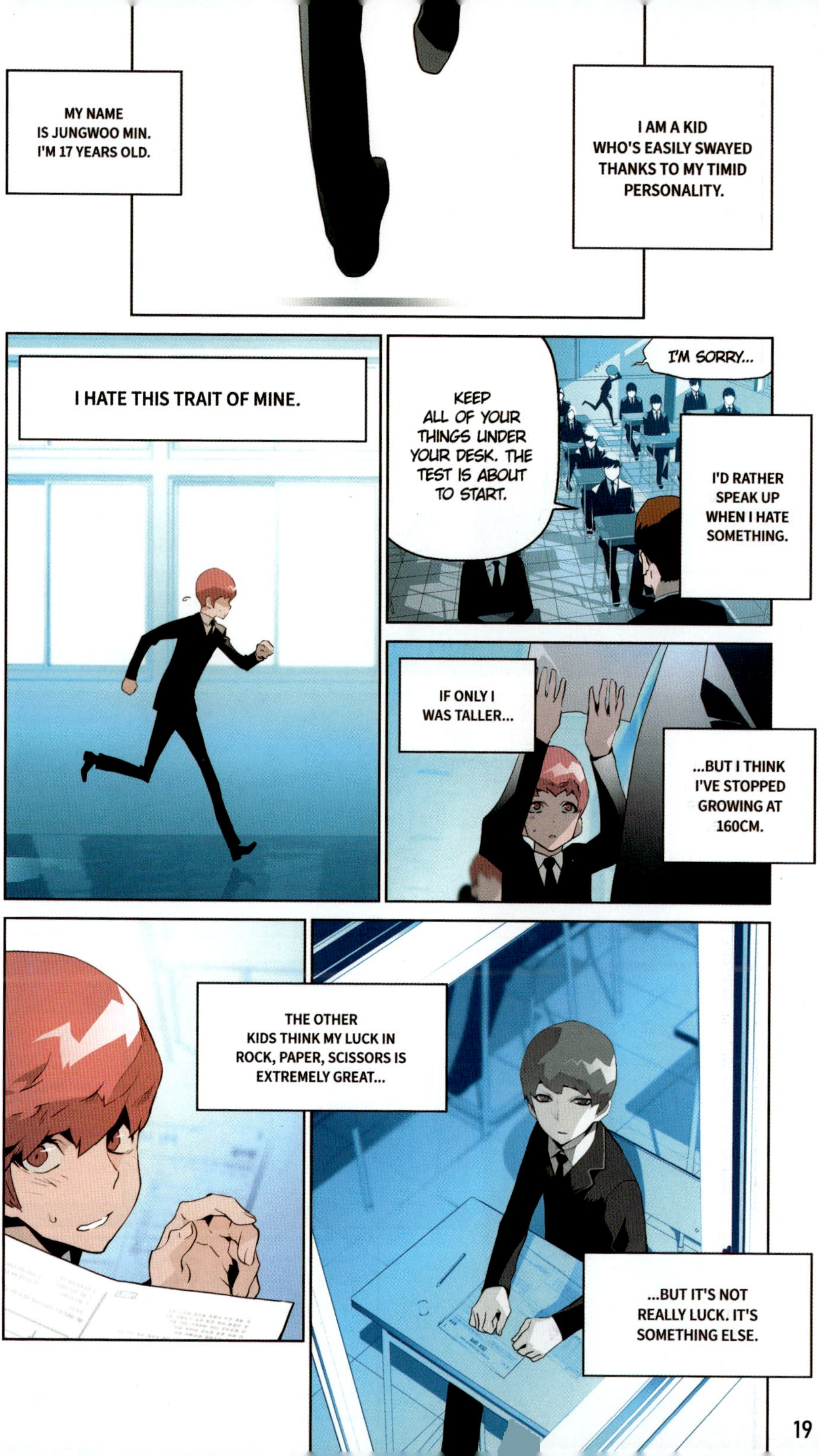
MY NAME IS JUNGWOO MIN. I'M 17 YEARS OLD.
I AM A KID WHO'S EASILY SWAYED THANKS TO MY TIMID PERSONALITY.
I HATE THIS TRAIT OF MINE.
KEEP ALL OF YOUR THINGS UNDER YOUR DESK. THE TEST IS ABOUT TO START.
I'M SORRY...
I'D RATHER SPEAK UP WHEN I HATE SOMETHING.
IF ONLY I WAS TALLER...
...BUT I THINK I'VE STOPPED GROWING AT 160CM.
THE OTHER KIDS THINK MY LUCK IN ROCK, PAPER, SCISSORS IS EXTREMELY GREAT...
...BUT IT'S NOT REALLY LUCK. IT'S SOMETHING ELSE.

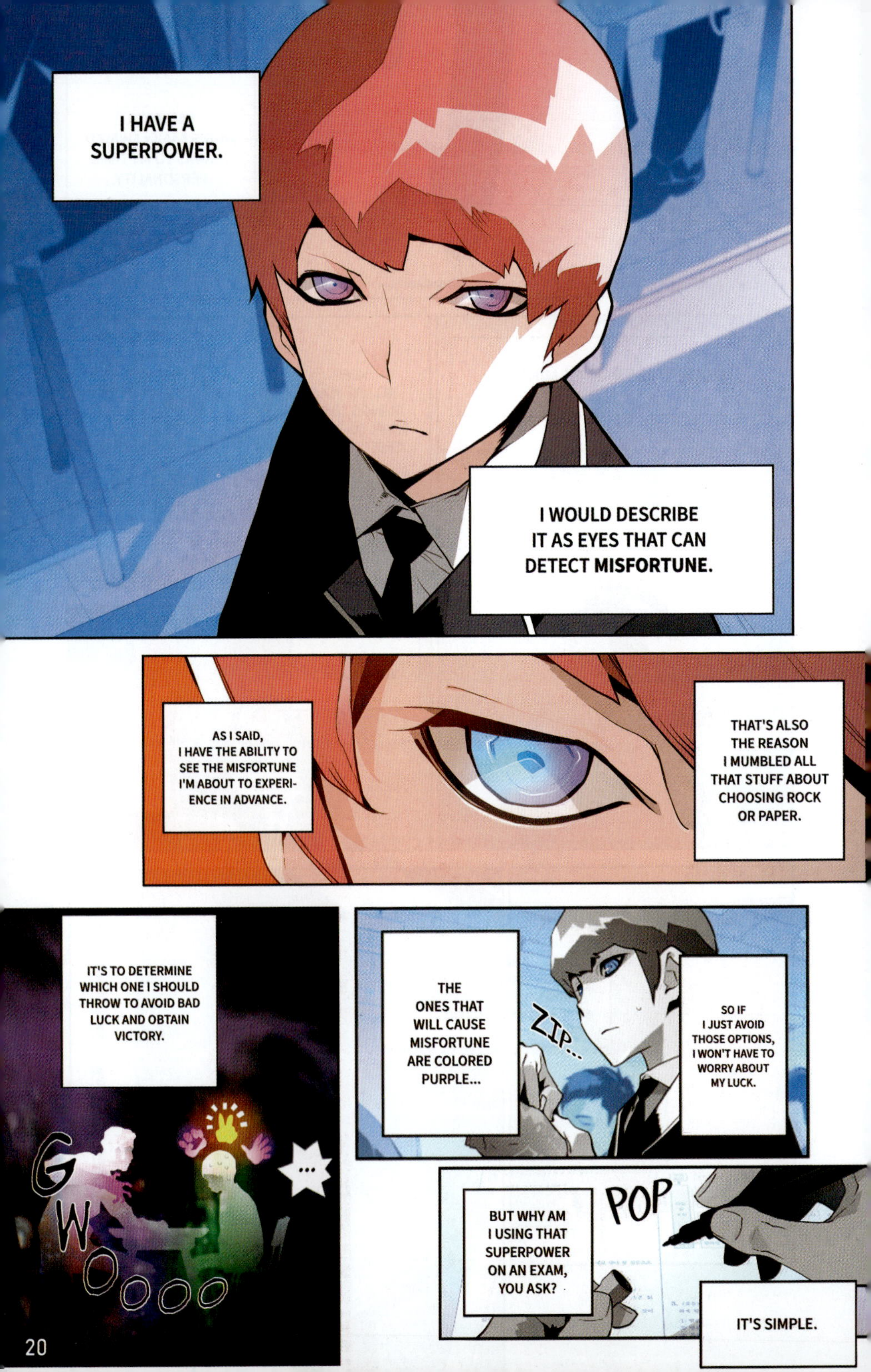
I HAVE A SUPERPOWER.
I WOULD DESCRIBE IT AS EYES THAT CAN DETECT **MISFORTUNE.**
AS I SAID, I HAVE THE ABILITY TO SEE THE MISFORTUNE I'M ABOUT TO EXPERIENCE IN ADVANCE.
THAT'S ALSO THE REASON I MUMBLED ALL THAT STUFF ABOUT CHOOSING ROCK OR PAPER.
IT'S TO DETERMINE WHICH ONE I SHOULD THROW TO AVOID BAD LUCK AND OBTAIN VICTORY.
GWOOOOO
...
THE ONES THAT WILL CAUSE MISFORTUNE ARE COLORED PURPLE...
ZIP...
SO IF I JUST AVOID THOSE OPTIONS, I WON'T HAVE TO WORRY ABOUT MY LUCK.
BUT WHY AM I USING THAT SUPERPOWER ON AN EXAM, YOU ASK?
POP
IT'S SIMPLE.

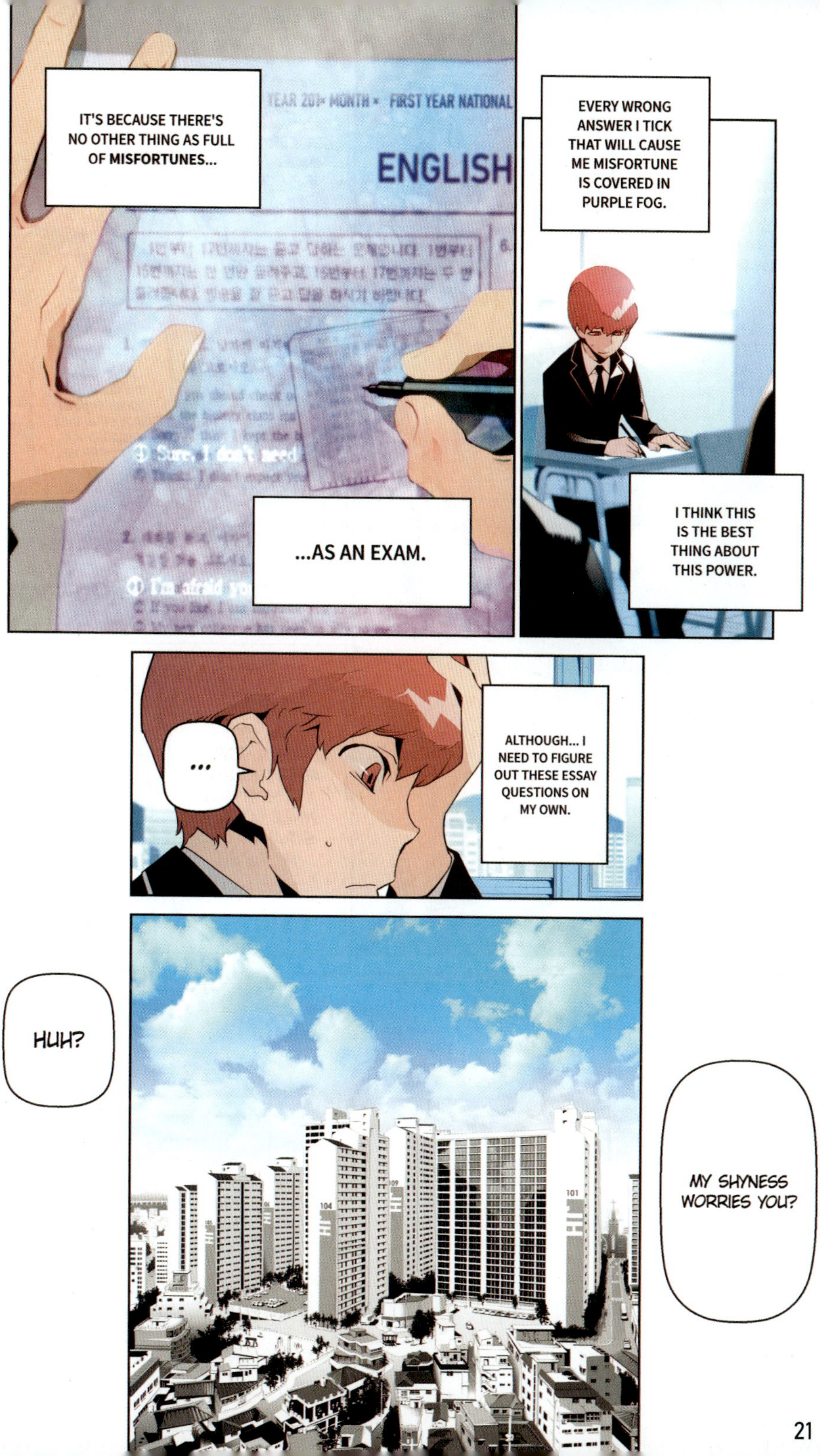
IT'S BECAUSE THERE'S NO OTHER THING AS FULL OF MISFORTUNES...
YEAR 201× MONTH × FIRST YEAR NATIONAL
ENGLISH
...AS AN EXAM.
EVERY WRONG ANSWER I TICK THAT WILL CAUSE ME MISFORTUNE IS COVERED IN PURPLE FOG.
I THINK THIS IS THE BEST THING ABOUT THIS POWER.
...
ALTHOUGH... I NEED TO FIGURE OUT THESE ESSAY QUESTIONS ON MY OWN.
HUH?
MY SHYNESS WORRIES YOU?

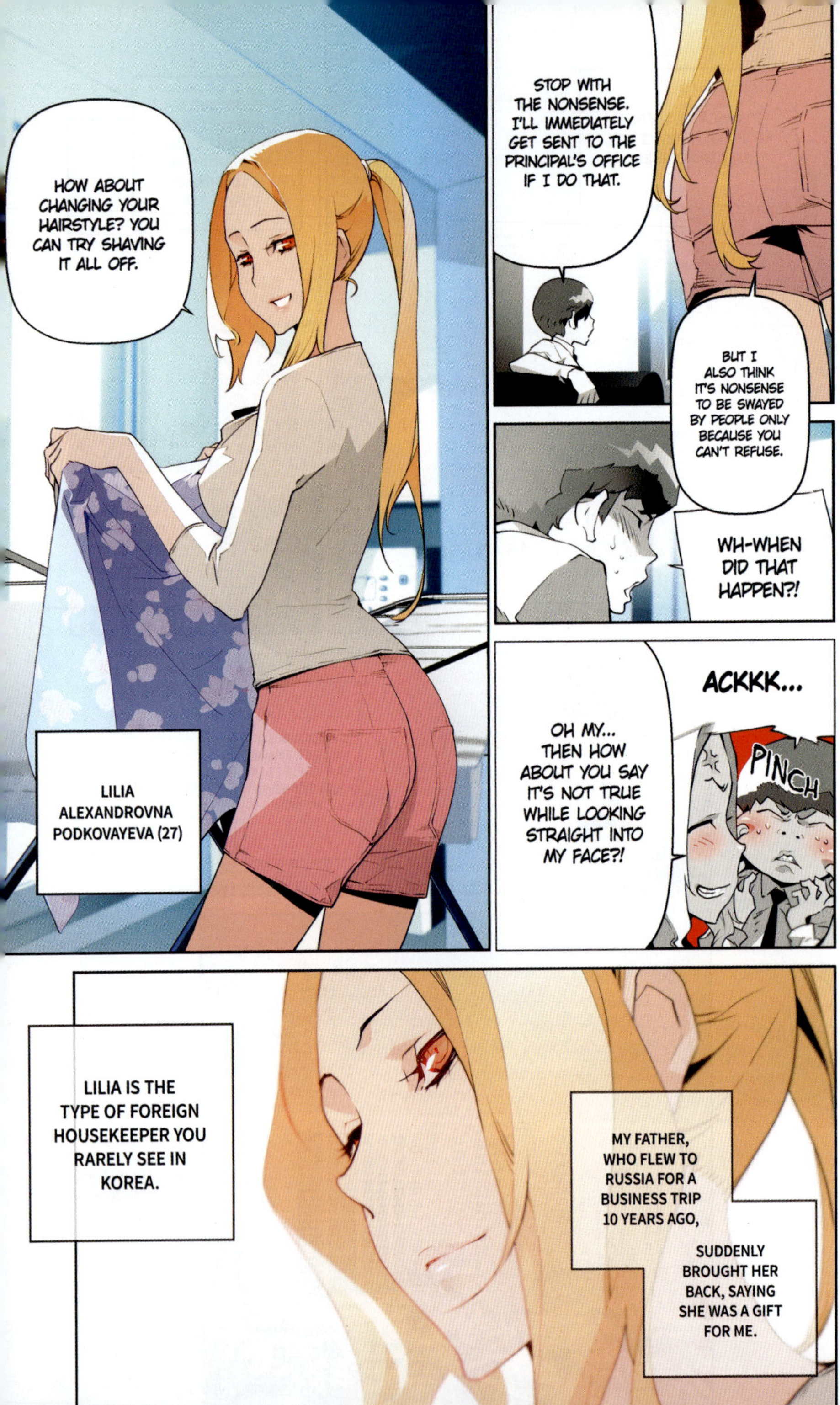
HOW ABOUT CHANGING YOUR HAIRSTYLE? YOU CAN TRY SHAVING IT ALL OFF.
LILIA ALEXANDROVNA PODKOVAYEVA (27)
STOP WITH THE NONSENSE. I'LL IMMEDIATELY GET SENT TO THE PRINCIPAL'S OFFICE IF I DO THAT.
BUT I ALSO THINK IT'S NONSENSE TO BE SWAYED BY PEOPLE ONLY BECAUSE YOU CAN'T REFUSE.
WH-WHEN DID THAT HAPPEN?!
ACKKK...
OH MY... THEN HOW ABOUT YOU SAY IT'S NOT TRUE WHILE LOOKING STRAIGHT INTO MY FACE?!
PINCH
LILIA IS THE TYPE OF FOREIGN HOUSEKEEPER YOU RARELY SEE IN KOREA.
MY FATHER, WHO FLEW TO RUSSIA FOR A BUSINESS TRIP 10 YEARS AGO,
SUDDENLY BROUGHT HER BACK, SAYING SHE WAS A GIFT FOR ME.

SHE'S QUITE TOUGH, BUT THE WAY SHE DOES THE LAUNDRY OR CLEANING IS SOMETHING A MACHINE CAN'T COPY. SHE'S WELL-ROUNDED.
I MADE A STRAWBERRY SMOOTHIE. WOULD YOU LIKE SOME?
SURE.
NEITHER DAD NOR LILIA HAVE EVER DISCLOSED TO ME WHAT SHE DID BEFORE COMING HERE.
BUT IF I HAD TO POINT OUT A FLAW...
...
GULP...
THIS... IS... STRAW-BERRY...?
EVEN THE COLOR IS DIFFERENT...
CRACK
SHE'S DISGUSTINGLY BAD AT COOKING.
WHAT DO YOU WANT TO EAT? I'LL MAKE EVERYTHING YOU WANT TODAY.
COME TO THINK OF IT, YOUNG MASTER IS DONE WITH HIS EXAMS, AM I RIGHT?
I'M THINKING...
I DON'T REALLY WANT ANYTHING IN PARTICULAR.
ESPECIALLY NOT YOUR COOKING...
PIERCE
HERE, YOUNG MASTER.
SAY "AH..."
LIFT
I DON'T REALLY WANT TO EAT AN APPLE SKEWERED BY A JACK KNIFE.

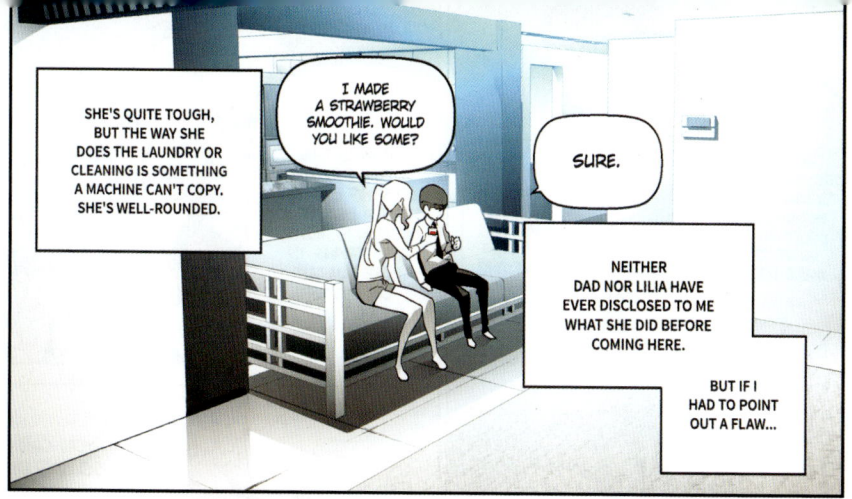

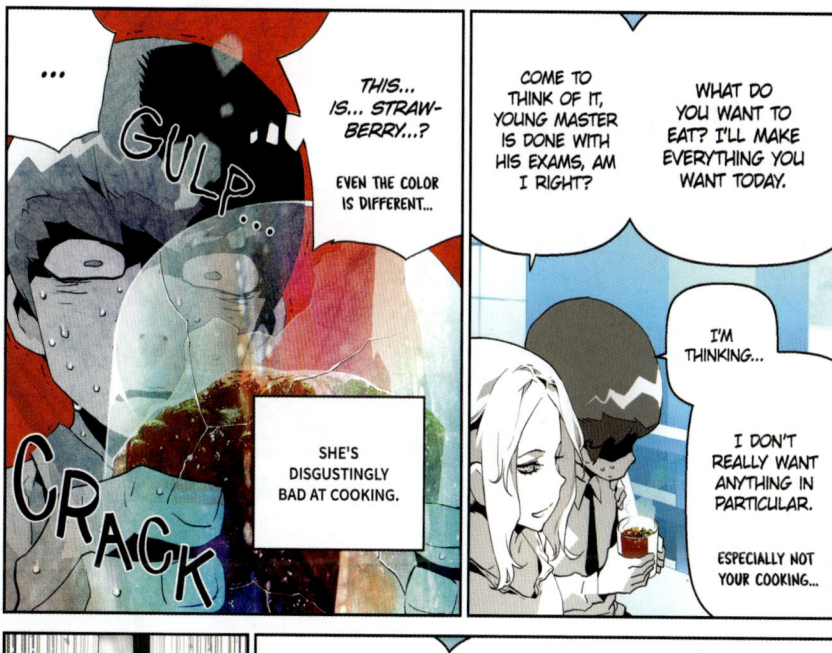

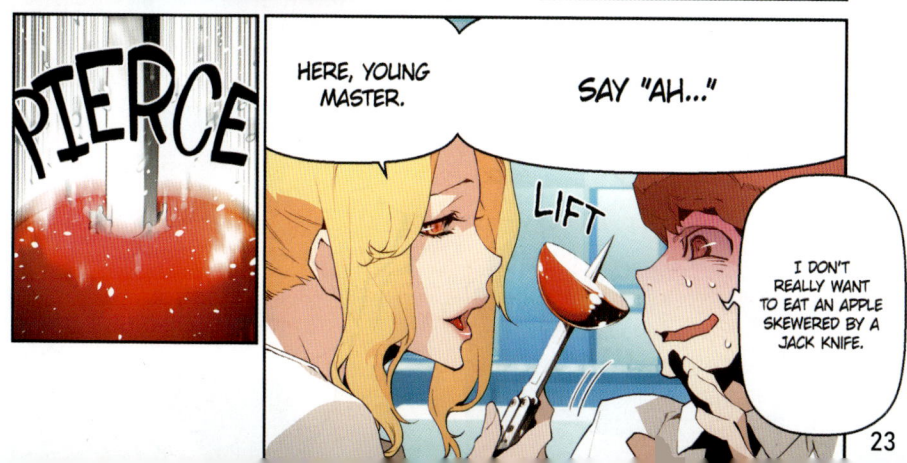

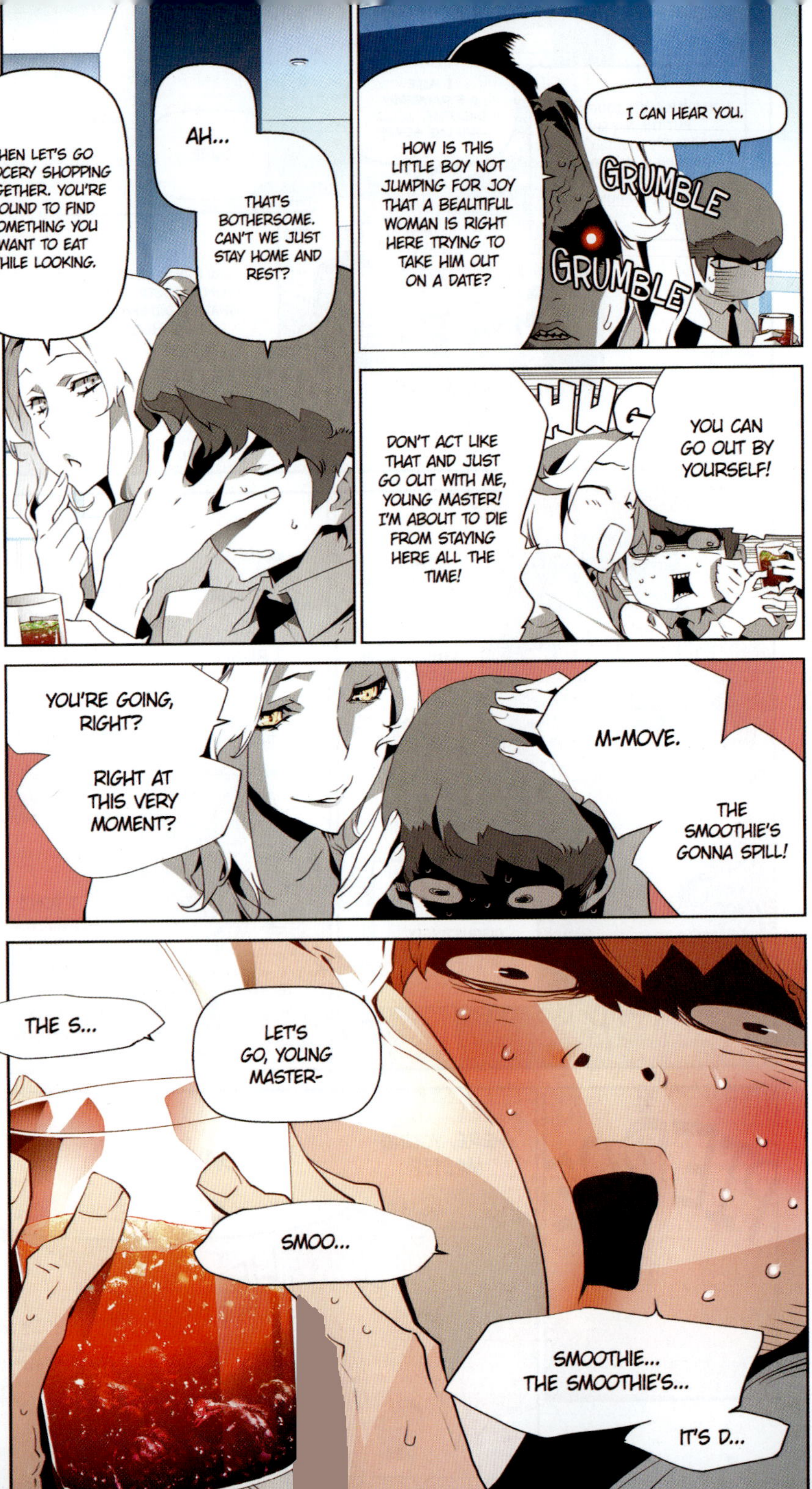
THEN LET'S GO GROCERY SHOPPING TOGETHER. YOU'RE BOUND TO FIND SOMETHING YOU WANT TO EAT WHILE LOOKING.
AH...
THAT'S BOTHERSOME. CAN'T WE JUST STAY HOME AND REST?
HOW IS THIS LITTLE BOY NOT JUMPING FOR JOY THAT A BEAUTIFUL WOMAN IS RIGHT HERE TRYING TO TAKE HIM OUT ON A DATE?
I CAN HEAR YOU.
GRUMBLE
GRUMBLE
DON'T ACT LIKE THAT AND JUST GO OUT WITH ME, YOUNG MASTER! I'M ABOUT TO DIE FROM STAYING HERE ALL THE TIME!
HUG
YOU CAN GO OUT BY YOURSELF!
YOU'RE GOING, RIGHT?
RIGHT AT THIS VERY MOMENT?
M-MOVE.
THE SMOOTHIE'S GONNA SPILL!
THE S...
LET'S GO, YOUNG MASTER-
SMOO...
SMOOTHIE... THE SMOOTHIE'S...
IT'S D...

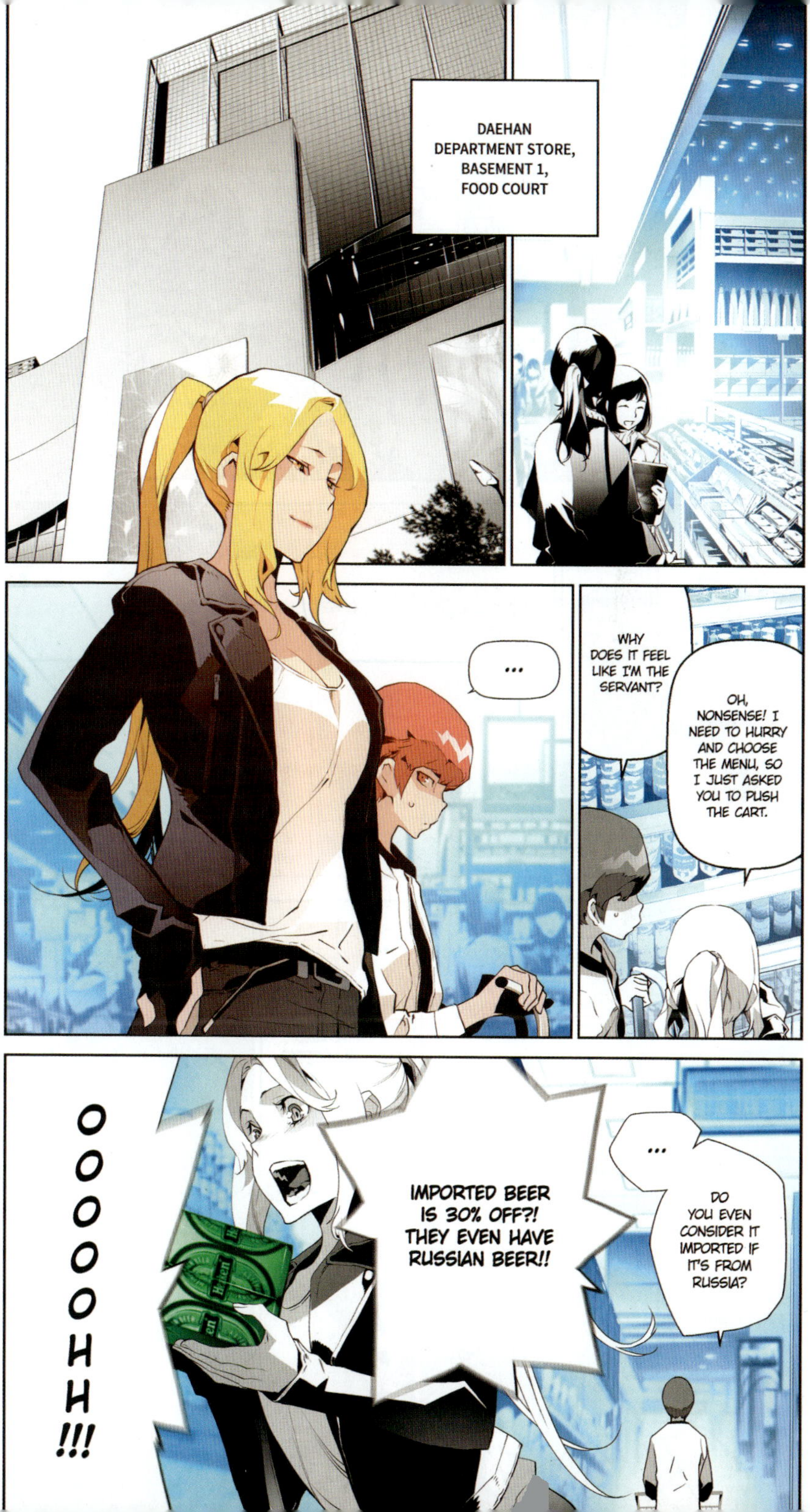
DAEHAN DEPARTMENT STORE, BASEMENT 1, FOOD COURT
...
WHY DOES IT FEEL LIKE I'M THE SERVANT?
OH, NONSENSE! I NEED TO HURRY AND CHOOSE THE MENU, SO I JUST ASKED YOU TO PUSH THE CART.
OOOOOOHHH!!!
IMPORTED BEER IS 30% OFF?! THEY EVEN HAVE RUSSIAN BEER!!
...
DO YOU EVEN CONSIDER IT IMPORTED IF IT'S FROM RUSSIA?

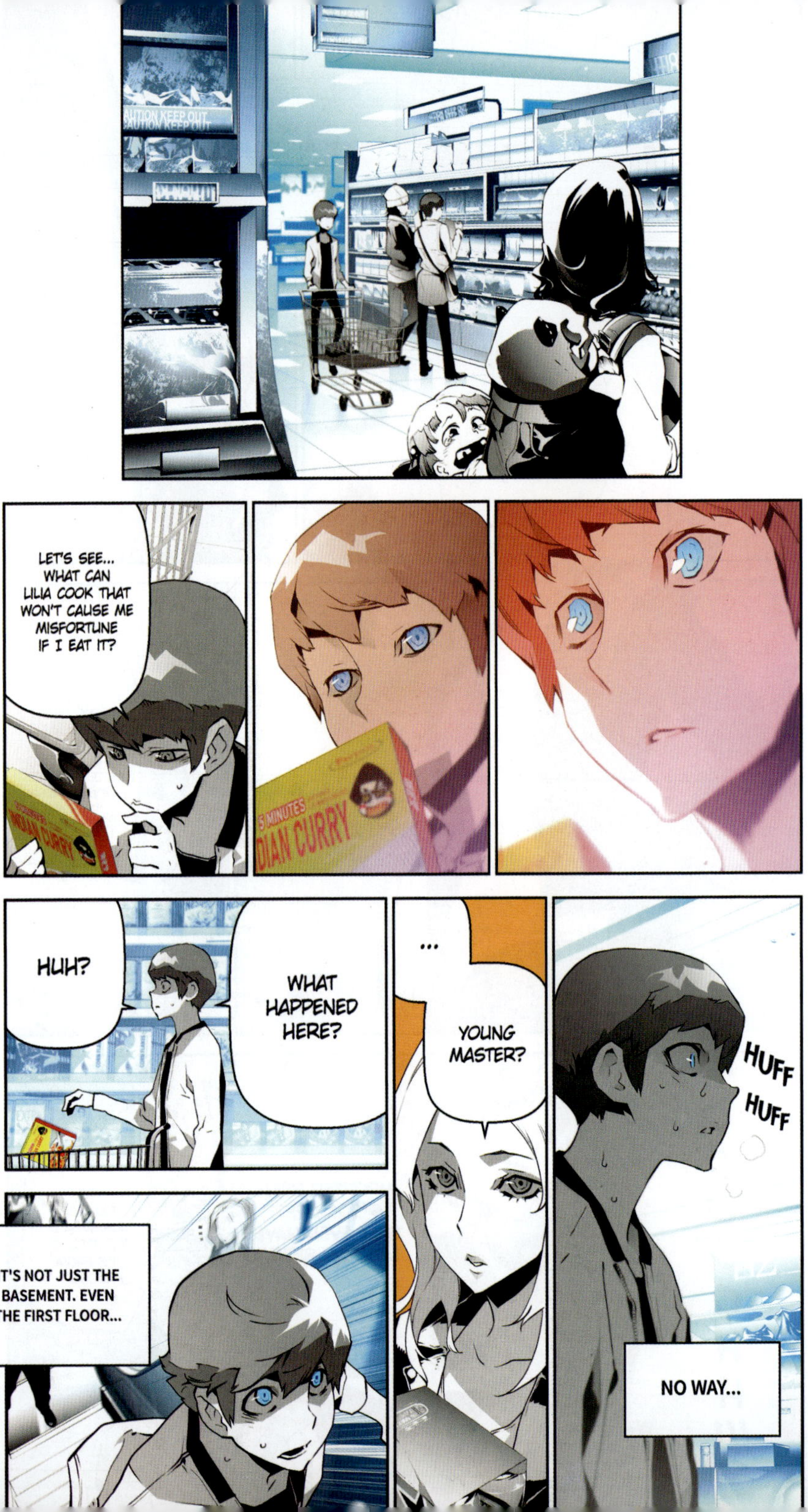
AUTION KEEP OUT
AUTION KEEP OUT
LET'S SEE... WHAT CAN LILIA COOK THAT WON'T CAUSE ME MISFORTUNE IF I EAT IT?
INDIAN CURRY
5 MINUTES
DIAN CURRY
HUH?
WHAT HAPPENED HERE?
...
YOUNG MASTER?
HUFF
HUFF
IT'S NOT JUST THE BASEMENT. EVEN THE FIRST FLOOR...
NO WAY...

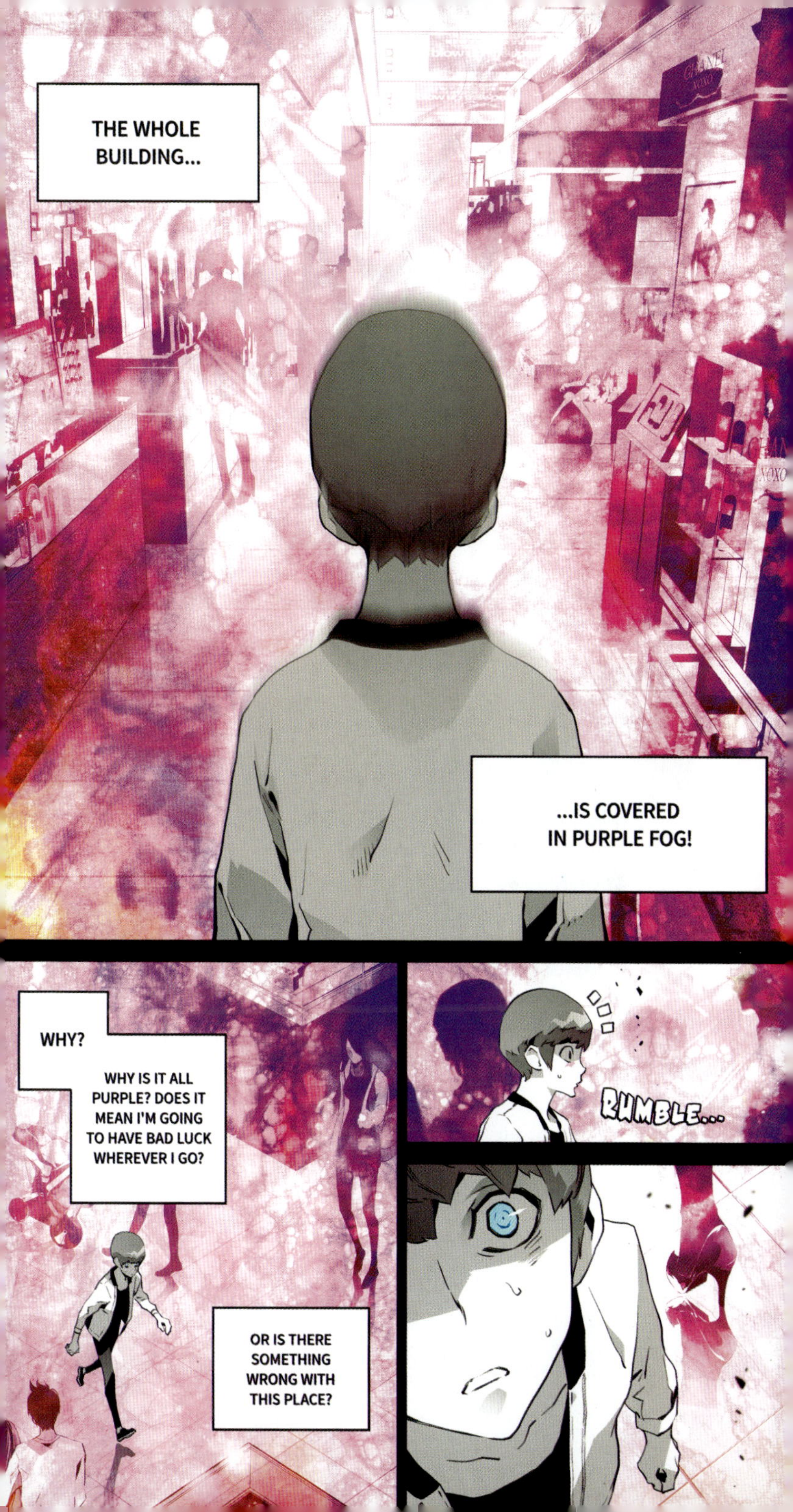
THE WHOLE BUILDING...
...IS COVERED IN PURPLE FOG!
WHY?
WHY IS IT ALL PURPLE? DOES IT MEAN I'M GOING TO HAVE BAD LUCK WHEREVER I GO?
OR IS THERE SOMETHING WRONG WITH THIS PLACE?
RUMBLE...

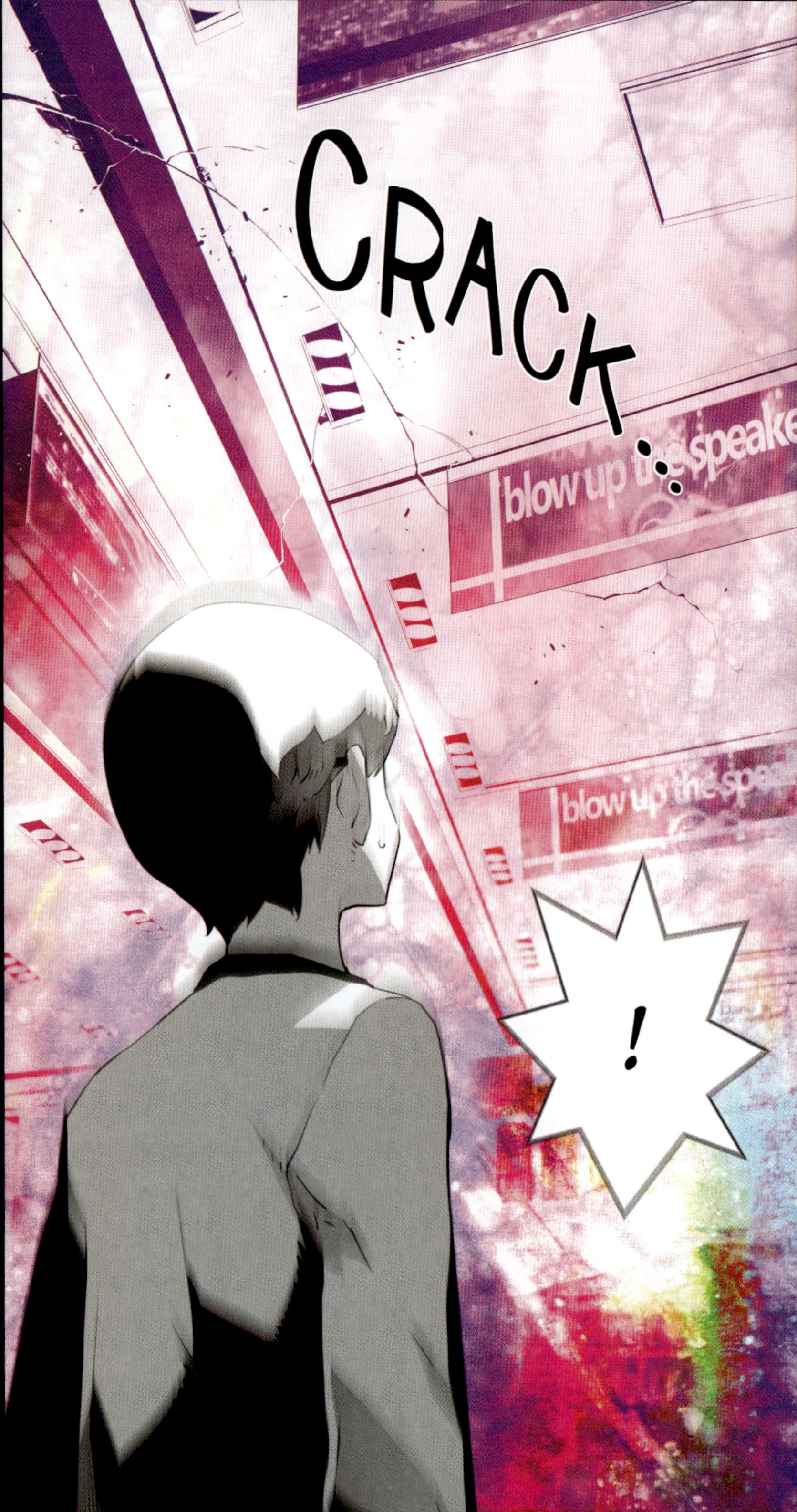
CRACK...
!

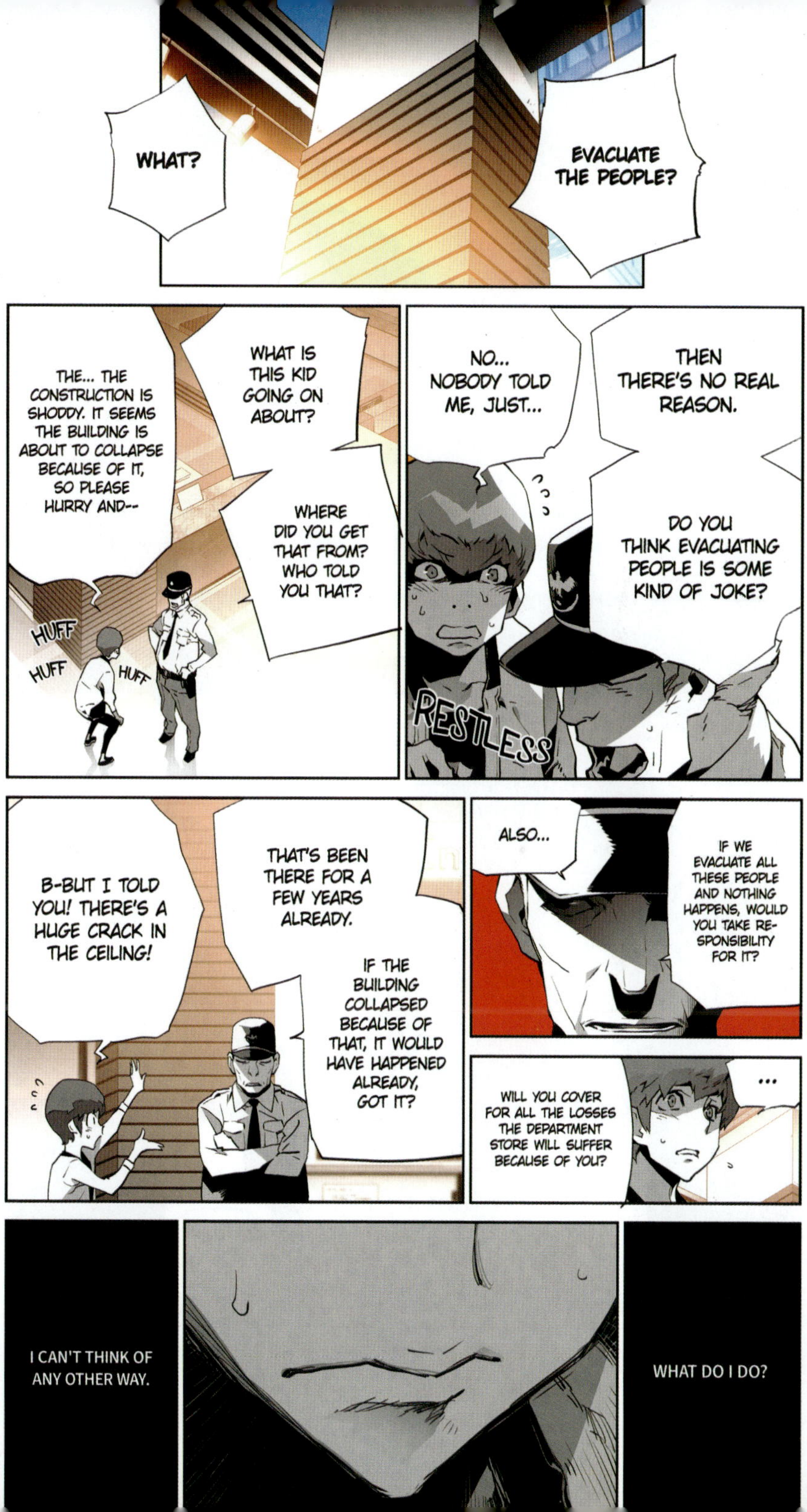
WHAT?
EVACUATE THE PEOPLE?
THE... THE CONSTRUCTION IS SHODDY. IT SEEMS THE BUILDING IS ABOUT TO COLLAPSE BECAUSE OF IT, SO PLEASE HURRY AND--
WHAT IS THIS KID GOING ON ABOUT?
WHERE DID YOU GET THAT FROM? WHO TOLD YOU THAT?
HUFF
HUFF
HUFF
NO... NOBODY TOLD ME, JUST...
THEN THERE'S NO REAL REASON.
DO YOU THINK EVACUATING PEOPLE IS SOME KIND OF JOKE?
RESTLESS
B-BUT I TOLD YOU! THERE'S A HUGE CRACK IN THE CEILING!
THAT'S BEEN THERE FOR A FEW YEARS ALREADY.
IF THE BUILDING COLLAPSED BECAUSE OF THAT, IT WOULD HAVE HAPPENED ALREADY, GOT IT?
ALSO...
IF WE EVACUATE ALL THESE PEOPLE AND NOTHING HAPPENS, WOULD YOU TAKE RESPONSIBILITY FOR IT?
WILL YOU COVER FOR ALL THE LOSSES THE DEPARTMENT STORE WILL SUFFER BECAUSE OF YOU?
...
I CAN'T THINK OF ANY OTHER WAY.
WHAT DO I DO?

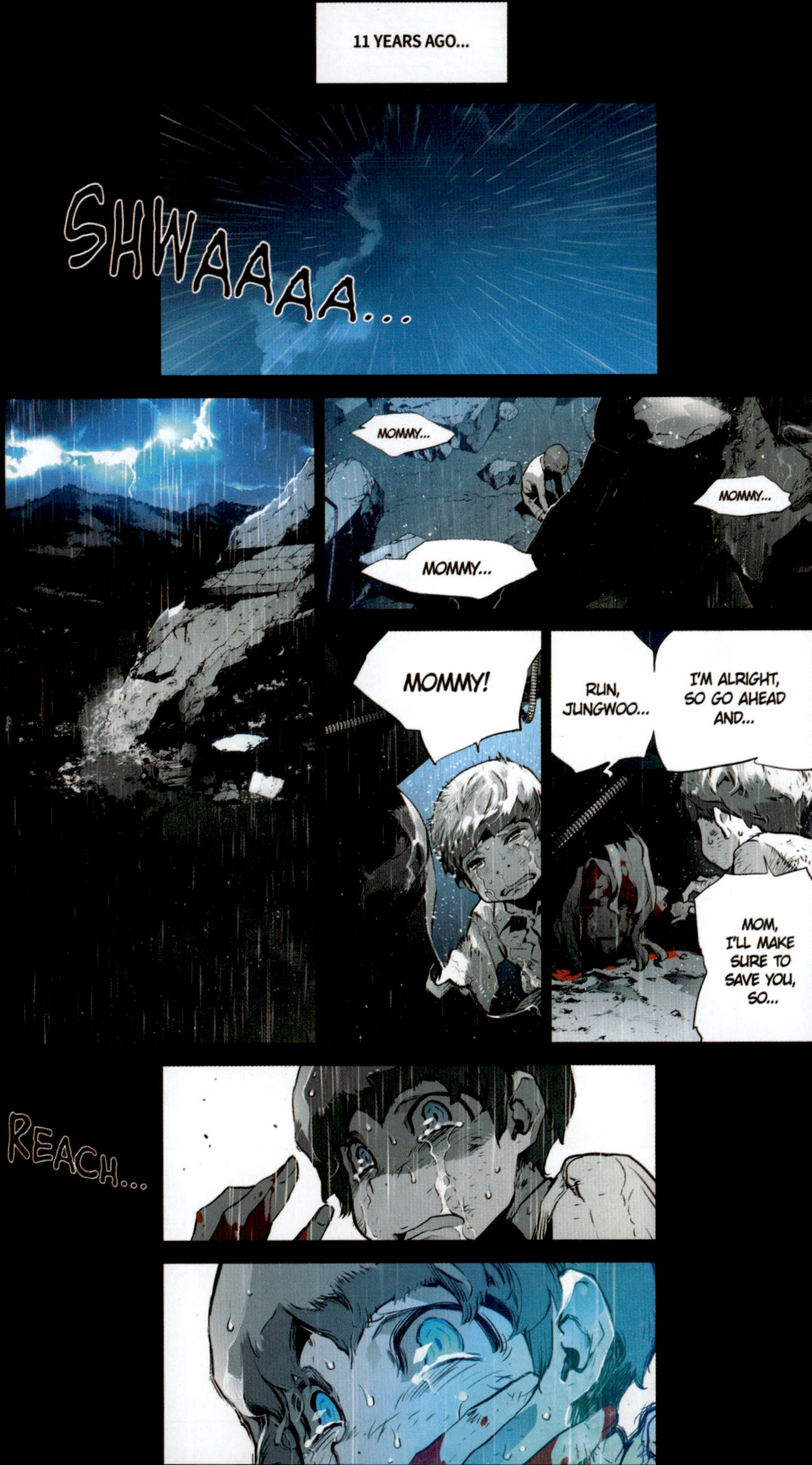
11 YEARS AGO...
SHWAAAAA...
MOMMY...
MOMMY...
MOMMY...
MOMMY!
RUN, JUNGWOO...
I'M ALRIGHT, SO GO AHEAD AND...
MOM, I'LL MAKE SURE TO SAVE YOU, SO...
REACH...

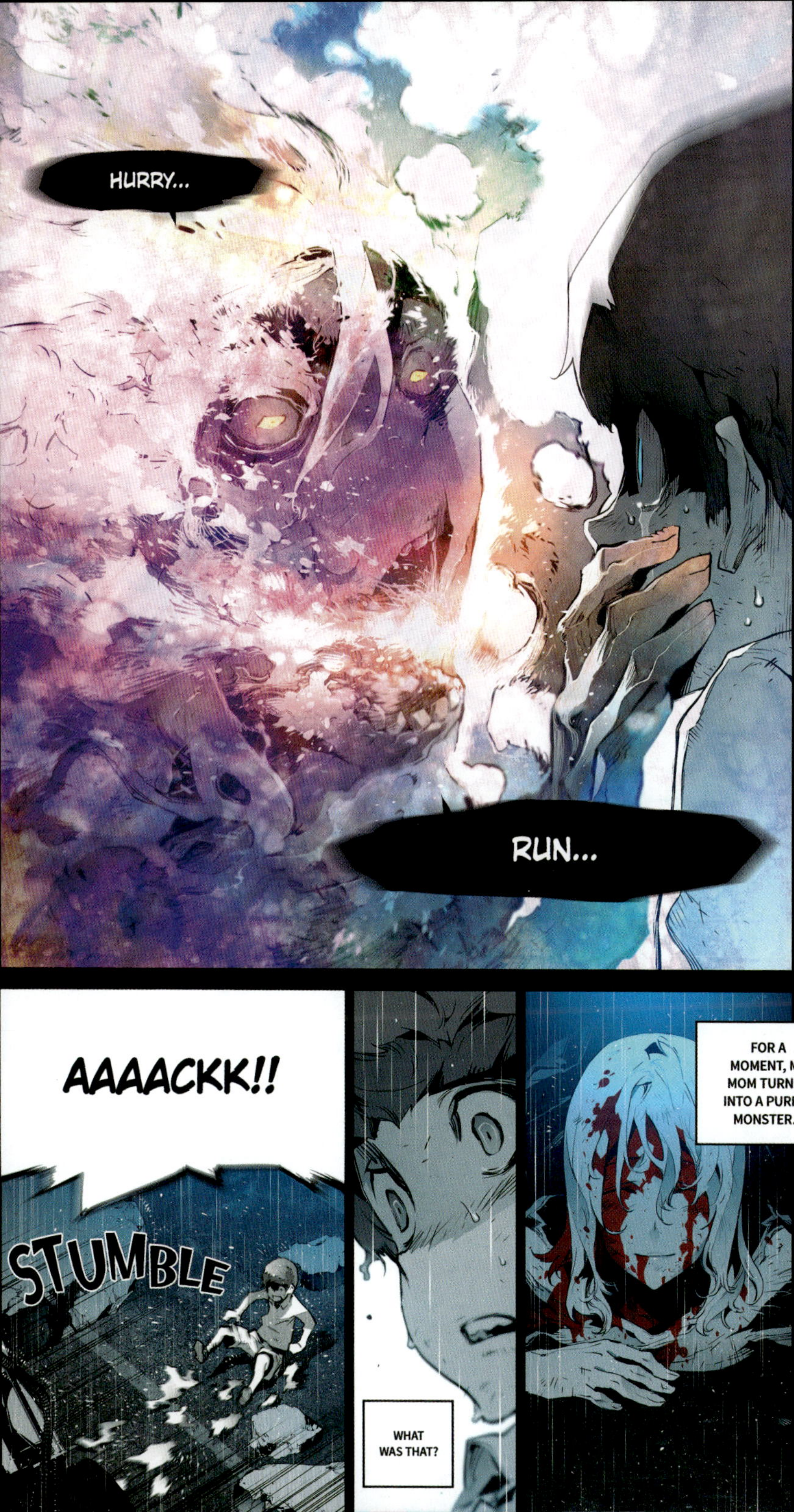
HURRY...
RUN...
AAAACKK!!
STUMBLE
WHAT WAS THAT?
FOR A MOMENT, MY MOM TURNED INTO A PURPLE MONSTER...

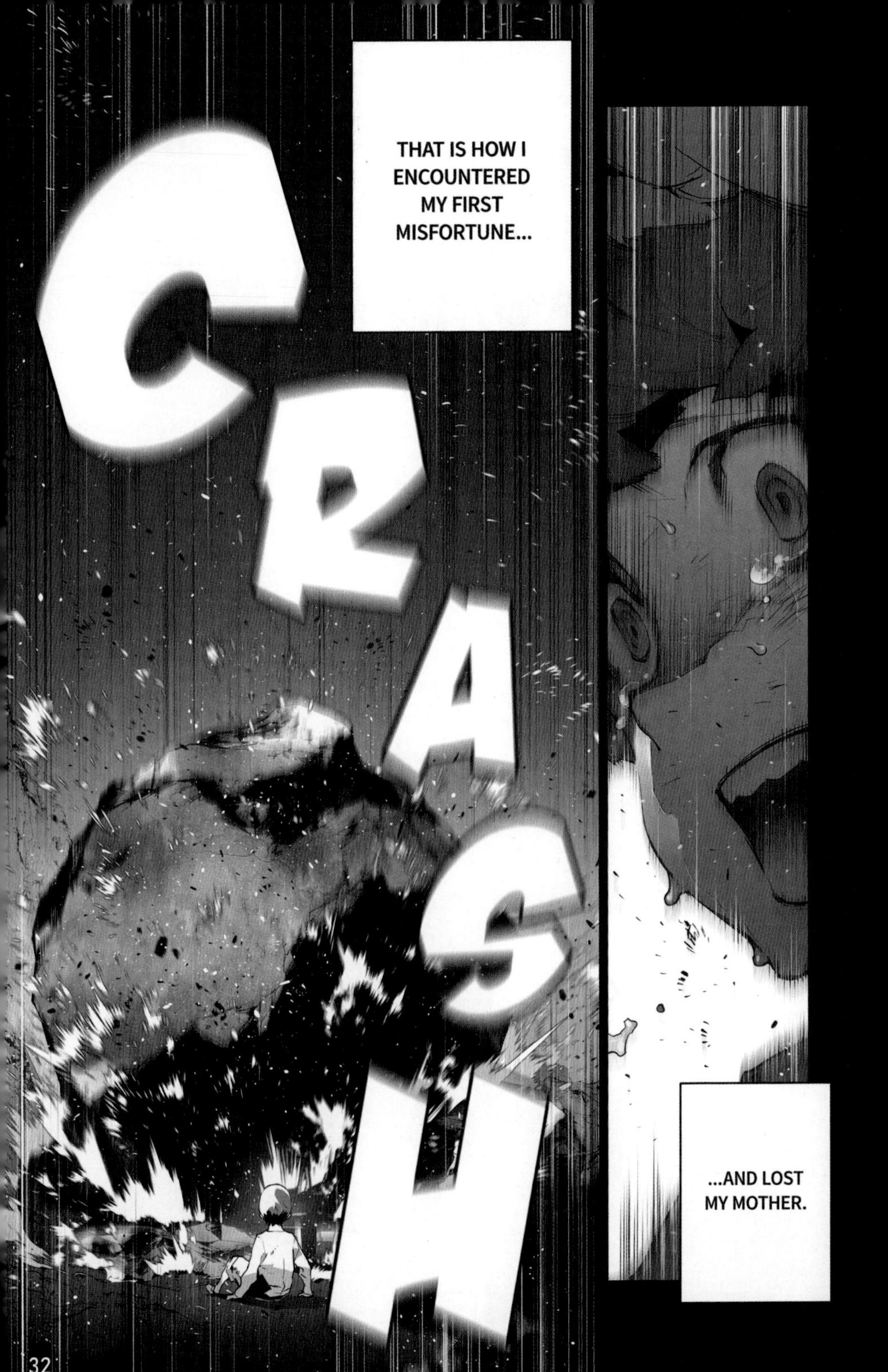
THAT IS HOW I ENCOUNTERED MY FIRST MISFORTUNE...
CRASH
...AND LOST MY MOTHER.

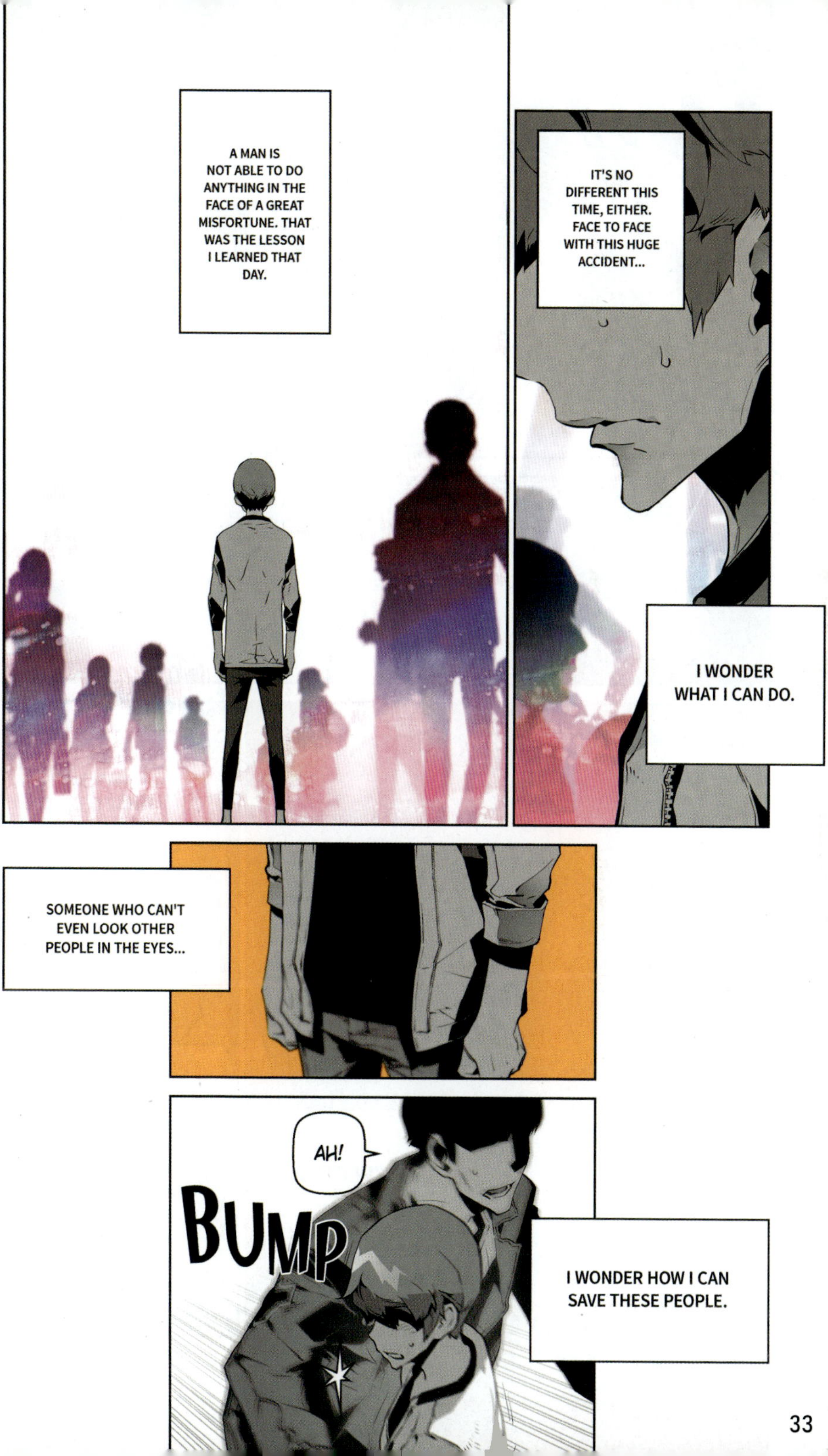
A MAN IS NOT ABLE TO DO ANYTHING IN THE FACE OF A GREAT MISFORTUNE. THAT WAS THE LESSON I LEARNED THAT DAY.
IT'S NO DIFFERENT THIS TIME, EITHER. FACE TO FACE WITH THIS HUGE ACCIDENT...
I WONDER WHAT I CAN DO.
SOMEONE WHO CAN'T EVEN LOOK OTHER PEOPLE IN THE EYES...
AH!
BUMP
I WONDER HOW I CAN SAVE THESE PEOPLE.

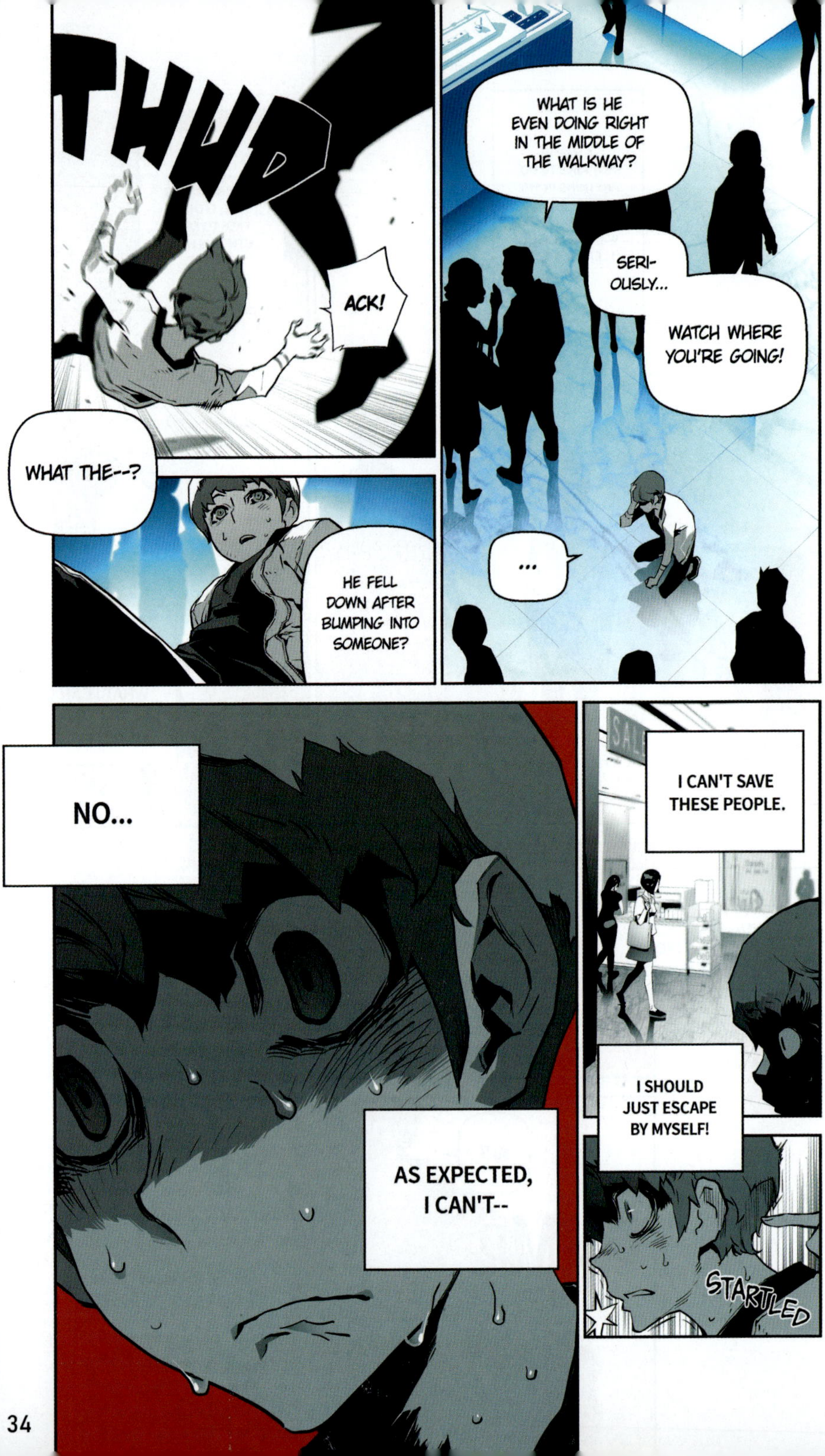

THUD
ACK!
WHAT THE--?
HE FELL DOWN AFTER BUMPING INTO SOMEONE?
WHAT IS HE EVEN DOING RIGHT IN THE MIDDLE OF THE WALKWAY?
SERI-OUSLY...
WATCH WHERE YOU'RE GOING!
...
NO...
AS EXPECTED, I CAN'T--
I CAN'T SAVE THESE PEOPLE.
I SHOULD JUST ESCAPE BY MYSELF!
STARTLED

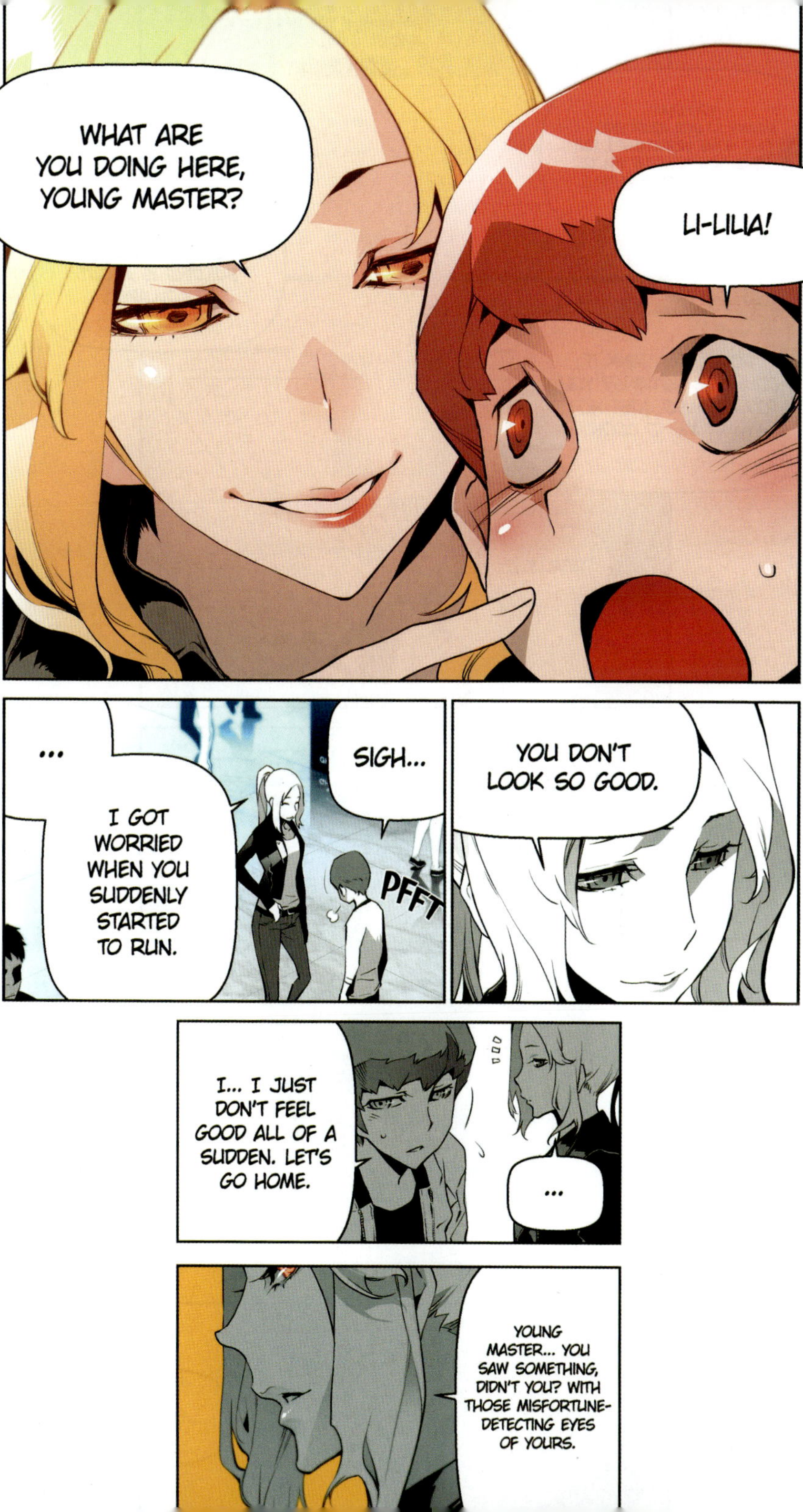
WHAT ARE YOU DOING HERE, YOUNG MASTER?
LI-LILIA!
...
I GOT WORRIED WHEN YOU SUDDENLY STARTED TO RUN.
SIGH...
PFFT
YOU DON'T LOOK SO GOOD.
I... I JUST DON'T FEEL GOOD ALL OF A SUDDEN. LET'S GO HOME.
...
YOUNG MASTER... YOU SAW SOMETHING, DIDN'T YOU? WITH THOSE MISFORTUNE-DETECTING EYES OF YOURS.

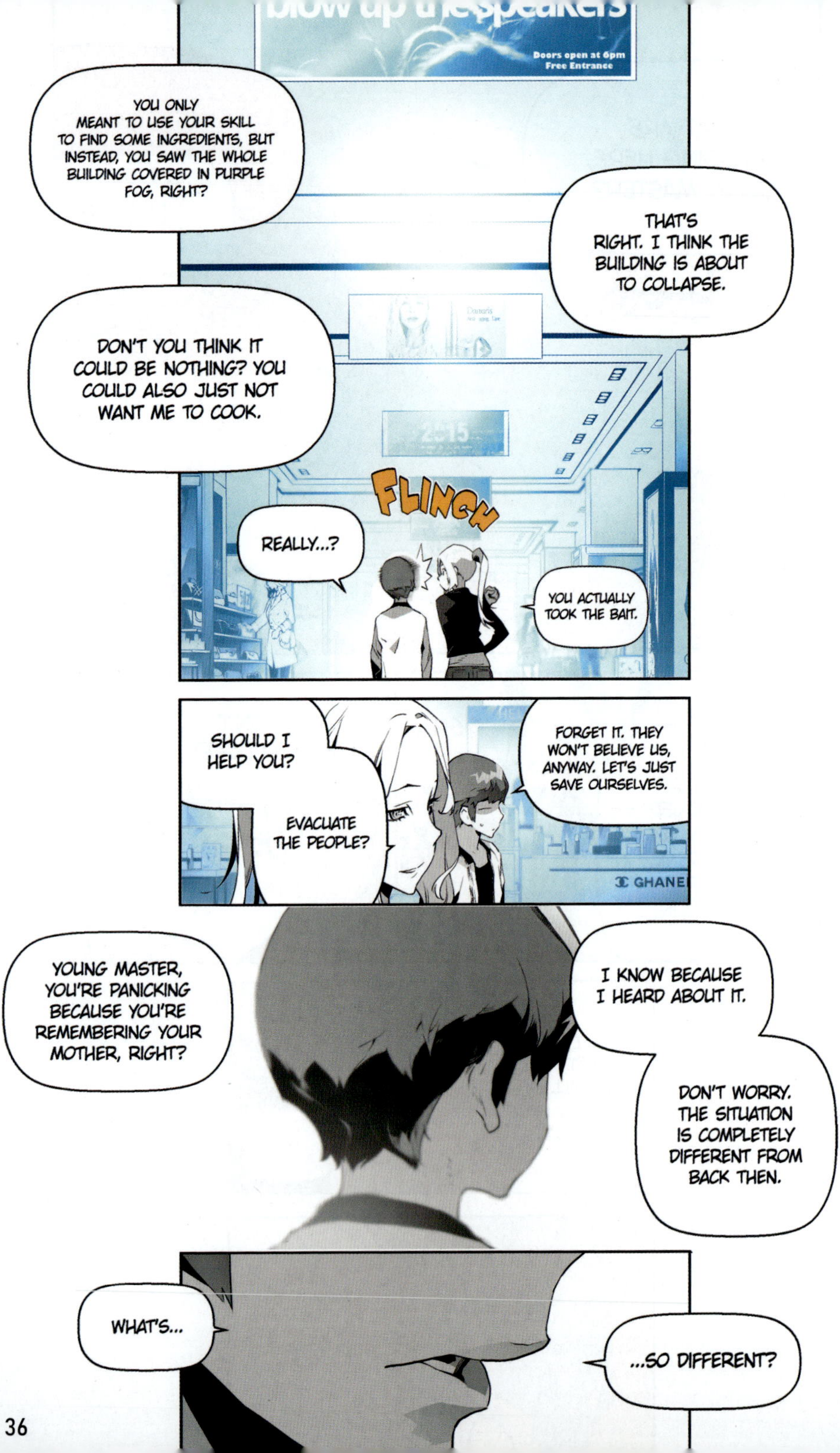

blow up the speakers
Doors open at 6pm
Free Entrance
YOU ONLY MEANT TO USE YOUR SKILL TO FIND SOME INGREDIENTS, BUT INSTEAD, YOU SAW THE WHOLE BUILDING COVERED IN PURPLE FOG, RIGHT?
THAT'S RIGHT. I THINK THE BUILDING IS ABOUT TO COLLAPSE.
DON'T YOU THINK IT COULD BE NOTHING? YOU COULD ALSO JUST NOT WANT ME TO COOK.
FLINCH
REALLY...?
YOU ACTUALLY TOOK THE BAIT.
SHOULD I HELP YOU?
EVACUATE THE PEOPLE?
FORGET IT. THEY WON'T BELIEVE US, ANYWAY. LET'S JUST SAVE OURSELVES.
GHANEL
YOUNG MASTER, YOU'RE PANICKING BECAUSE YOU'RE REMEMBERING YOUR MOTHER, RIGHT?
I KNOW BECAUSE I HEARD ABOUT IT.
DON'T WORRY. THE SITUATION IS COMPLETELY DIFFERENT FROM BACK THEN.
WHAT'S...
...SO DIFFERENT?

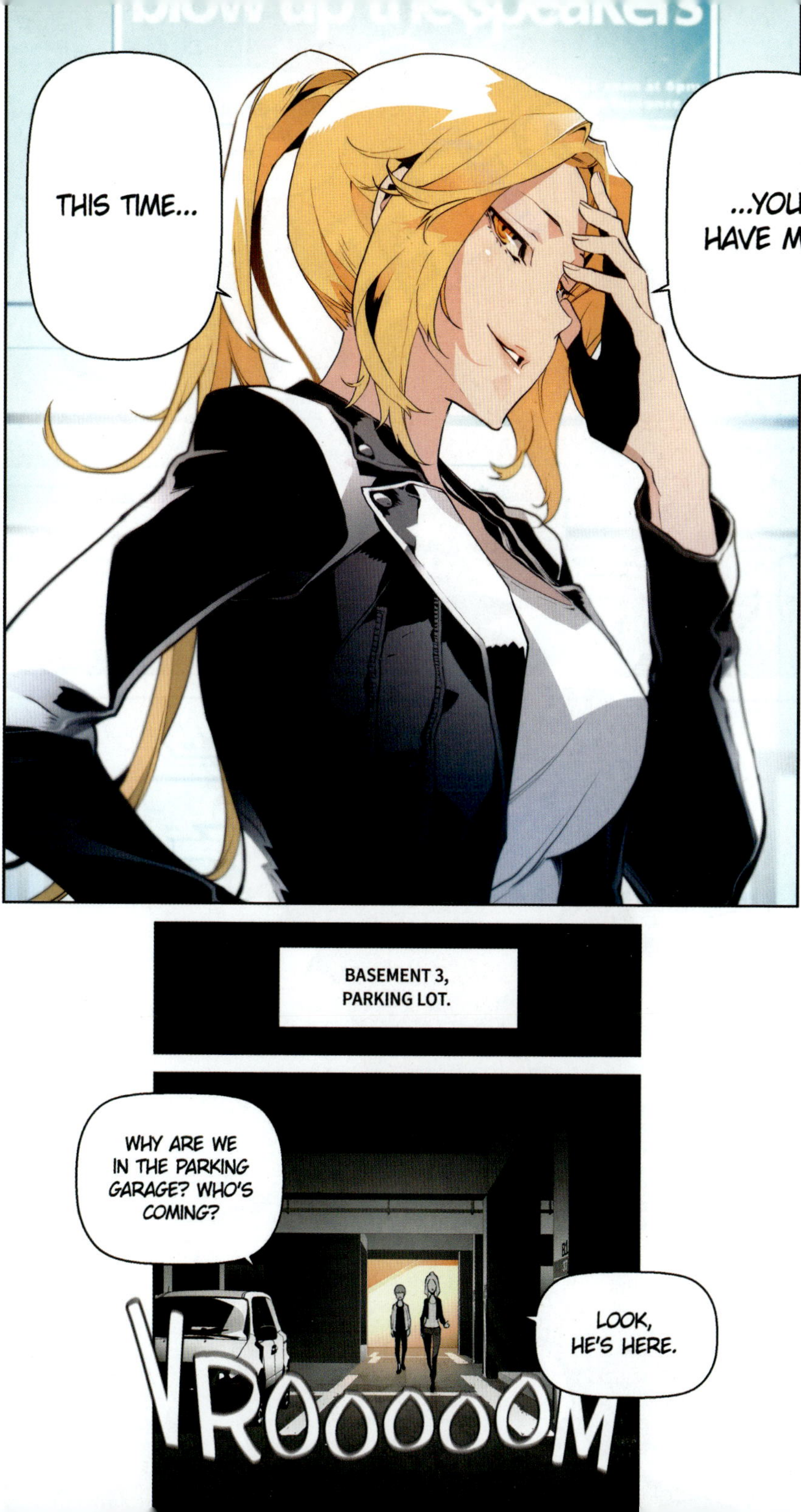
THIS TIME...
...YOU HAVE ME.
BASEMENT 3, PARKING LOT.
WHY ARE WE IN THE PARKING GARAGE? WHO'S COMING?
LOOK, HE'S HERE.
VROOOOOM

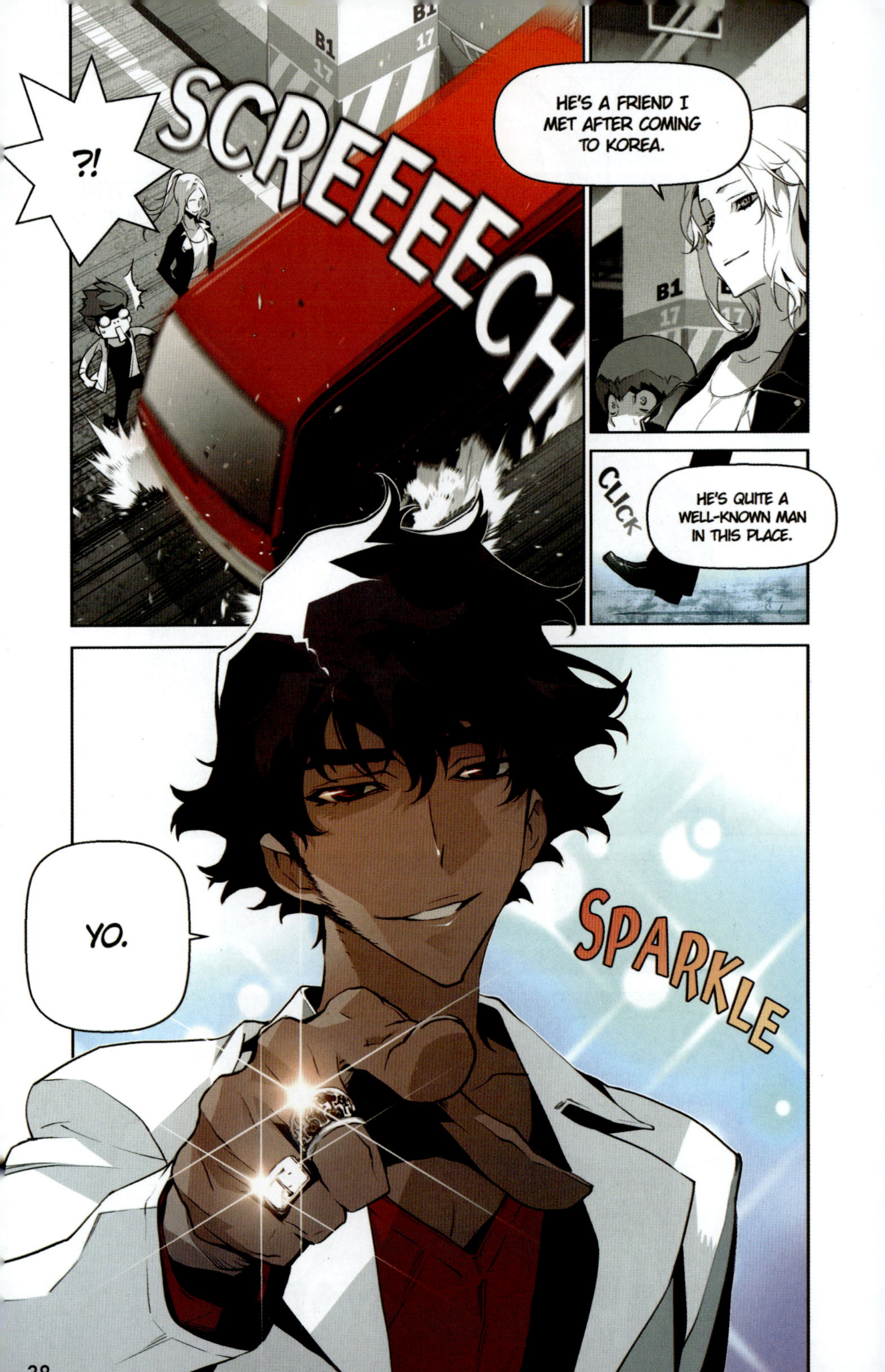
?!
SCREEEEECH
HE'S A FRIEND I MET AFTER COMING TO KOREA.
CLICK
HE'S QUITE A WELL-KNOWN MAN IN THIS PLACE.
YO.
SPARKLE

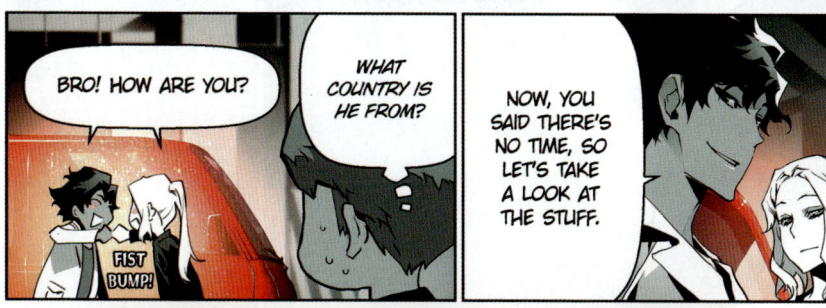

A... FOREIGNER?

...

BRO! HOW ARE YOU?

FIST BUMP!

WHAT COUNTRY IS HE FROM?

NOW, YOU SAID THERE'S NO TIME, SO LET'S TAKE A LOOK AT THE STUFF.

HUH... ...?

WHAT ON EARTH...

...IS ALL OF THIS?

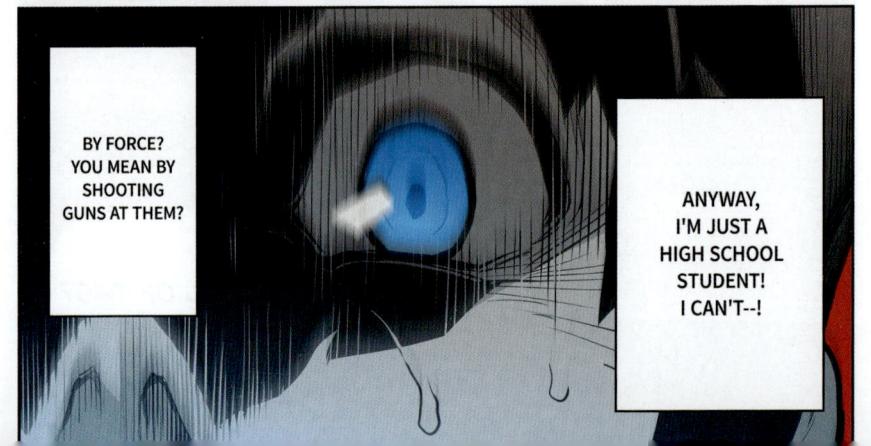

"IF THEY DON'T LISTEN WHEN WE ASK THEM NICELY, WE'LL JUST KICK THEM OUT BY FORCE."

CLICK

"HUH?"

THE CAR'S FILLED WITH GUNS...

NO WAY... ARE THESE ALL REAL GUNS?!

"BY FORCE? YOU MEAN BY SHOOTING GUNS AT THEM?"

"ANYWAY, I'M JUST A HIGH SCHOOL STUDENT! I CAN'T--!"

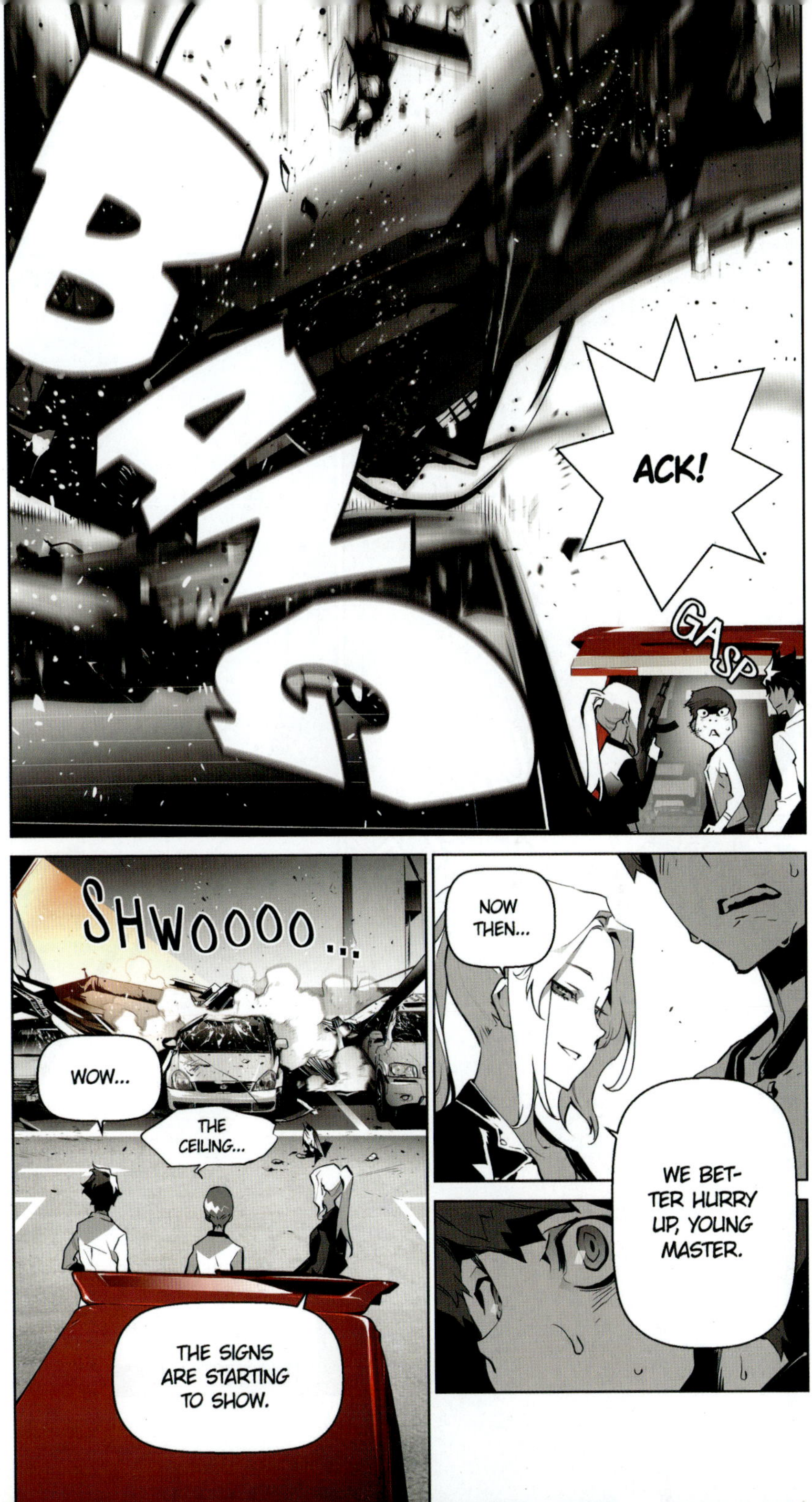
BANG
ACK!
GASP
SHWOOOO...
WOW...
THE CEILING...
THE SIGNS ARE STARTING TO SHOW.
NOW THEN...
WE BETTER HURRY UP, YOUNG MASTER.

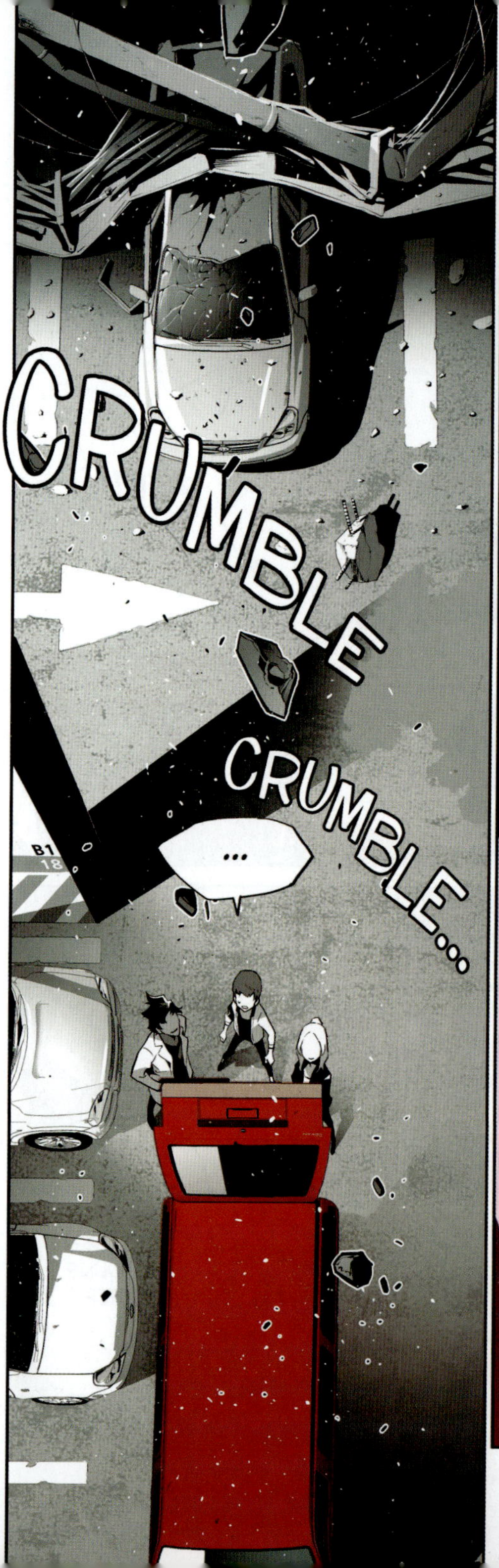
CRUMBLE
CRUMBLE
CRUMBLE...
...
B1
18
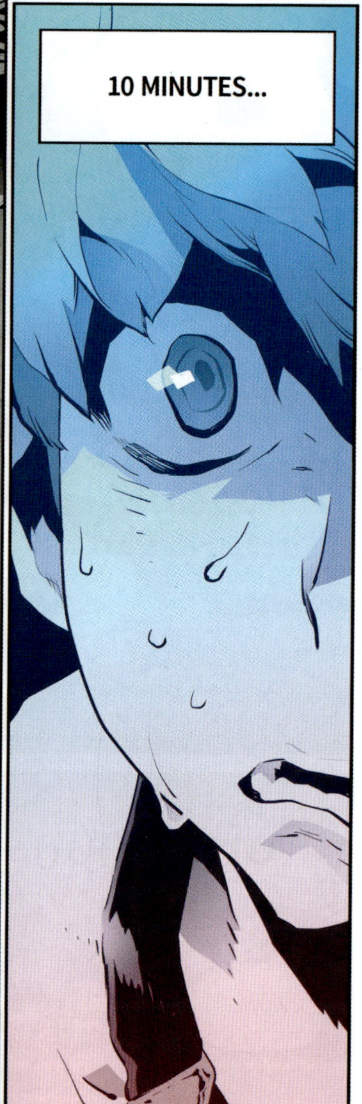
10 MINUTES...
...BEFORE THE DEPARTMENT STORE COLLAPSES.

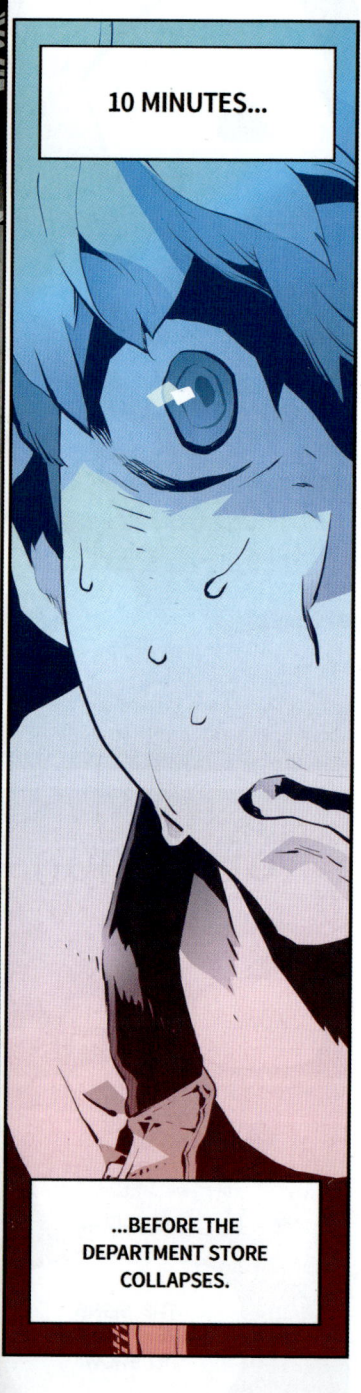

TERROR MAN

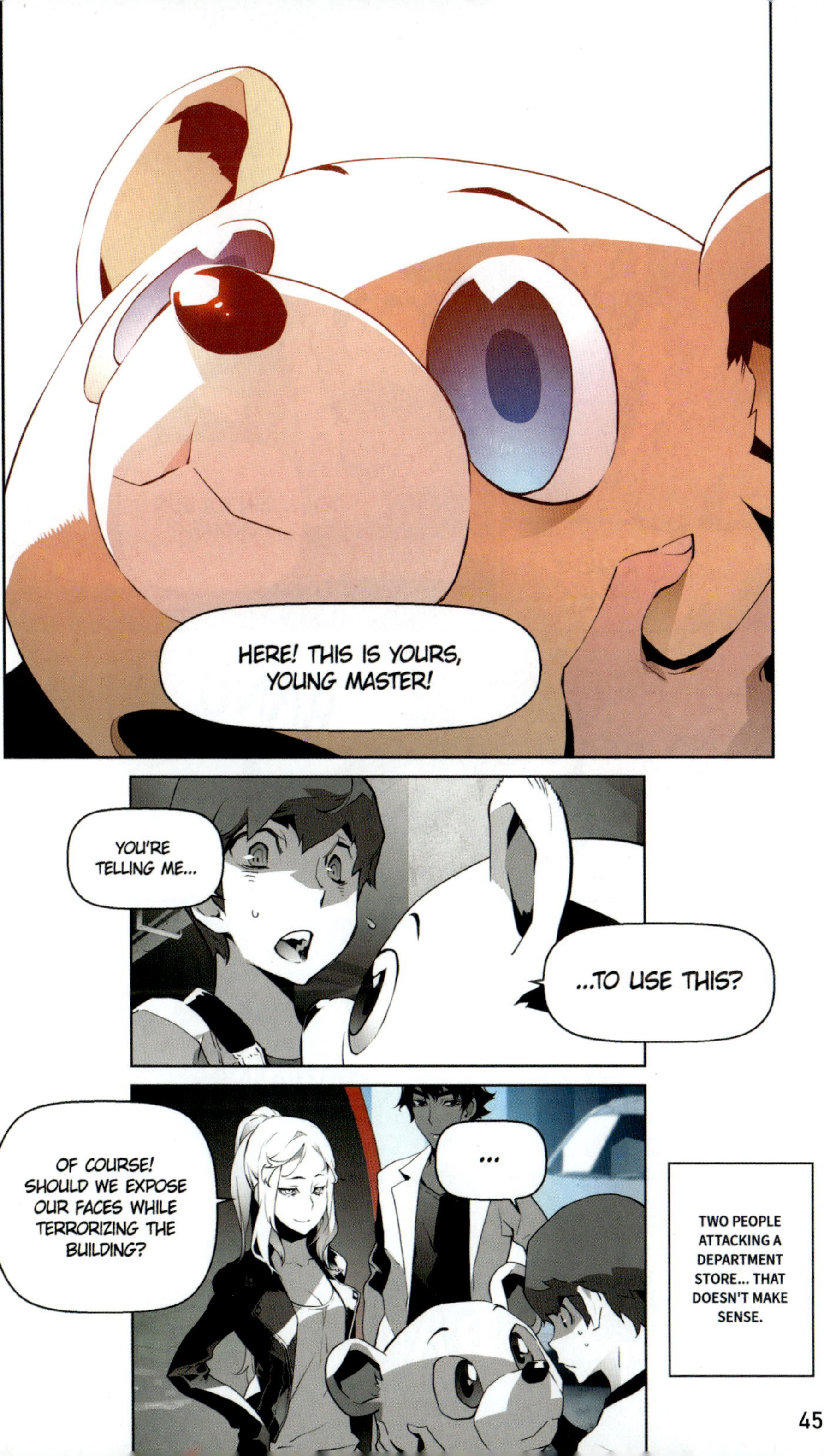
HERE! THIS IS YOURS, YOUNG MASTER!
YOU'RE TELLING ME...
...TO USE THIS?
OF COURSE! SHOULD WE EXPOSE OUR FACES WHILE TERRORIZING THE BUILDING?
...
TWO PEOPLE ATTACKING A DEPARTMENT STORE... THAT DOESN'T MAKE SENSE.

"WHAT'S THIS?"

"WE HAVE TO GO IN AND CAUSE A RUCKUS, SO EVERYONE GETS OUT QUICKLY."

"ISN'T A GUN ENOUGH?"

"A SMOKE GRENADE."

"SURE, IF WE HAD REAL GUNS."

BANG BANG BANG

"UNFORTUNATELY, THESE ARE JUST BB GUNS."

"OH..."

BANG BANG BANG BANG

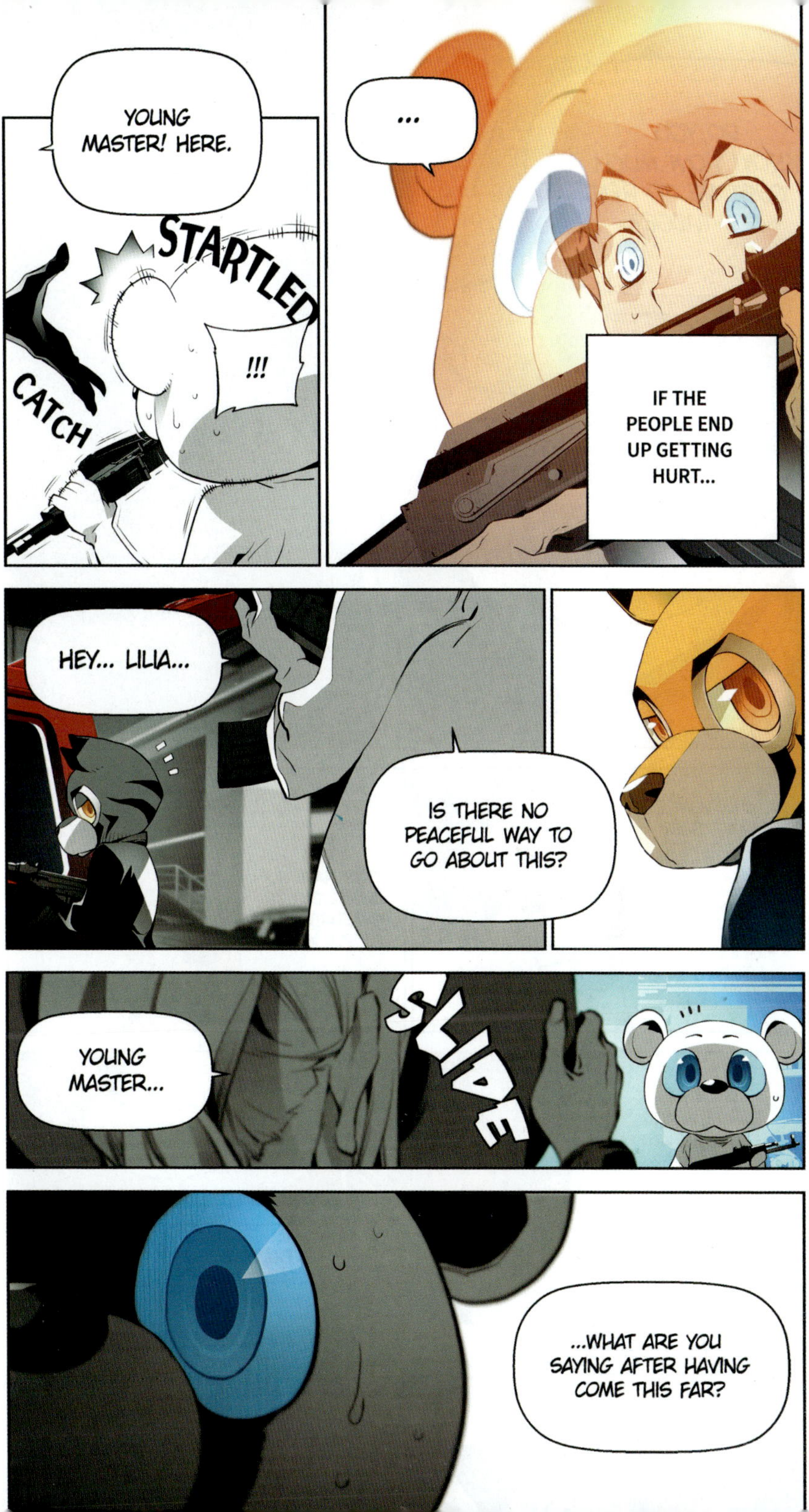
YOUNG MASTER! HERE.
STARTLED
!!!
CATCH
...
IF THE PEOPLE END UP GETTING HURT...
HEY... LILIA...
IS THERE NO PEACEFUL WAY TO GO ABOUT THIS?
YOUNG MASTER...
SLIDE
...WHAT ARE YOU SAYING AFTER HAVING COME THIS FAR?

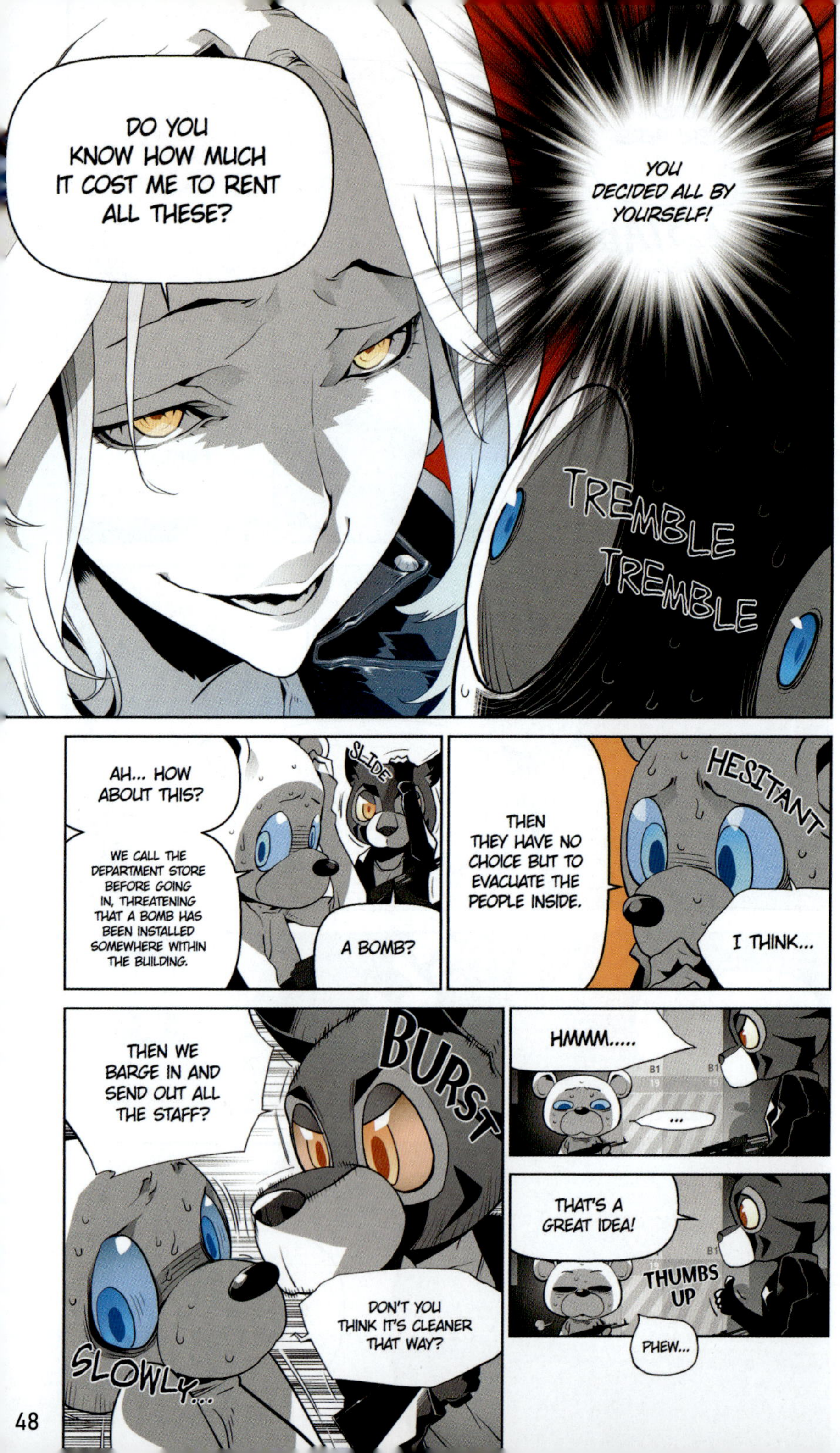
DO YOU KNOW HOW MUCH IT COST ME TO RENT ALL THESE?
YOU DECIDED ALL BY YOURSELF!
TREMBLE TREMBLE
AH... HOW ABOUT THIS?
WE CALL THE DEPARTMENT STORE BEFORE GOING IN, THREATENING THAT A BOMB HAS BEEN INSTALLED SOMEWHERE WITHIN THE BUILDING.
SLIDE
A BOMB?
THEN THEY HAVE NO CHOICE BUT TO EVACUATE THE PEOPLE INSIDE.
HESITANT
I THINK...
THEN WE BARGE IN AND SEND OUT ALL THE STAFF?
BURST
DON'T YOU THINK IT'S CLEANER THAT WAY?
SLOWLY...
HMMM.....
...
THAT'S A GREAT IDEA!
THUMBS UP
PHEW...

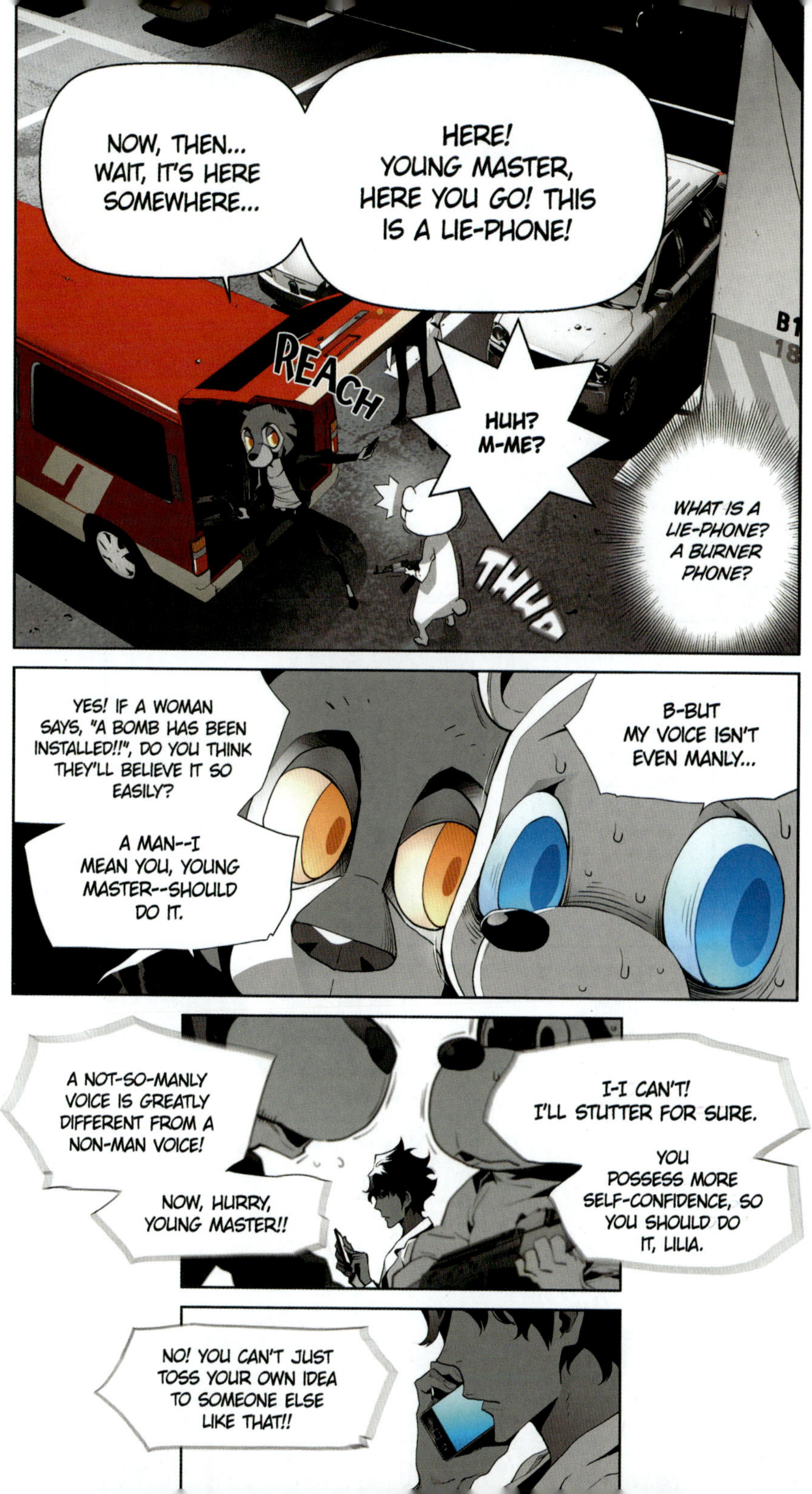
NOW, THEN... WAIT, IT'S HERE SOMEWHERE...
HERE! YOUNG MASTER, HERE YOU GO! THIS IS A LIE-PHONE!
REACH
HUH? M-ME?
WHAT IS A LIE-PHONE? A BURNER PHONE?
THUD
B1
YES! IF A WOMAN SAYS, "A BOMB HAS BEEN INSTALLED!!", DO YOU THINK THEY'LL BELIEVE IT SO EASILY?
A MAN--I MEAN YOU, YOUNG MASTER--SHOULD DO IT.
B-BUT MY VOICE ISN'T EVEN MANLY...
A NOT-SO-MANLY VOICE IS GREATLY DIFFERENT FROM A NON-MAN VOICE!
NOW, HURRY, YOUNG MASTER!!
I-I CAN'T! I'LL STUTTER FOR SURE.
YOU POSSESS MORE SELF-CONFIDENCE, SO YOU SHOULD DO IT, LILIA.
NO! YOU CAN'T JUST TOSS YOUR OWN IDEA TO SOMEONE ELSE LIKE THAT!!

HELLO, SOMEBODY INSTALLED A BOMB INSIDE THE DEPARTMENT STORE, Y'KNOW.

WITHIN AN HOUR, LEAVE A SACK FILLED WITH 15 KILOS OF 50,000 WON BILLS 100 METERS AWAY FROM THE FRONT ENTRANCE OF THE DEPARTMENT STORE, Y'GOT IT?

AY, THAT GUY ALREADY WENT INSIDE THE BUILDIN'! Y'THINK I'M JOKING?

'NYWAYS, IT WILL BLOW UP AFTER AN HOUR, Y'GOT IT?!

CHUNGCHEONG DIALECT?

IF YOU'RE GOING TO DO THAT, THEN YOU MIGHT AS WELL DO IT IN THE SEOUL DIALECT. THAT WAS WAY TOO OBVIOUS.

I'M FROM CHUNGCHEONG, SO I CAN'T SPEAK IN SEOUL DIALECT, Y'KNOW.

WHAT DO YOU MEAN? I ALREADY TAUGHT YOU.

WASN'T THAT RUSSIAN?

NICE, BONGCHUN! YOU DID GREAT!!

YO!

HIGH FIVE

I THOUGHT THAT WAS DUBBED FOR A MOMENT...

IS THIS WHAT THEY MEANT BY A MULTICULTURAL SOCIETY...?

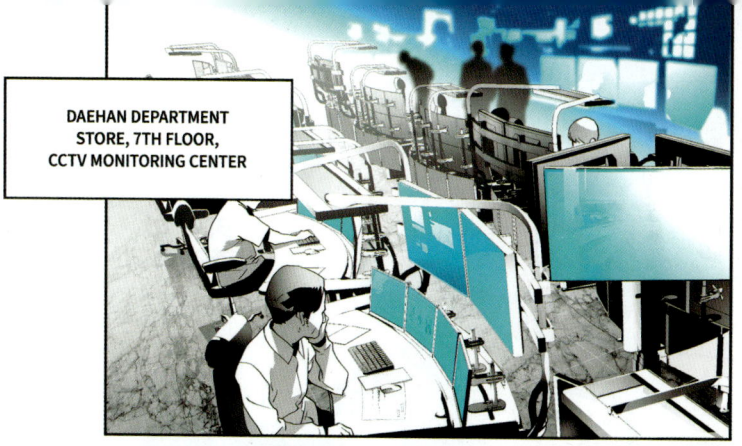

DAEHAN DEPARTMENT STORE, 7TH FLOOR, CCTV MONITORING CENTER

A BOMB, ALL OF A SUDDEN...

CLICK

WHAT'S THAT ABOUT?

A MAN WHO SOUNDS LIKE HE'S FROM CHUNGCHEONG CALLED AND SAID THERE'S A BOMB IN THE BUILDING AND TOLD US TO HAND OVER MONEY.

THEY MUST BE BORED. NOW HURRY AND ROLL THE DICE. IT'S YOUR TURN.

OH, SHOOT!!

MAYBE YOU CALLED THE WRONG NUMBER?

NAH, I CALLED THE RIGHT ONE.

THERE'S NO REACTION...

YEAH...

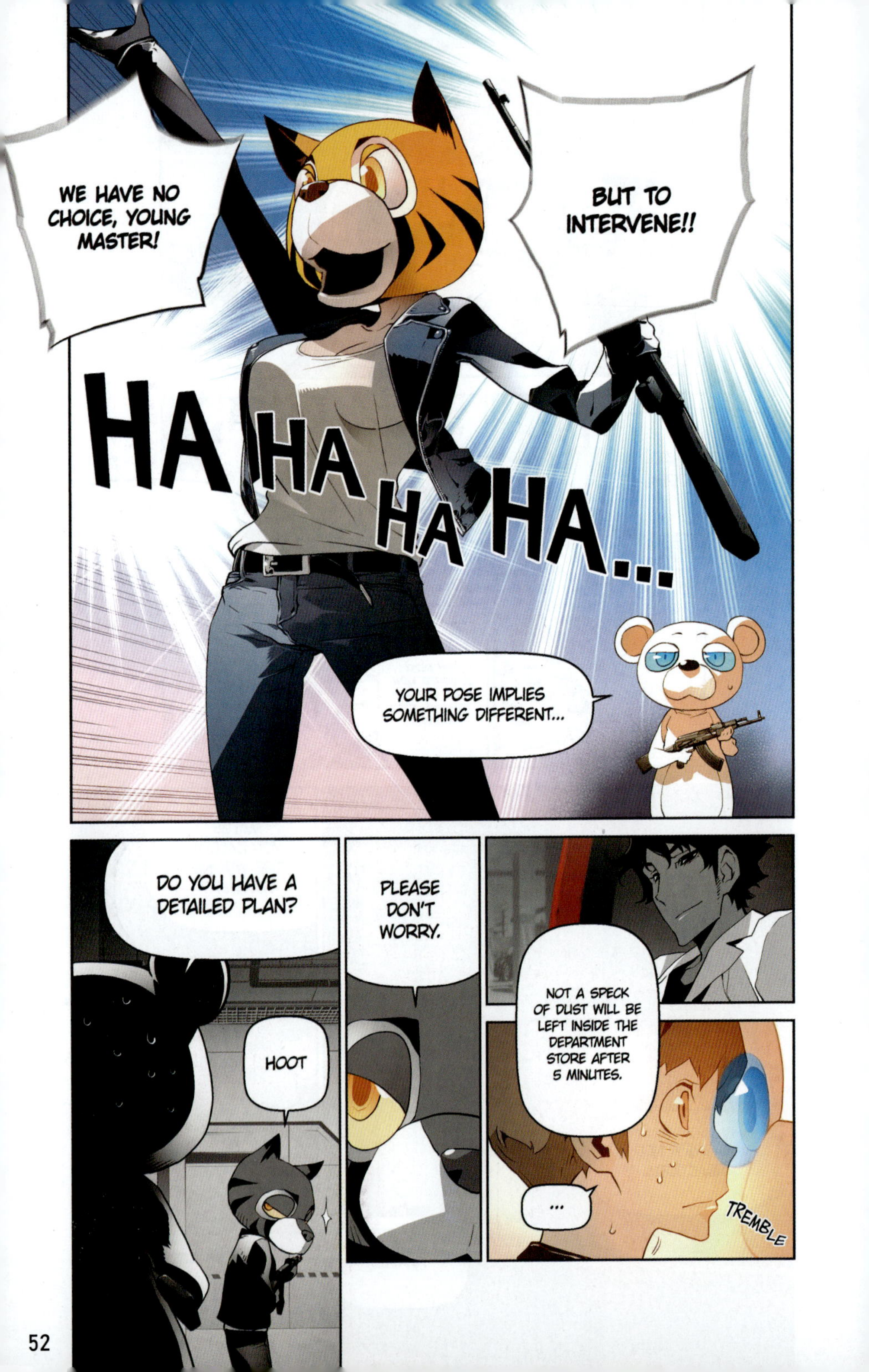
WE HAVE NO CHOICE, YOUNG MASTER!
BUT TO INTERVENE!!
HA HA HA HA...
YOUR POSE IMPLIES SOMETHING DIFFERENT...
DO YOU HAVE A DETAILED PLAN?
PLEASE DON'T WORRY.
HOOT
NOT A SPECK OF DUST WILL BE LEFT INSIDE THE DEPARTMENT STORE AFTER 5 MINUTES.
...
TREMBLE

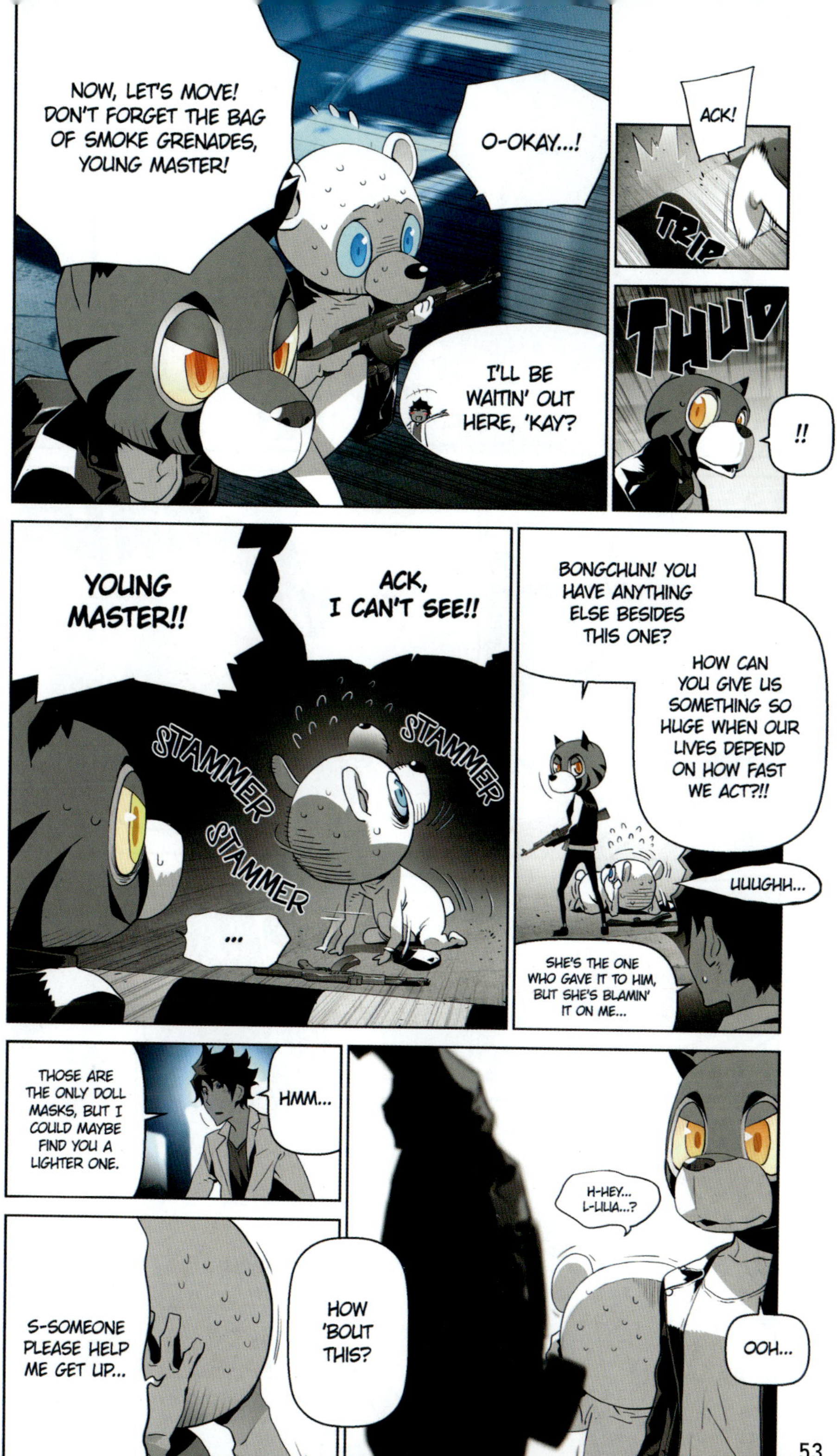
NOW, LET'S MOVE! DON'T FORGET THE BAG OF SMOKE GRENADES, YOUNG MASTER!
O-OKAY...!
I'LL BE WAITIN' OUT HERE, 'KAY?
ACK!
TRIP
THUD
!!
YOUNG MASTER!!
ACK, I CAN'T SEE!!
STAMMER
STAMMER
STAMMER
...
BONGCHUN! YOU HAVE ANYTHING ELSE BESIDES THIS ONE?
HOW CAN YOU GIVE US SOMETHING SO HUGE WHEN OUR LIVES DEPEND ON HOW FAST WE ACT?!!
UUUGHH...
SHE'S THE ONE WHO GAVE IT TO HIM, BUT SHE'S BLAMIN' IT ON ME...
THOSE ARE THE ONLY DOLL MASKS, BUT I COULD MAYBE FIND YOU A LIGHTER ONE.
HMM...
S-SOMEONE PLEASE HELP ME GET UP...
HOW 'BOUT THIS?
H-HEY... L-LILIA...?
OOH...

PSSSHHT

?

SHOOOOO

BUMP

TSSSSS

FIRE!!

AAAHH!

AAAAHH!!

HUH...??

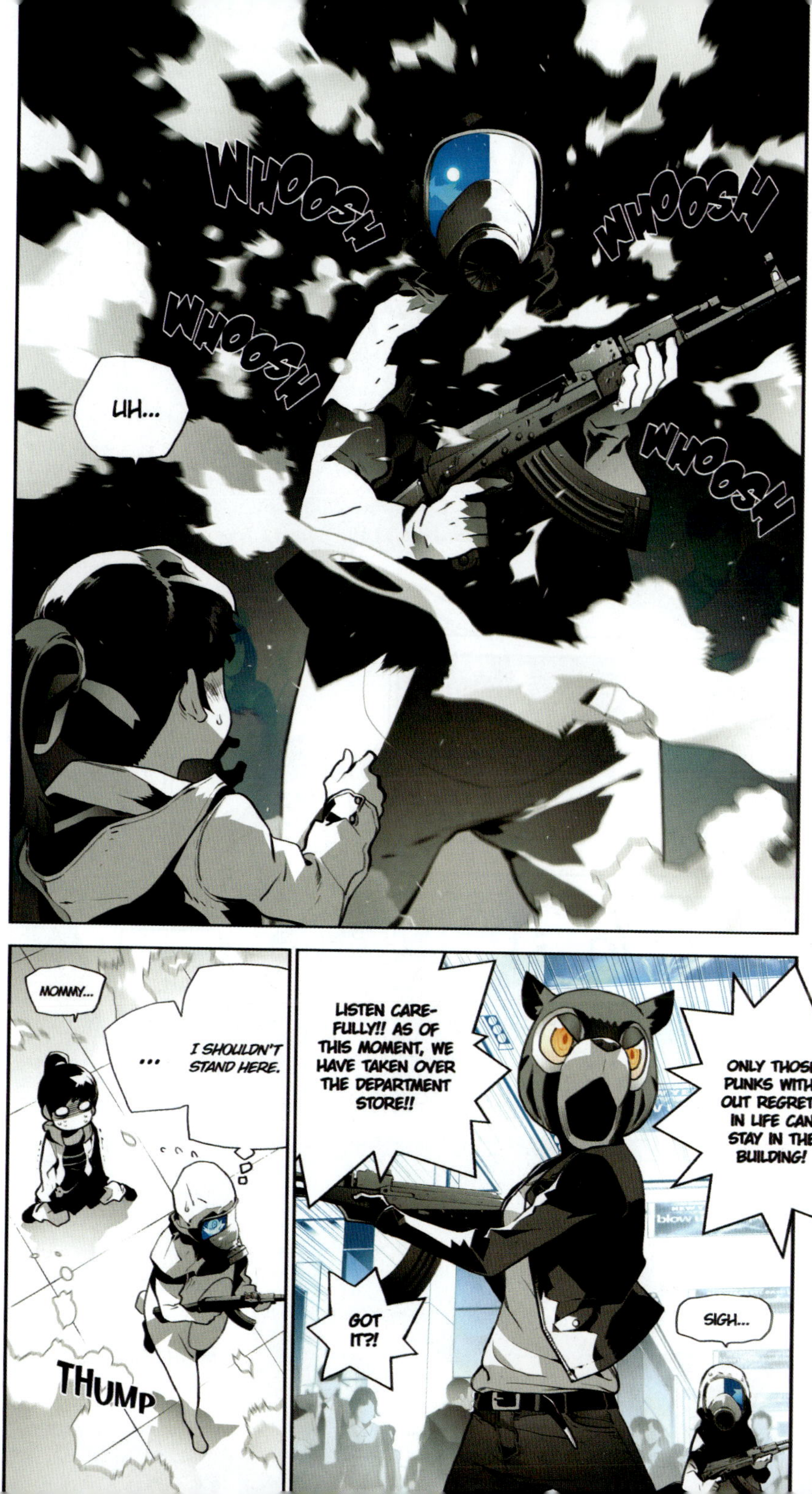
WHOOSH
WHOOSH
WHOOSH
UH...
WHOOSH
MOMMY...
...
I SHOULDN'T STAND HERE.
THUMP
LISTEN CARE-FULLY!! AS OF THIS MOMENT, WE HAVE TAKEN OVER THE DEPARTMENT STORE!!
ONLY THOSE PUNKS WITH-OUT REGRETS IN LIFE CAN STAY IN THE BUILDING!
GOT IT?!
SIGH...

EVERYONE ELSE... GET LOST!!

CLICK

WH-WHAT IS THIS? SOME KIND OF EVENT?

A BOMB SALE?

UNLIMITED SALE?

I DON'T THINK SO. LET'S JUST LEAVE.

SHUFFLE
SHUFFLE

AH...

WHAT ARE YOU DOING JUST STANDING AROUND?! SEEMS LIKE YOUR LIFE ISN'T ALL THAT PRECIOUS, HUH?!

JOLT

THE OLD LADY...

...MIGHT GET HURT.

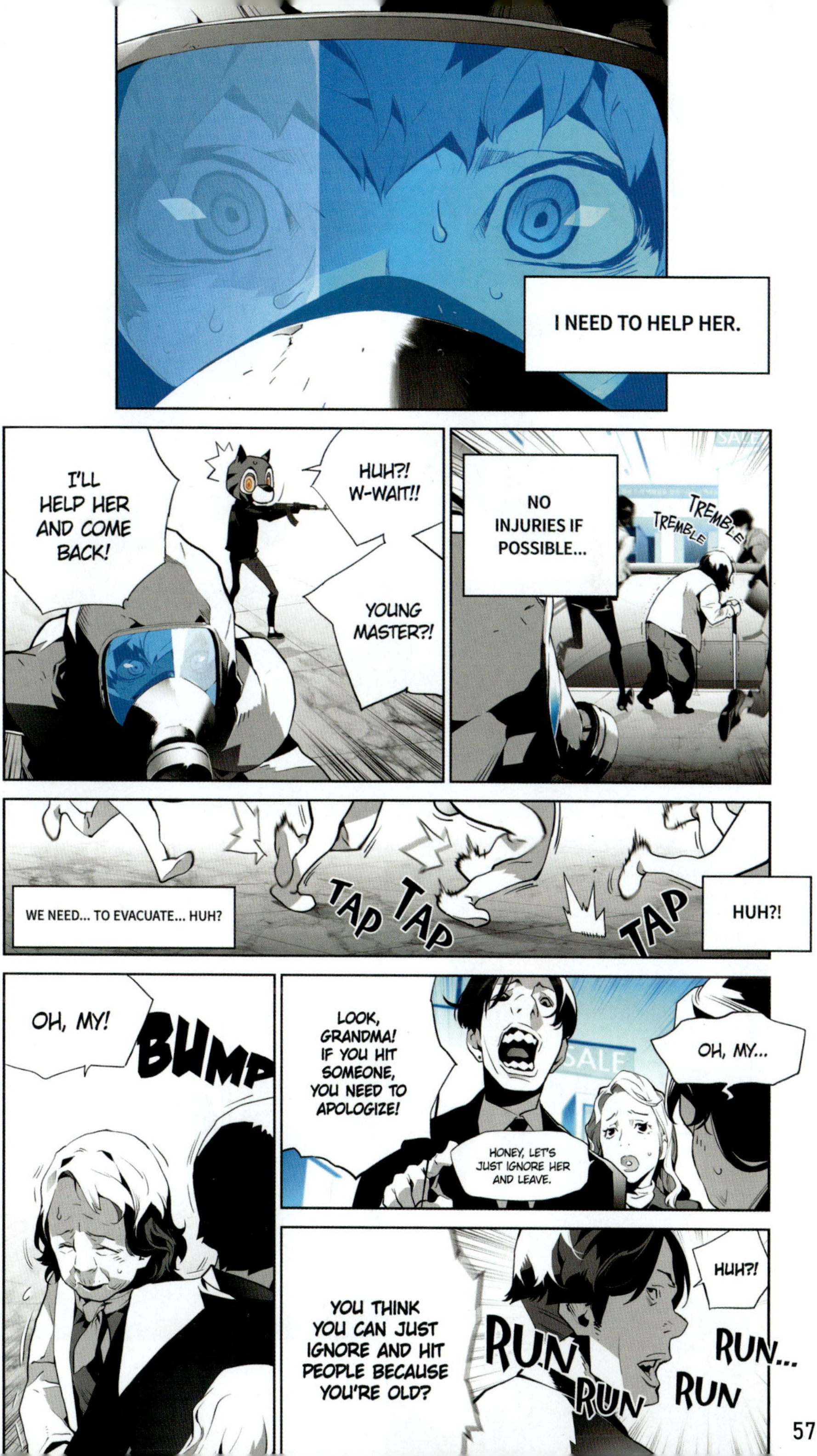

I NEED TO HELP HER.
I'LL HELP HER AND COME BACK!
HUH?! W-WAIT!!
YOUNG MASTER?!
NO INJURIES IF POSSIBLE...
TREMBLE
TREMBLE
SALE
WE NEED... TO EVACUATE... HUH?
TAP
TAP
TAP
HUH?!
OH, MY!
BUMP
LOOK, GRANDMA! IF YOU HIT SOMEONE, YOU NEED TO APOLOGIZE!
SALE
OH, MY...
HONEY, LET'S JUST IGNORE HER AND LEAVE.
YOU THINK YOU CAN JUST IGNORE AND HIT PEOPLE BECAUSE YOU'RE OLD?
HUH?!
RUN
RUN
RUN...
RUN

WHAM

OOF!

!!

H-HONEY!

AAAAAHHH!!

THUD

AH.

| I-I'M SORRY... I... IT'S... | THE TERRORIST KILLED MY BOYFRIEND!! | EEK!! |

MUMBLE MUMBLE

| I-I JUST...!! | !! | **TREMBLE TREMBLE** | NO! THIS PERSON'S NOT D--!! |

AAAH!!

HELP!!

SOMEBODY CALL THE POLICE!

HUH...!

N-NO...

HEY...

SOMEONE REPORT HIM!

THERE'S A TERRORIST HERE!

TERROR...

...IST?

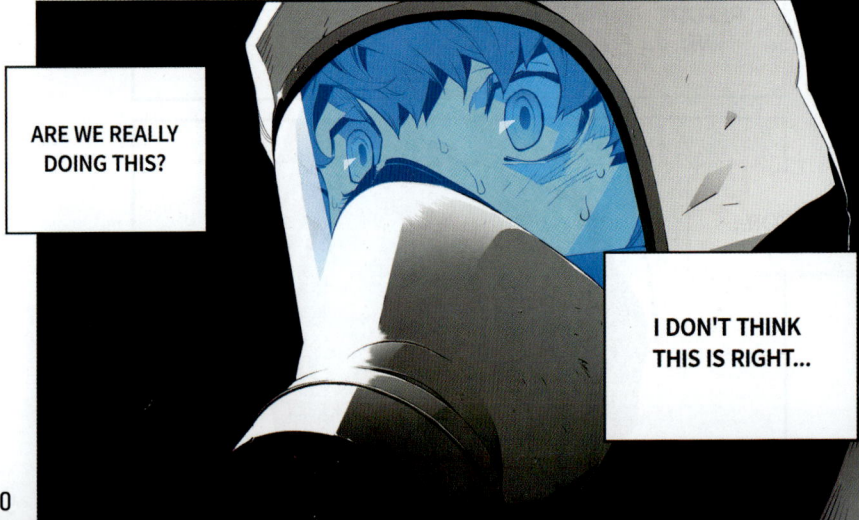

YOUNG MASTER!!

APPEAR

LI-LILIA!

EXACTLY WHAT WE NEEDED!

WHAT...?!

THUMBS UP

...

AS EXPECTED, YOU DO WHAT YOU NEED TO DO WHEN YOU HAVE TO!!

IF WE GO TO ANOTHER FLOOR AND CREATE A FUSS JUST LIKE THIS, EVERYONE WILL LEAVE ON THEIR OWN.

LET'S FINISH THIS BEFORE THE POLICE COME.

ARE WE REALLY DOING THIS?

I DON'T THINK THIS IS RIGHT...

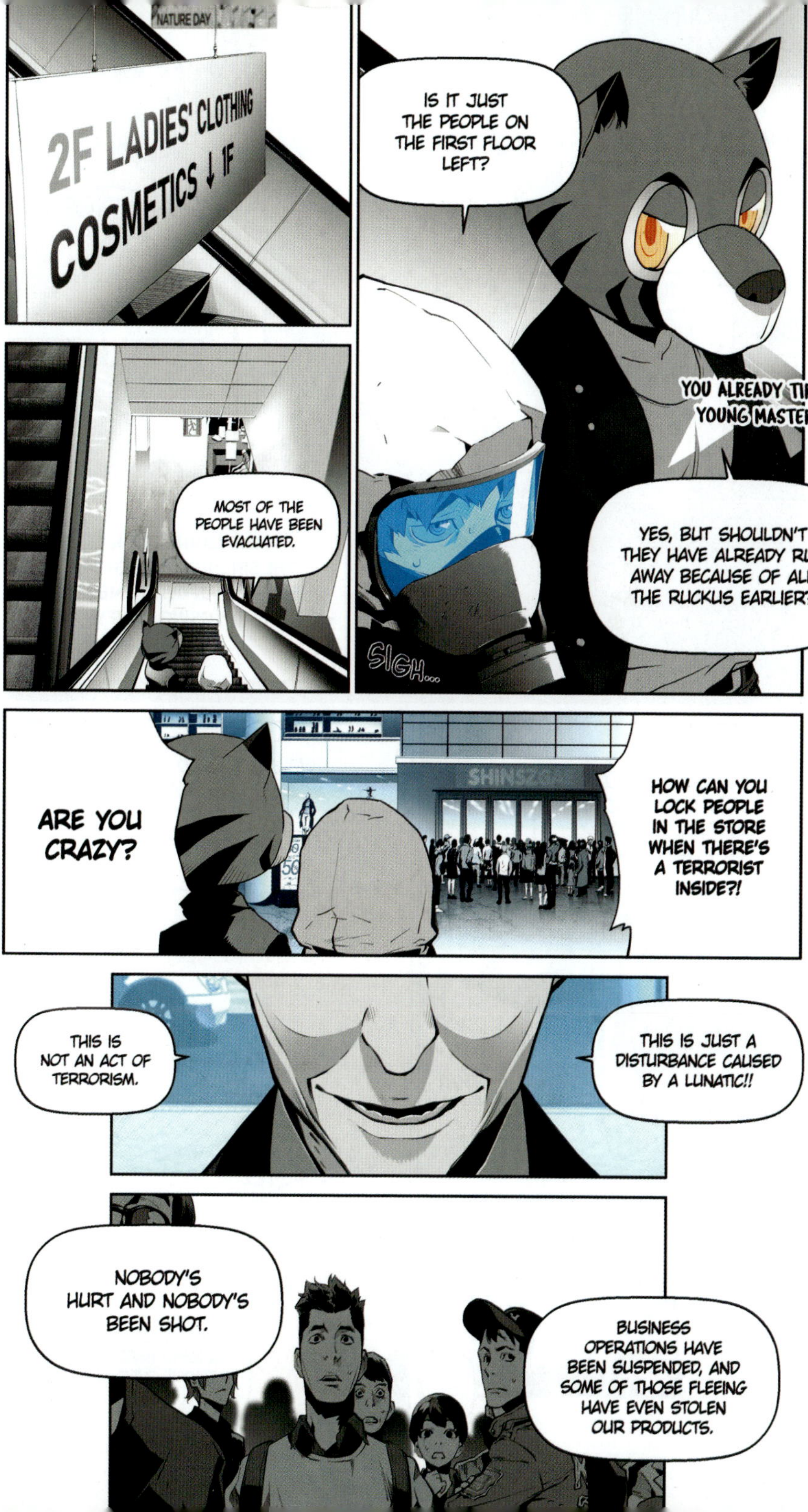
NATURE DAY
2F LADIES' CLOTHING
COSMETICS ↓ 1F
IS IT JUST THE PEOPLE ON THE FIRST FLOOR LEFT?
YOU ALREADY TIRED, YOUNG MASTER?
MOST OF THE PEOPLE HAVE BEEN EVACUATED.
YES, BUT SHOULDN'T THEY HAVE ALREADY RUN AWAY BECAUSE OF ALL THE RUCKUS EARLIER?
SIGH...
ARE YOU CRAZY?
HOW CAN YOU LOCK PEOPLE IN THE STORE WHEN THERE'S A TERRORIST INSIDE?!
THIS IS NOT AN ACT OF TERRORISM.
THIS IS JUST A DISTURBANCE CAUSED BY A LUNATIC!!
NOBODY'S HURT AND NOBODY'S BEEN SHOT.
BUSINESS OPERATIONS HAVE BEEN SUSPENDED, AND SOME OF THOSE FLEEING HAVE EVEN STOLEN OUR PRODUCTS.

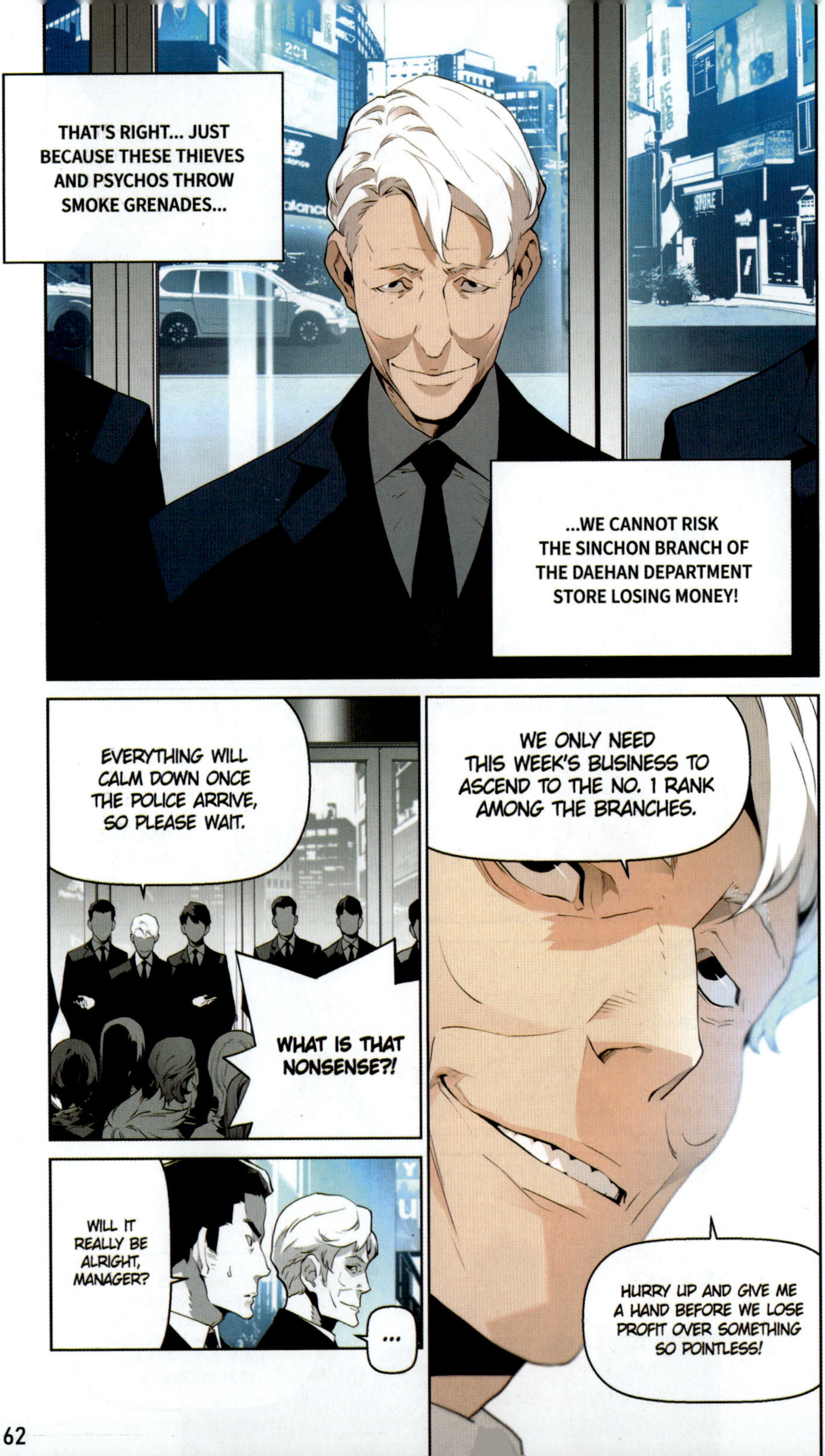
THAT'S RIGHT... JUST BECAUSE THESE THIEVES AND PSYCHOS THROW SMOKE GRENADES...
...WE CANNOT RISK THE SINCHON BRANCH OF THE DAEHAN DEPARTMENT STORE LOSING MONEY!
EVERYTHING WILL CALM DOWN ONCE THE POLICE ARRIVE, SO PLEASE WAIT.
WHAT IS THAT NONSENSE?!
WE ONLY NEED THIS WEEK'S BUSINESS TO ASCEND TO THE NO. 1 RANK AMONG THE BRANCHES.
WILL IT REALLY BE ALRIGHT, MANAGER?
...
HURRY UP AND GIVE ME A HAND BEFORE WE LOSE PROFIT OVER SOMETHING SO POINTLESS!

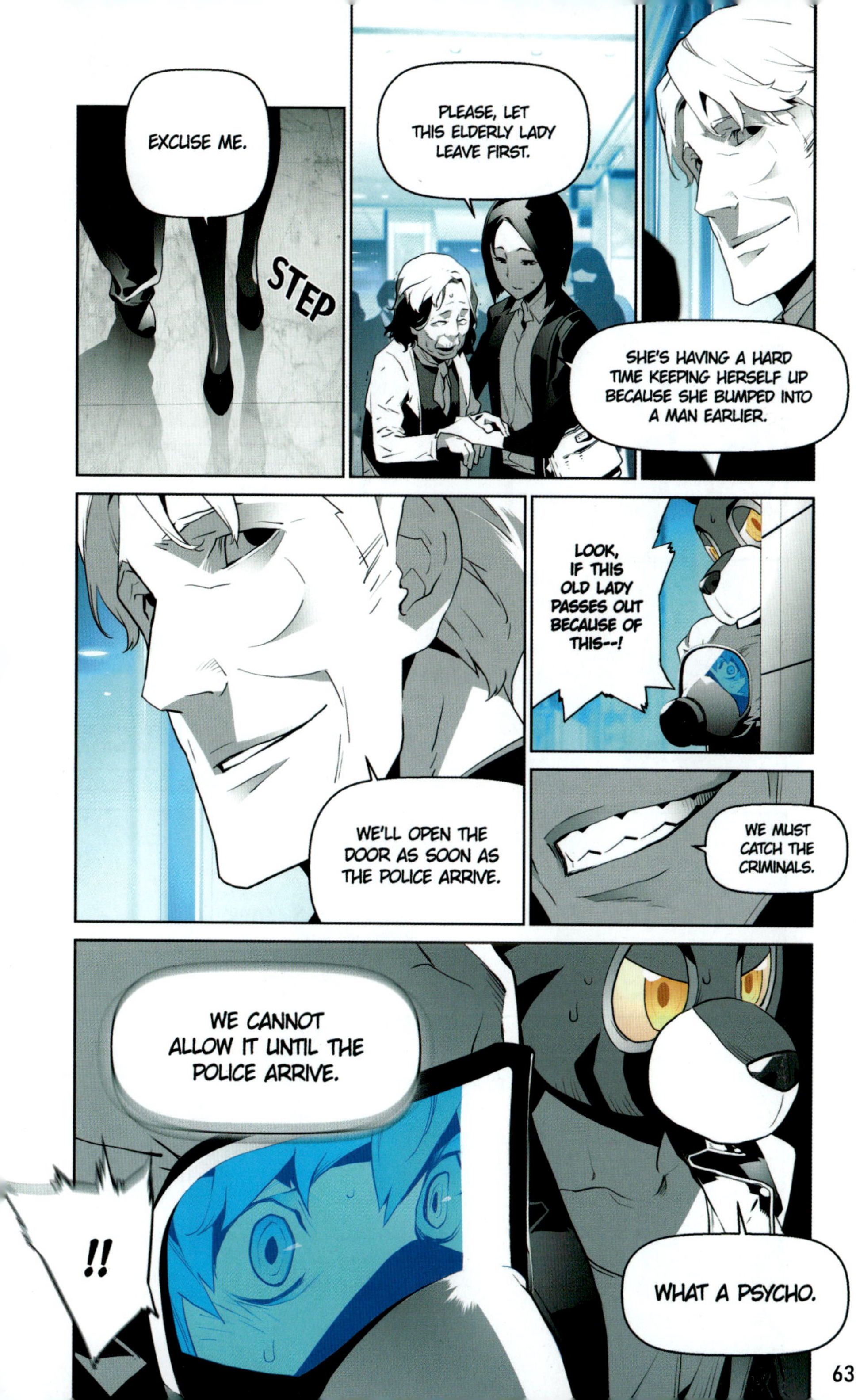
EXCUSE ME.
STEP
PLEASE, LET THIS ELDERLY LADY LEAVE FIRST.
SHE'S HAVING A HARD TIME KEEPING HERSELF UP BECAUSE SHE BUMPED INTO A MAN EARLIER.
WE'LL OPEN THE DOOR AS SOON AS THE POLICE ARRIVE.
LOOK, IF THIS OLD LADY PASSES OUT BECAUSE OF THIS--!
WE MUST CATCH THE CRIMINALS.
WE CANNOT ALLOW IT UNTIL THE POLICE ARRIVE.
!!
WHAT A PSYCHO.

RUMBLE...

?!

YOUNG MASTER, IS THIS--?!

!!

WHAT THE--?

WHAT'S THAT NOISE?!

AT THIS RATE...

CRACK...

CRACK...

...IT'LL COLLAPSE IN NO TIME!!

NO!

AT THIS RATE, EVERYONE WILL DIE.

BY ANY MEANS...

WE NEED TO PREVENT THAT FROM HAPPENING!

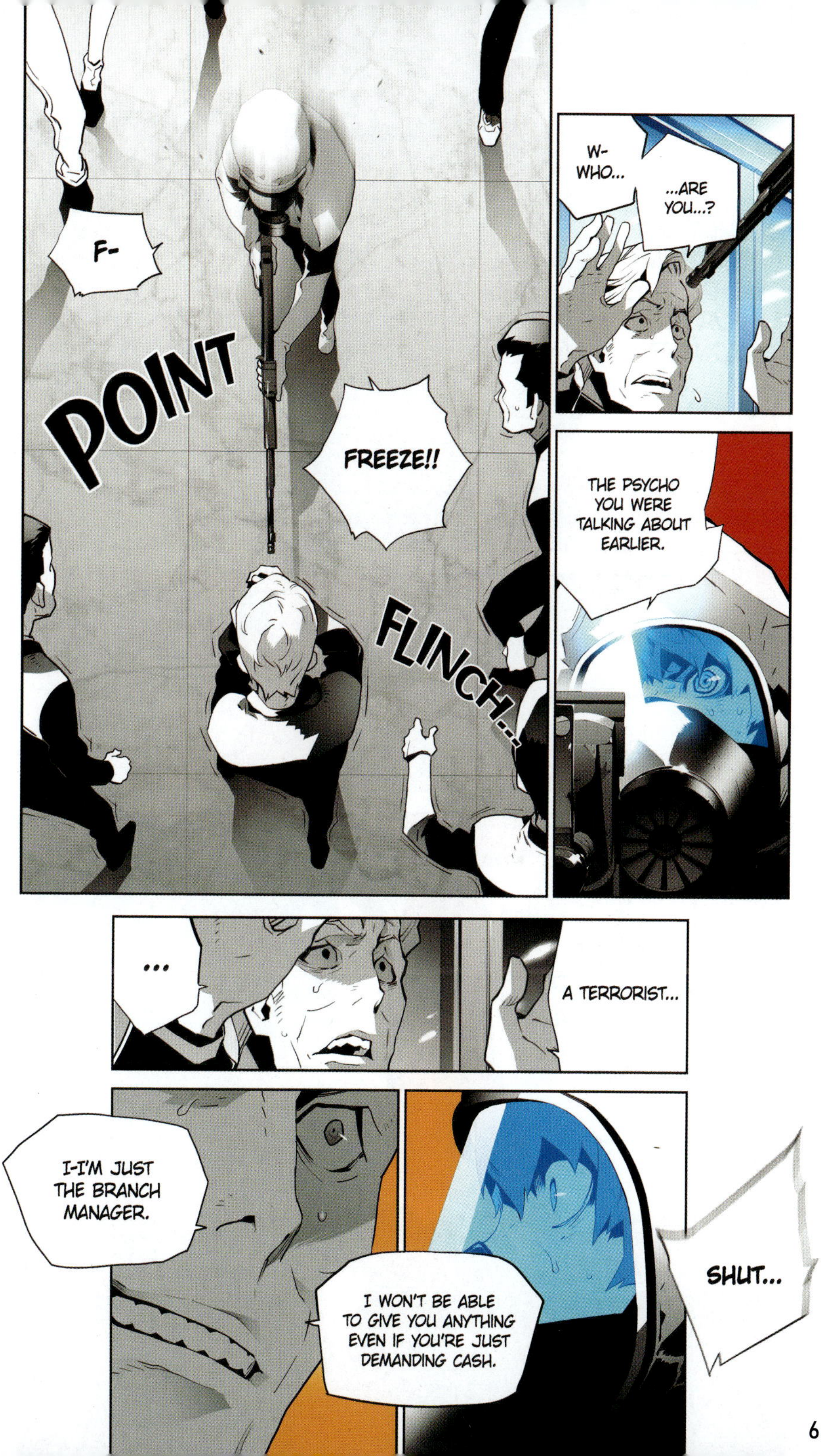
F-
POINT
FREEZE!!
FLINCH...
W-
WHO...
...ARE
YOU...?
THE PSYCHO
YOU WERE
TALKING ABOUT
EARLIER.
...
A TERRORIST...
I-I'M JUST
THE BRANCH
MANAGER.
I WON'T BE ABLE
TO GIVE YOU ANYTHING
EVEN IF YOU'RE JUST
DEMANDING CASH.
SHUT...

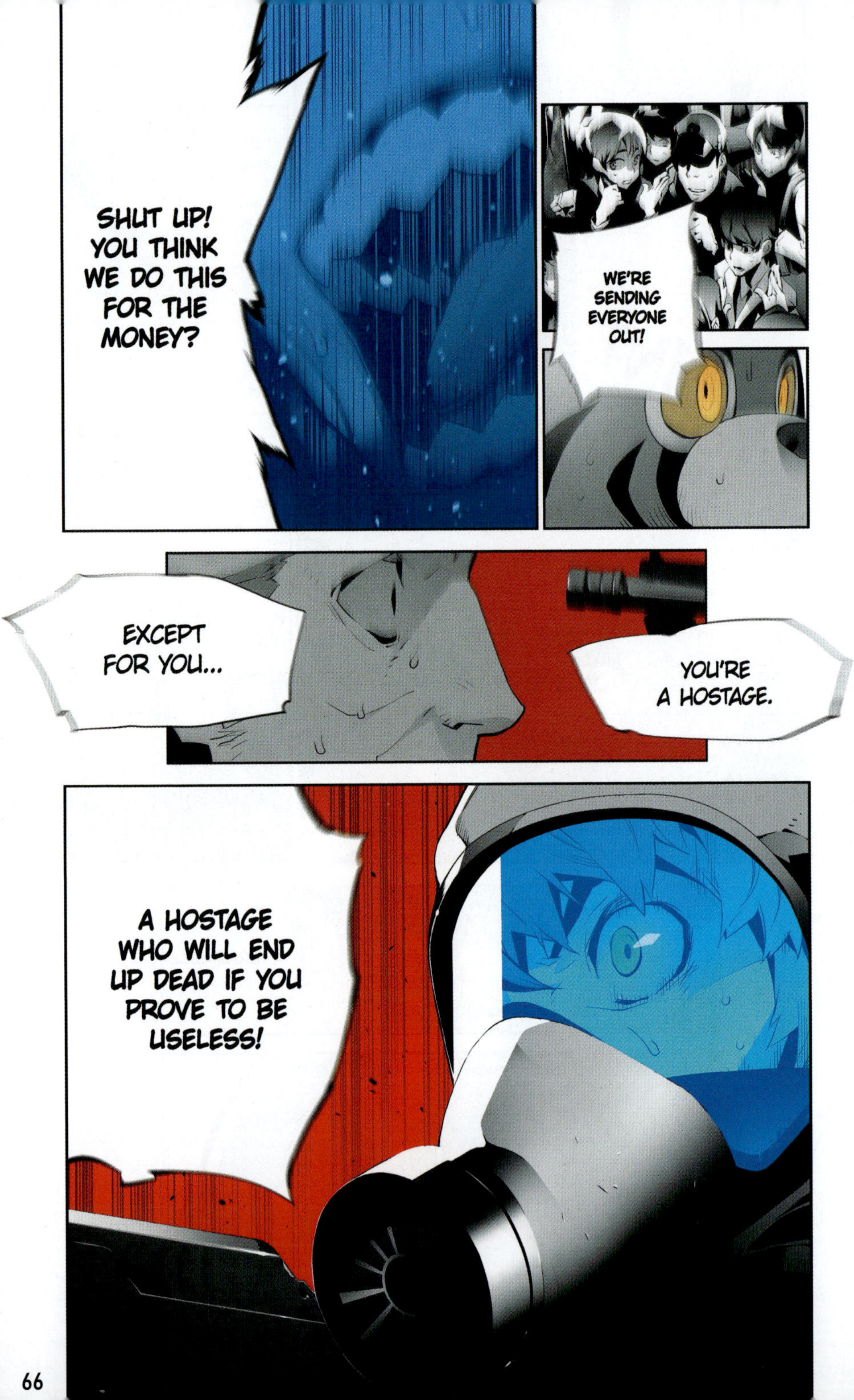
SHUT UP! YOU THINK WE DO THIS FOR THE MONEY?
WE'RE SENDING EVERYONE OUT!
EXCEPT FOR YOU...
YOU'RE A HOSTAGE.
A HOSTAGE WHO WILL END UP DEAD IF YOU PROVE TO BE USELESS!

TERROR MAN

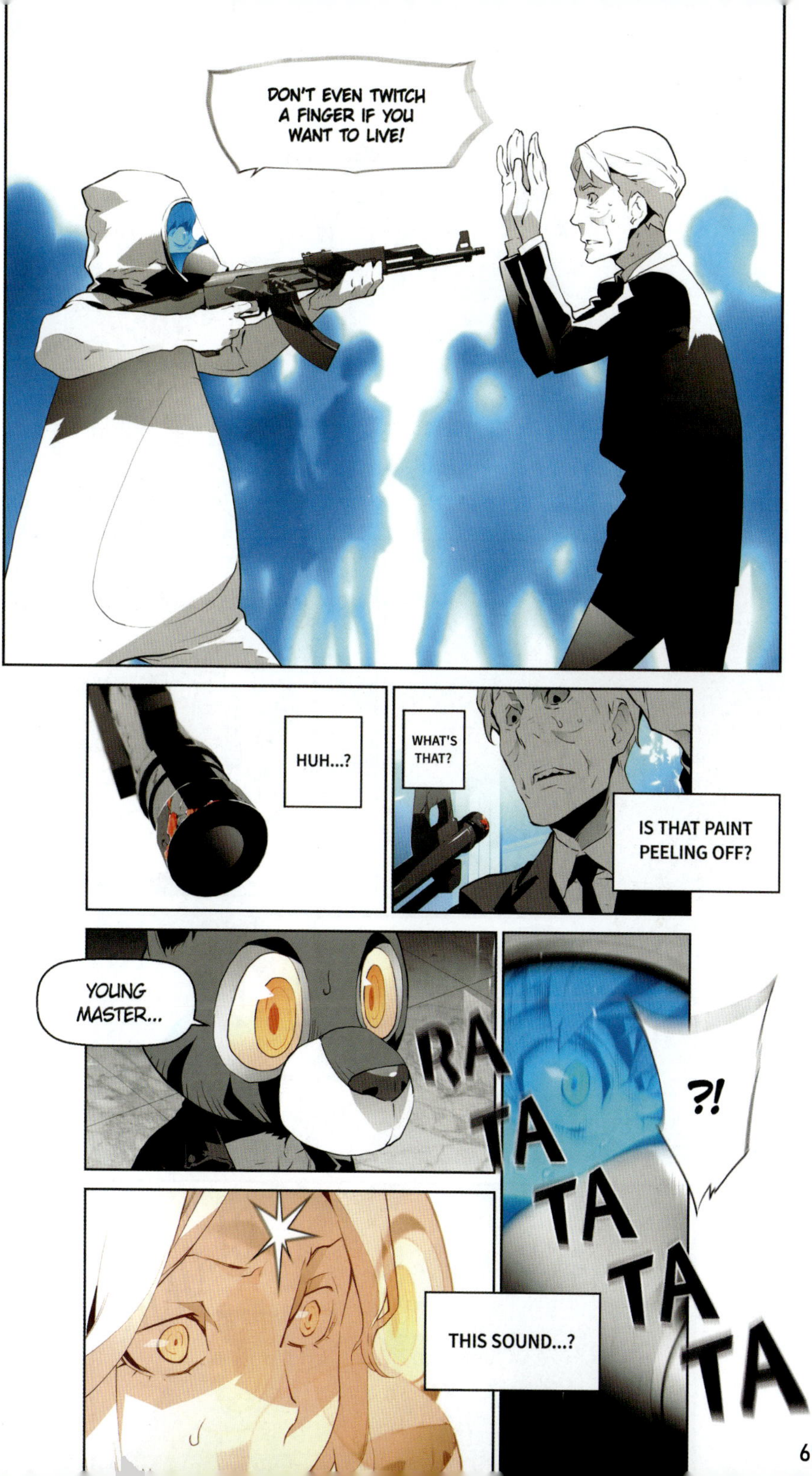
DON'T EVEN TWITCH A FINGER IF YOU WANT TO LIVE!
HUH...?
WHAT'S THAT?
IS THAT PAINT PEELING OFF?
YOUNG MASTER...
RA TA TA TA TA TA
?!
THIS SOUND...?

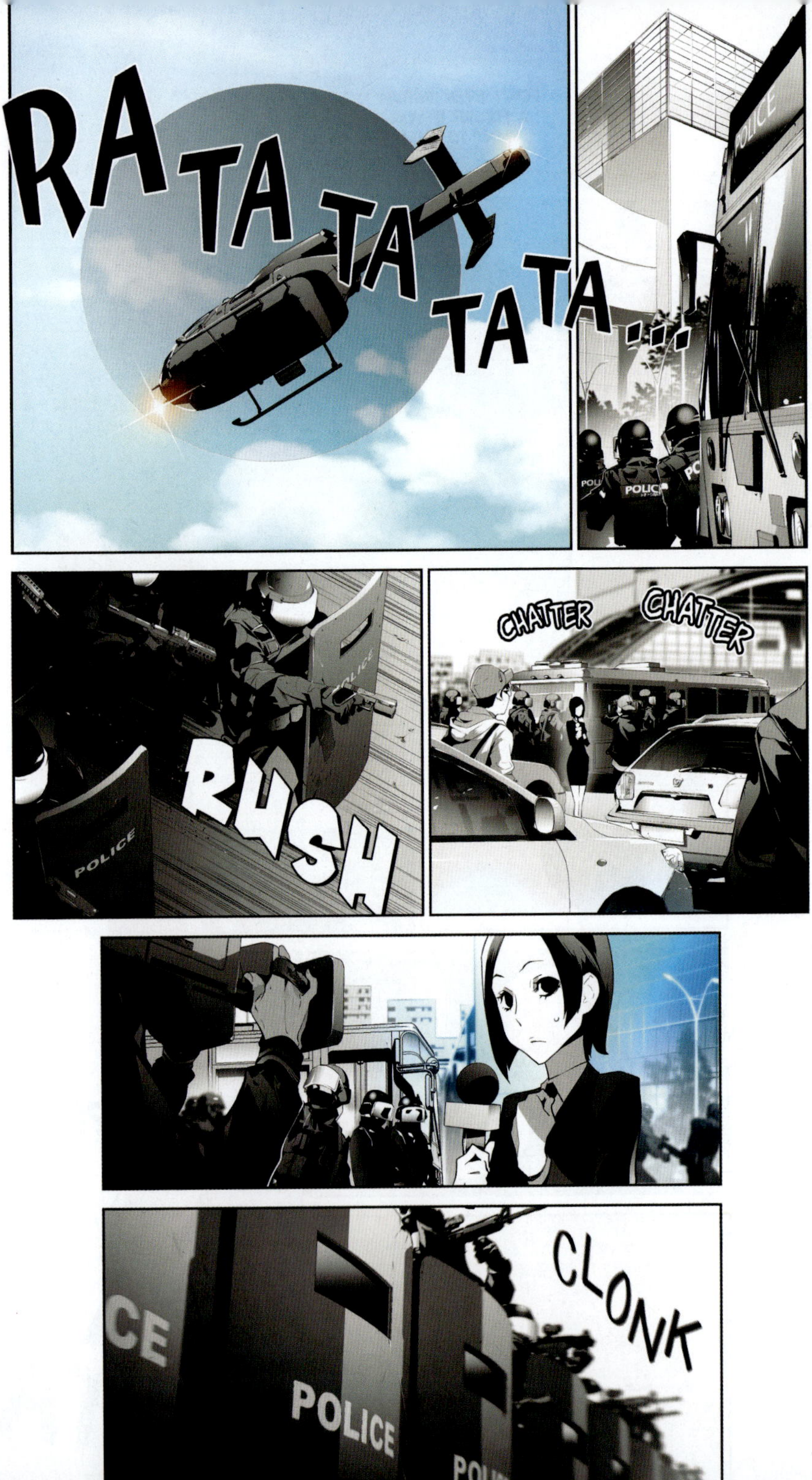
RATATATATATA...!!
POLICE
POLICE
RUSH
POLICE
CHATTER
CHATTER
CLONK
POLICE
POLICE

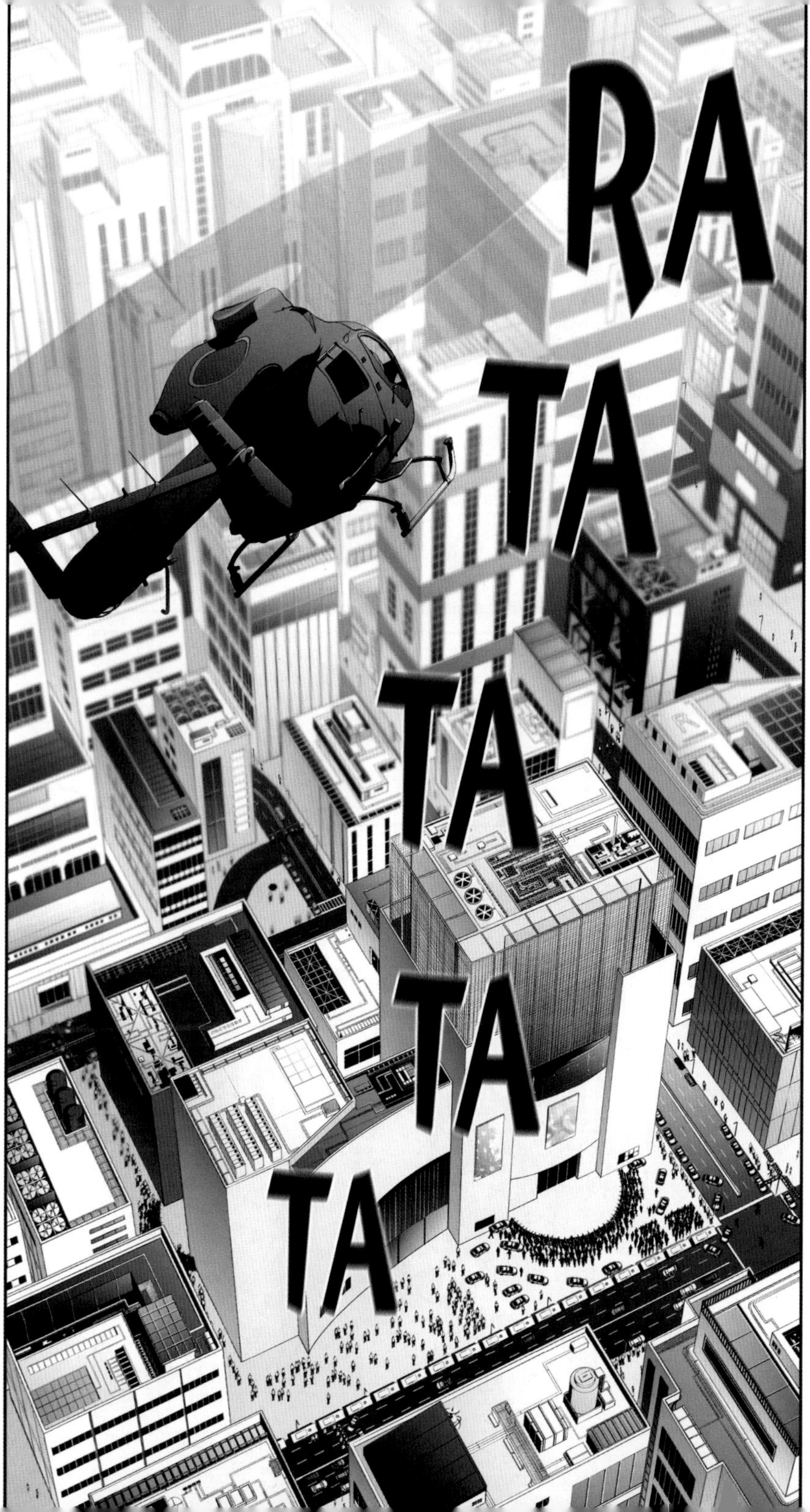
RA TA TA TA TA TA TA

IT'S THE POLICE!

THE POLICE ARE HERE!!

CHATTER CHATTER

CHATTER CHATTER

AH...

...

THAT QUICKLY?!

CLICK

!!

RUSH

S- STOP!!

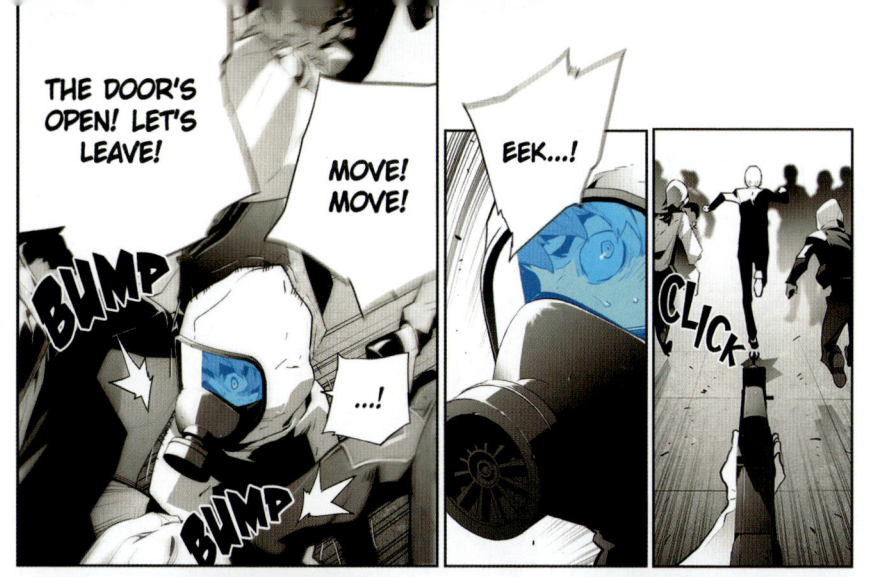

THE DOOR'S OPEN! LET'S LEAVE!

MOVE! MOVE!

EEK...!

BUMP

BUMP

...!

CLICK

AIM

SINK...

!

WHAT ARE YOU GOING TO DO WITH A BB GUN?

LILIA!

FORGET IT.

JUST LET THEM GO.

73

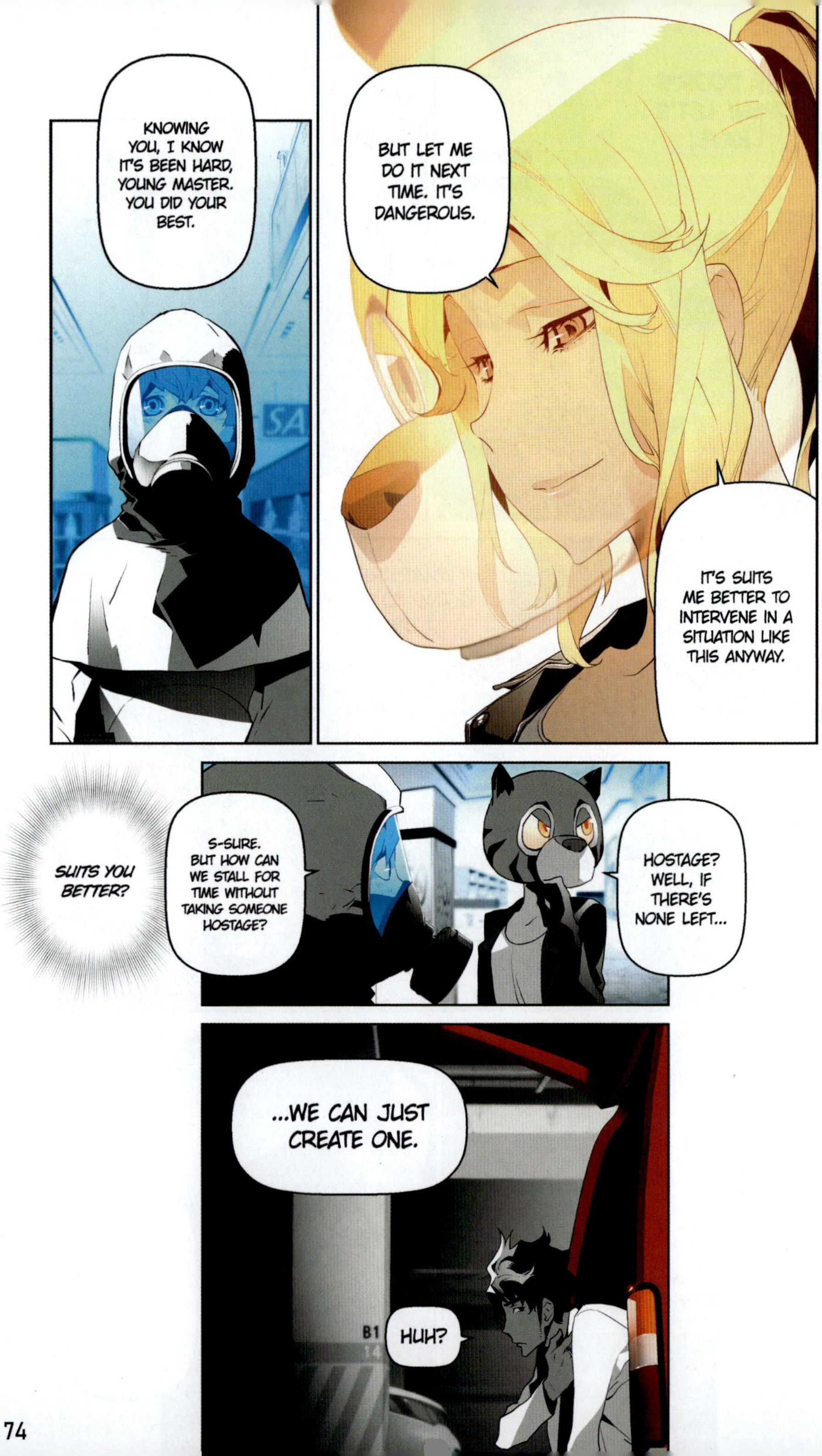
BUT LET ME DO IT NEXT TIME. IT'S DANGEROUS.
IT'S SUITS ME BETTER TO INTERVENE IN A SITUATION LIKE THIS ANYWAY.
KNOWING YOU, I KNOW IT'S BEEN HARD, YOUNG MASTER. YOU DID YOUR BEST.
HOSTAGE? WELL, IF THERE'S NONE LEFT...
S-SURE. BUT HOW CAN WE STALL FOR TIME WITHOUT TAKING SOMEONE HOSTAGE?
SUITS YOU BETTER?
...WE CAN JUST CREATE ONE.
B1
HUH?

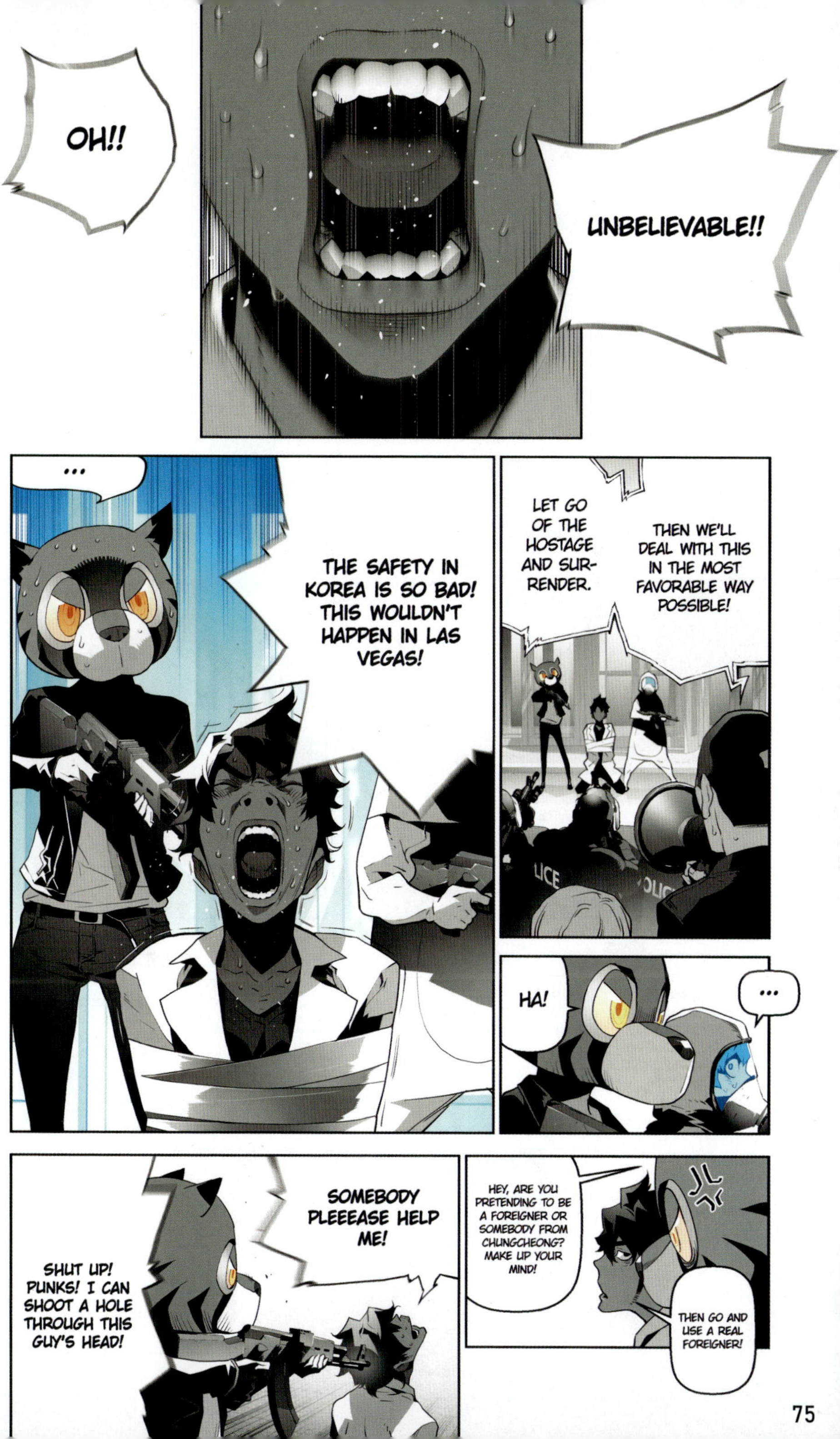
OH!!
UNBELIEVABLE!!
...
THE SAFETY IN KOREA IS SO BAD! THIS WOULDN'T HAPPEN IN LAS VEGAS!
LET GO OF THE HOSTAGE AND SUR-RENDER.
THEN WE'LL DEAL WITH THIS IN THE MOST FAVORABLE WAY POSSIBLE!
LICE
OLICE
HA!
...
SOMEBODY PLEEEASE HELP ME!
SHUT UP! PUNKS! I CAN SHOOT A HOLE THROUGH THIS GUY'S HEAD!
HEY, ARE YOU PRETENDING TO BE A FOREIGNER OR SOMEBODY FROM CHUNGCHEONG? MAKE UP YOUR MIND!
THEN GO AND USE A REAL FOREIGNER!

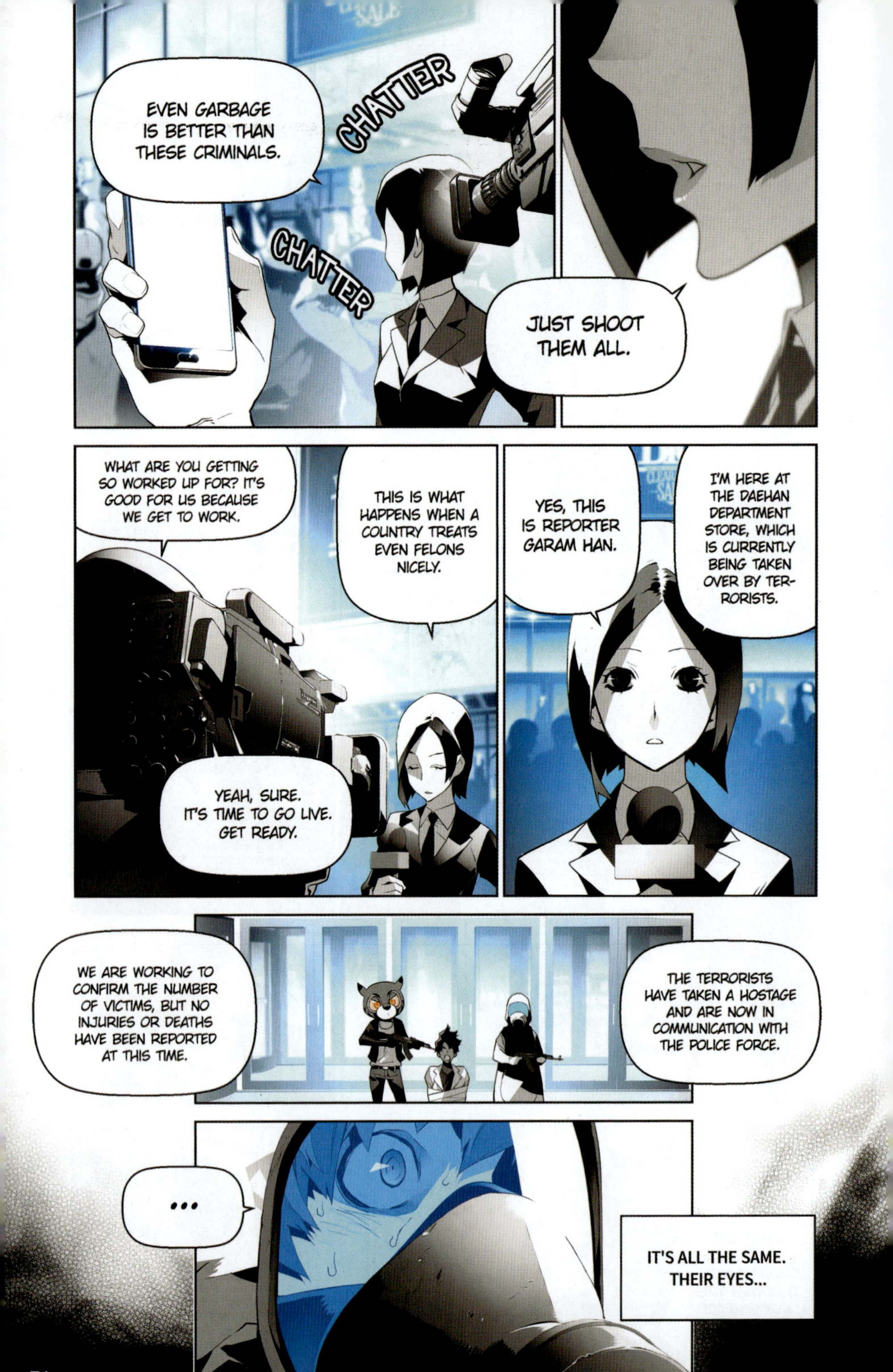
EVEN GARBAGE IS BETTER THAN THESE CRIMINALS.
CHATTER
CHATTER
JUST SHOOT THEM ALL.
WHAT ARE YOU GETTING SO WORKED UP FOR? IT'S GOOD FOR US BECAUSE WE GET TO WORK.
THIS IS WHAT HAPPENS WHEN A COUNTRY TREATS EVEN FELONS NICELY.
YEAH, SURE. IT'S TIME TO GO LIVE. GET READY.
YES, THIS IS REPORTER GARAM HAN.
I'M HERE AT THE DAEHAN DEPARTMENT STORE, WHICH IS CURRENTLY BEING TAKEN OVER BY TER-RORISTS.
WE ARE WORKING TO CONFIRM THE NUMBER OF VICTIMS, BUT NO INJURIES OR DEATHS HAVE BEEN REPORTED AT THIS TIME.
THE TERRORISTS HAVE TAKEN A HOSTAGE AND ARE NOW IN COMMUNICATION WITH THE POLICE FORCE.
...
IT'S ALL THE SAME. THEIR EYES...

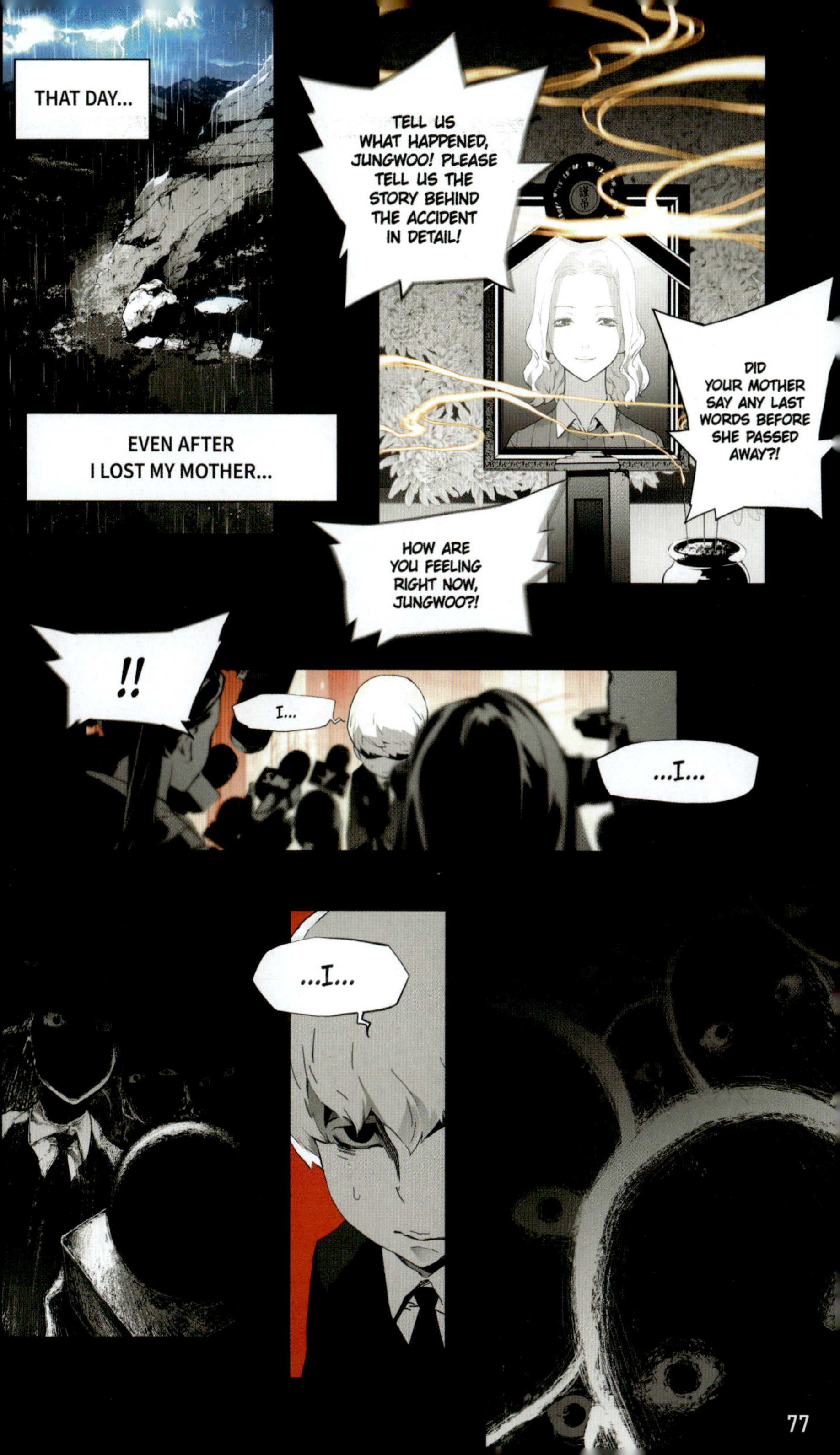
THAT DAY...
EVEN AFTER I LOST MY MOTHER...
TELL US WHAT HAPPENED, JUNGWOO! PLEASE TELL US THE STORY BEHIND THE ACCIDENT IN DETAIL!
DID YOUR MOTHER SAY ANY LAST WORDS BEFORE SHE PASSED AWAY?!
HOW ARE YOU FEELING RIGHT NOW, JUNGWOO?!
!!
I...
...I...
...I...

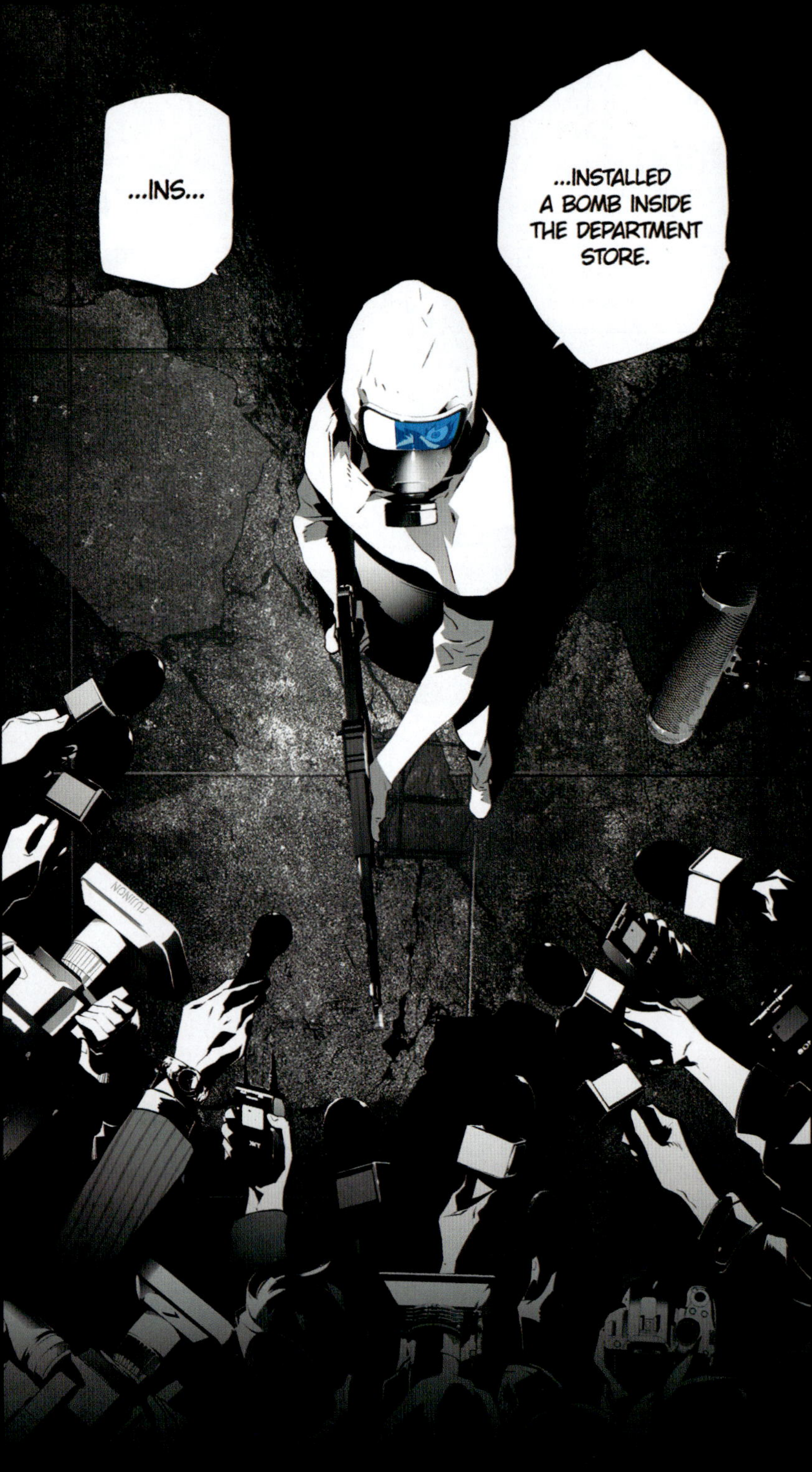
...INSTALLED A BOMB INSIDE THE DEPARTMENT STORE.
...INS...

!

IT WILL BLOW UP...

...NOT JUST IN THE DEPARTMENT STORE, BUT ALSO THE NEIGHBORING BUILDINGS!

I-IF YOU DON'T GIVE IN... TO OUR DEMANDS...

...WE WILL MERCILESSLY...

THAT'S A LIE!

I SAW IT! I SAW THE PAINT MARKS ON THE GUNS OF THOSE PUNKS!

THAT WAS ORIGINALLY ORANGE-COLORED PLASTIC, RIGHT?! RIGHT?!

I KNOW BECAUSE MY SON LOVES BB GUNS!

HOW DARE YOU ROB A STORE'S FORTUNE BY BARGING IN WITH BB GUNS?!!

SHOOT

MOVE... ... MOVE...

WHAT DID YOU SAY?

I CAN'T HEAR YOU VERY WELL.

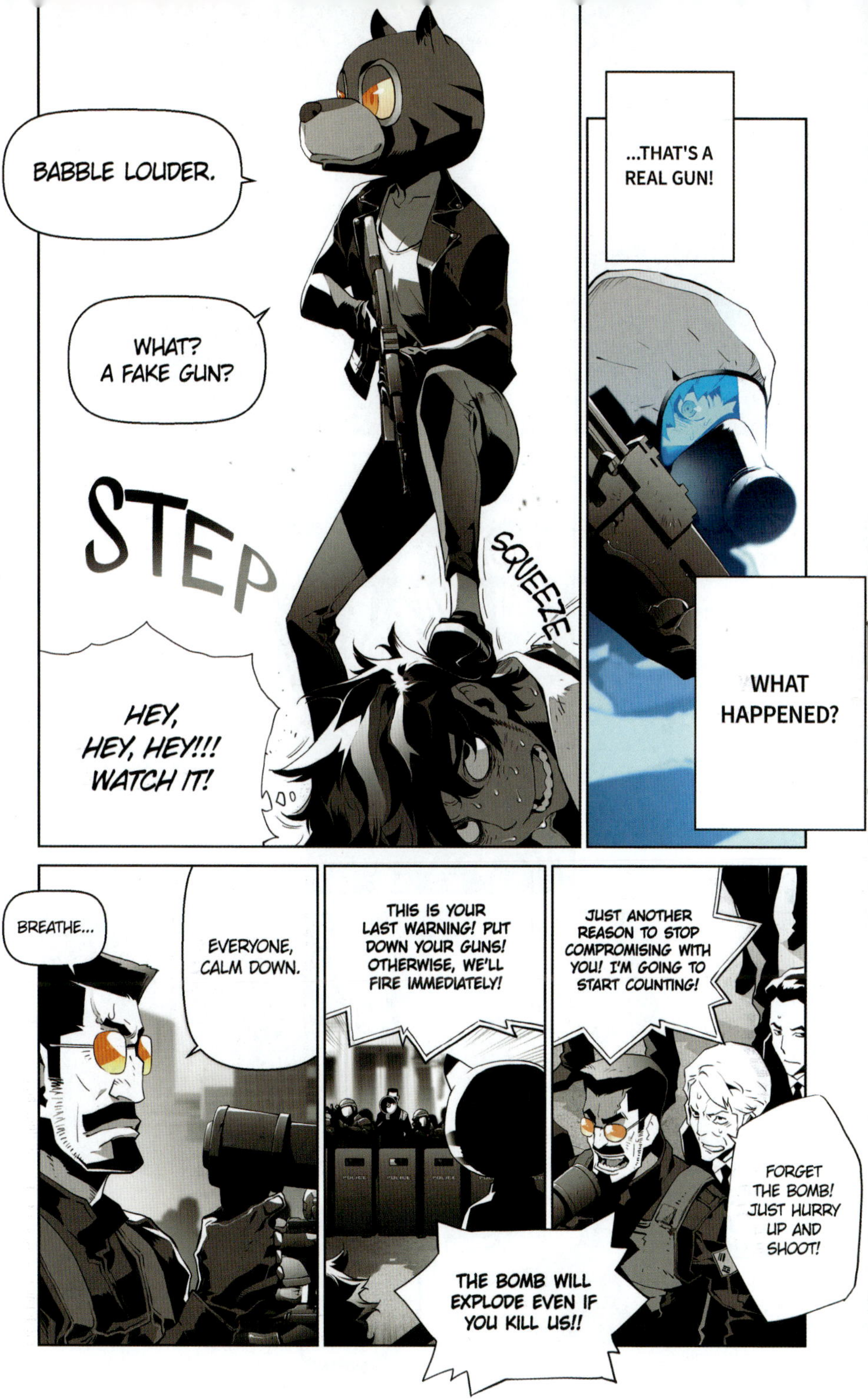
BABBLE LOUDER.
WHAT? A FAKE GUN?
STEP
SQUEEZE
HEY, HEY, HEY!!! WATCH IT!
...THAT'S A REAL GUN!
WHAT HAPPENED?
BREATHE...
EVERYONE, CALM DOWN.
THIS IS YOUR LAST WARNING! PUT DOWN YOUR GUNS! OTHERWISE, WE'LL FIRE IMMEDIATELY!
THE BOMB WILL EXPLODE EVEN IF YOU KILL US!!
JUST ANOTHER REASON TO STOP COMPROMISING WITH YOU! I'M GOING TO START COUNTING!
FORGET THE BOMB! JUST HURRY UP AND SHOOT!

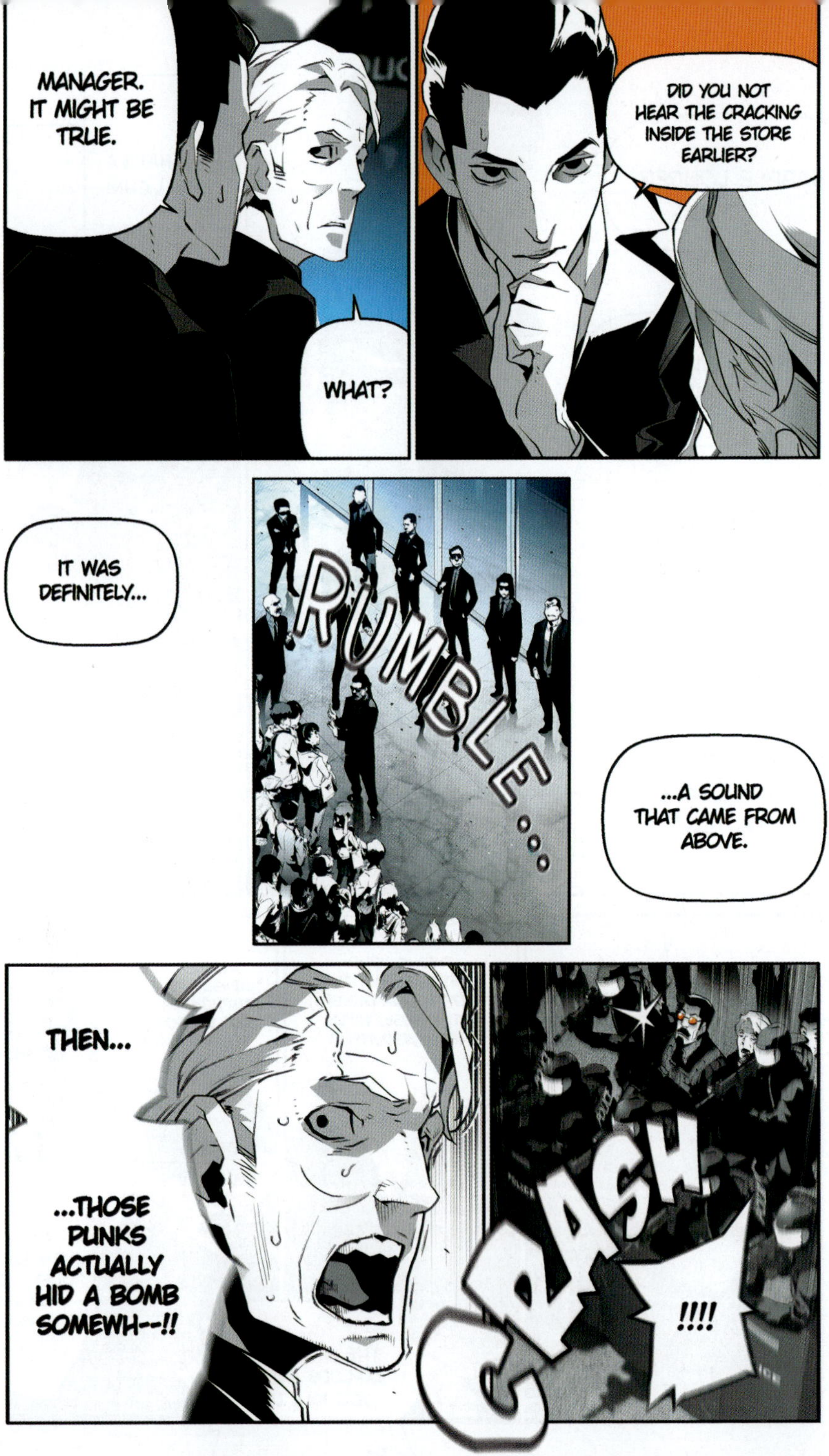
MANAGER. IT MIGHT BE TRUE.
WHAT?
DID YOU NOT HEAR THE CRACKING INSIDE THE STORE EARLIER?
IT WAS DEFINITELY...
RUMBLE...
...A SOUND THAT CAME FROM ABOVE.
THEN...
...THOSE PUNKS ACTUALLY HID A BOMB SOMEWH--!!
CRASH
!!!!

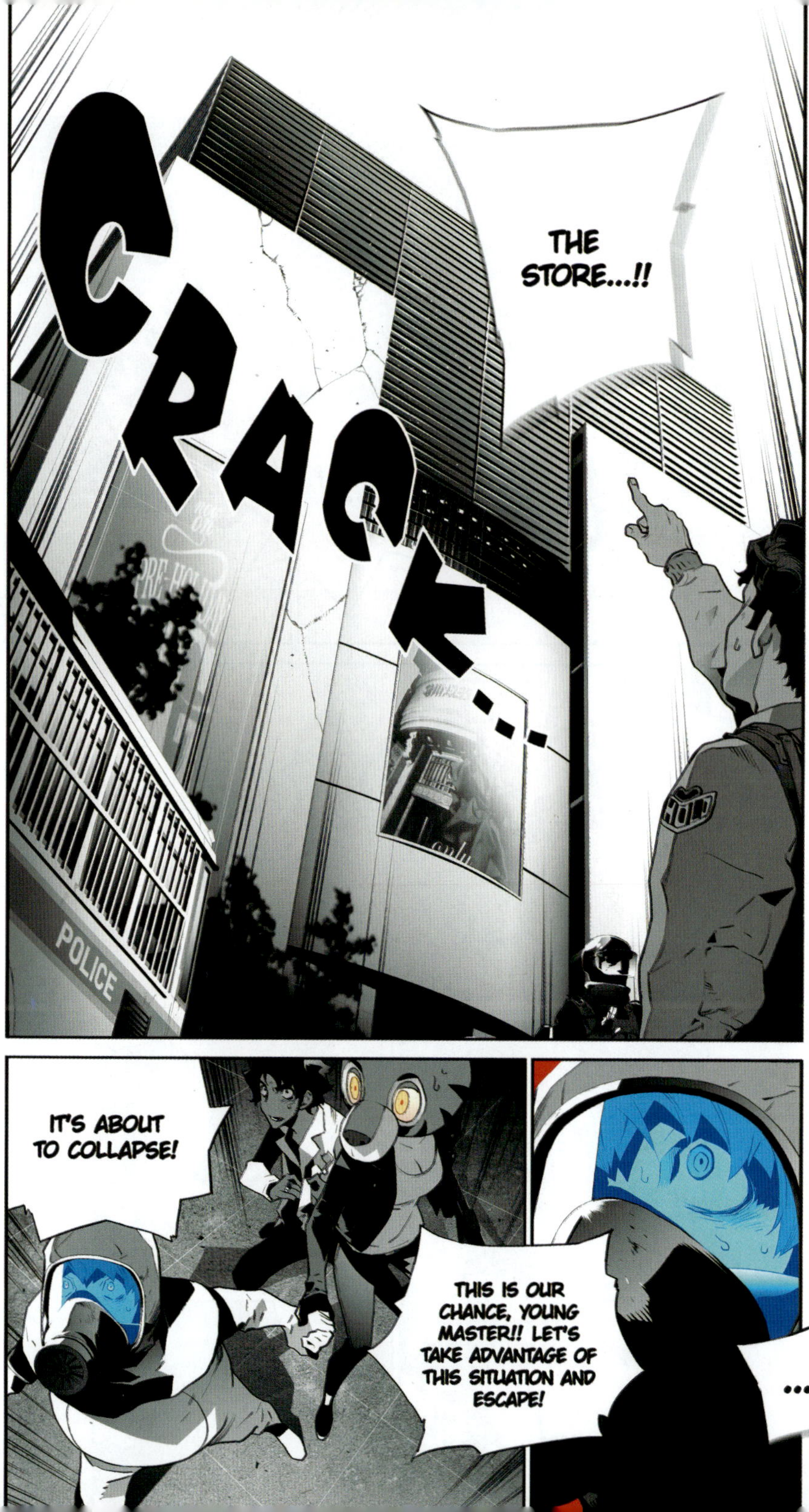

CRACK...
THE STORE...!!
PRE-HOLIDAY
POLICE
IT'S ABOUT TO COLLAPSE!
THIS IS OUR CHANCE, YOUNG MASTER!! LET'S TAKE ADVANTAGE OF THIS SITUATION AND ESCAPE!
...!

CRACK CRACK CRASH

CRACK ...! CRUMBLE

COMMANDER!! GIVE US THE EVACUATION ORDER!!

EVERYONE, GET OUT!!

WAAAAH!!

BUMP

AAAH!

...!

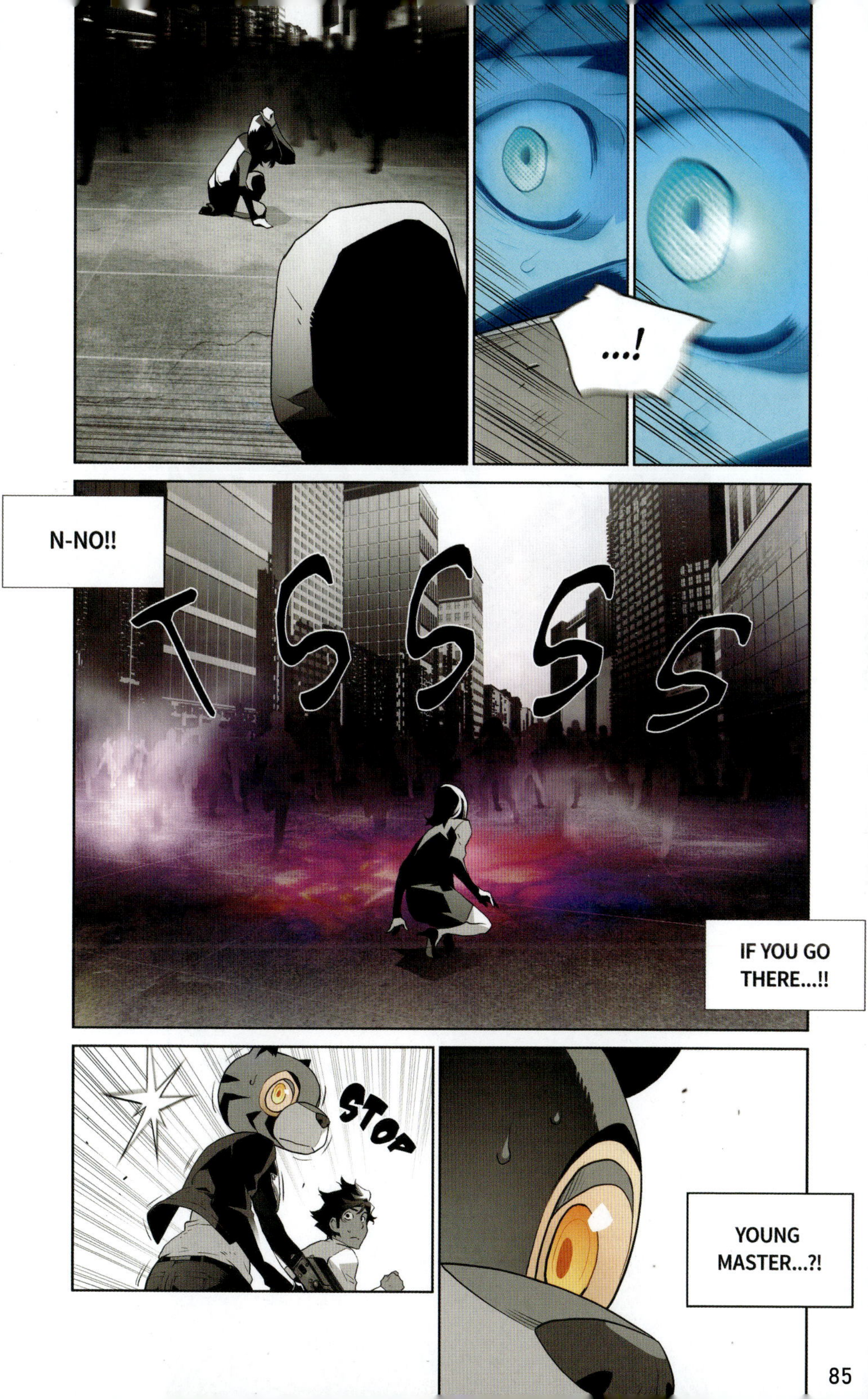
...!
N-NO!!
TSSSS
IF YOU GO THERE...!!
STOP
YOUNG MASTER...?!

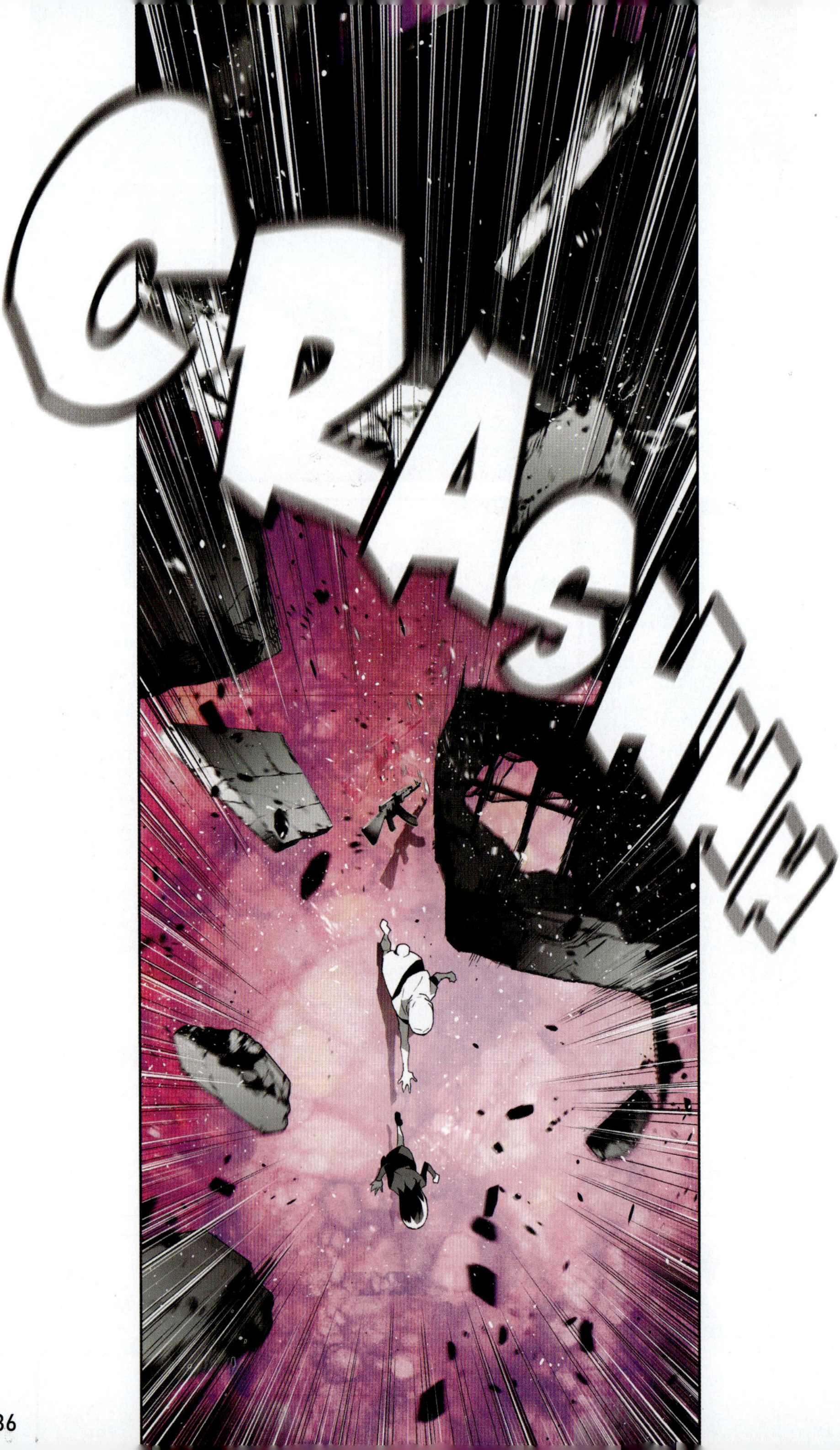
CRASH!!

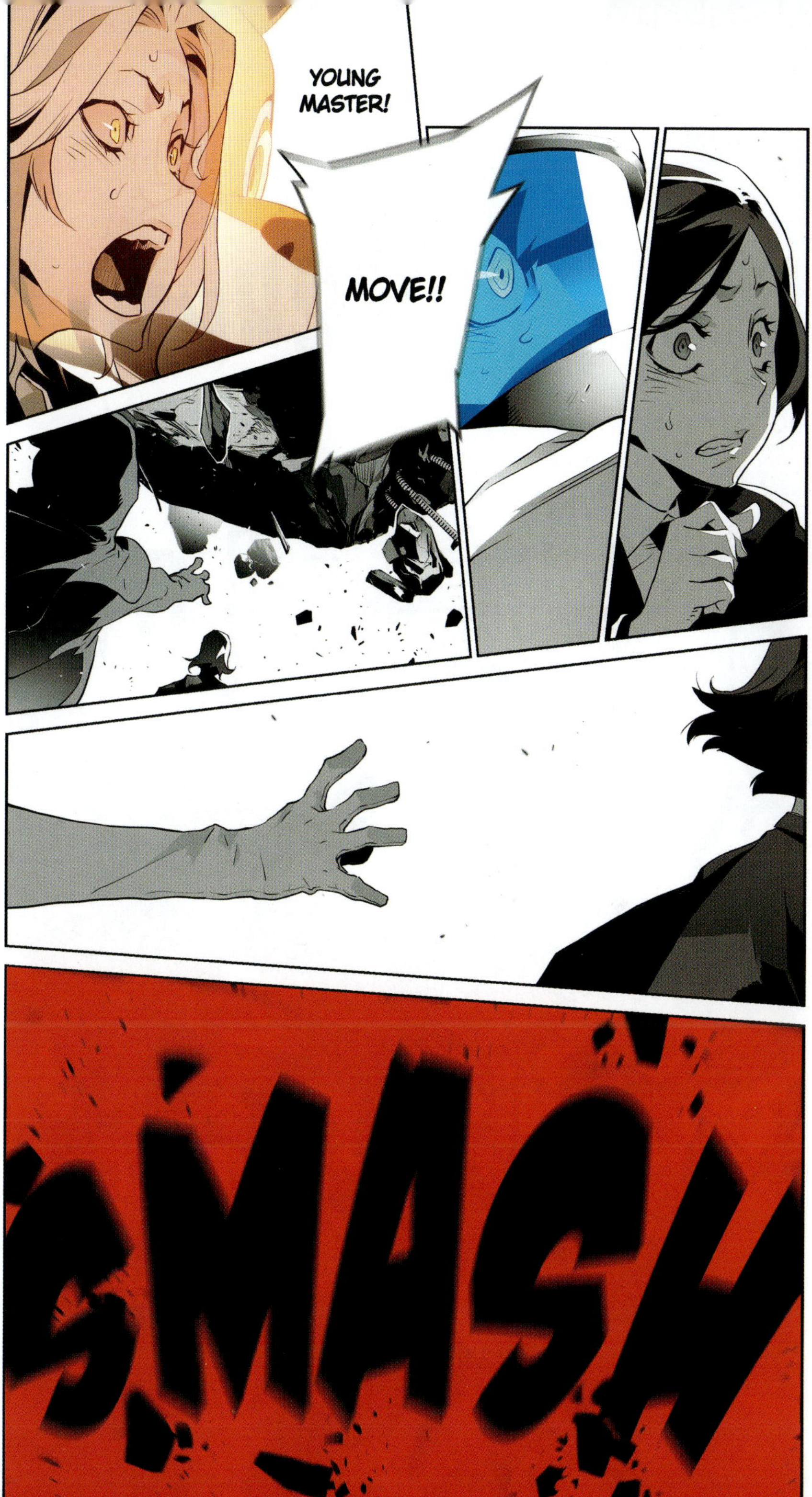
YOUNG MASTER!
MOVE!!
SMASH

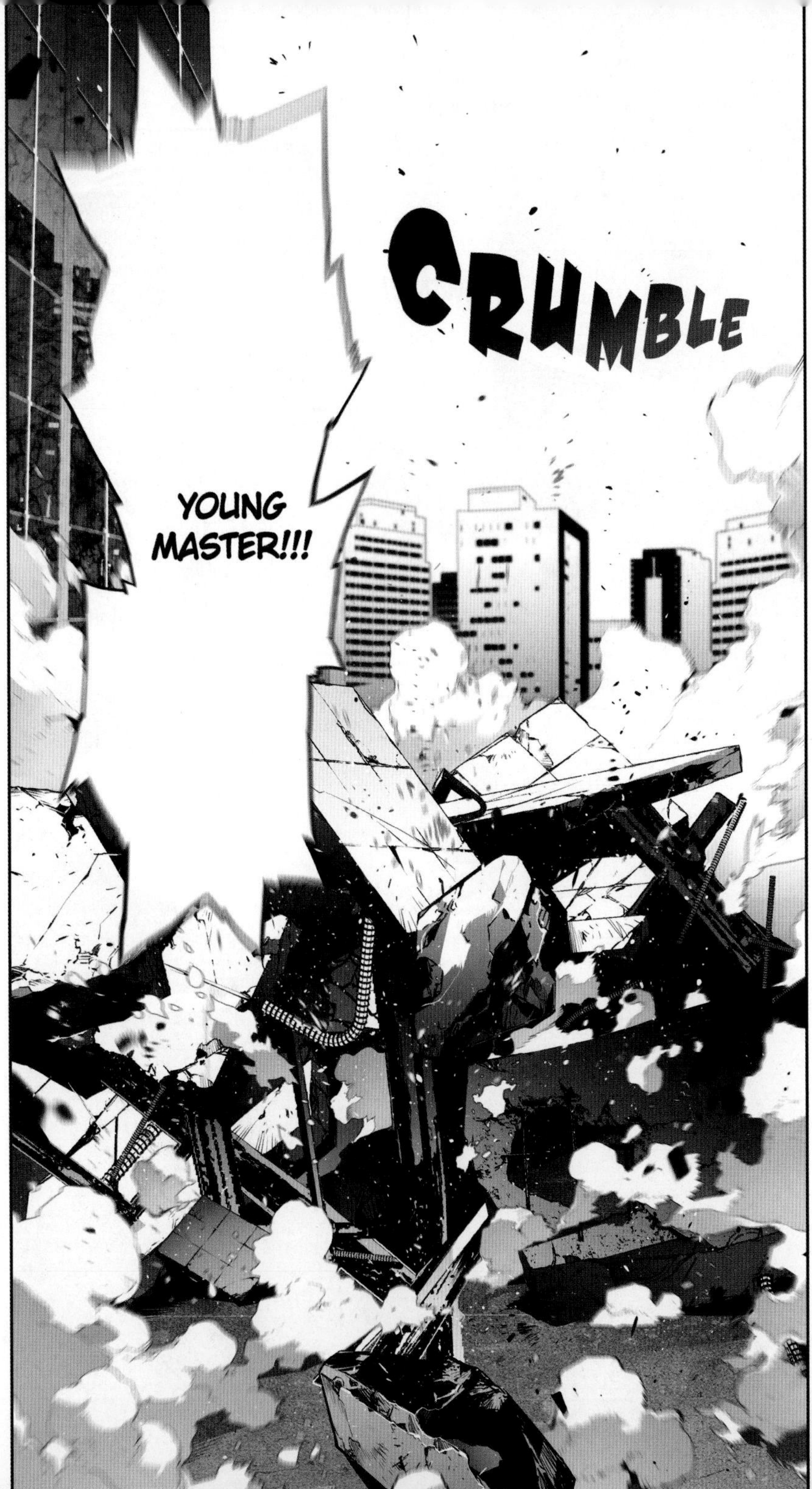
CRUMBLE
YOUNG MASTER!!!

TERROR MAN

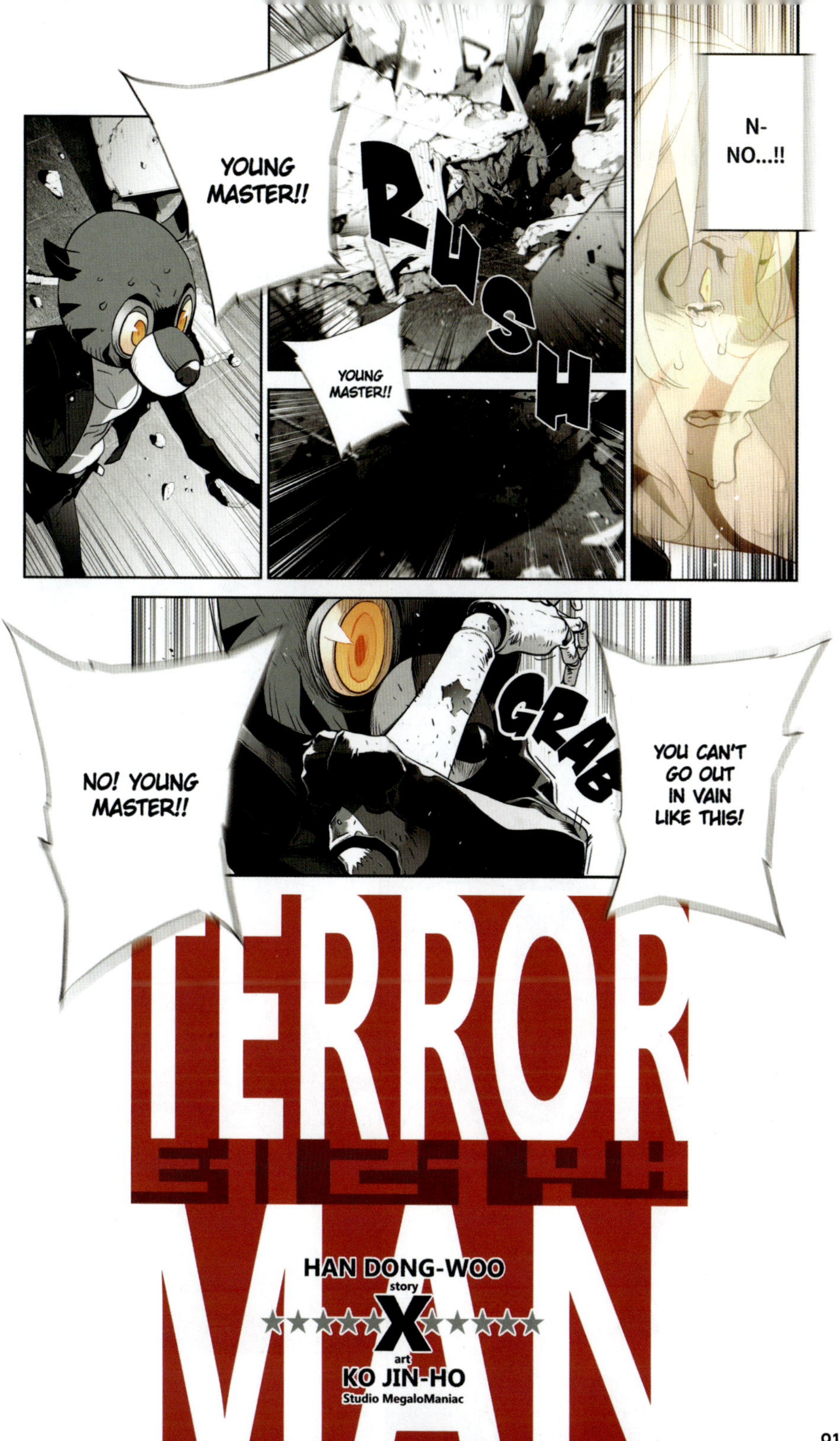
YOUNG MASTER!!
RUSH
YOUNG MASTER!!
N- NO...!!
NO! YOUNG MASTER!!
GRAB
YOU CAN'T GO OUT IN VAIN LIKE THIS!
TERROR MAN
HAN DONG-WOO
story
X
art
KO JIN-HO
Studio MegaloManiac

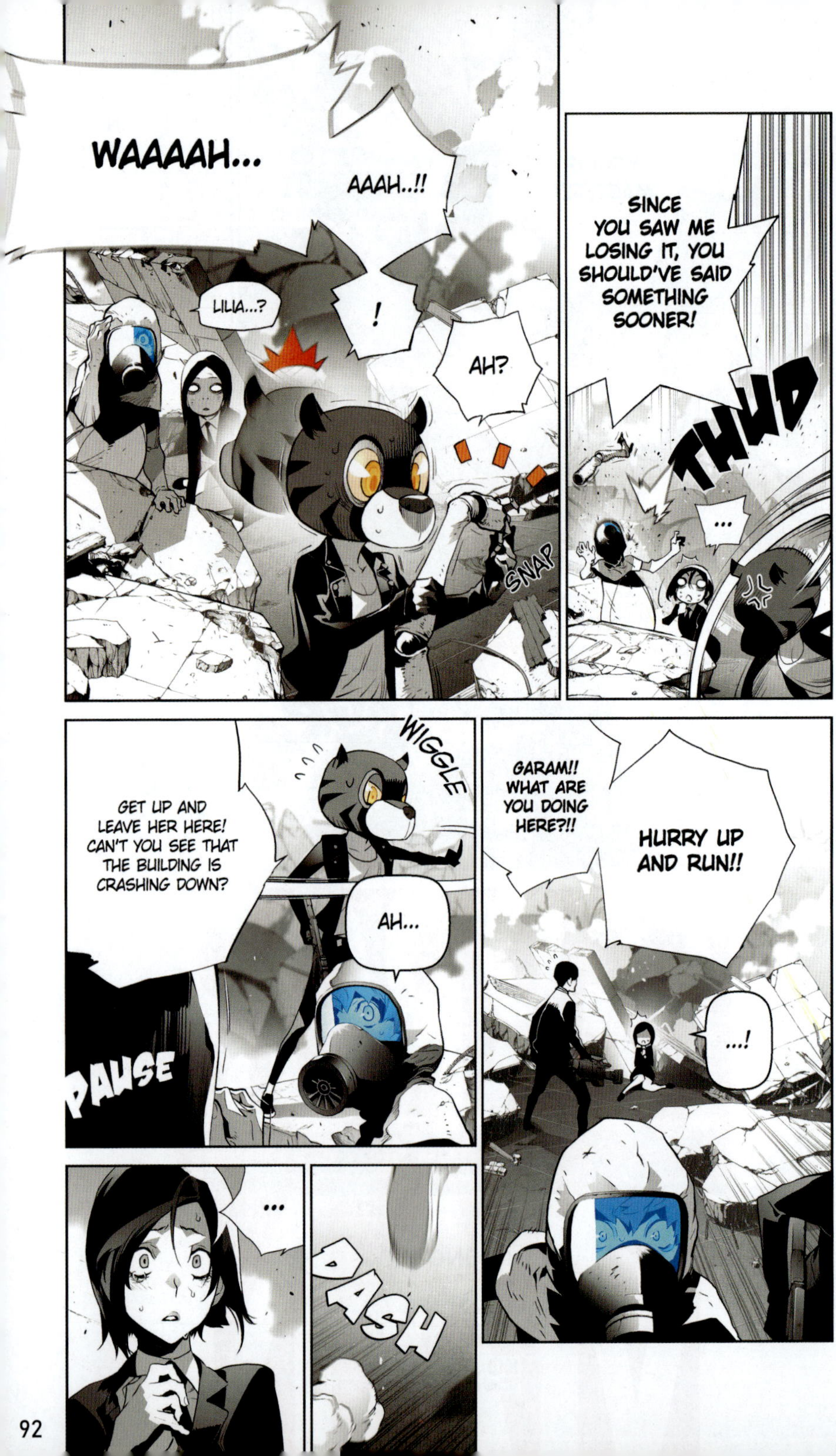
WAAAAH...
AAAH..!!
LILIA...?
!
AH?
SNAP
SINCE YOU SAW ME LOSING IT, YOU SHOULD'VE SAID SOMETHING SOONER!
THUD
...
WIGGLE
GET UP AND LEAVE HER HERE! CAN'T YOU SEE THAT THE BUILDING IS CRASHING DOWN?
AH...
PAUSE
GARAM!! WHAT ARE YOU DOING HERE?!!
HURRY UP AND RUN!!
...!
...
DASH

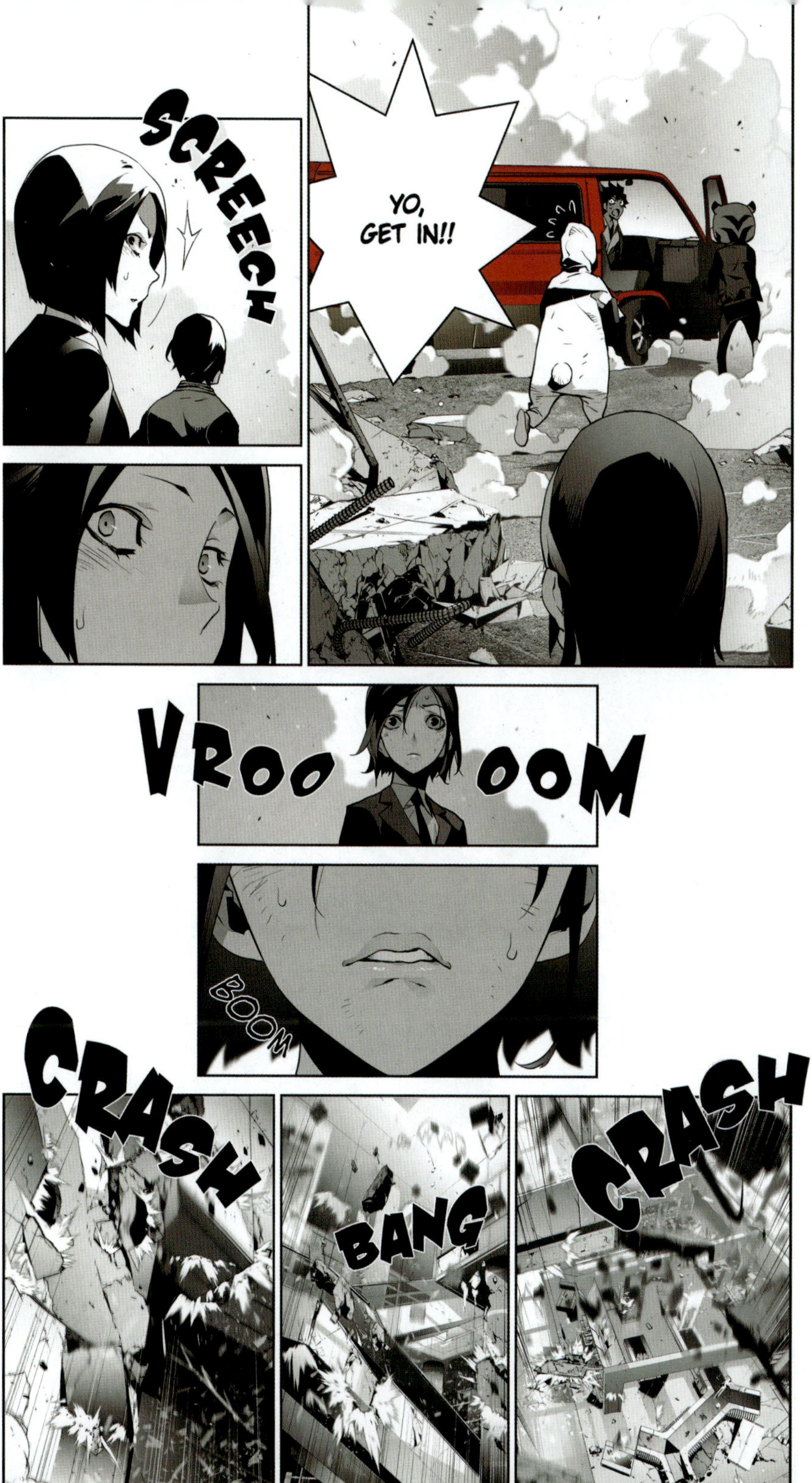
SCREEECH
YO, GET IN!!
VROOOOM
BOOM
CRASH
BANG
CRASH

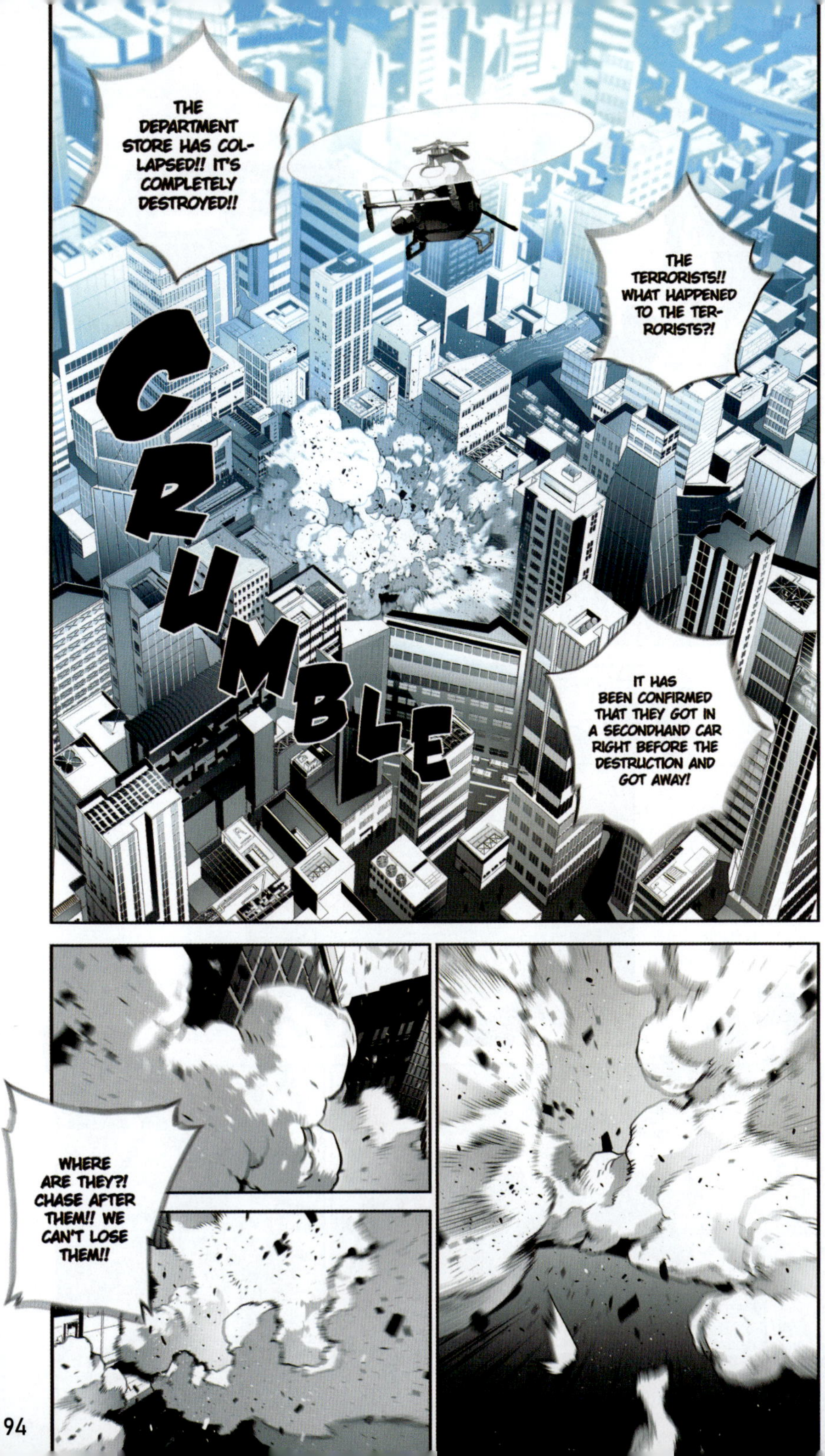
THE DEPARTMENT STORE HAS COL-LAPSED!! IT'S COMPLETELY DESTROYED!!
THE TERRORISTS!! WHAT HAPPENED TO THE TER-RORISTS?!
CRUMBLE
IT HAS BEEN CONFIRMED THAT THEY GOT IN A SECONDHAND CAR RIGHT BEFORE THE DESTRUCTION AND GOT AWAY!
WHERE ARE THEY?! CHASE AFTER THEM!! WE CAN'T LOSE THEM!!

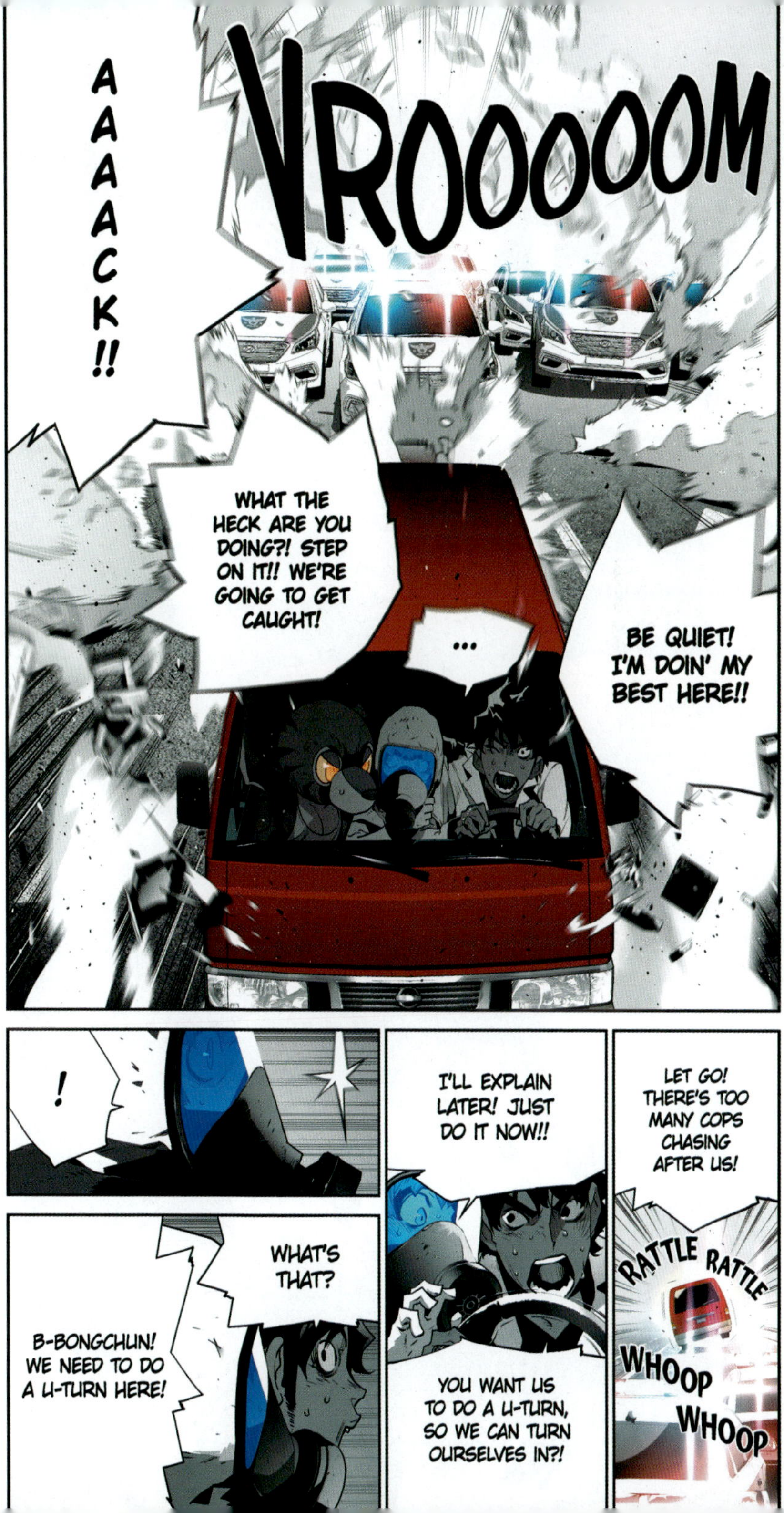
VROOOOOM
AAAAACK!!
WHAT THE HECK ARE YOU DOING?! STEP ON IT!! WE'RE GOING TO GET CAUGHT!
...
BE QUIET! I'M DOIN' MY BEST HERE!!
!
B-BONGCHUN! WE NEED TO DO A U-TURN HERE!
WHAT'S THAT?
I'LL EXPLAIN LATER! JUST DO IT NOW!!
YOU WANT US TO DO A U-TURN, SO WE CAN TURN OURSELVES IN?!
LET GO! THERE'S TOO MANY COPS CHASING AFTER US!
RATTLE RATTLE
WHOOP WHOOP

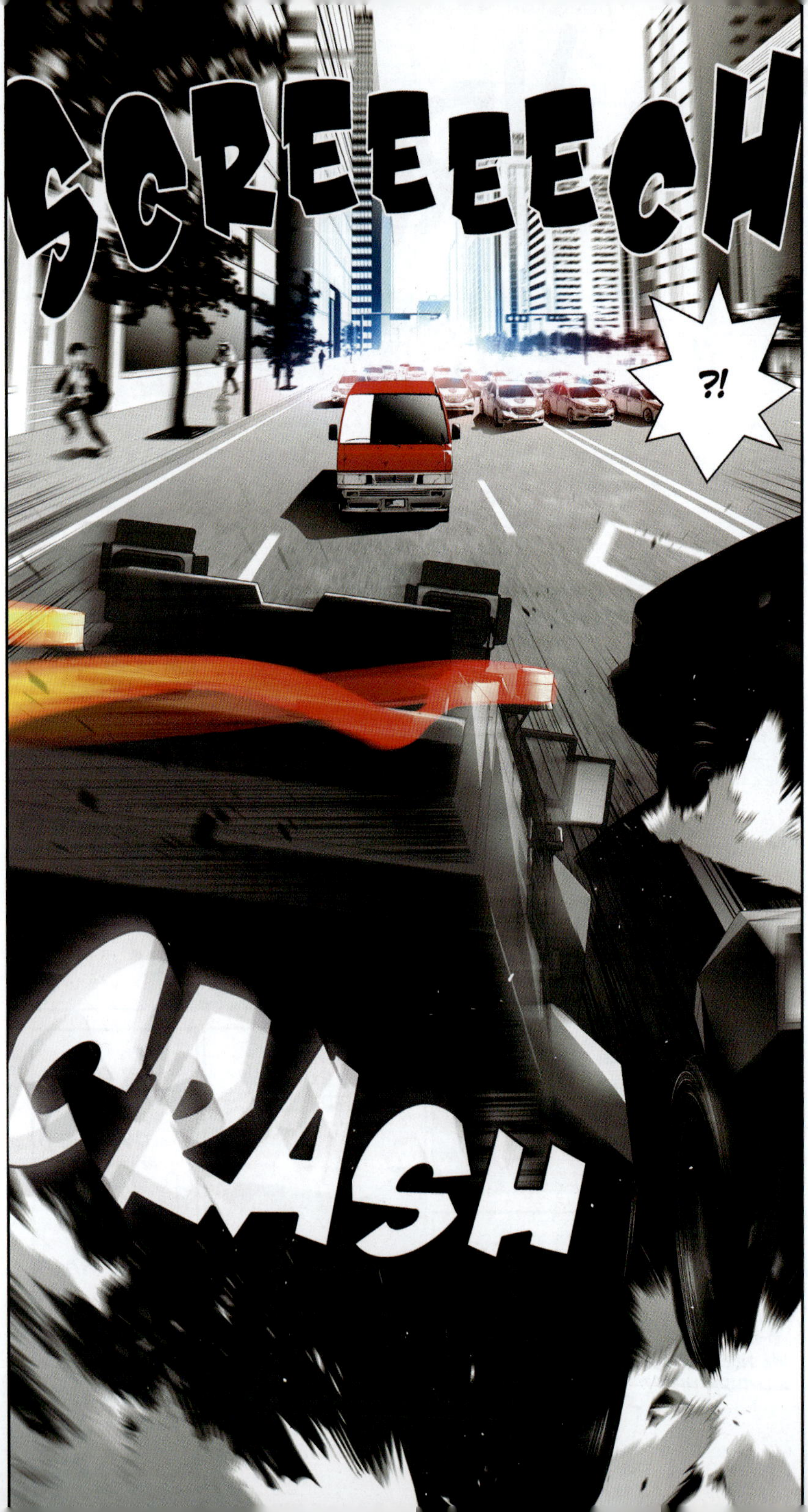
SCREEECH
?!
CRASH

DAMN IT! MOVE! I'LL DRIVE!

WHAT?

WHAT??

STEP ON THE BRAKES!

AH, SERIOUSLY?!

AAAAH!

SCREEECH

VROOOOM

OMG!!

CRASH

SCREEECH

HEY, THERE'S PEOPLE HERE!!

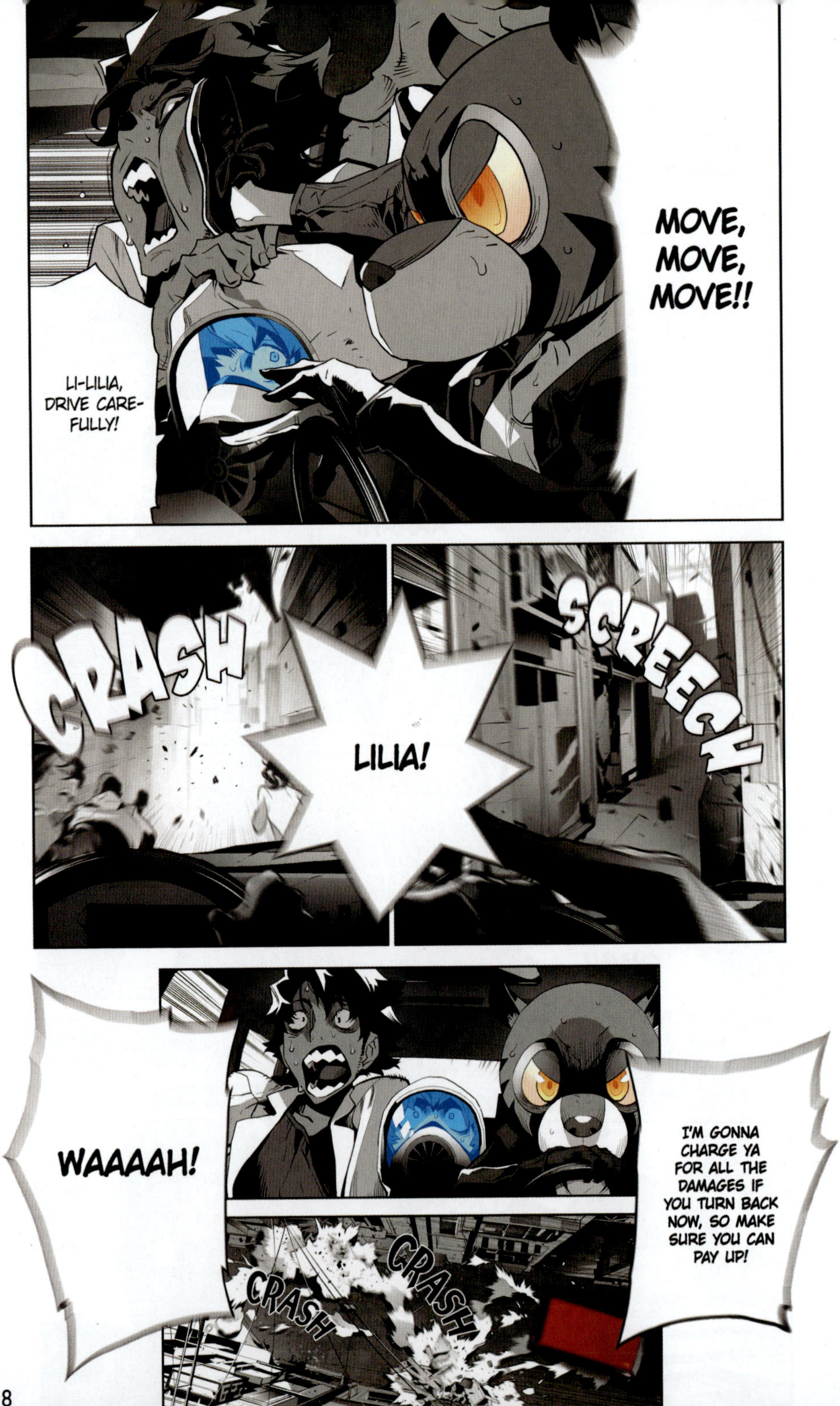
MOVE, MOVE, MOVE!!
LI-LILIA, DRIVE CARE-FULLY!
CRASH
SCREECH
LILIA!
I'M GONNA CHARGE YA FOR ALL THE DAMAGES IF YOU TURN BACK NOW, SO MAKE SURE YOU CAN PAY UP!
WAAAAH!
CRASH
CRASH

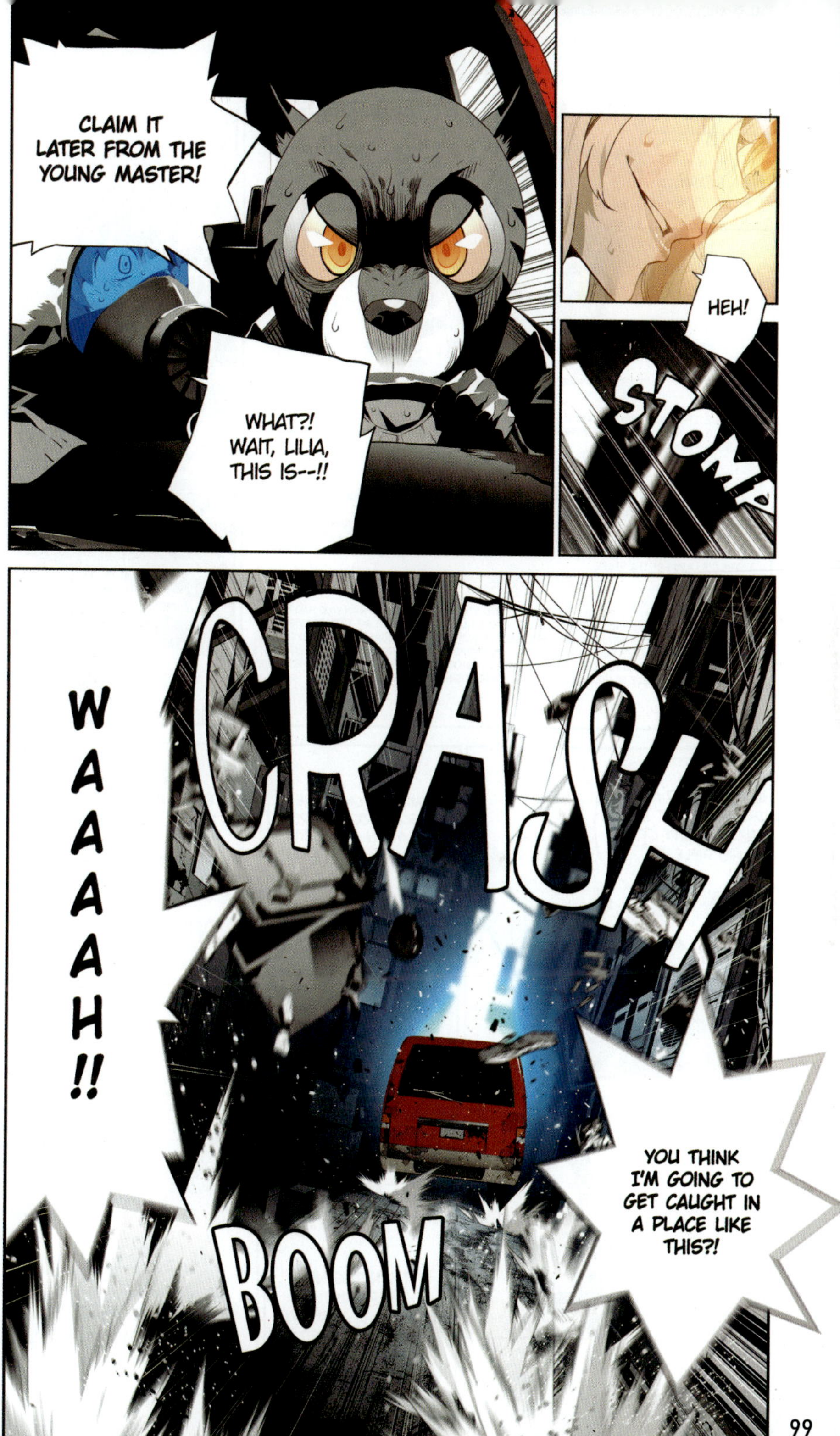
CLAIM IT LATER FROM THE YOUNG MASTER!
WHAT?! WAIT, LILIA, THIS IS--!!
HEH!
STOMP
CRASH
WAAAAAH!!
YOU THINK I'M GOING TO GET CAUGHT IN A PLACE LIKE THIS?!
BOOM

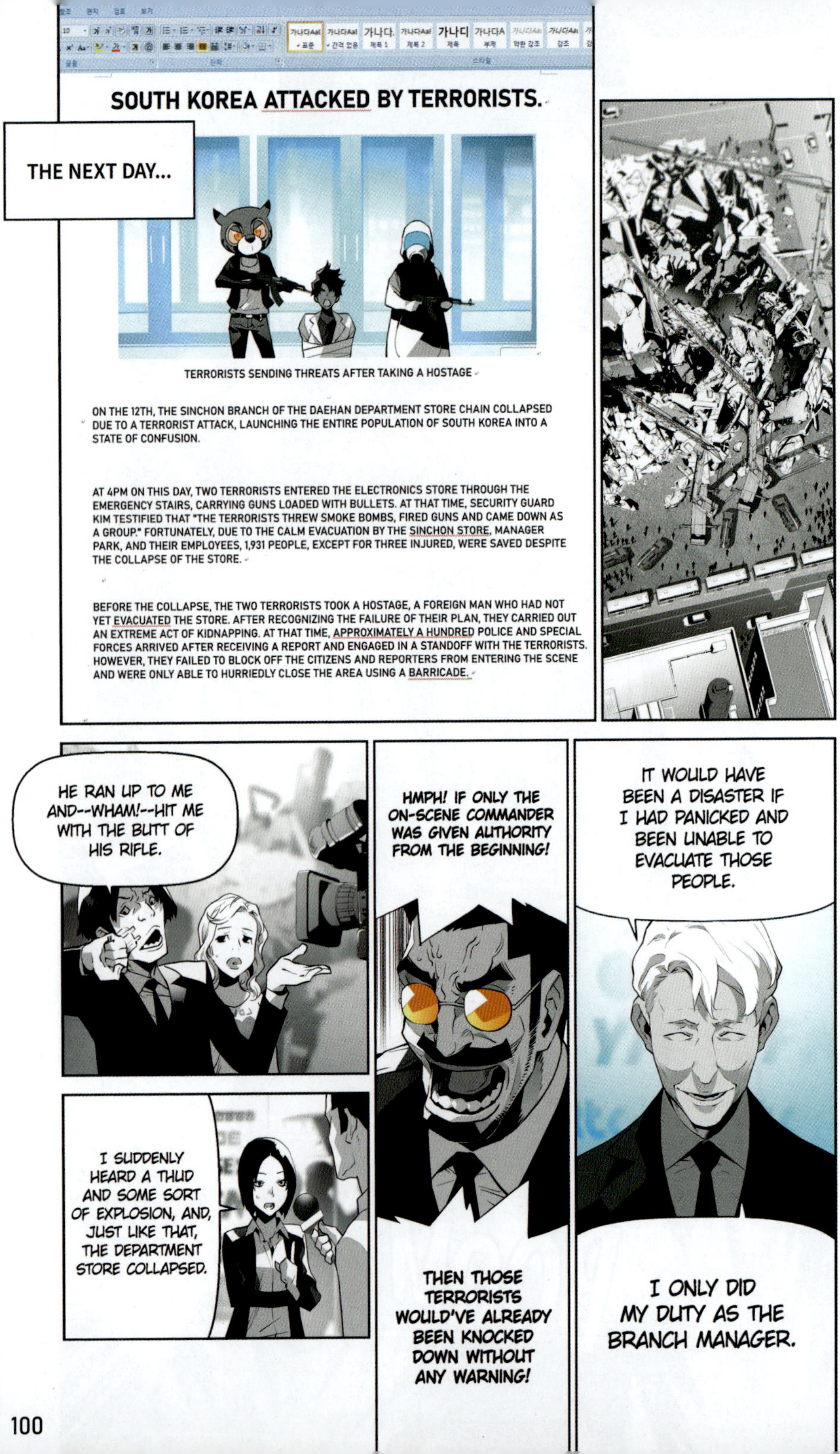
THE NEXT DAY...
SOUTH KOREA ATTACKED BY TERRORISTS.
TERRORISTS SENDING THREATS AFTER TAKING A HOSTAGE
ON THE 12TH, THE SINCHON BRANCH OF THE DAEHAN DEPARTMENT STORE CHAIN COLLAPSED DUE TO A TERRORIST ATTACK, LAUNCHING THE ENTIRE POPULATION OF SOUTH KOREA INTO A STATE OF CONFUSION.
AT 4PM ON THIS DAY, TWO TERRORISTS ENTERED THE ELECTRONICS STORE THROUGH THE EMERGENCY STAIRS, CARRYING GUNS LOADED WITH BULLETS. AT THAT TIME, SECURITY GUARD KIM TESTIFIED THAT "THE TERRORISTS THREW SMOKE BOMBS, FIRED GUNS AND CAME DOWN AS A GROUP." FORTUNATELY, DUE TO THE CALM EVACUATION BY THE SINCHON STORE, MANAGER PARK, AND THEIR EMPLOYEES, 1,931 PEOPLE, EXCEPT FOR THREE INJURED, WERE SAVED DESPITE THE COLLAPSE OF THE STORE.
BEFORE THE COLLAPSE, THE TWO TERRORISTS TOOK A HOSTAGE, A FOREIGN MAN WHO HAD NOT YET EVACUATED THE STORE. AFTER RECOGNIZING THE FAILURE OF THEIR PLAN, THEY CARRIED OUT AN EXTREME ACT OF KIDNAPPING. AT THAT TIME, APPROXIMATELY A HUNDRED POLICE AND SPECIAL FORCES ARRIVED AFTER RECEIVING A REPORT AND ENGAGED IN A STANDOFF WITH THE TERRORISTS. HOWEVER, THEY FAILED TO BLOCK OFF THE CITIZENS AND REPORTERS FROM ENTERING THE SCENE AND WERE ONLY ABLE TO HURRIEDLY CLOSE THE AREA USING A BARRICADE.
HE RAN UP TO ME AND--WHAM!--HIT ME WITH THE BUTT OF HIS RIFLE.
I SUDDENLY HEARD A THUD AND SOME SORT OF EXPLOSION, AND, JUST LIKE THAT, THE DEPARTMENT STORE COLLAPSED.
HMPH! IF ONLY THE ON-SCENE COMMANDER WAS GIVEN AUTHORITY FROM THE BEGINNING!
THEN THOSE TERRORISTS WOULD'VE ALREADY BEEN KNOCKED DOWN WITHOUT ANY WARNING!
IT WOULD HAVE BEEN A DISASTER IF I HAD PANICKED AND BEEN UNABLE TO EVACUATE THOSE PEOPLE.
I ONLY DID MY DUTY AS THE BRANCH MANAGER.

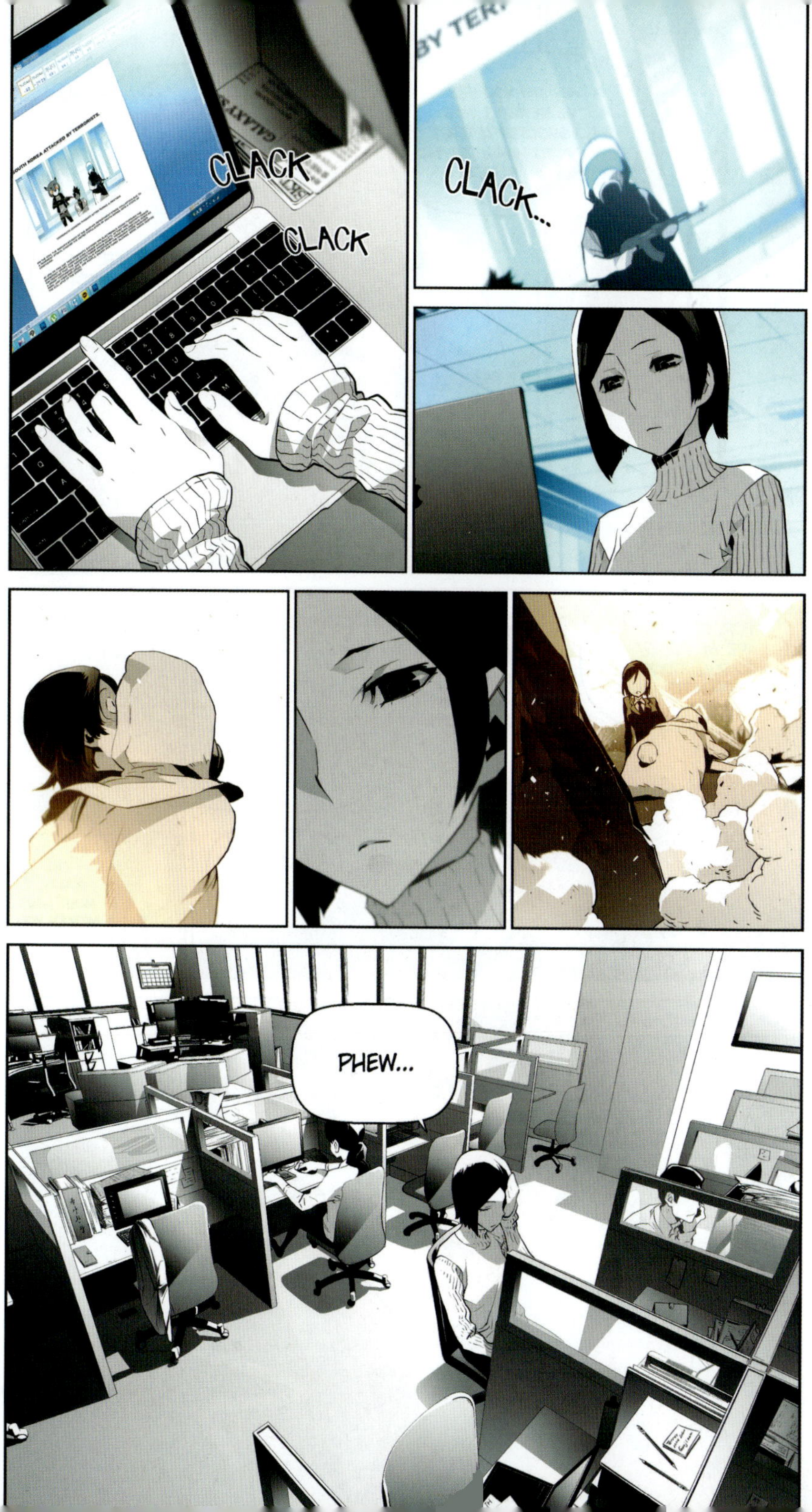
CLACK
CLACK
CLACK...
PHEW...

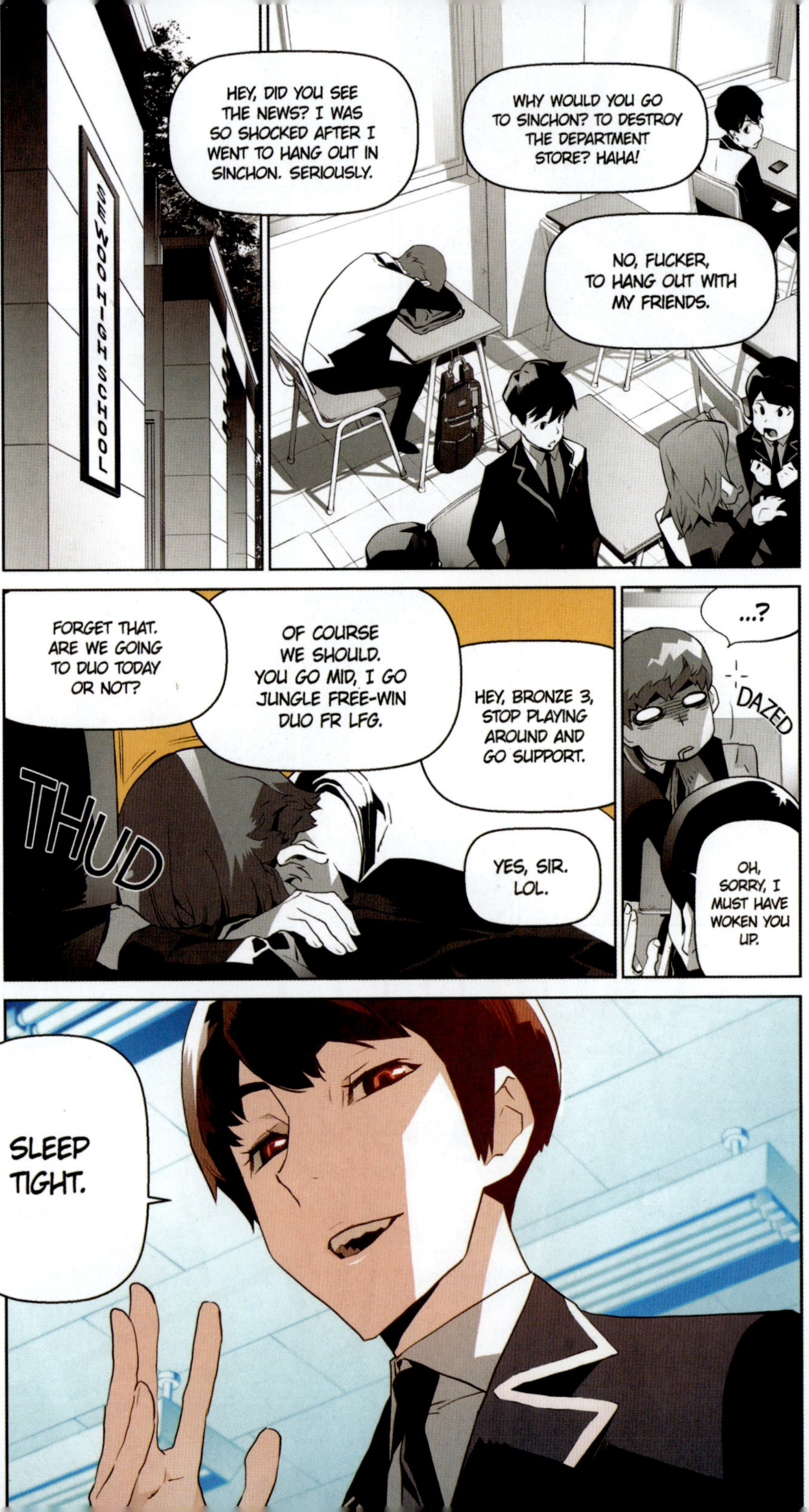
SEWOO HIGH SCHOOL
HEY, DID YOU SEE THE NEWS? I WAS SO SHOCKED AFTER I WENT TO HANG OUT IN SINCHON. SERIOUSLY.
WHY WOULD YOU GO TO SINCHON? TO DESTROY THE DEPARTMENT STORE? HAHA!
NO, FUCKER, TO HANG OUT WITH MY FRIENDS.
FORGET THAT. ARE WE GOING TO DUO TODAY OR NOT?
OF COURSE WE SHOULD. YOU GO MID, I GO JUNGLE FREE-WIN DUO FR LFG.
HEY, BRONZE 3, STOP PLAYING AROUND AND GO SUPPORT.
YES, SIR. LOL.
THUD
...?
DAZED
OH, SORRY, I MUST HAVE WOKEN YOU UP.
SLEEP TIGHT.

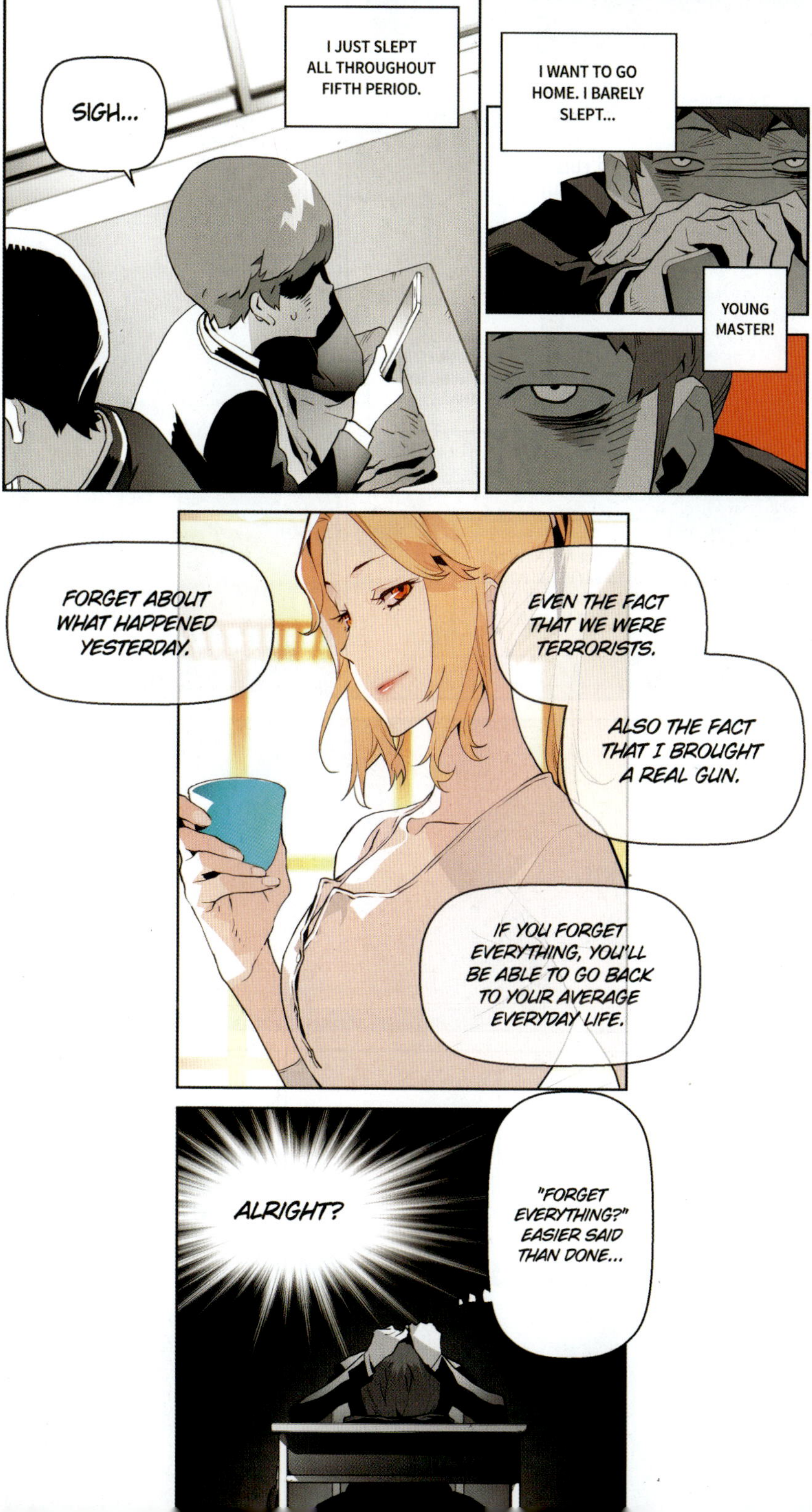
I JUST SLEPT ALL THROUGHOUT FIFTH PERIOD.
SIGH...
I WANT TO GO HOME. I BARELY SLEPT...
YOUNG MASTER!
FORGET ABOUT WHAT HAPPENED YESTERDAY.
EVEN THE FACT THAT WE WERE TERRORISTS.
ALSO THE FACT THAT I BROUGHT A REAL GUN.
IF YOU FORGET EVERYTHING, YOU'LL BE ABLE TO GO BACK TO YOUR AVERAGE EVERYDAY LIFE.
ALRIGHT?
"FORGET EVERYTHING?" EASIER SAID THAN DONE...

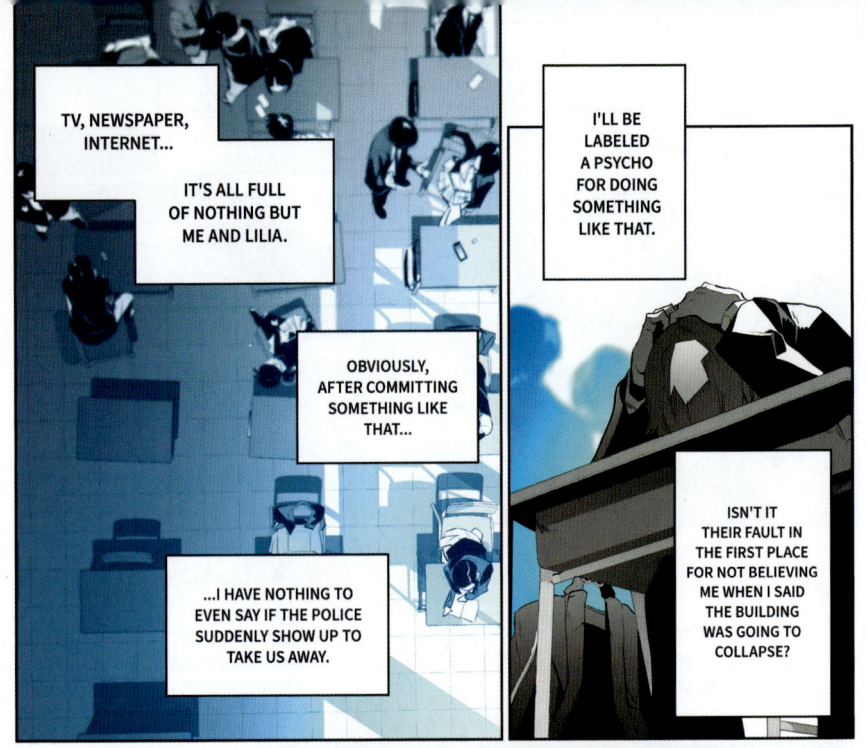

TV, NEWSPAPER, INTERNET...

IT'S ALL FULL OF NOTHING BUT ME AND LILIA.

I'LL BE LABELED A PSYCHO FOR DOING SOMETHING LIKE THAT.

OBVIOUSLY, AFTER COMMITTING SOMETHING LIKE THAT...

ISN'T IT THEIR FAULT IN THE FIRST PLACE FOR NOT BELIEVING ME WHEN I SAID THE BUILDING WAS GOING TO COLLAPSE?

...I HAVE NOTHING TO EVEN SAY IF THE POLICE SUDDENLY SHOW UP TO TAKE US AWAY.

STILL...

...RATHER THAN A THOUSAND DEATHS...

...ISN'T IT BETTER THAT WE GET FRAMED INSTEAD?

HEY, WEEKLY DUTY.

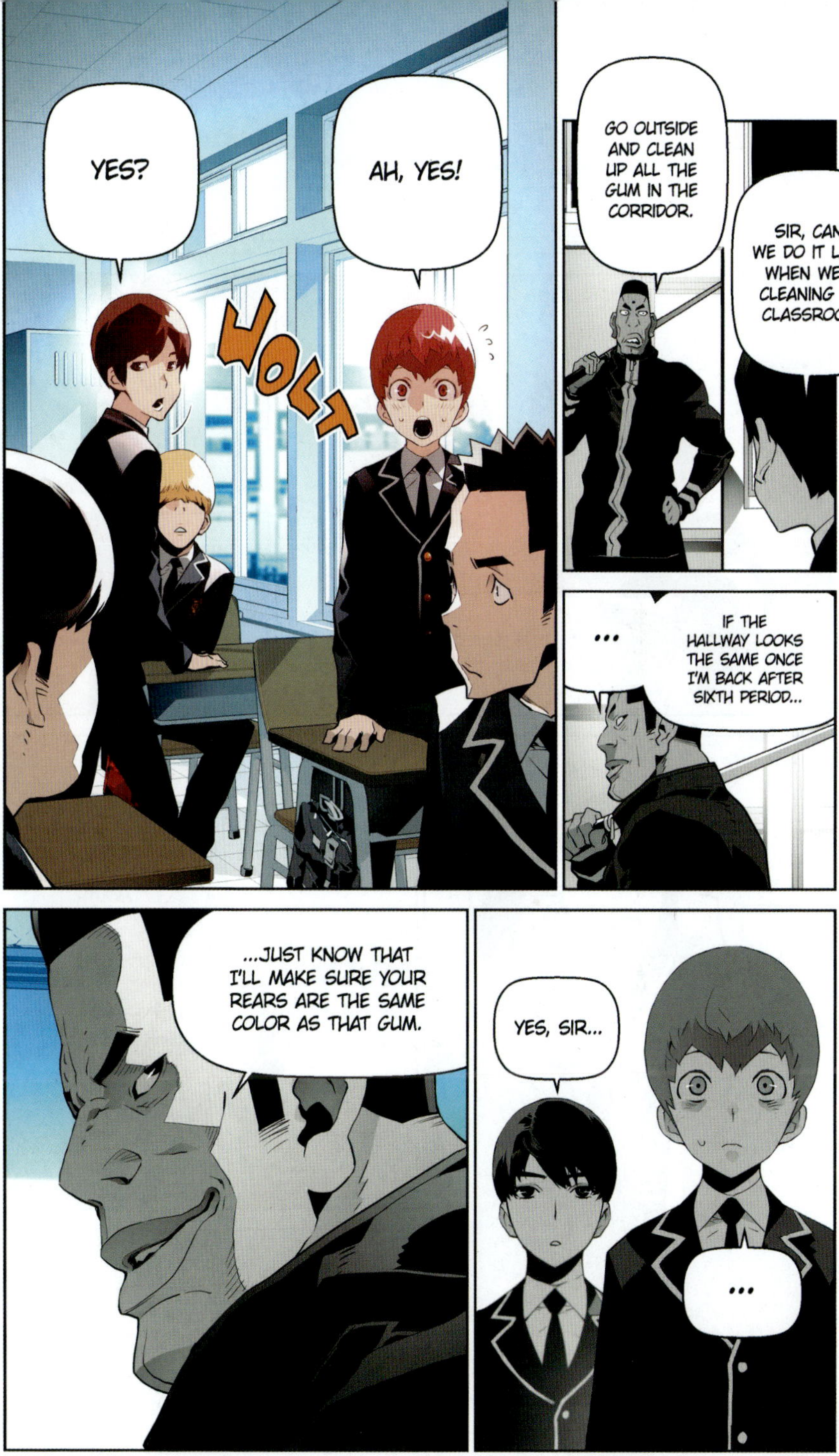
YES?
AH, YES!
JOLT
GO OUTSIDE AND CLEAN UP ALL THE GUM IN THE CORRIDOR.
SIR, CAN'T WE DO IT LATER WHEN WE'RE CLEANING THE CLASSROOM?
...
IF THE HALLWAY LOOKS THE SAME ONCE I'M BACK AFTER SIXTH PERIOD...
...JUST KNOW THAT I'LL MAKE SURE YOUR REARS ARE THE SAME COLOR AS THAT GUM.
YES, SIR...
...

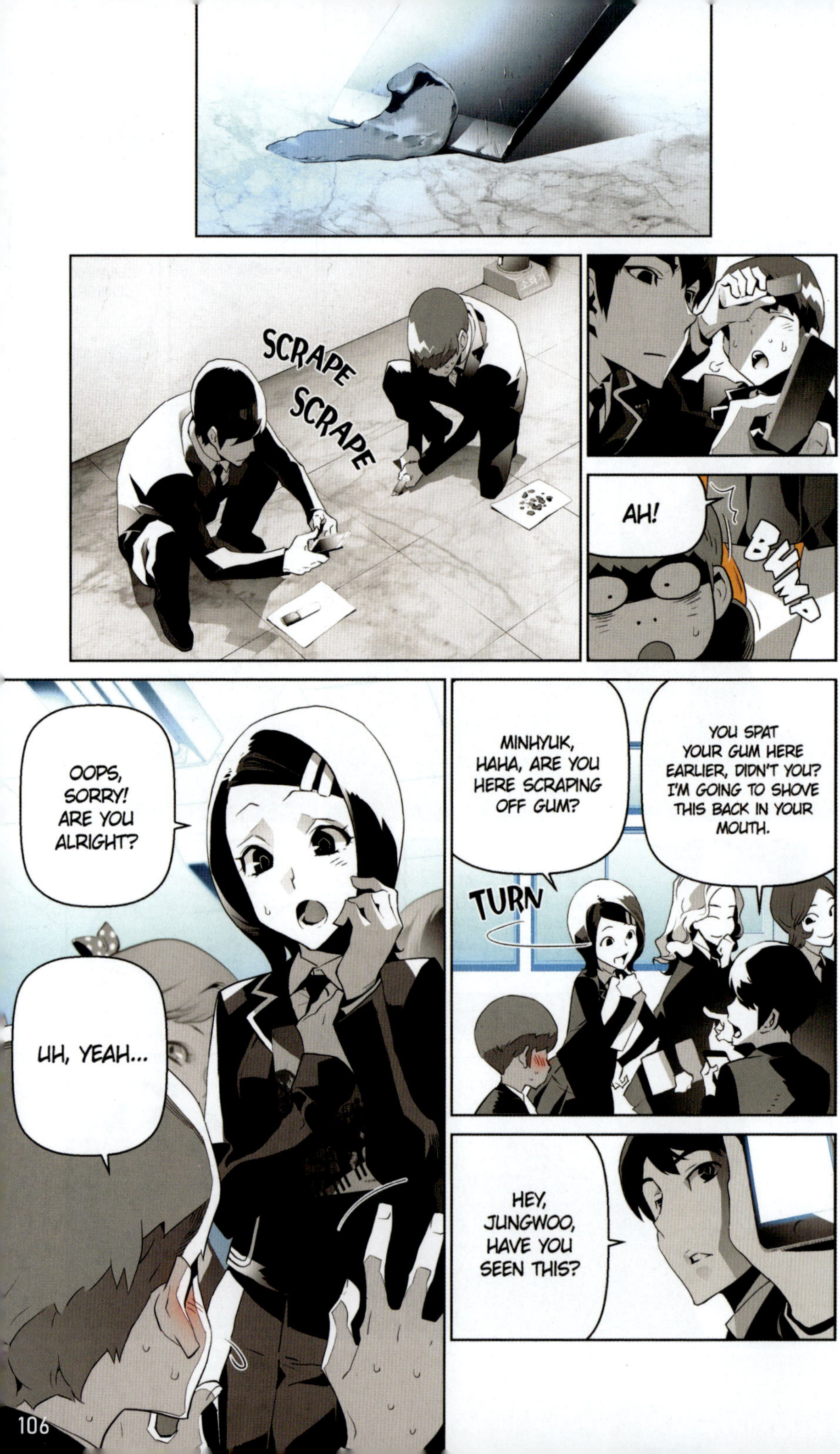
SCRAPE
SCRAPE
AH!
BUMP
OOPS, SORRY! ARE YOU ALRIGHT?
UH, YEAH...
MINHYUK, HAHA, ARE YOU HERE SCRAPING OFF GUM?
YOU SPAT YOUR GUM HERE EARLIER, DIDN'T YOU? I'M GOING TO SHOVE THIS BACK IN YOUR MOUTH.
TURN
HEY, JUNGWOO, HAVE YOU SEEN THIS?

NO MATTER HOW YOU LOOK AT IT, DON'T YOU THINK THESE GUYS ARE NUTS? HOW CAN THESE TWO ALONE DESTROY A DEPARTMENT STORE?

!!

I-I DON'T KNOW!! I DON'T KNOW WHO THOSE TWO ARE!

WHO SAID ANYTHING ABOUT THEIR IDENTITIES? YOU'RE OVERREACTING ALL OF A SUDDEN.

THE BELL RANG. LET'S STOP THIS AND GO.

...

SIGH... THIS IS TIRING.

LILIA WAS RIGHT.

I SHOULD JUST FORGET EVERYTHING AND GO BACK TO HOW IT ORIGINALLY WAS.

IF I STOP THINKING ABOUT IT AND JUST LIVE MY LIFE...

BAAAM

?!

SCREEEEECH

AAAACKK!! WHAT'S HAPPENING?!

AAAAH!

S-SOMEBODY HELP US!!

HA... HA...

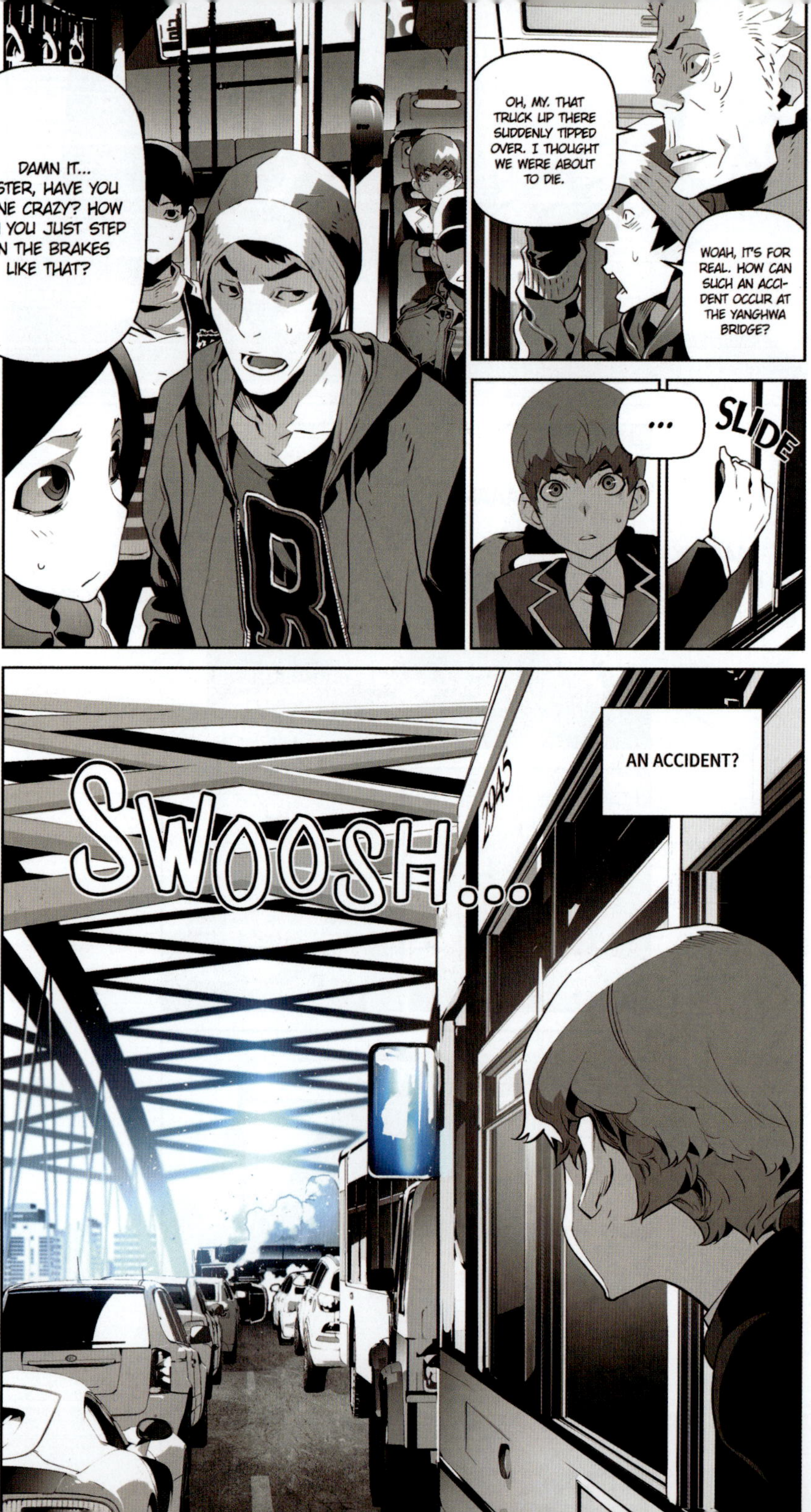
DAMN IT... MISTER, HAVE YOU GONE CRAZY? HOW CAN YOU JUST STEP ON THE BRAKES LIKE THAT?
OH, MY. THAT TRUCK UP THERE SUDDENLY TIPPED OVER. I THOUGHT WE WERE ABOUT TO DIE.
WOAH, IT'S FOR REAL. HOW CAN SUCH AN ACCI-DENT OCCUR AT THE YANGHWA BRIDGE?
...
SLIDE
SWOOSH...
2945
AN ACCIDENT?

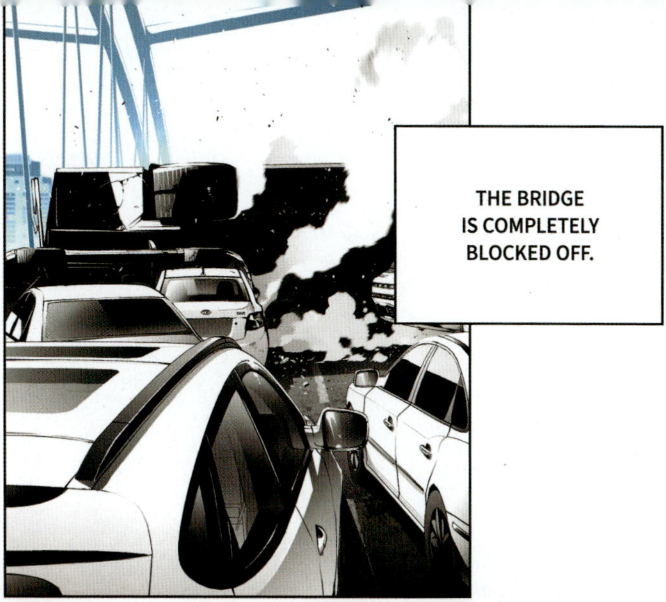
THE BRIDGE
IS COMPLETELY
BLOCKED OFF.

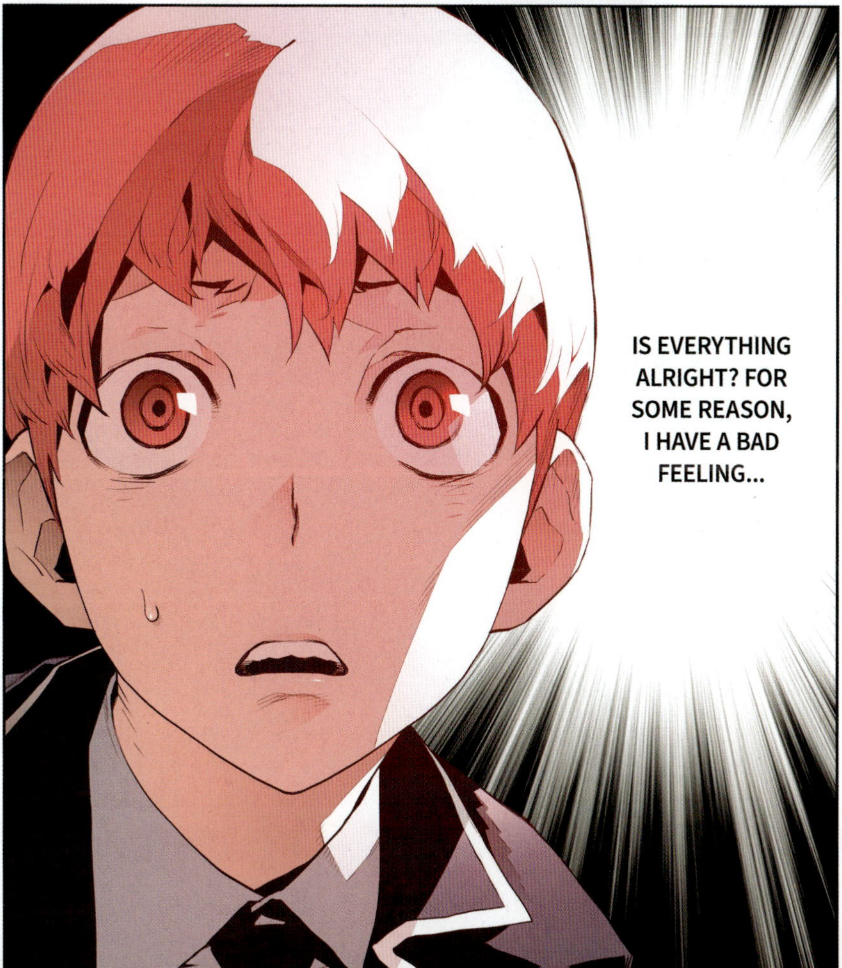
IS EVERYTHING
ALRIGHT? FOR
SOME REASON,
I HAVE A BAD
FEELING...

TERROR MAN

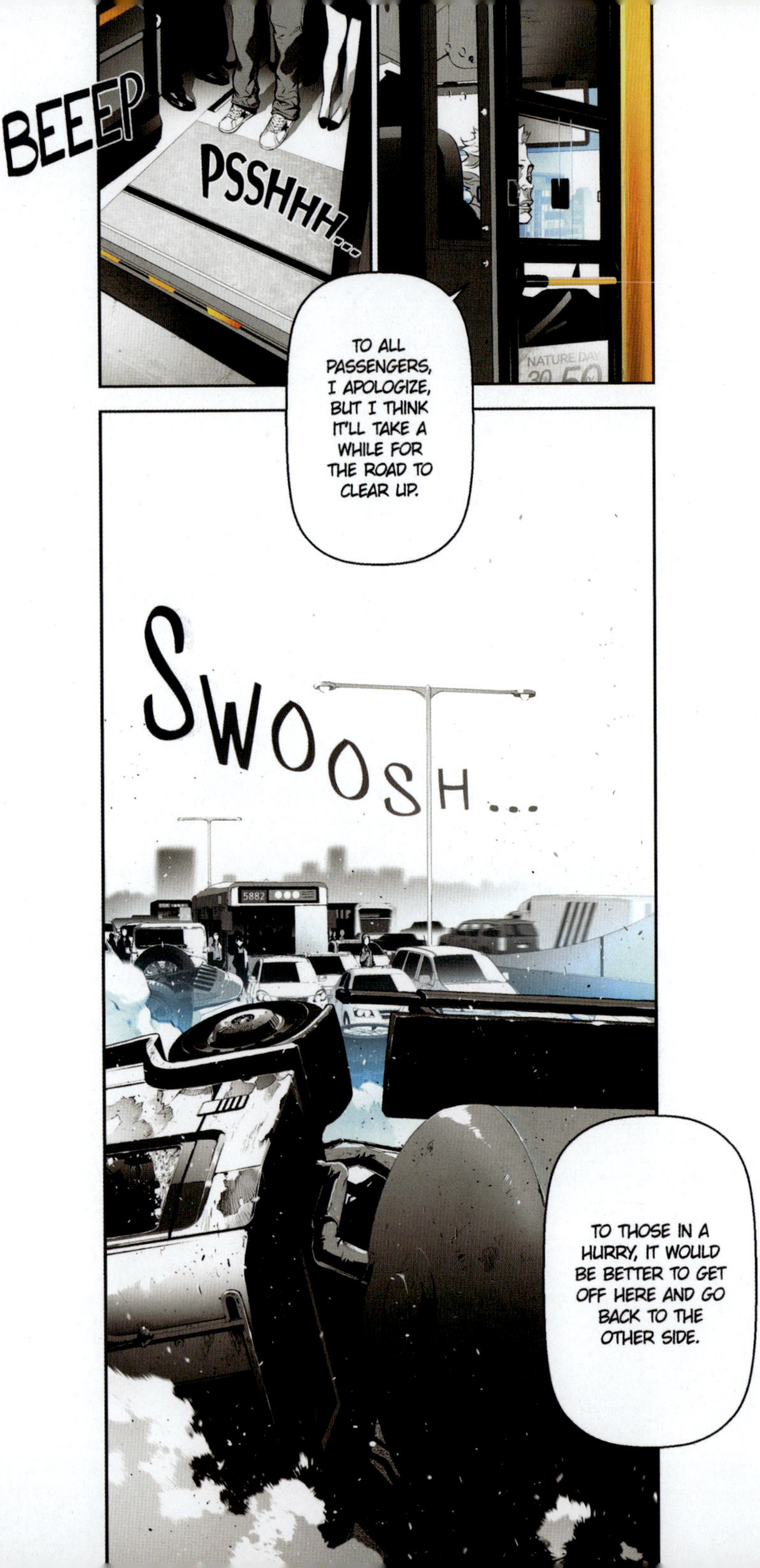
BEEEP
PSSHHH...
TO ALL PASSENGERS, I APOLOGIZE, BUT I THINK IT'LL TAKE A WHILE FOR THE ROAD TO CLEAR UP.
SWOOSH...
TO THOSE IN A HURRY, IT WOULD BE BETTER TO GET OFF HERE AND GO BACK TO THE OTHER SIDE.

AH, HOW ANNOYING FOR AN ACCIDENT TO OCCUR LIKE THAT.

YES, BOSS. THERE'S AN ACCIDENT HERE AT THE YANGHWA BRIDGE, SO...

WHAT DO I DO?

SHOULD I ALSO JUST GET OFF AND WALK?

MY HOUSE IS RIGHT NEARBY...

I ALSO DON'T SEE ANY PURPLE FOG OR ANYTHING...

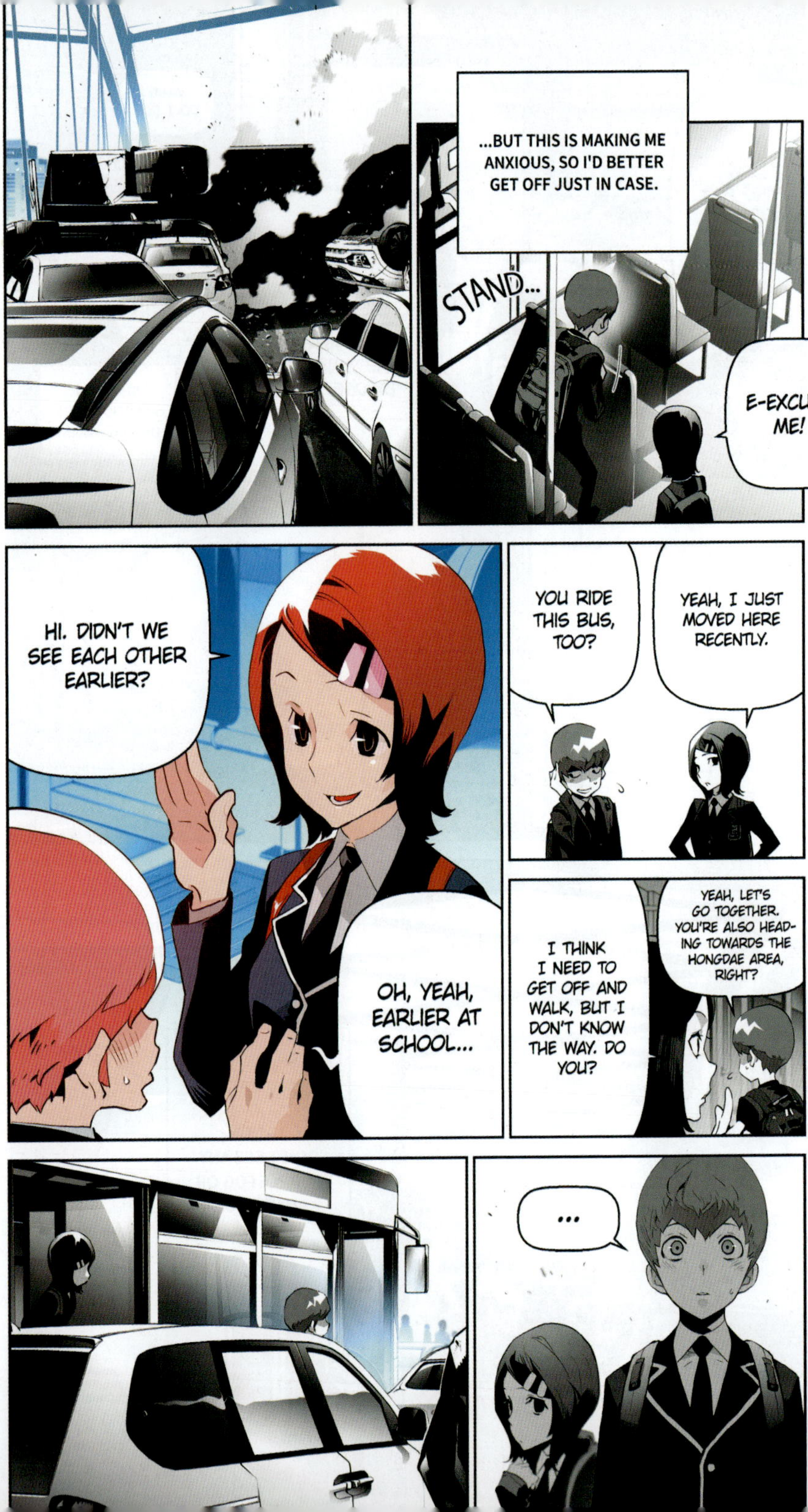
...BUT THIS IS MAKING ME ANXIOUS, SO I'D BETTER GET OFF JUST IN CASE.
STAND...
E-EXCUSE ME!
HI. DIDN'T WE SEE EACH OTHER EARLIER?
OH, YEAH, EARLIER AT SCHOOL...
YOU RIDE THIS BUS, TOO?
YEAH, I JUST MOVED HERE RECENTLY.
I THINK I NEED TO GET OFF AND WALK, BUT I DON'T KNOW THE WAY. DO YOU?
YEAH, LET'S GO TOGETHER. YOU'RE ALSO HEADING TOWARDS THE HONGDAE AREA, RIGHT?
...

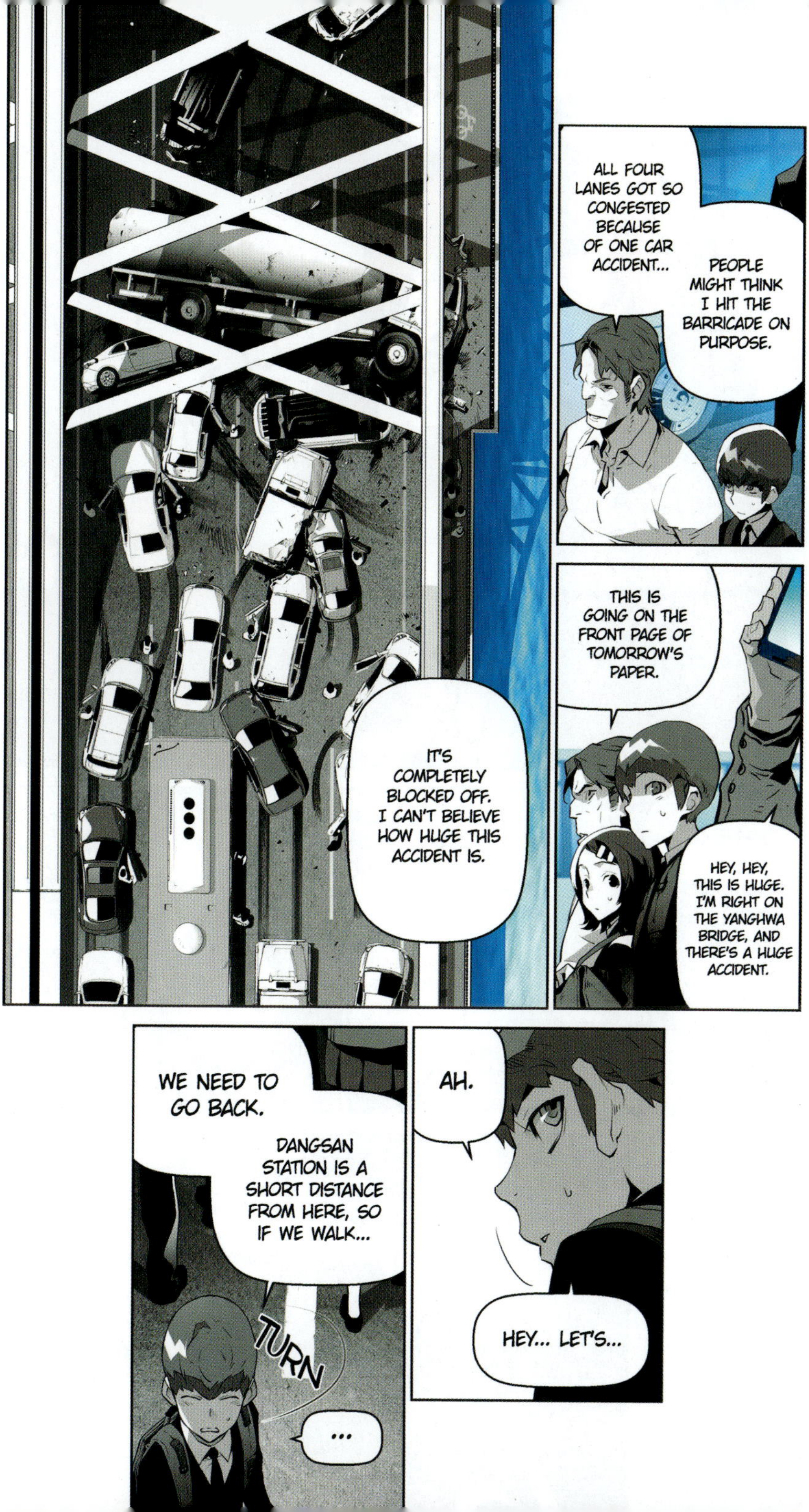
ALL FOUR LANES GOT SO CONGESTED BECAUSE OF ONE CAR ACCIDENT...
PEOPLE MIGHT THINK I HIT THE BARRICADE ON PURPOSE.
IT'S COMPLETELY BLOCKED OFF. I CAN'T BELIEVE HOW HUGE THIS ACCIDENT IS.
THIS IS GOING ON THE FRONT PAGE OF TOMORROW'S PAPER.
HEY, HEY, THIS IS HUGE. I'M RIGHT ON THE YANGHWA BRIDGE, AND THERE'S A HUGE ACCIDENT.
WE NEED TO GO BACK.
DANGSAN STATION IS A SHORT DISTANCE FROM HERE, SO IF WE WALK...
TURN
...
AH.
HEY... LET'S...

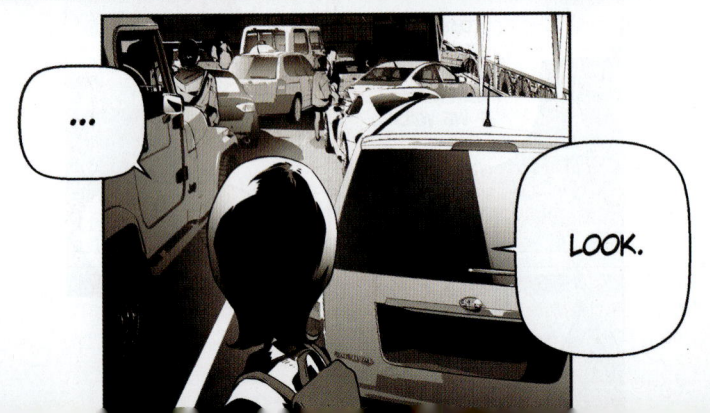

CLICK

CLICK CLICK CLICK

H-HEY...

AH!

SORRY. I LIKE TAKING PICTURES, SO...

I-IT'S FINE. LET'S GO.

WHERE DID THAT HUGE CAMERA COME FROM? YOU CARRY THAT IN YOUR BAG?

HUH?

...

LOOK.

INSIDE THAT CAR...

CREAAAK

SOMEONE'S IN THERE.

HUH?!

SOMEONE'S INSIDE THAT CAR! AND IT LOOKS LIKE IT'S ABOUT TO FALL!

?!

I'M FINE. MOMMY'S FINE, SO HURRY AND GET OUT OF THE CAR.

NO!!! I'LL STAY WITH YOU, MOMMY!

PLEASE LISTEN TO ME, ALRIGHT?

TILT TILT

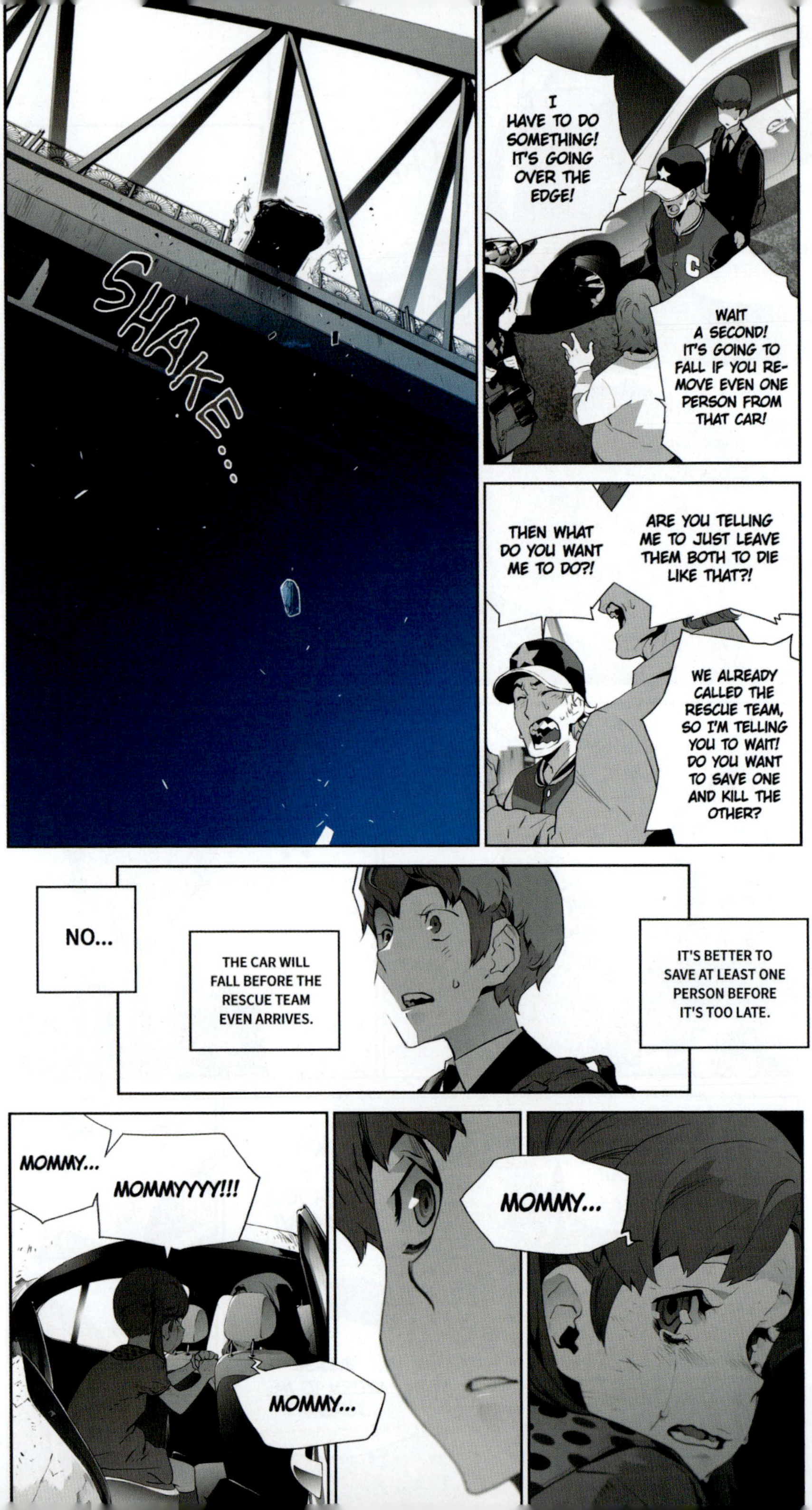

SHAKE...
I HAVE TO DO SOMETHING! IT'S GOING OVER THE EDGE!
WAIT A SECOND! IT'S GOING TO FALL IF YOU RE-MOVE EVEN ONE PERSON FROM THAT CAR!
ARE YOU TELLING ME TO JUST LEAVE THEM BOTH TO DIE LIKE THAT?!
THEN WHAT DO YOU WANT ME TO DO?!
WE ALREADY CALLED THE RESCUE TEAM, SO I'M TELLING YOU TO WAIT! DO YOU WANT TO SAVE ONE AND KILL THE OTHER?
NO...
THE CAR WILL FALL BEFORE THE RESCUE TEAM EVEN ARRIVES.
IT'S BETTER TO SAVE AT LEAST ONE PERSON BEFORE IT'S TOO LATE.
MOMMY...
MOMMYYYY!!!
MOMMY...
MOMMY...

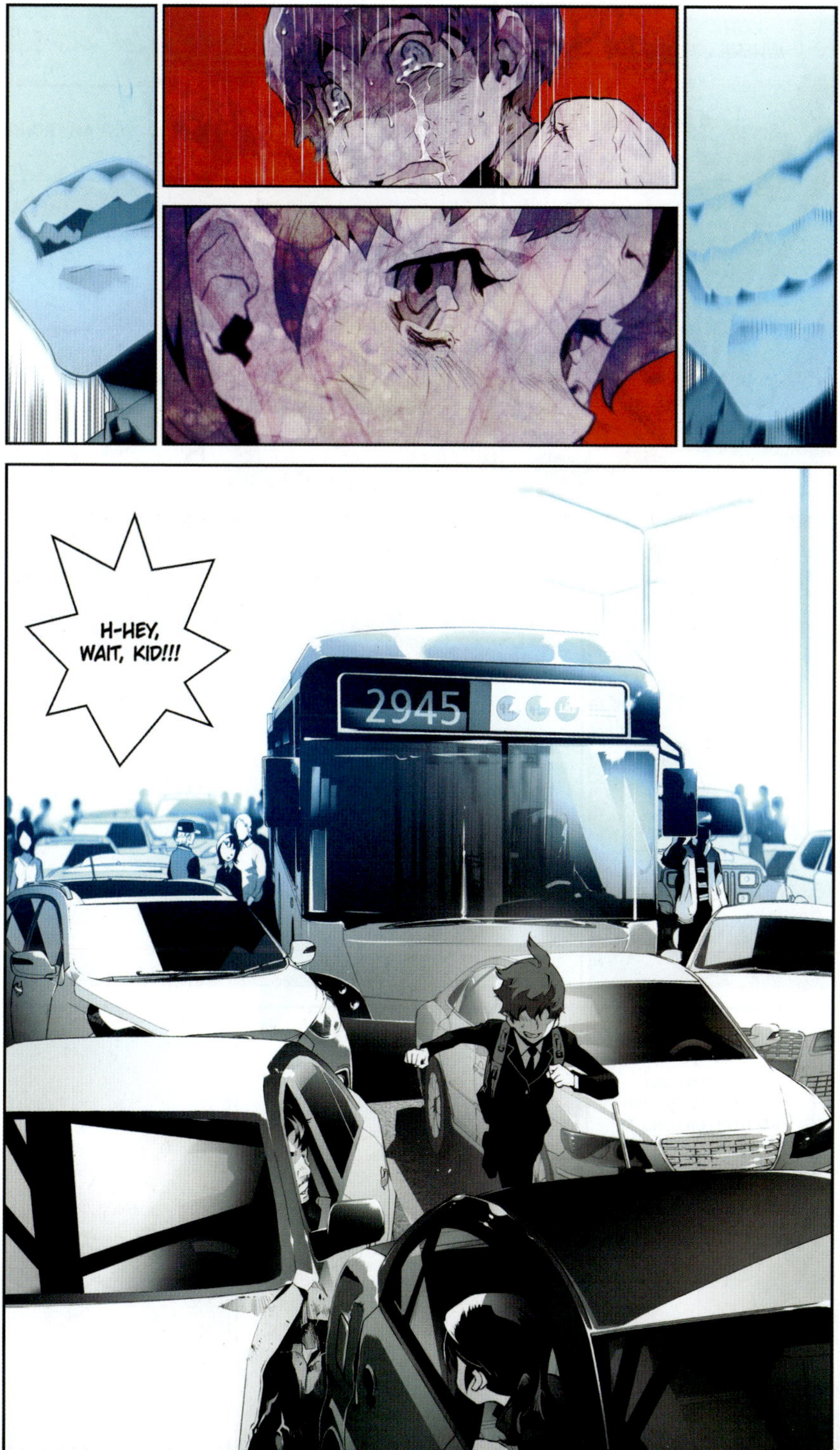

H-HEY, WAIT, KID!!!
2945

HUH? WHERE...?

WHAT AM I DOING?

WHY AM I RUNNING?

NO WAY... HE'S TRYING TO SAVE THOSE PEOPLE?

BECAUSE IT'S NOT PURPLE? BECAUSE I'M NOT IN DANGER?

CLENCH

J- JUST BEAR WITH IT FOR A BIT LONGER. ALRIGHT?

I'LL SAVE YOU.

TWITCH TWITCH

I SAID THAT, BUT I WON'T BE ABLE TO HOLD ON FOR LONG. AT LEAST THE CHILD CAN...

CREAK...

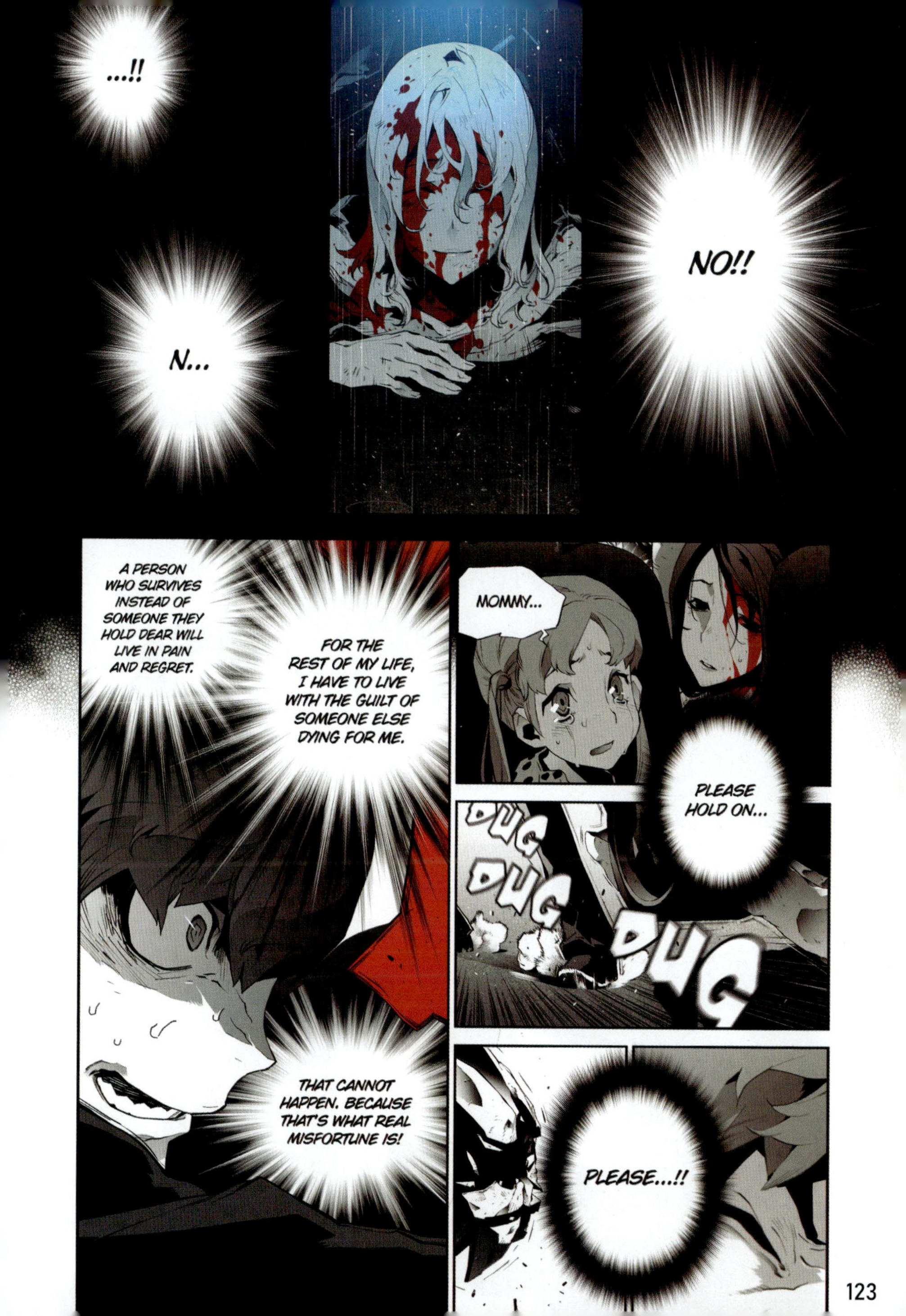
...!!
NO!!
N...
A PERSON WHO SURVIVES INSTEAD OF SOMEONE THEY HOLD DEAR WILL LIVE IN PAIN AND REGRET.
FOR THE REST OF MY LIFE, I HAVE TO LIVE WITH THE GUILT OF SOMEONE ELSE DYING FOR ME.
MOMMY...
PLEASE HOLD ON...
DUG
DUG
DUG
THAT CANNOT HAPPEN. BECAUSE THAT'S WHAT REAL MISFORTUNE IS!
PLEASE...!!

EVERYONE, PLEASE COME OVER HERE AND HELP ME!

UUUUGH!!

CREAK...

!

YOU...!

MY NAME'S NOT "YOU." IT'S MINJI. MINJI LEE.

LET'S PULL ALTOGETHER ON THE COUNT OF THREE!!

ONE, TWO, THREE!!

ONE, TWO, THREE!!

JUST A BIT MORE!

HEAVE-HO!

HUH...?!

WAAAH!!

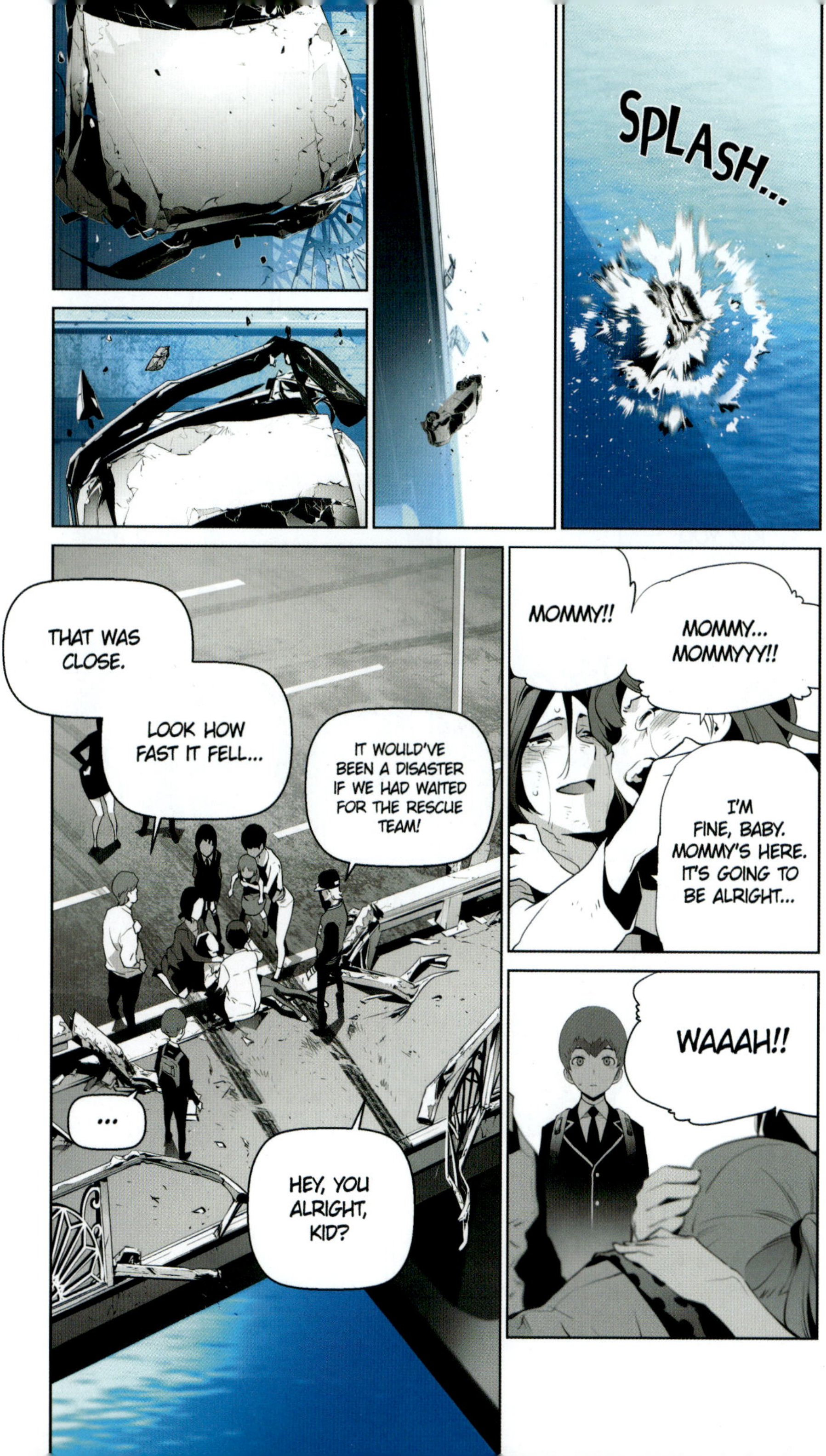
SPLASH...
THAT WAS CLOSE.
LOOK HOW FAST IT FELL...
IT WOULD'VE BEEN A DISASTER IF WE HAD WAITED FOR THE RESCUE TEAM!
...
HEY, YOU ALRIGHT, KID?
MOMMY!!
MOMMY... MOMMYYY!!
I'M FINE, BABY. MOMMY'S HERE. IT'S GOING TO BE ALRIGHT...
WAAAH!!

THANK GOODNESS. SERIOUSLY...

KID, YOU DID GREAT!!

STARTLE

YOU SAVED THAT WOMAN!!

YOU WERE AMAZING!!

N-NO...

ALL I DID WAS JUMP IN...

THE YOUNG BOY HAS GUTS!! HE DESERVES AN AWARD!

YOU WERE THE BEST, YOUNG MAN.

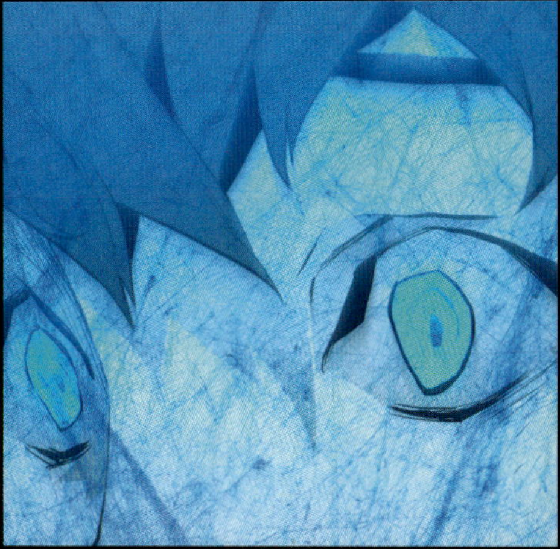
…
?!

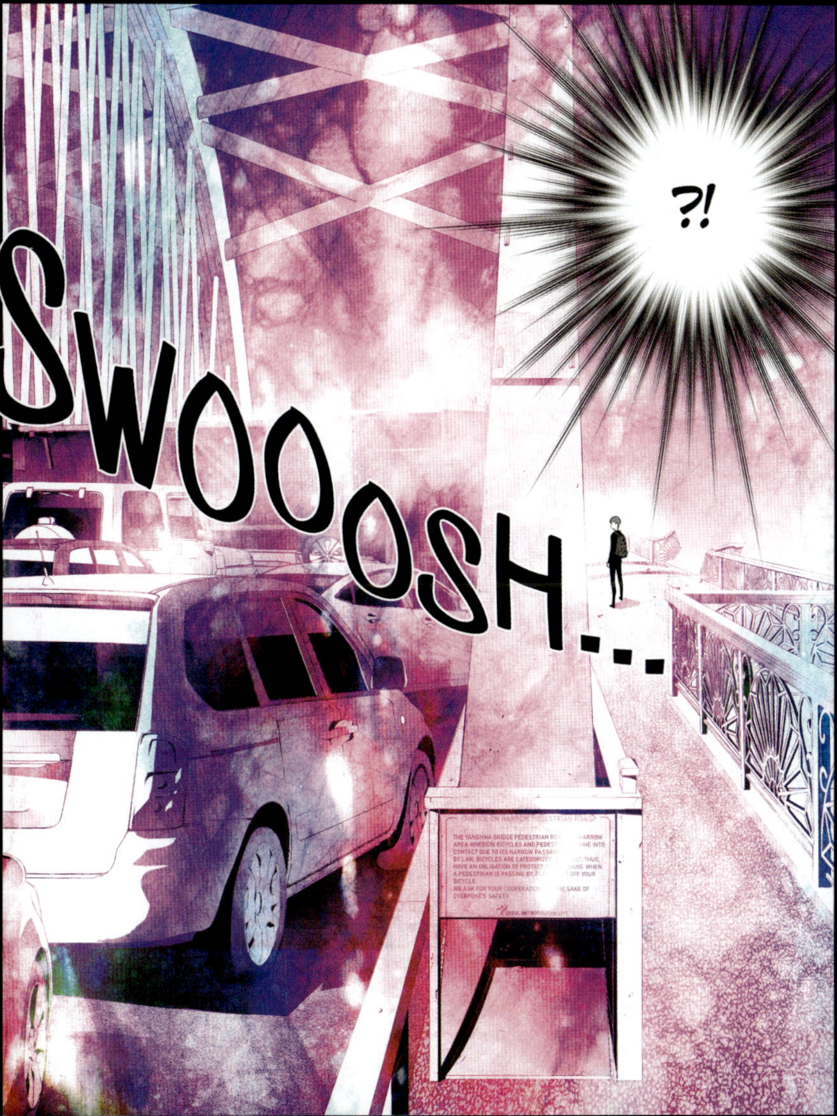
?!
SWOOOSH…

TERROR MAN

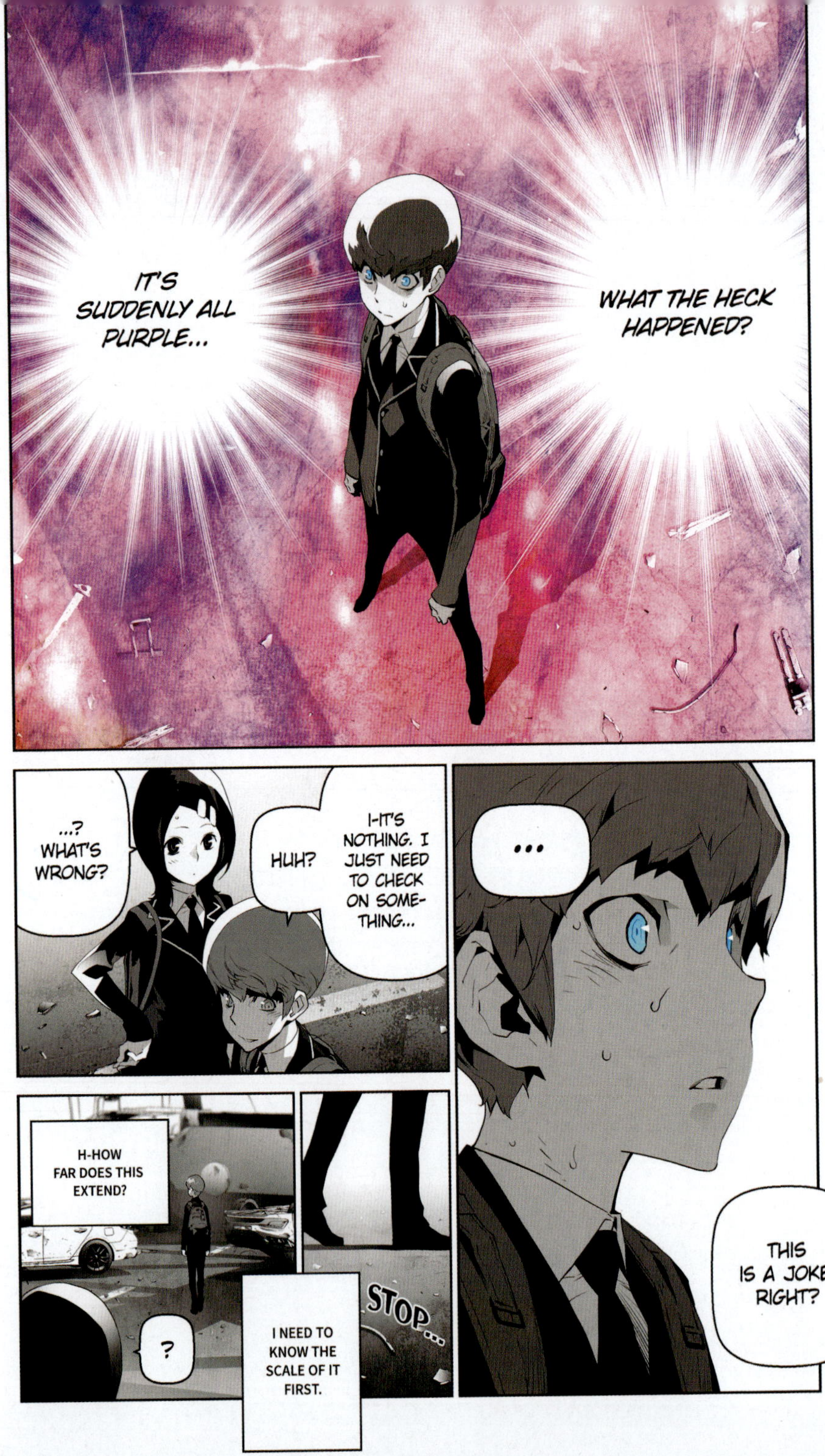
IT'S SUDDENLY ALL PURPLE...
WHAT THE HECK HAPPENED?
...? WHAT'S WRONG?
HUH?
I-IT'S NOTHING. I JUST NEED TO CHECK ON SOME-THING...
...
THIS IS A JOKE, RIGHT?
H-HOW FAR DOES THIS EXTEND?
?
STOP...
I NEED TO KNOW THE SCALE OF IT FIRST.

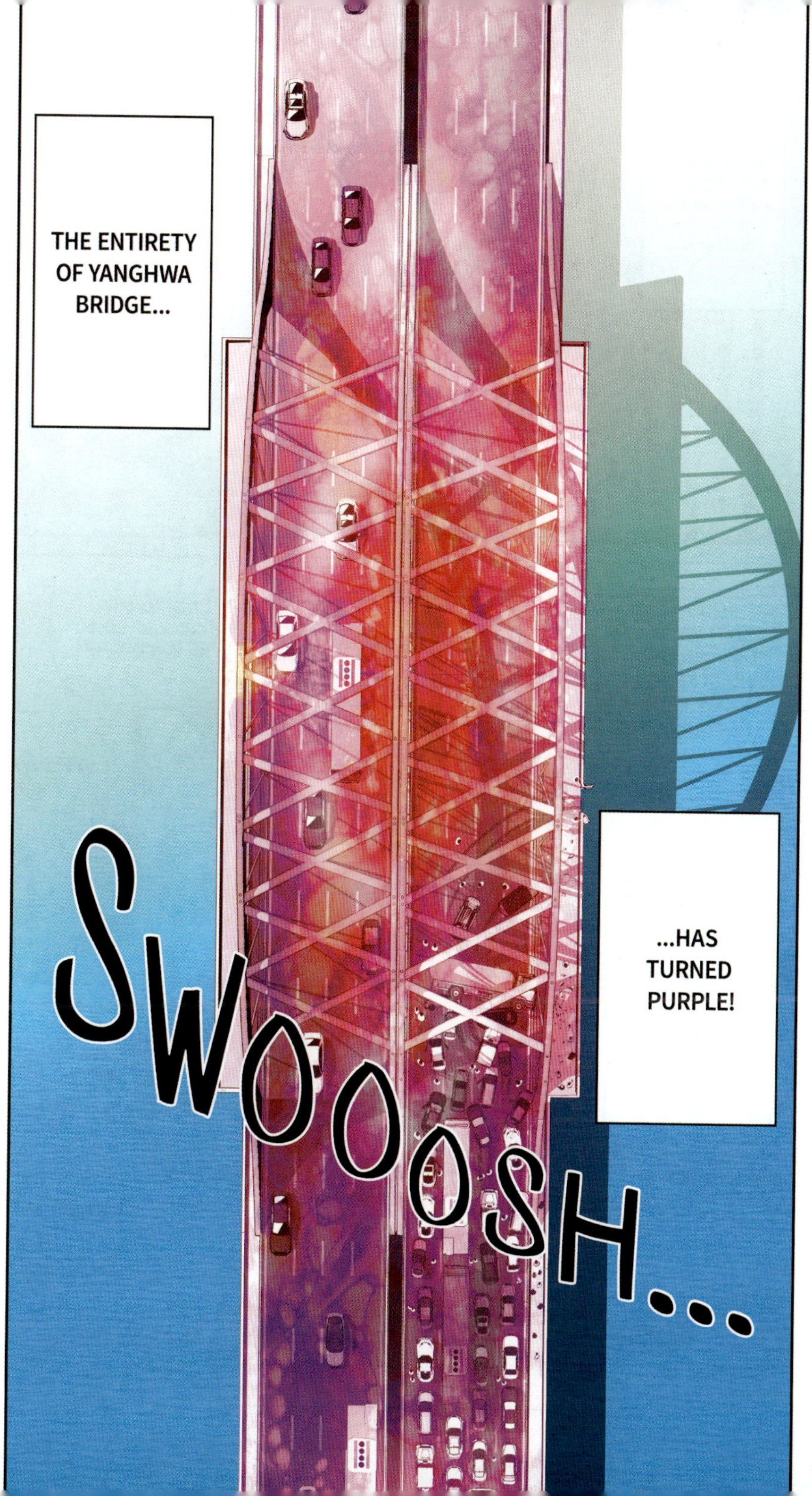
THE ENTIRETY OF YANGHWA BRIDGE...
SWOOOSH...
...HAS TURNED PURPLE!

IF THIS BRIDGE COLLAPSES LIKE THE DEPARTMENT STORE YESTERDAY...

WHINGGGG...

E-EXCUSE ME...

HUH?

H-HOW ABOUT WE ALL TURN AROUND AND GO BACK ALONG WITH THAT LADY?

WE NEED TO ESCORT HER TO THE HOSPITAL QUICKLY.

YOU WANT US ALL TO LEAVE THE BRIDGE ALTOGETHER? IT'LL BE FASTER WAITING FOR THE RESCUE TEAM TO PULL OUT THE VEHICLES.

THE ROAD WILL CLEAR UP SOON, SO DON'T WORRY.

HE'S RIGHT, KID.

THE CARS HAVE CONGESTED THE WHOLE LENGTH OF THE BRIDGE, BUT THE RESCUE TEAM WILL COORDINATE EVERYTHING SOON ENOUGH.

...

LEAVE THE REST TO THE ADULTS.

WHAT DO I DO?

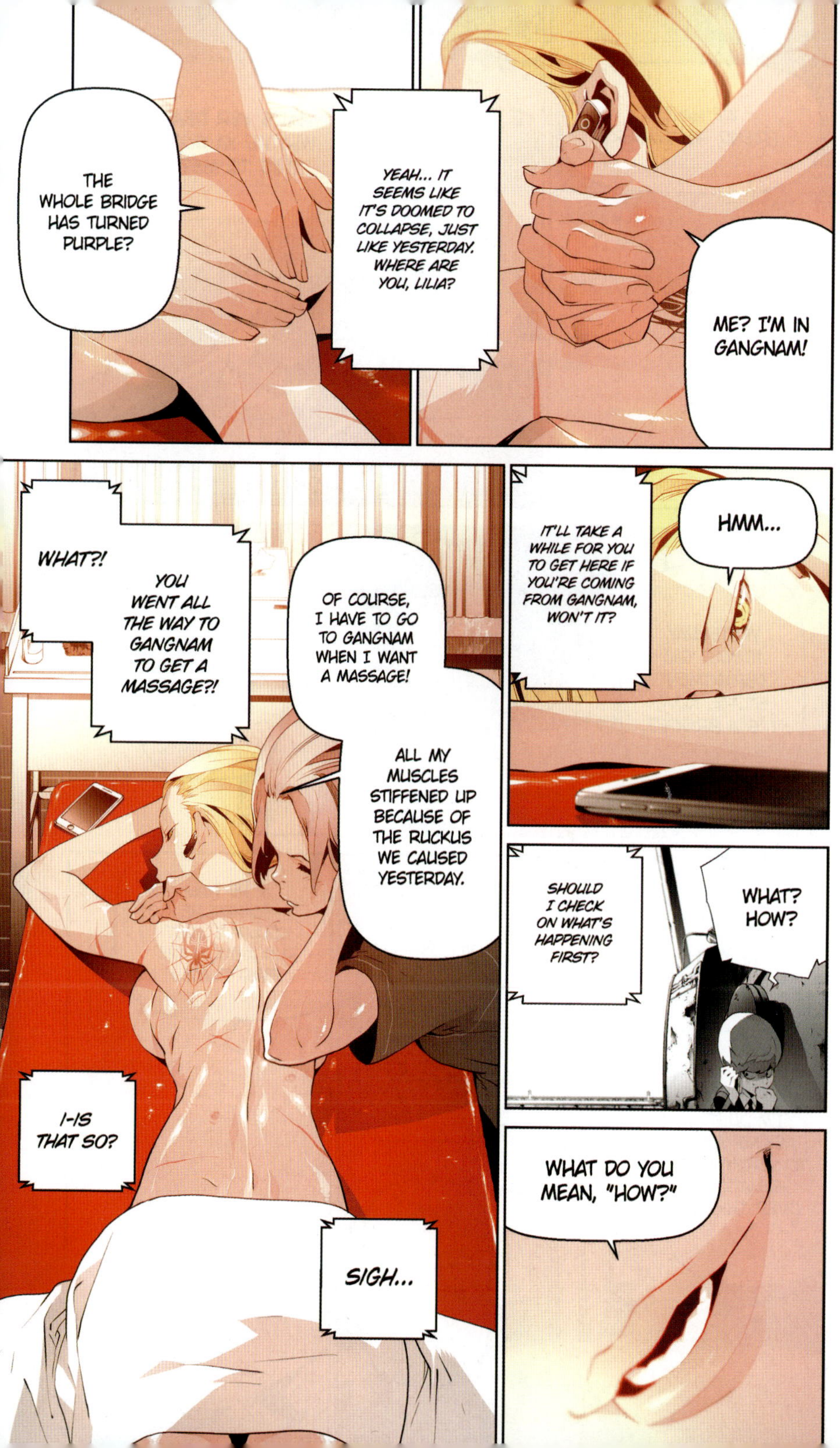
THE WHOLE BRIDGE HAS TURNED PURPLE?
YEAH... IT SEEMS LIKE IT'S DOOMED TO COLLAPSE, JUST LIKE YESTERDAY. WHERE ARE YOU, LILIA?
ME? I'M IN GANGNAM!
WHAT?!
YOU WENT ALL THE WAY TO GANGNAM TO GET A MASSAGE?!
OF COURSE, I HAVE TO GO TO GANGNAM WHEN I WANT A MASSAGE!
ALL MY MUSCLES STIFFENED UP BECAUSE OF THE RUCKUS WE CAUSED YESTERDAY.
I-IS THAT SO?
SIGH...
IT'LL TAKE A WHILE FOR YOU TO GET HERE IF YOU'RE COMING FROM GANGNAM, WON'T IT?
HMM...
SHOULD I CHECK ON WHAT'S HAPPENING FIRST?
WHAT? HOW?
WHAT DO YOU MEAN, "HOW?"

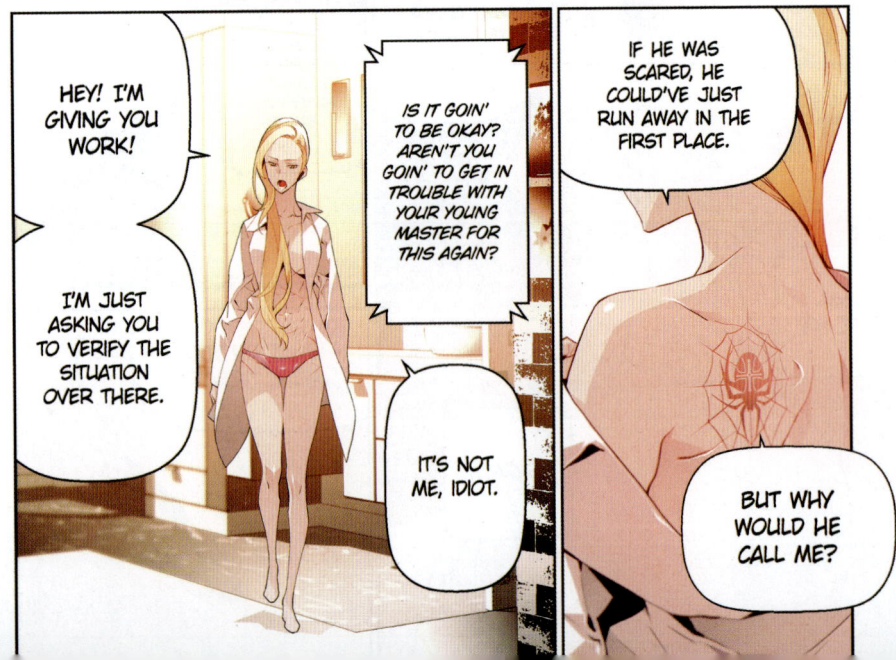

"WE HAVE A FRIEND, REMEMBER?"

"AH, SERIOUSLY!"

"WHAT'S YER DEAL?! WHY'RE YA DOIN' THIS TO ME?!"

"YESTERDAY, IT WAS THE DEPARTMENT STORE. NOW, IT'S A BRIDGE?"

"ARE YOU ACTUAL TERRORISTS OR SOMETHIN'?"

"HEY! I'M GIVING YOU WORK!"

"I'M JUST ASKING YOU TO VERIFY THE SITUATION OVER THERE."

IS IT GOIN' TO BE OKAY? AREN'T YOU GOIN' TO GET IN TROUBLE WITH YOUR YOUNG MASTER FOR THIS AGAIN?

"IF HE WAS SCARED, HE COULD'VE JUST RUN AWAY IN THE FIRST PLACE."

"IT'S NOT ME, IDIOT."

"BUT WHY WOULD HE CALL ME?"

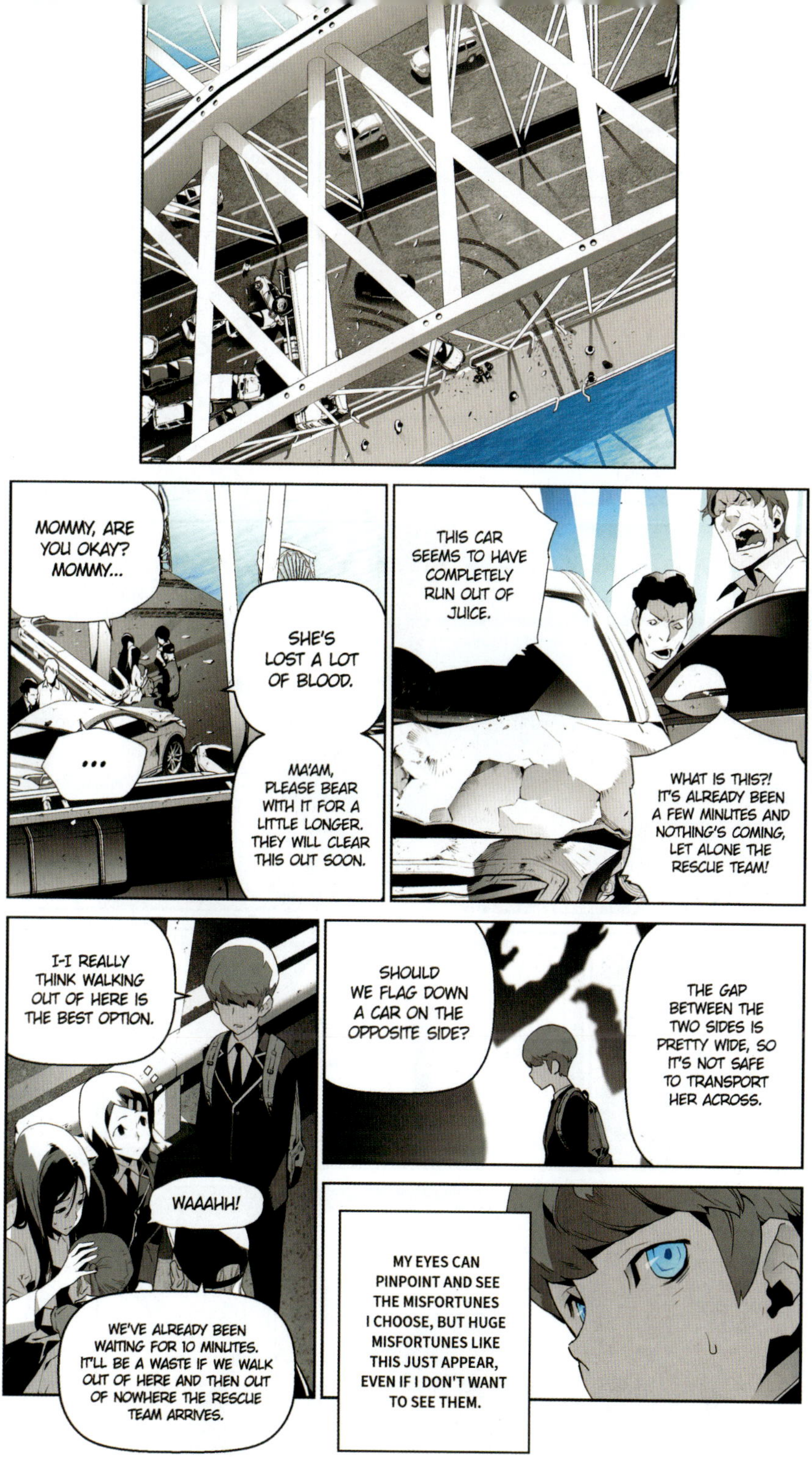
MOMMY, ARE YOU OKAY? MOMMY...
...
SHE'S LOST A LOT OF BLOOD.
MA'AM, PLEASE BEAR WITH IT FOR A LITTLE LONGER. THEY WILL CLEAR THIS OUT SOON.
THIS CAR SEEMS TO HAVE COMPLETELY RUN OUT OF JUICE.
WHAT IS THIS?! IT'S ALREADY BEEN A FEW MINUTES AND NOTHING'S COMING, LET ALONE THE RESCUE TEAM!
I-I REALLY THINK WALKING OUT OF HERE IS THE BEST OPTION.
WAAAHH!
WE'VE ALREADY BEEN WAITING FOR 10 MINUTES. IT'LL BE A WASTE IF WE WALK OUT OF HERE AND THEN OUT OF NOWHERE THE RESCUE TEAM ARRIVES.
SHOULD WE FLAG DOWN A CAR ON THE OPPOSITE SIDE?
THE GAP BETWEEN THE TWO SIDES IS PRETTY WIDE, SO IT'S NOT SAFE TO TRANSPORT HER ACROSS.
MY EYES CAN PINPOINT AND SEE THE MISFORTUNES I CHOOSE, BUT HUGE MISFORTUNES LIKE THIS JUST APPEAR, EVEN IF I DON'T WANT TO SEE THEM.

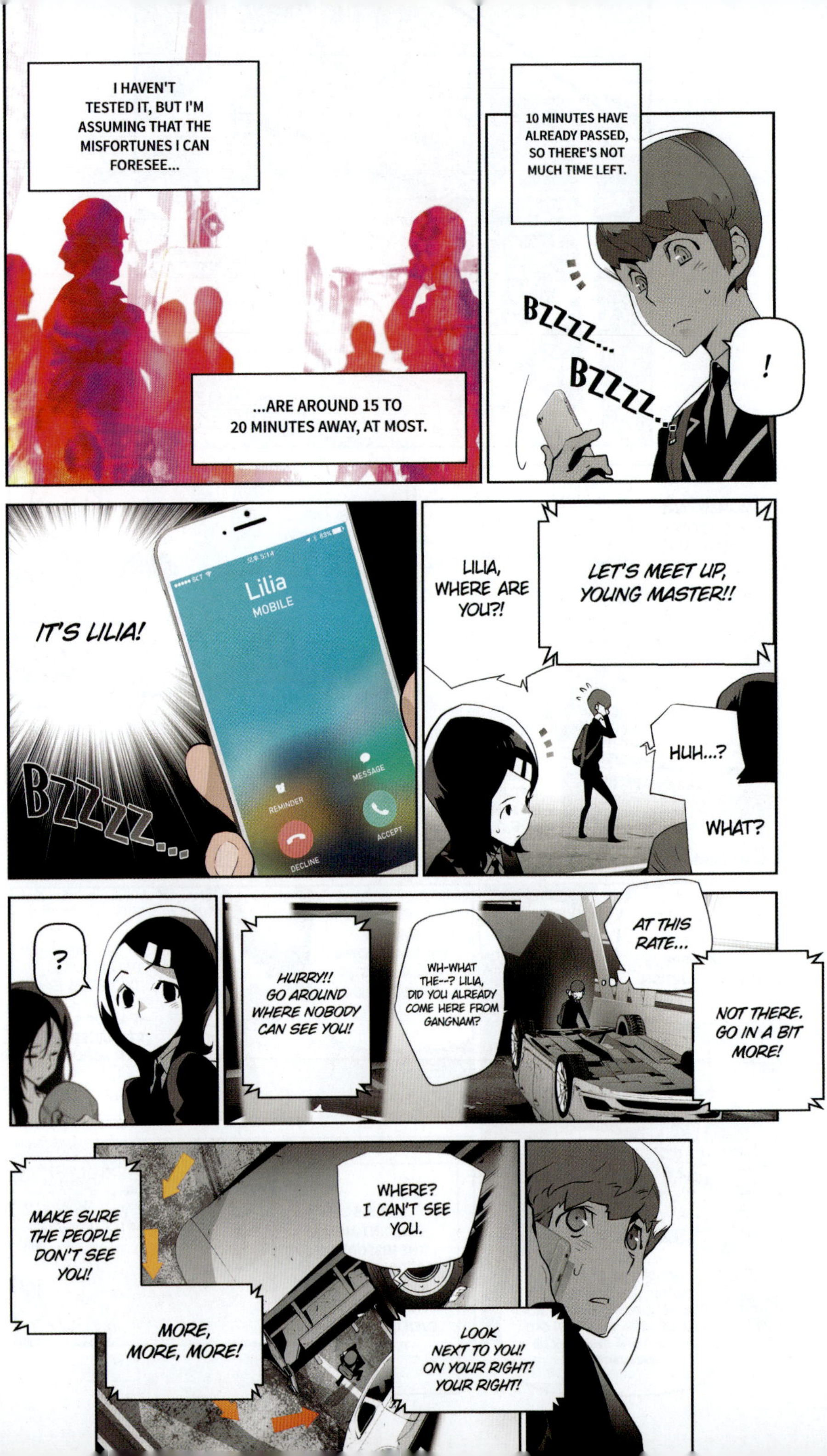
I HAVEN'T TESTED IT, BUT I'M ASSUMING THAT THE MISFORTUNES I CAN FORESEE...
...ARE AROUND 15 TO 20 MINUTES AWAY, AT MOST.
10 MINUTES HAVE ALREADY PASSED, SO THERE'S NOT MUCH TIME LEFT.
BZZZZ...
BZZZZ...
!
IT'S LILIA!
Lilia
MOBILE
REMINDER
MESSAGE
DECLINE
ACCEPT
BZZZZZ...
LET'S MEET UP, YOUNG MASTER!!
LILIA, WHERE ARE YOU?!
HUH...?
WHAT?
?
AT THIS RATE...
WH-WHAT THE--? LILIA, DID YOU ALREADY COME HERE FROM GANGNAM?
HURRY!! GO AROUND WHERE NOBODY CAN SEE YOU!
NOT THERE. GO IN A BIT MORE!
MAKE SURE THE PEOPLE DON'T SEE YOU!
MORE, MORE, MORE!
WHERE? I CAN'T SEE YOU.
LOOK NEXT TO YOU! ON YOUR RIGHT! YOUR RIGHT!

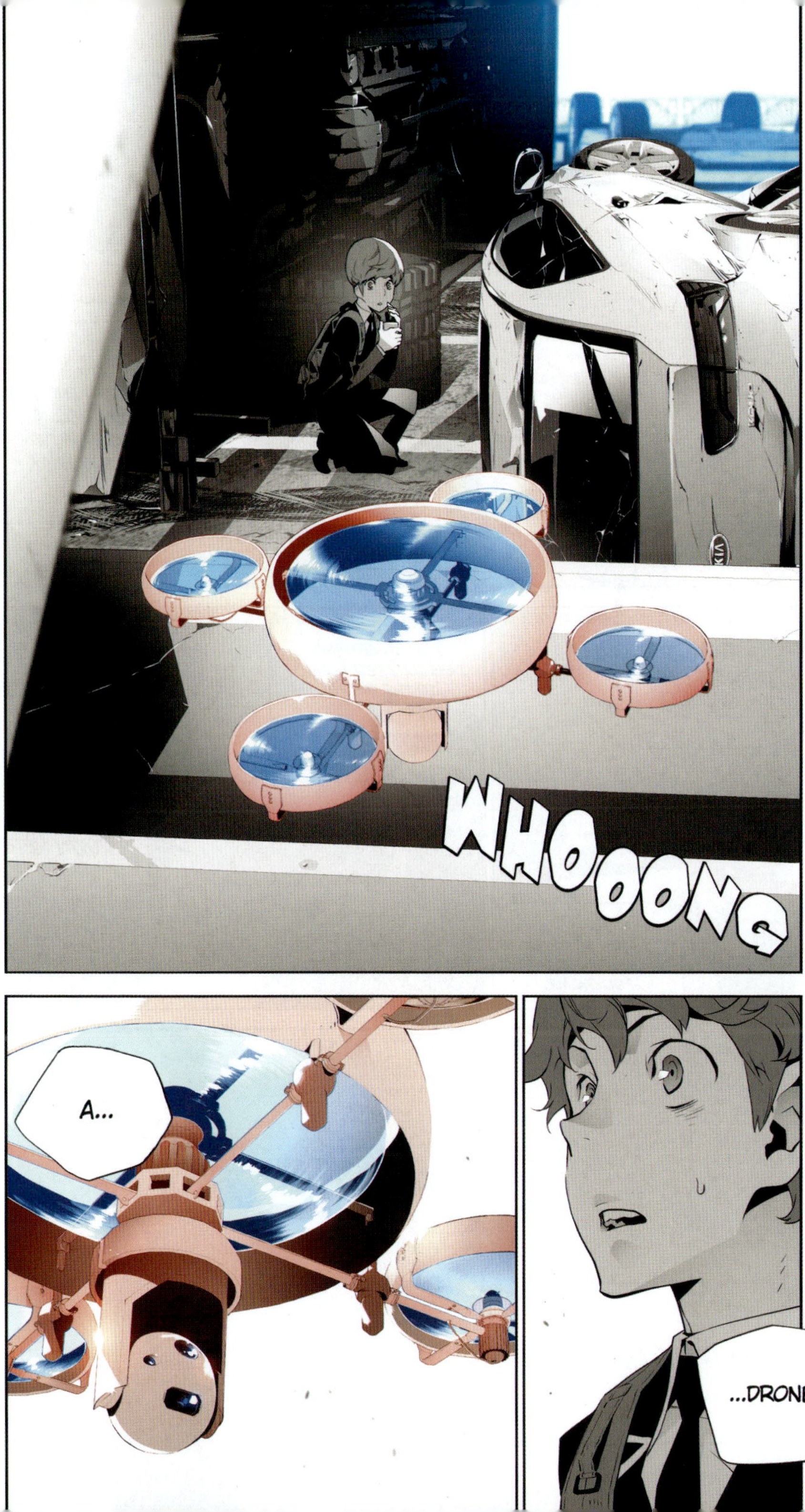
WHOOOONG
A...
...DRONE?

WHY ARE YOU SO SURPRISED? HOW LAME.

THIS IS A DRONE BONGCHUN DEVELOPED HIMSELF.

I CAN EVEN CONTROL IT FROM UP TO 30 KM AWAY.

TH-THAT'S AMAZING, BUT... HOW...?

WHOONG...

IT'S SOMETHING I DISCOVERED THANKS TO THE DRONE.

...

COME DOWN HERE.

FIRST, I HAVE TO SHOW YOU SOMETHING. FOLLOW ME.

WHOOONG

HURRY, HURRY!!

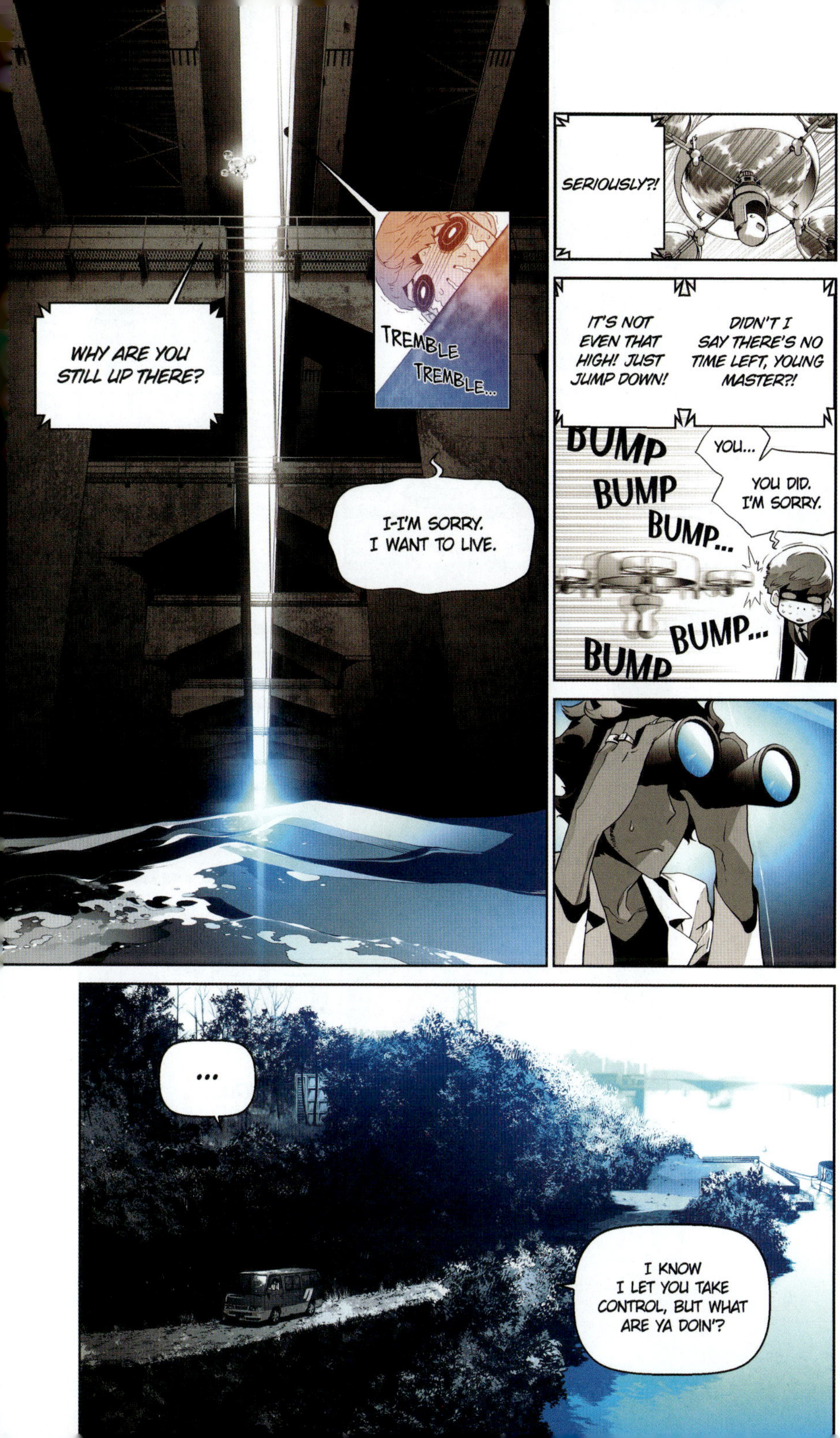

WHY ARE YOU STILL UP THERE?
TREMBLE TREMBLE...
I-I'M SORRY. I WANT TO LIVE.
SERIOUSLY?!
IT'S NOT EVEN THAT HIGH! JUST JUMP DOWN!
DIDN'T I SAY THERE'S NO TIME LEFT, YOUNG MASTER?!
BUMP BUMP BUMP...
YOU...
YOU DID. I'M SORRY.
BUMP... BUMP
...
I KNOW I LET YOU TAKE CONTROL, BUT WHAT ARE YA DOIN'?

LIKE THIS?

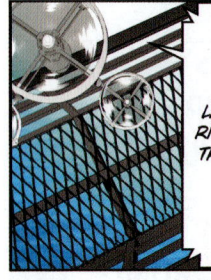

MY FOOT SLIPPED! LILIA, SAVE ME!

STRUGGLE

SHAKE SHAKE SHAKE

...DAMN IT!

QUIVER QUIVER QUIVER...

LAND HERE, RIGHT UNDER THE BRIDGE.

JUST JUMP DOWN!

SLIP

WAAAH!!

THUD

ACK!

GREAT! NOW, LOOK HERE.

OWWW...

LILIA, YOU...

FREEZE

...!

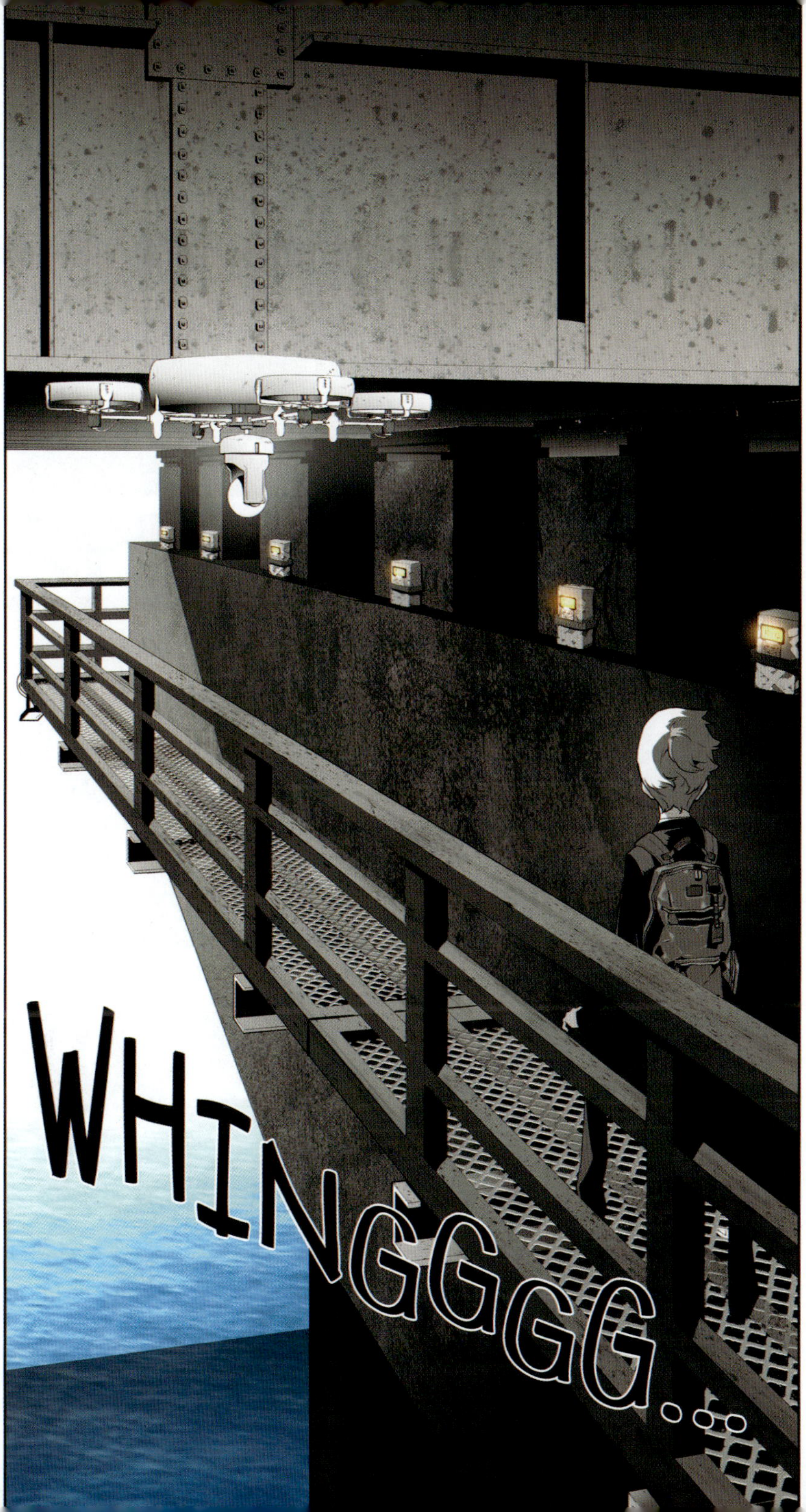
WHINGGGG...

W-WHAT...

...IS ALL THIS?

TIME BOMBS.

...

I DON'T KNOW ABOUT THE DEPARTMENT STORE, BUT IT SEEMS LIKE SOMEBODY IS TRYING TO DESTROY THE YANGHWA BRIDGE ON PURPOSE.

YOU NEED TO DECIDE, YOUNG MASTER.

STARTLED

DO YOU WANT TO SAVE THOSE PEOPLE FROM A SITUATION I CAN'T DIRECTLY HELP YOU WITH, ALL WITHIN 10 MINUTES?

OR DO YOU WANT TO RUN AWAY TO SAFETY?

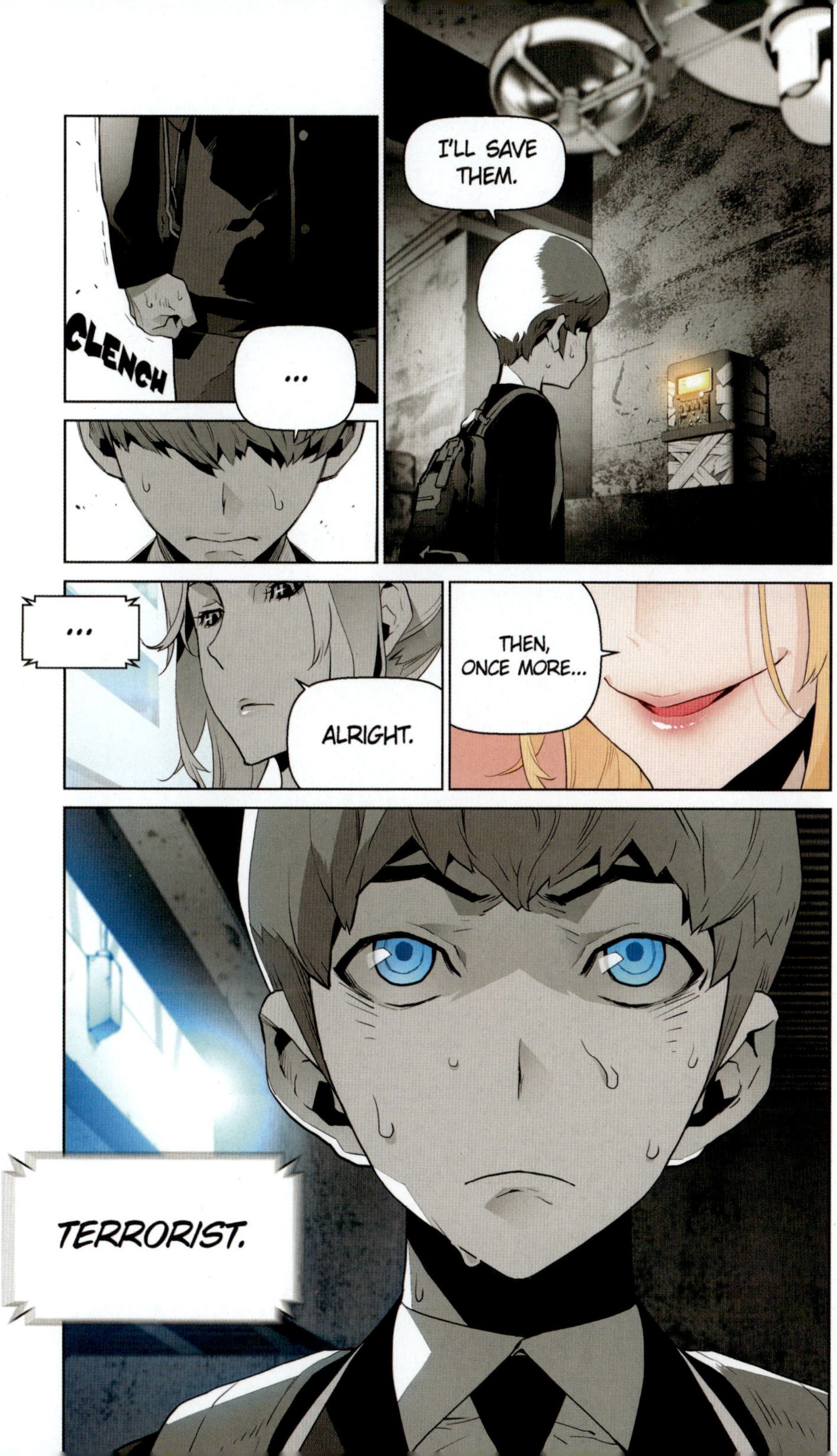
I'LL SAVE THEM.
CLENCH
...
...
ALRIGHT.
THEN, ONCE MORE...
TERRORIST.

TERROR MAN

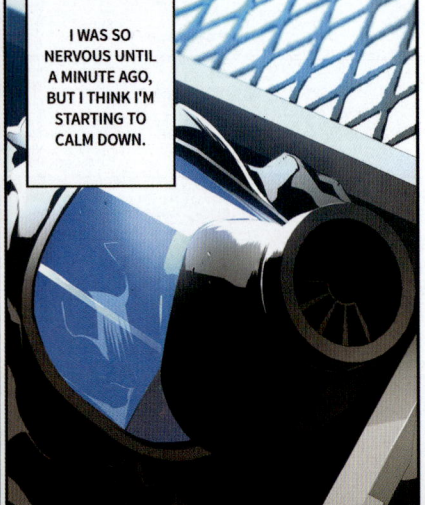

146

I'LL BE CONTROLLIN' THE DRONE 'TIL LILIA ARRIVES.

HOW'S THE STUFF I SENT YA?

ARE THE EARPHONES WORKIN' WELL?

ZINGGG...

YES.

TICK

LET'S DO OUR BEST, YOUNG MASTER.

EQUIPMENT?

LILIA'S UPDATED VIA VIDEO CALL, BUT SHE WON'T BE ABLE TO PAY ATTENTION NOW 'CAUSE SHE'S DRIVIN'.

VROOOM

EVEN IF I'M ASSISTIN' USIN' THE DRONE, Y'ALL'RE BY YOURSELVES THERE. LET'S JUST FOLLOW LILIA'S PLAN AND GET OUT.

I'LL JUST MAKE A SCENE AND WHEN I SEE THE PEOPLE RUNNING AWAY, I'LL ESCAPE. IS THAT RIGHT?

CLICK

I WAS SO NERVOUS UNTIL A MINUTE AGO, BUT I THINK I'M STARTING TO CALM DOWN.

THAT'S RIGHT.

HAVE I GOTTEN USED TO IT?

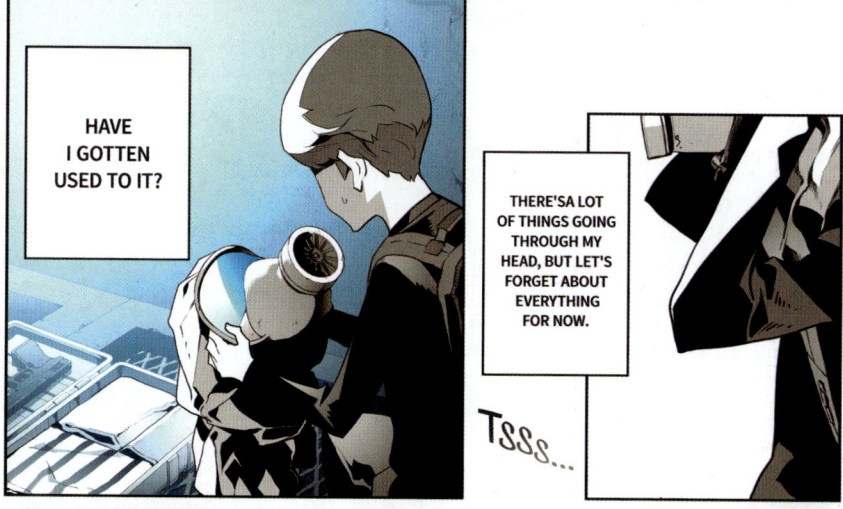

THERE'S A LOT OF THINGS GOING THROUGH MY HEAD, BUT LET'S FORGET ABOUT EVERYTHING FOR NOW.

TSSS...

AT LEAST FOR NOW...

...BECOMING A TERRORIST IS PRIORITY!

HUH?

WHAT'S THAT?

A... DRONE?

WHAT'S WRONG?

...

H-HOLD ON...

THE THING IT'S CARRYING...

WHAT'S THIS ALL OF A SUDDEN?!

EVERYONE, DUCK!

WHINGGG

AAAAH!!

DU DU DU DU

RIFLES?!

BANG BANG BANG

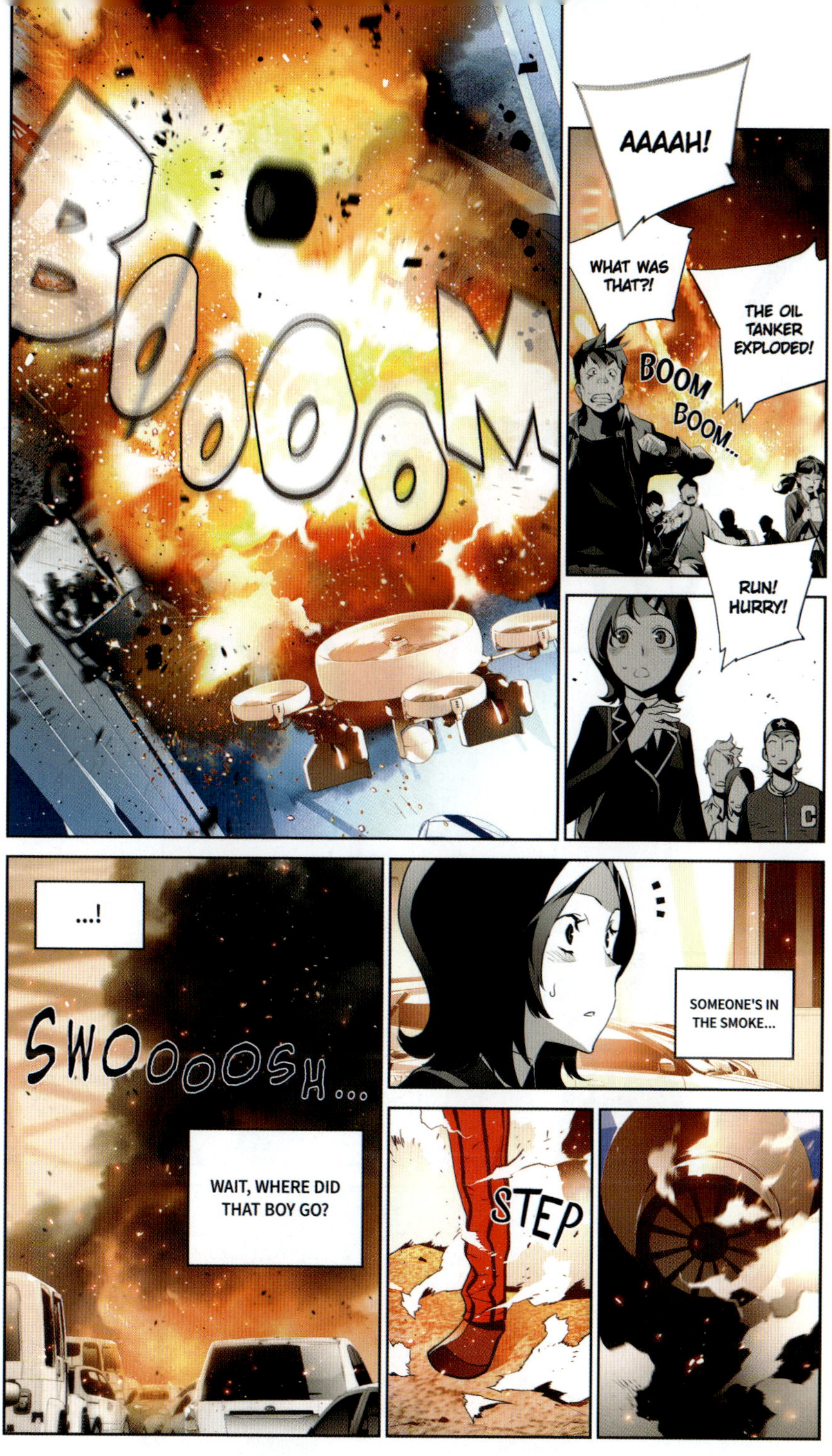
BOOOOOM
AAAAH!
WHAT WAS THAT?!
THE OIL TANKER EXPLODED!
BOOM BOOM...
RUN! HURRY!
...!
SWOOOOSH...
WAIT, WHERE DID THAT BOY GO?
SOMEONE'S IN THE SMOKE...
STEP

SWOOOOSH...

WHAT THE--? WHO IS THAT?

PIERROT?

ARE THESE REALLY THE ONLY CLOTHES YOU HAD?

THAT'S NOT IMPORTANT. THIS IS MUCH BETTER THAN DOIN' A SHOOTOUT IN A SCHOOL UNIFORM.

LIFT YOUR GUN. LET THE SHOW BEGIN.

...

RAISE

"A GAS MASK AND A GUN..."

"..."

"DON'T TELL ME... IT'S THE SAME GUY FROM THE NEWS EARLIER THIS MORNING."

"EVERYONE, GET DOWN! IT'S A TERRORIST!"

"T-THE TERRORIST THAT ATTACKED THE DEPARTMENT STORE..."

PLOP

"W-WE CAN'T JUST GET DOWN! WE NEED TO RUN!"

RUSH

"HUH?"

"OH, R-REALLY?!"

"JUST PRETEND TO AIM. I'LL TAKE CARE OF THE REST."

WHOONG...

"LE-LET'S START."

THUMP THUMP THUMP...

DU DU DU

"KYAAAA!"

"...!"

DU DU

"KYAAA!"

DU ...

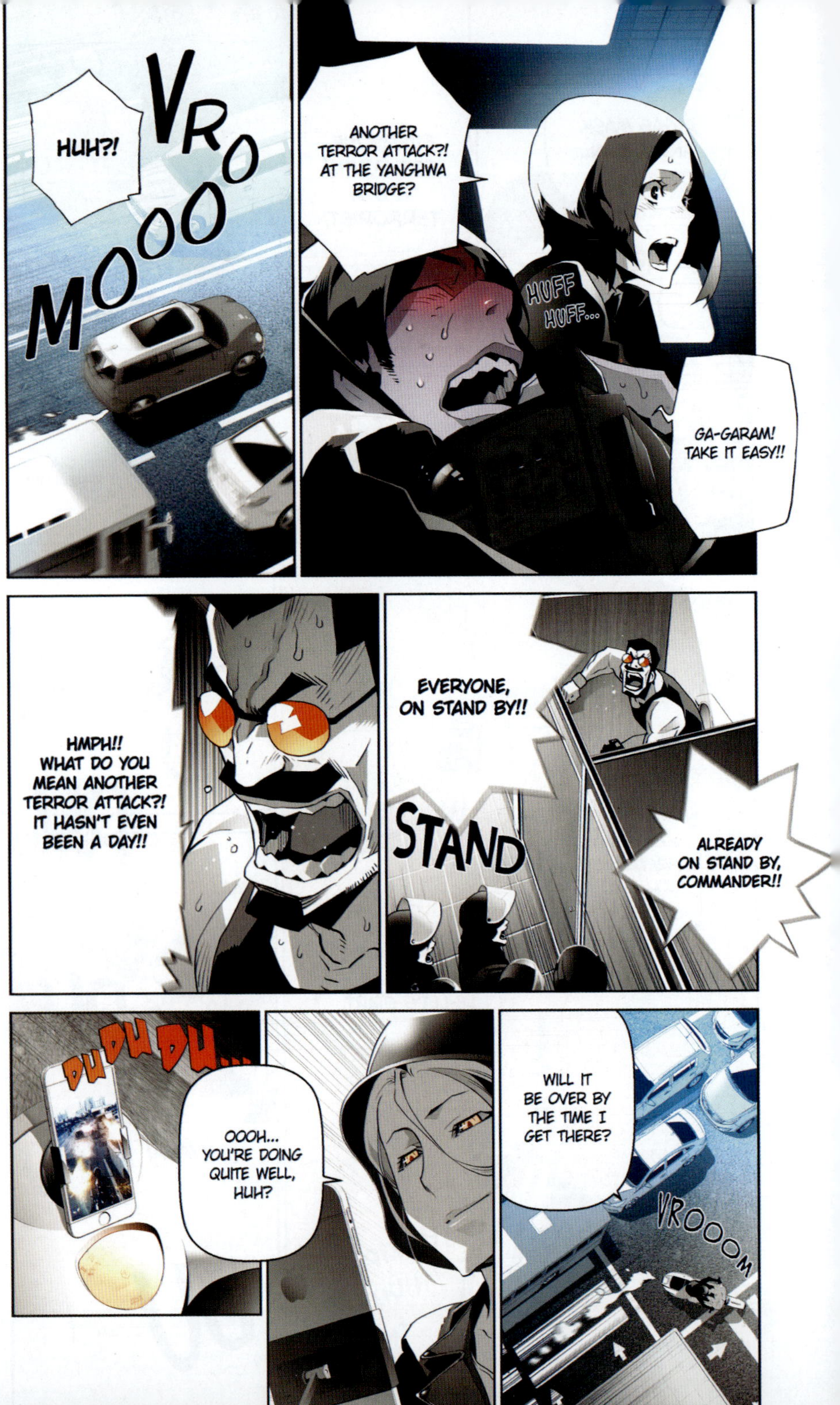
HUH?!
VROOOOOM
ANOTHER TERROR ATTACK?! AT THE YANGHWA BRIDGE?
HUFF HUFF...
GA-GARAM! TAKE IT EASY!!
HMPH!! WHAT DO YOU MEAN ANOTHER TERROR ATTACK?! IT HASN'T EVEN BEEN A DAY!!
EVERYONE, ON STAND BY!!
STAND
ALREADY ON STAND BY, COMMANDER!!
DUDUDU...
OOOH... YOU'RE DOING QUITE WELL, HUH?
WILL IT BE OVER BY THE TIME I GET THERE?
VROOOM

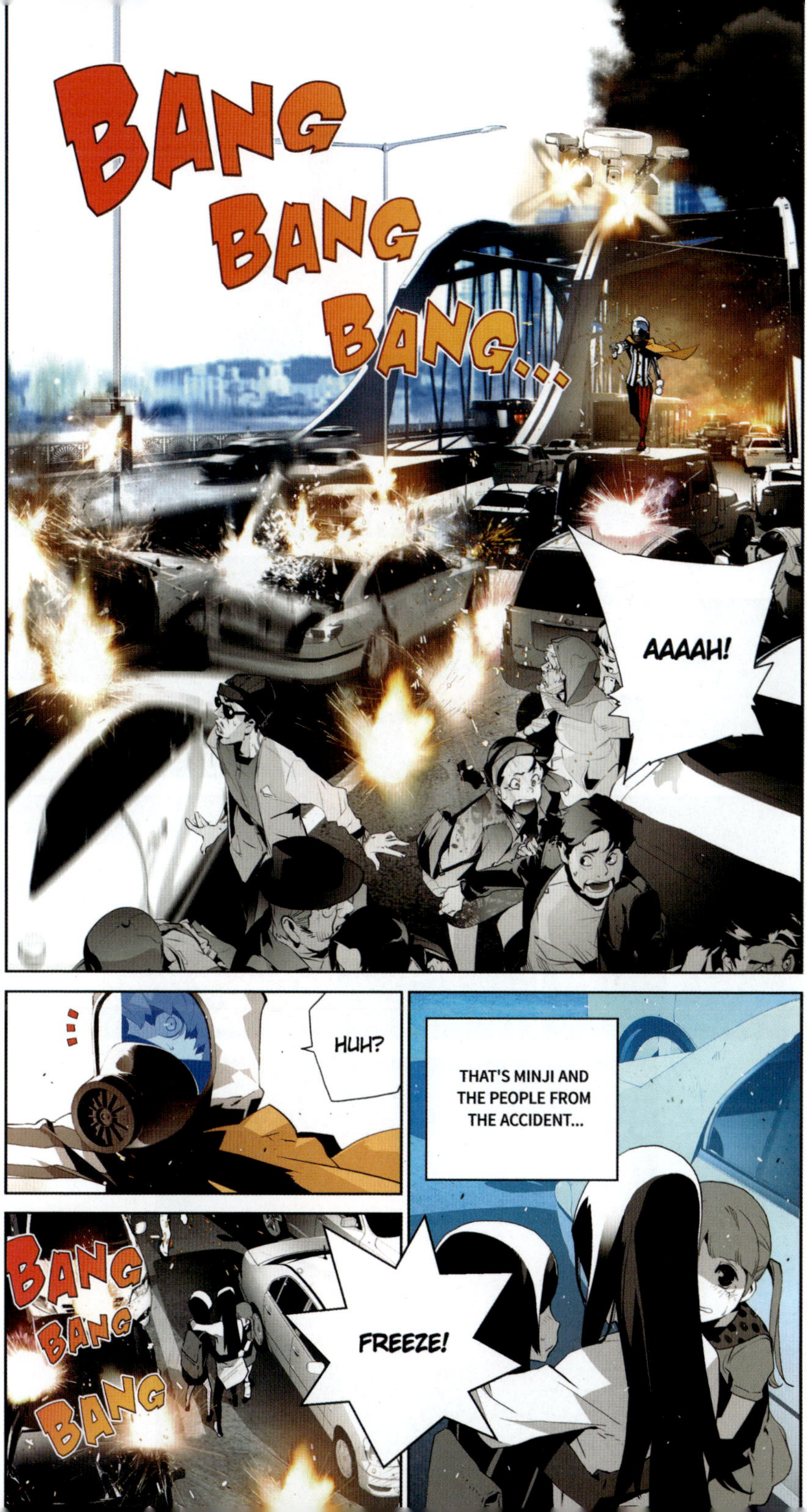
BANG
BANG
BANG...
AAAAH!
!!
HUH?
THAT'S MINJI AND THE PEOPLE FROM THE ACCIDENT...
BANG
BANG
BANG
FREEZE!

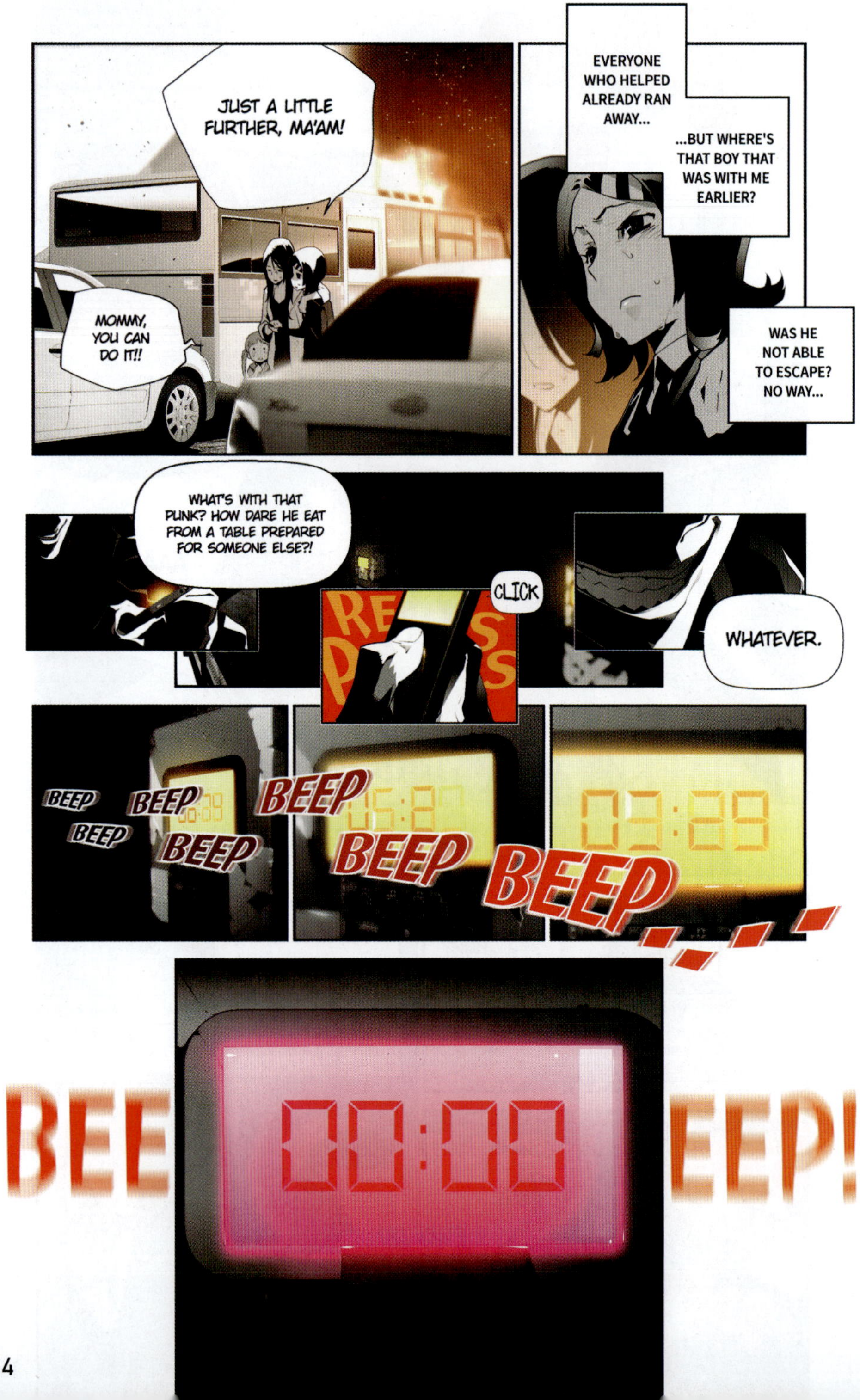
JUST A LITTLE FURTHER, MA'AM!
MOMMY, YOU CAN DO IT!!
EVERYONE WHO HELPED ALREADY RAN AWAY...
...BUT WHERE'S THAT BOY THAT WAS WITH ME EARLIER?
WAS HE NOT ABLE TO ESCAPE? NO WAY...
WHAT'S WITH THAT PUNK? HOW DARE HE EAT FROM A TABLE PREPARED FOR SOMEONE ELSE?!
CLICK
WHATEVER.
BEEP
BEEP
BEEP
BEEP
BEEP
BEEP
BEEP
03:29
00:00
BEE
EEP!

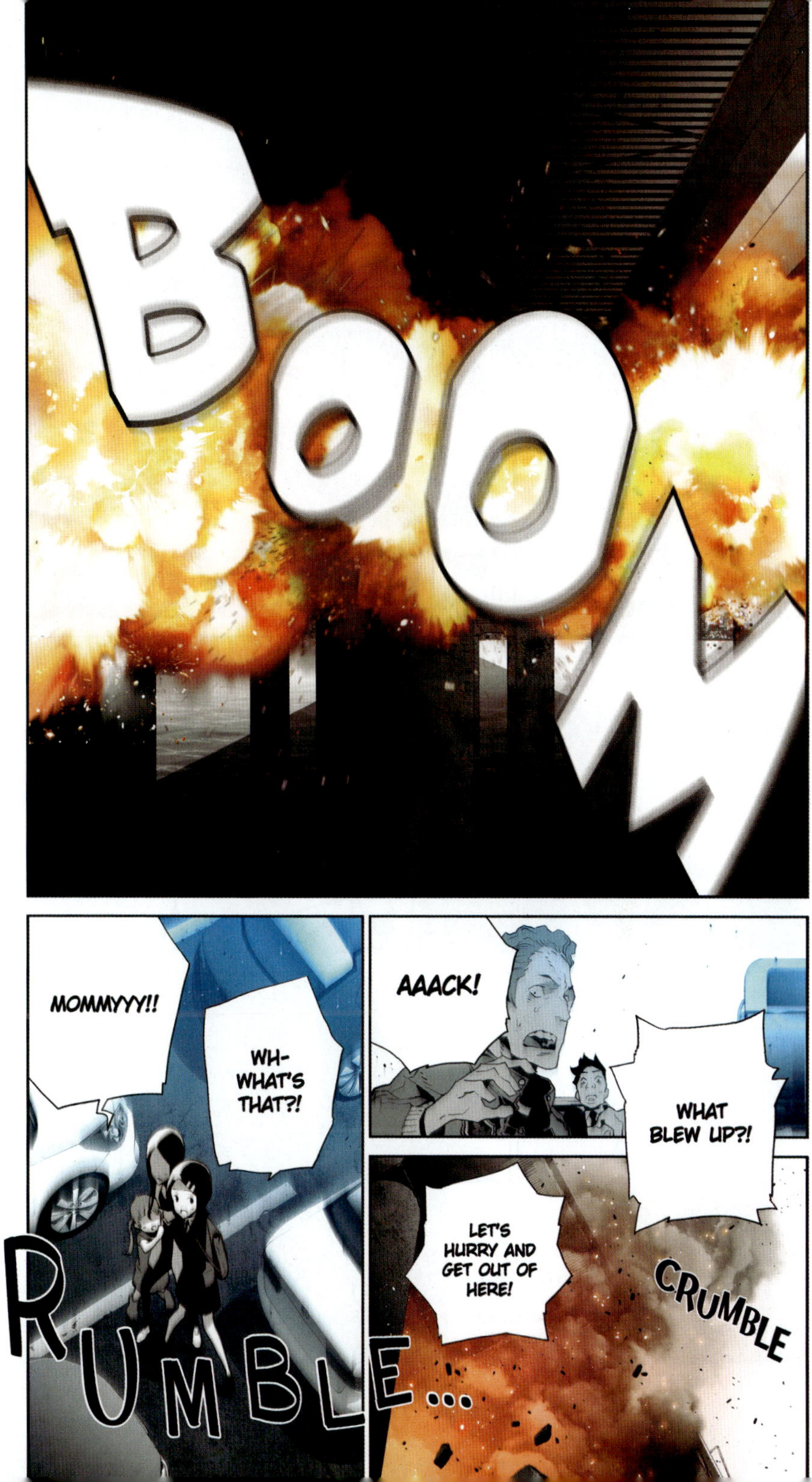
BOOOM
MOMMYYY!!
WH-
WHAT'S
THAT?!
RUMBLE...
AAACK!
WHAT
BLEW UP?!
LET'S
HURRY AND
GET OUT OF
HERE!
CRUMBLE

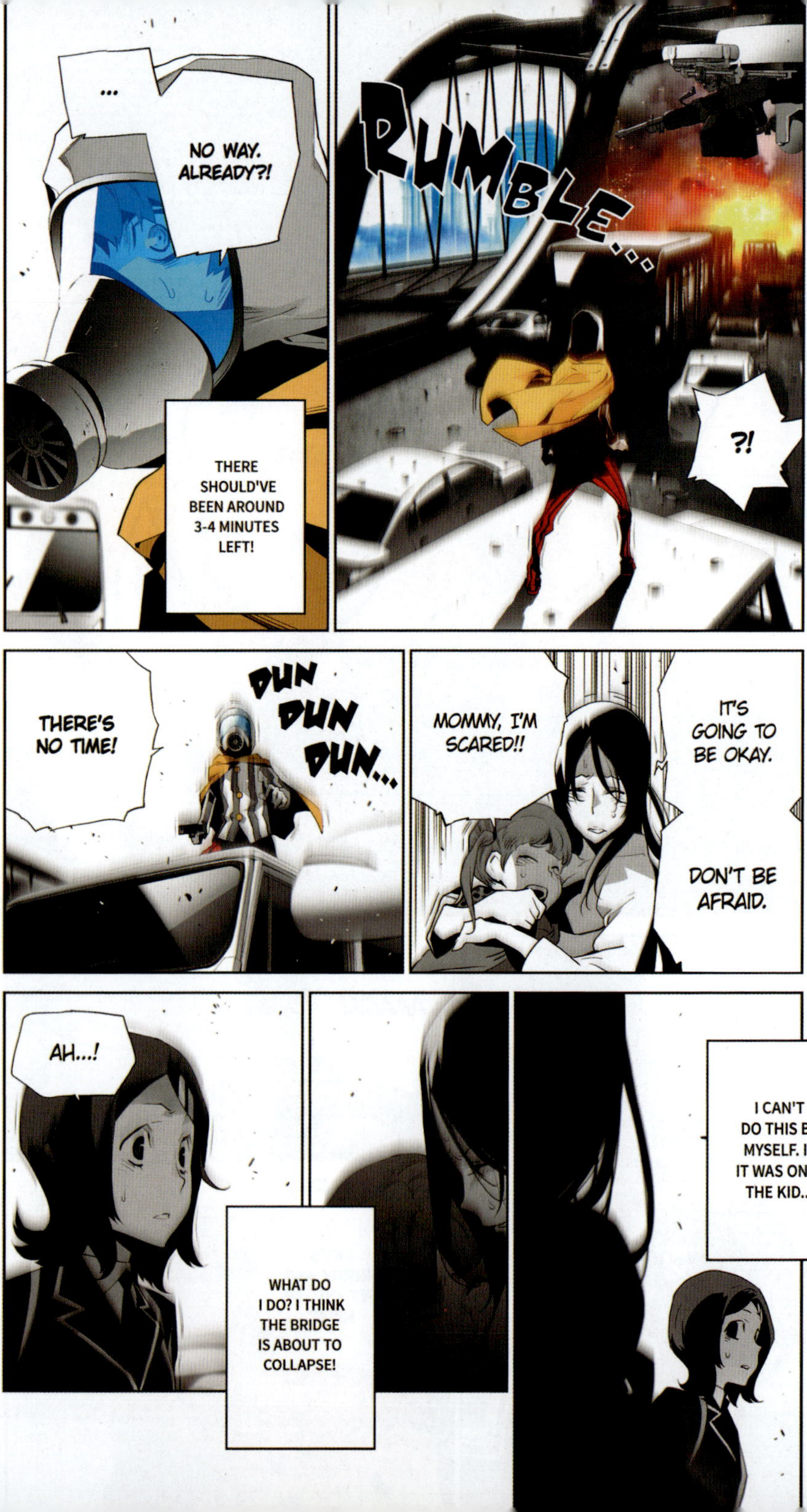
...
NO WAY. ALREADY?!
THERE SHOULD'VE BEEN AROUND 3-4 MINUTES LEFT!
RUMBLE...
?!
THERE'S NO TIME!
DUN DUN DUN...
MOMMY, I'M SCARED!!
IT'S GOING TO BE OKAY.
DON'T BE AFRAID.
AH...!
WHAT DO I DO? I THINK THE BRIDGE IS ABOUT TO COLLAPSE!
I CAN'T DO THIS BY MYSELF. IF IT WAS ONLY THE KID...

FLAP

POINT

W-WHAT...?

THE ENDS OF THE BRIDGE AREN'T PURPLE. IF THEY CAN MAKE IT THAT FAR...

...

157

WHAT ARE YOU DOING? HURRY UP!!	HUH? WHAT IS THIS GUY...? IS HE HELPING US? A TERRORIST?
...!	
STARTLED!!	
SWISH	

RUMBLE

...!

AH!

MOMMY, I'M SCARED...

CRACK...
CRACK...

LET'S HURRY UP, OKAY?

N-NO. I CAN'T THINK ABOUT ANYTHING ELSE RIGHT NOW.

PLEASE HANG IN THERE, MA'AM. LET'S JUST GET OFF THE BRIDGE.

ALRIGHT...

CLENCH

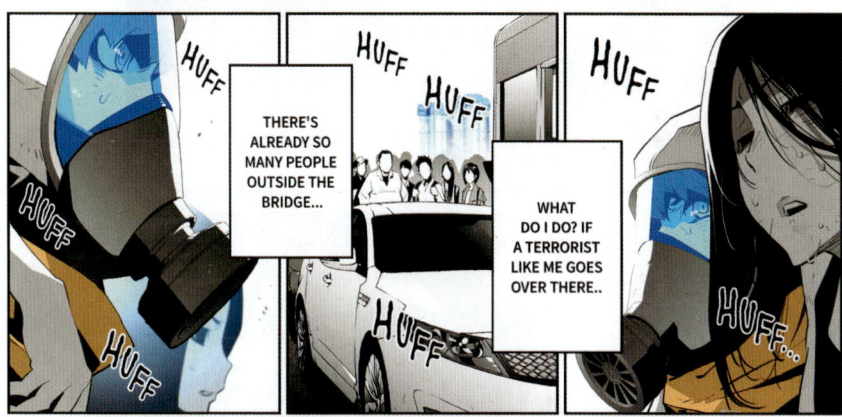

HUFF HUFF HUFF HUFF HUFF HUFF HUFF...

THERE'S ALREADY SO MANY PEOPLE OUTSIDE THE BRIDGE...

WHAT DO I DO? IF A TERRORIST LIKE ME GOES OVER THERE..

...IT WILL JUST CAUSE CHAOS.

THEN...!!

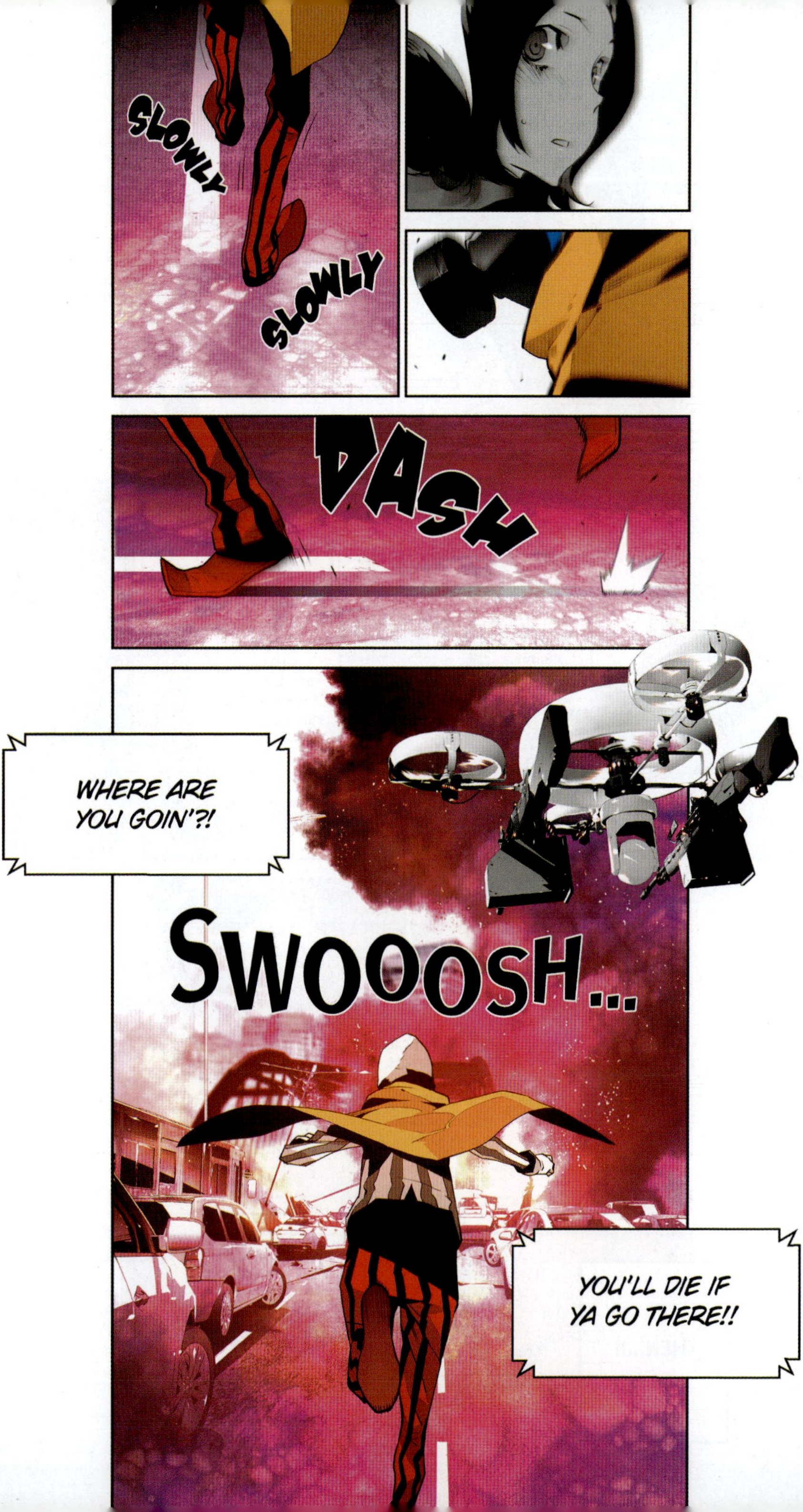
SLOWLY
SLOWLY
DASH
WHERE ARE YOU GOIN'?!
SWOOOSH...
YOU'LL DIE IF YA GO THERE!!

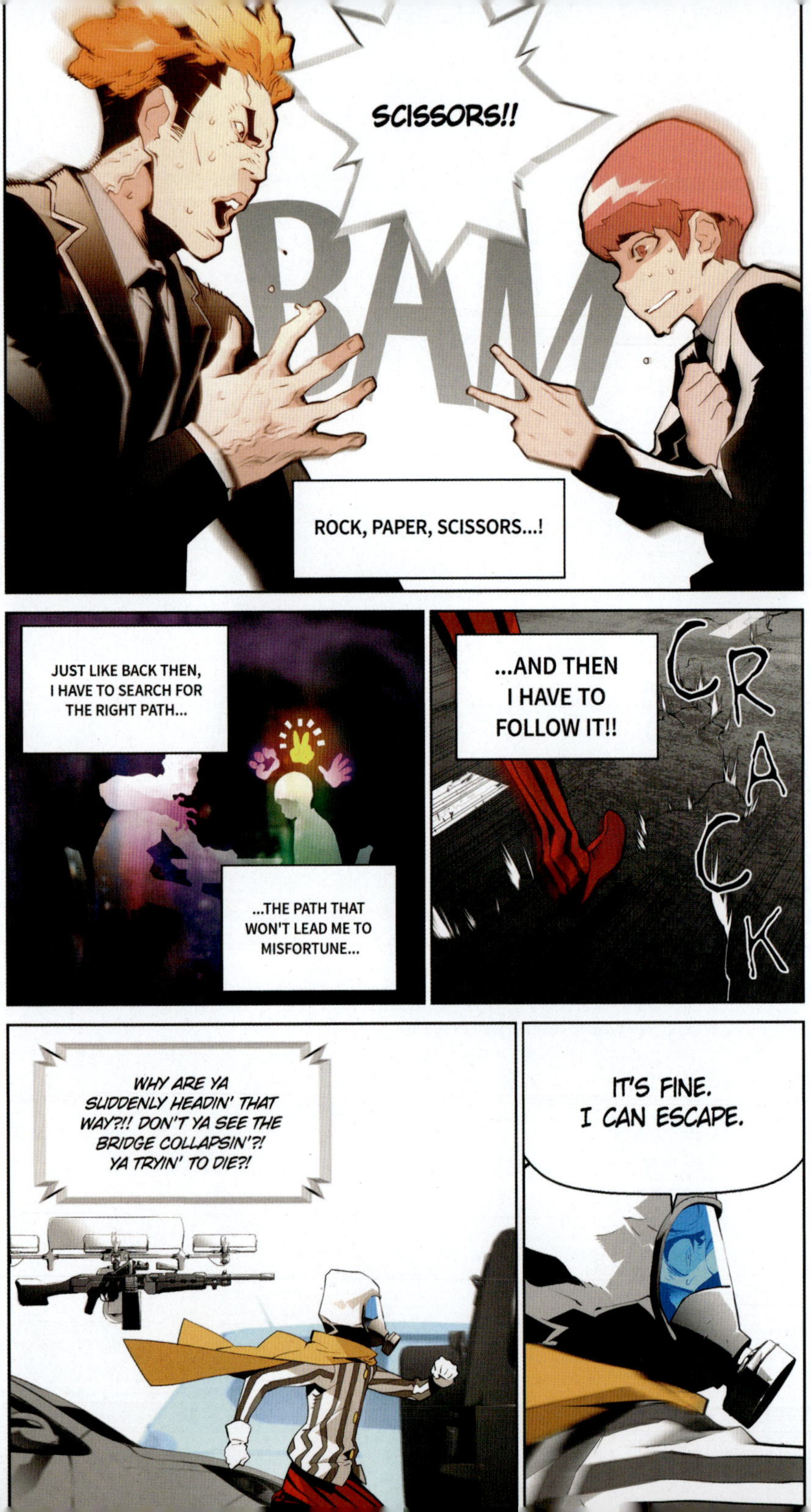
SCISSORS!!
BAM
ROCK, PAPER, SCISSORS...!
JUST LIKE BACK THEN, I HAVE TO SEARCH FOR THE RIGHT PATH...
...THE PATH THAT WON'T LEAD ME TO MISFORTUNE...
...AND THEN I HAVE TO FOLLOW IT!!
CRACK
WHY ARE YA SUDDENLY HEADIN' THAT WAY?!! DON'T YA SEE THE BRIDGE COLLAPSIN'?! YA TRYIN' TO DIE?!
IT'S FINE. I CAN ESCAPE.

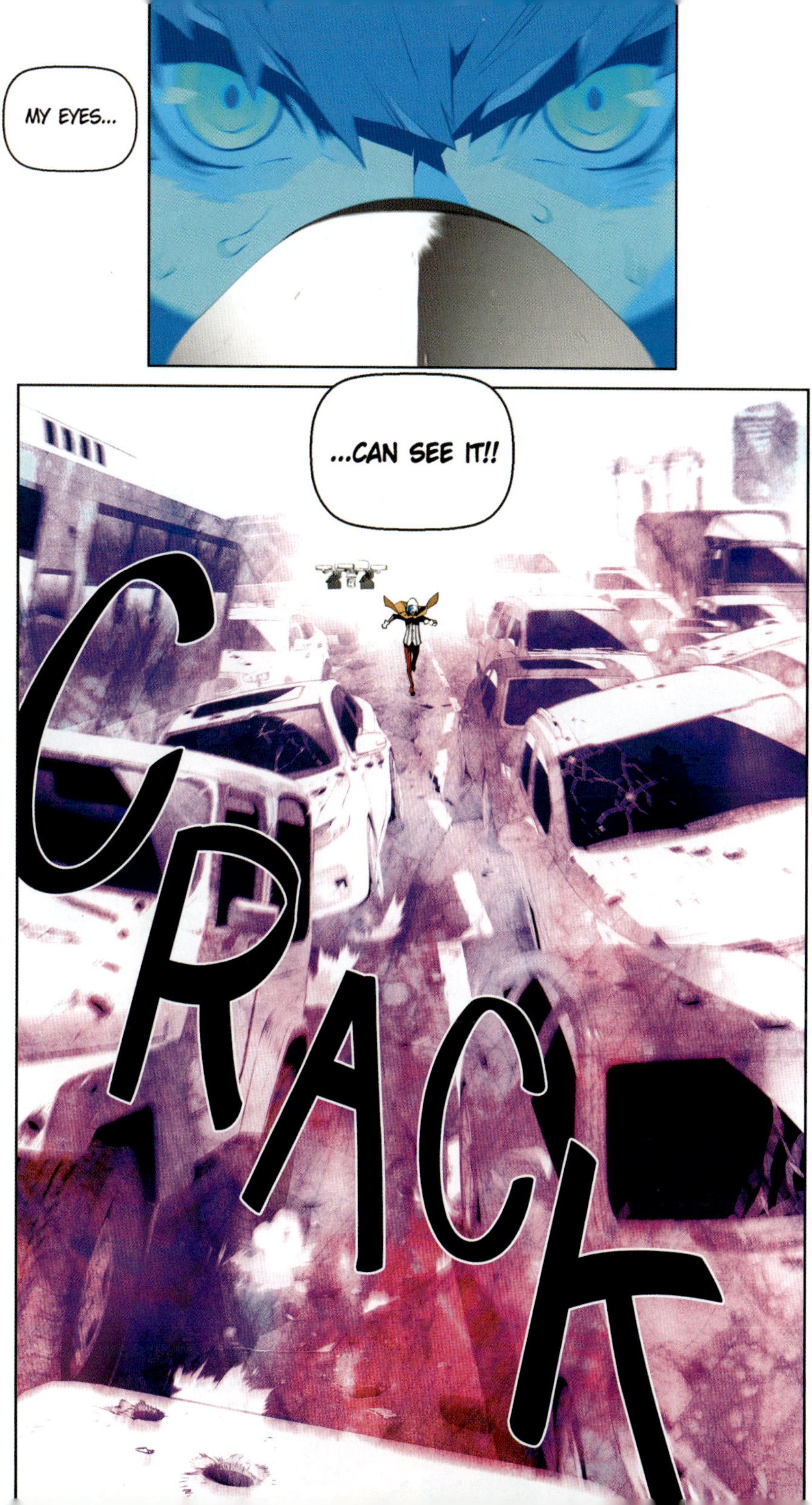
MY EYES...
...CAN SEE IT!!
CRACK

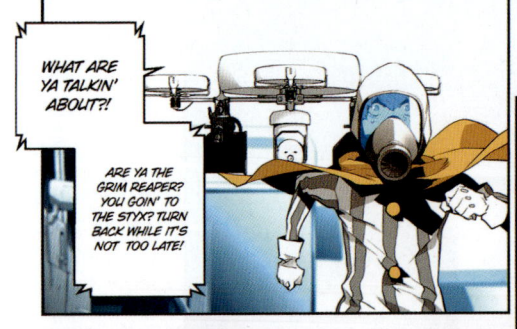

WHAT ARE YA TALKIN' ABOUT?!

ARE YA THE GRIM REAPER? YOU GOIN' TO THE STYX? TURN BACK WHILE IT'S NOT TOO LATE!

...STOP RIGHT HERE!

THAT'S IT!

I JUST NEED TO...

STEP...

GOODNESS!

STAGGER

CRASH

CRASH

CRACK

!!

HUH?!

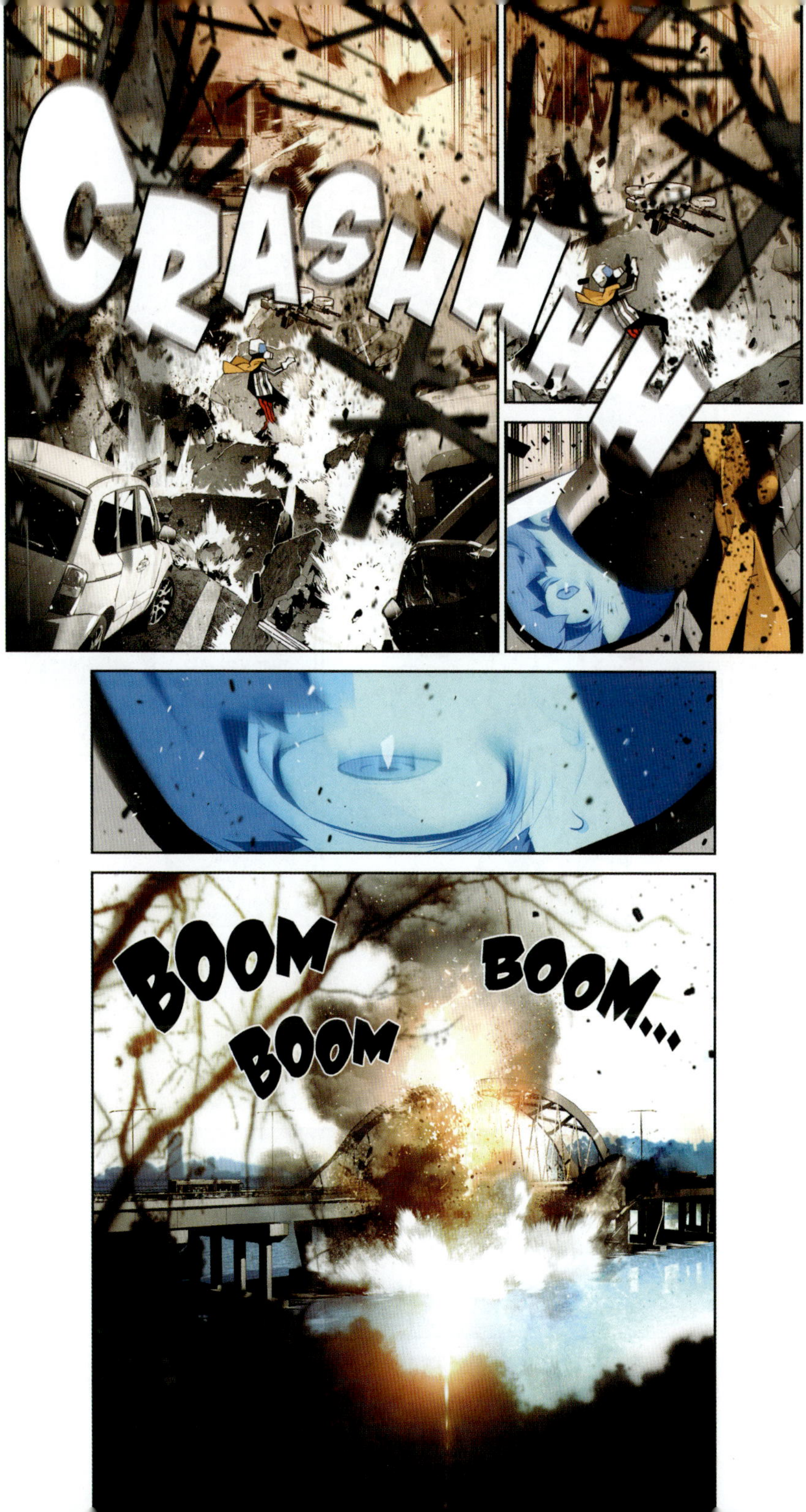
CRASHHHHH
BOOM
BOOM
BOOM...

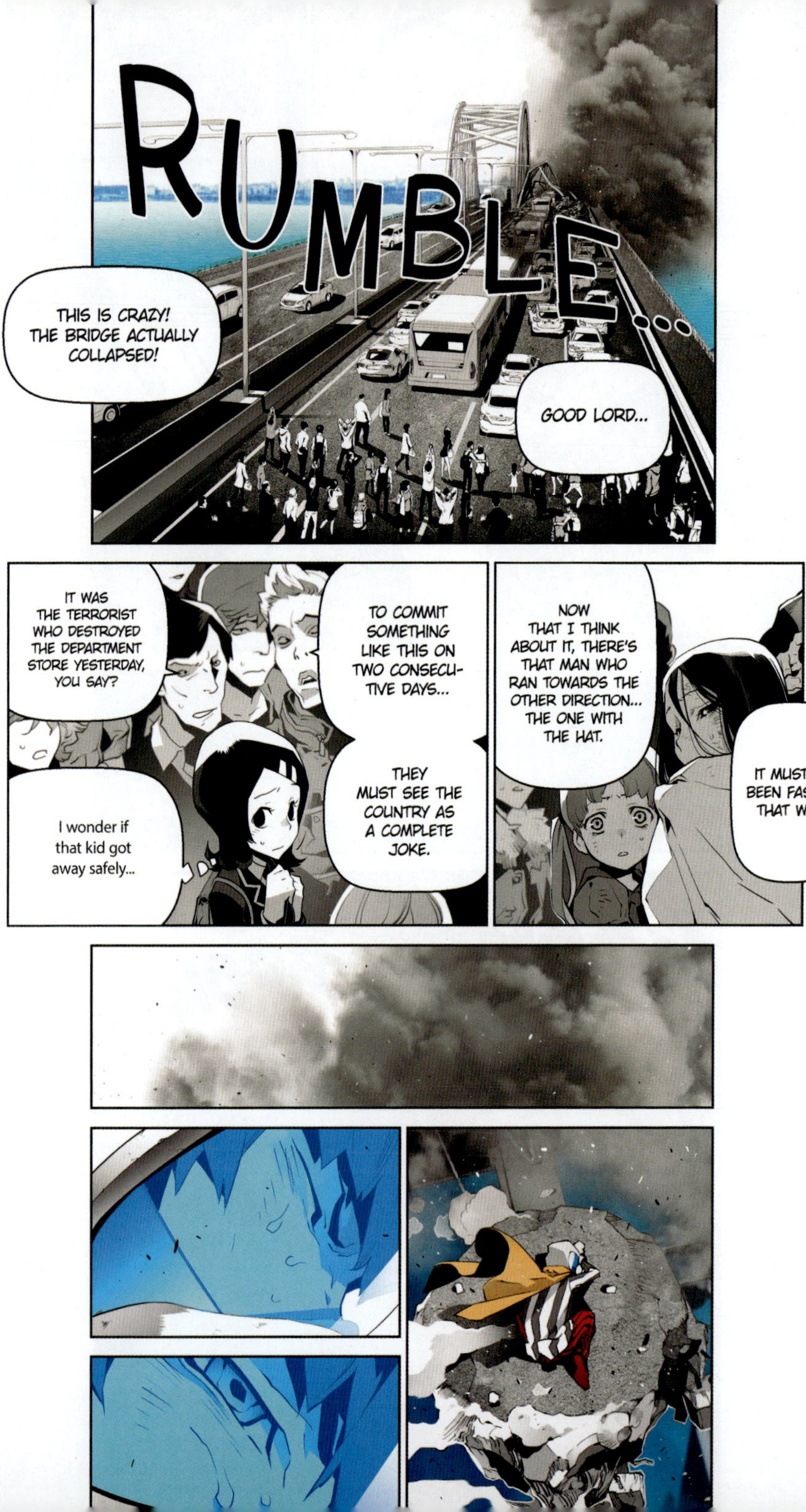
RUMBLE...
THIS IS CRAZY! THE BRIDGE ACTUALLY COLLAPSED!
GOOD LORD...
IT WAS THE TERRORIST WHO DESTROYED THE DEPARTMENT STORE YESTERDAY, YOU SAY?
TO COMMIT SOMETHING LIKE THIS ON TWO CONSECU-TIVE DAYS...
I wonder if that kid got away safely...
THEY MUST SEE THE COUNTRY AS A COMPLETE JOKE.
NOW THAT I THINK ABOUT IT, THERE'S THAT MAN WHO RAN TOWARDS THE OTHER DIRECTION... THE ONE WITH THE HAT.
IT MUST'VE BEEN FASTER THAT WAY.

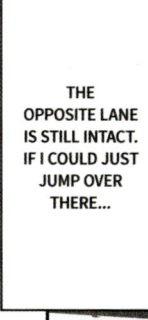

CRASH...

!!

CRACK...

I THIS THIS IS GOING TO COLLAPSE SOON...!

CRACK

THE OPPOSITE LANE IS STILL INTACT. IF I COULD JUST JUMP OVER THERE...

!!

JUMP

OOF...!!

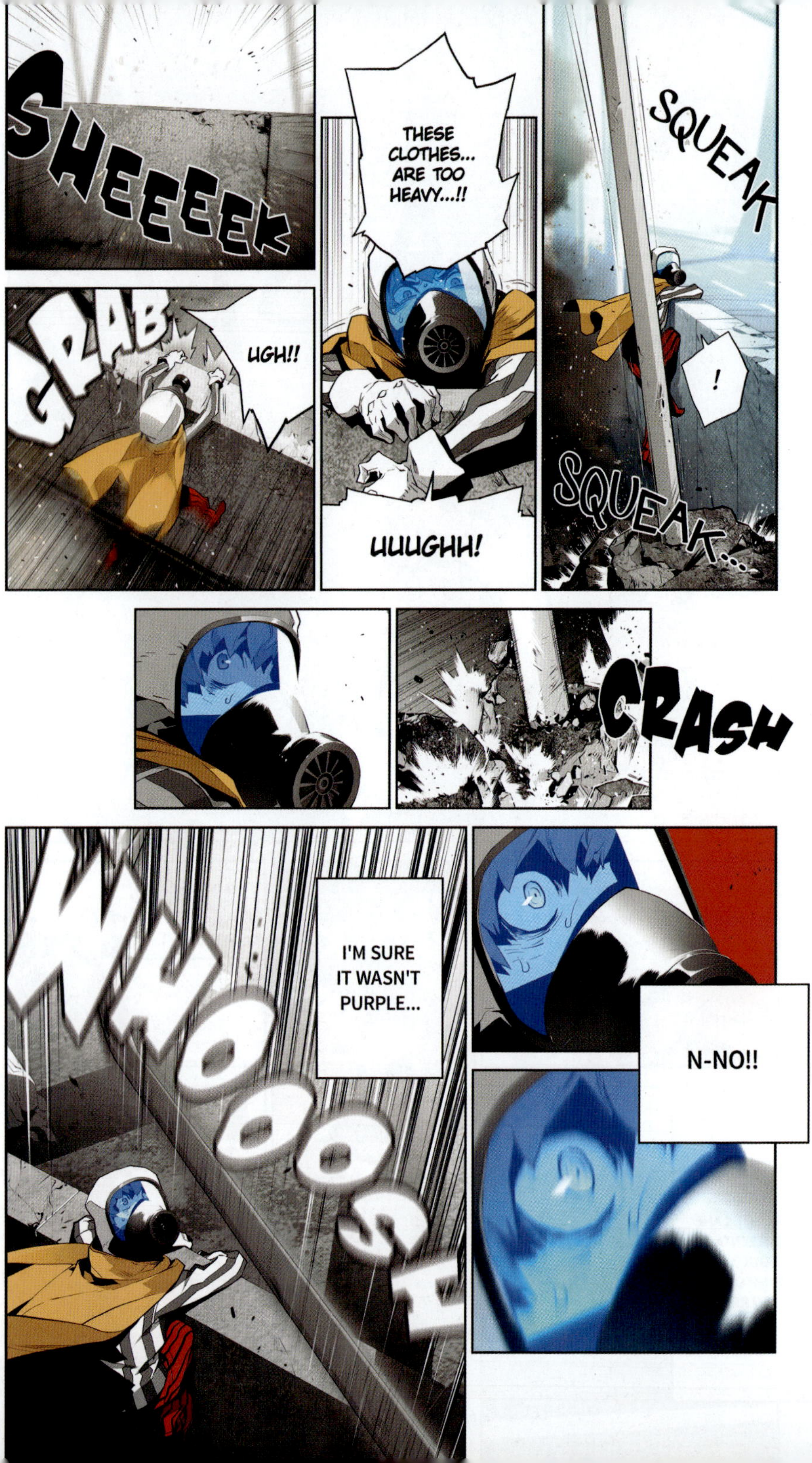
SHEEEEEK
THESE CLOTHES... ARE TOO HEAVY...!!
SQUEAK
GRAB
UGH!!
UUUGHH!
!
SQUEAK...
CRASH
WHOOOSH
I'M SURE IT WASN'T PURPLE...
N-NO!!

...!

CRUSH

THUD

BZZZT

THAT'S WHY YA SHOULD LISTEN TO ME.

I'LL BE FILIN' A REIMBURSEMENT REPORT ON THIS DRONE, TOO, SO MAKE SURE YOU GET OUT OF THIS.

BZZT...

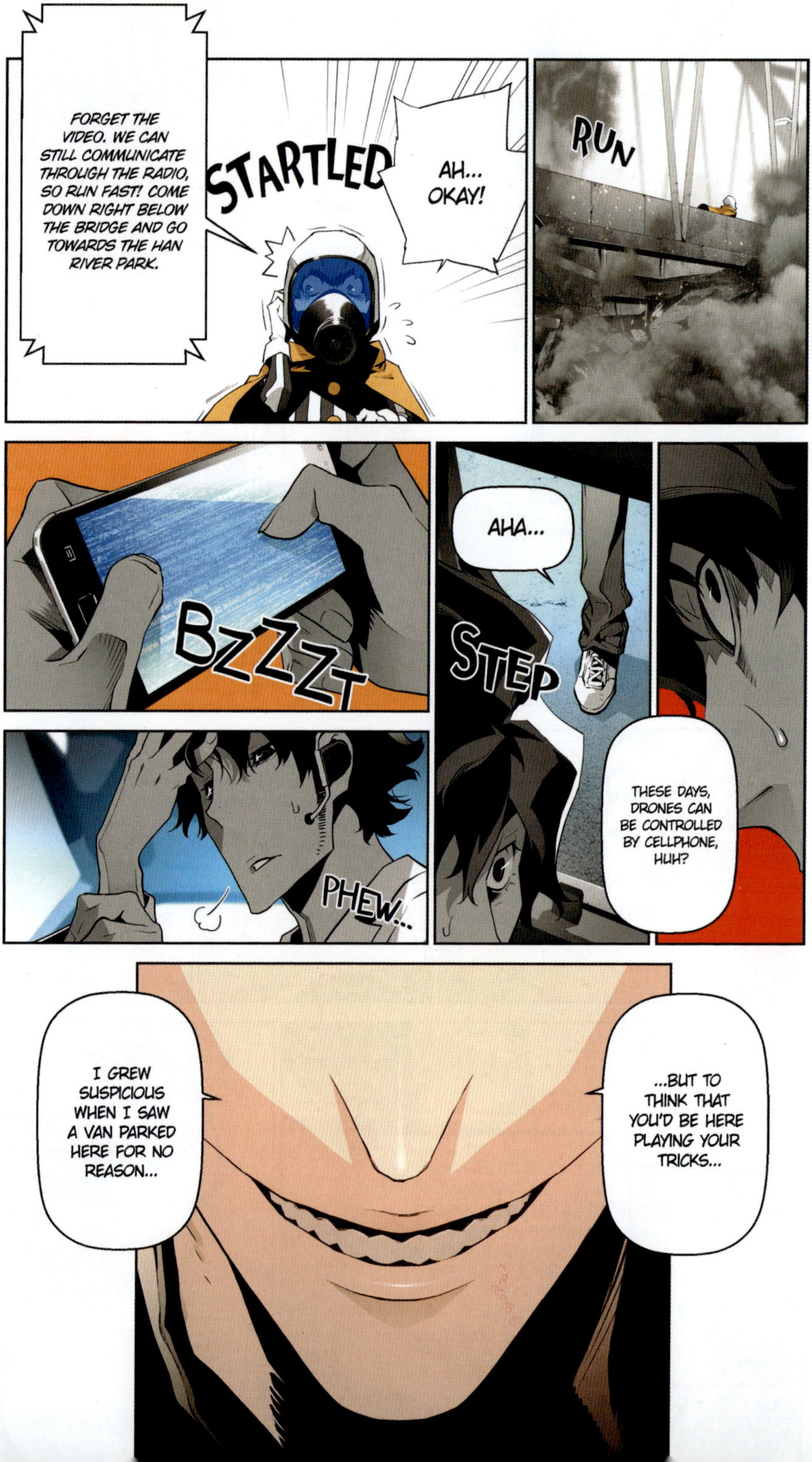
FORGET THE VIDEO. WE CAN STILL COMMUNICATE THROUGH THE RADIO, SO RUN FAST! COME DOWN RIGHT BELOW THE BRIDGE AND GO TOWARDS THE HAN RIVER PARK.
STARTLED
AH... OKAY!
RUN
BZZZT
PHEW...
AHA...
STEP
THESE DAYS, DRONES CAN BE CONTROLLED BY CELLPHONE, HUH?
I GREW SUSPICIOUS WHEN I SAW A VAN PARKED HERE FOR NO REASON...
...BUT TO THINK THAT YOU'D BE HERE PLAYING YOUR TRICKS...

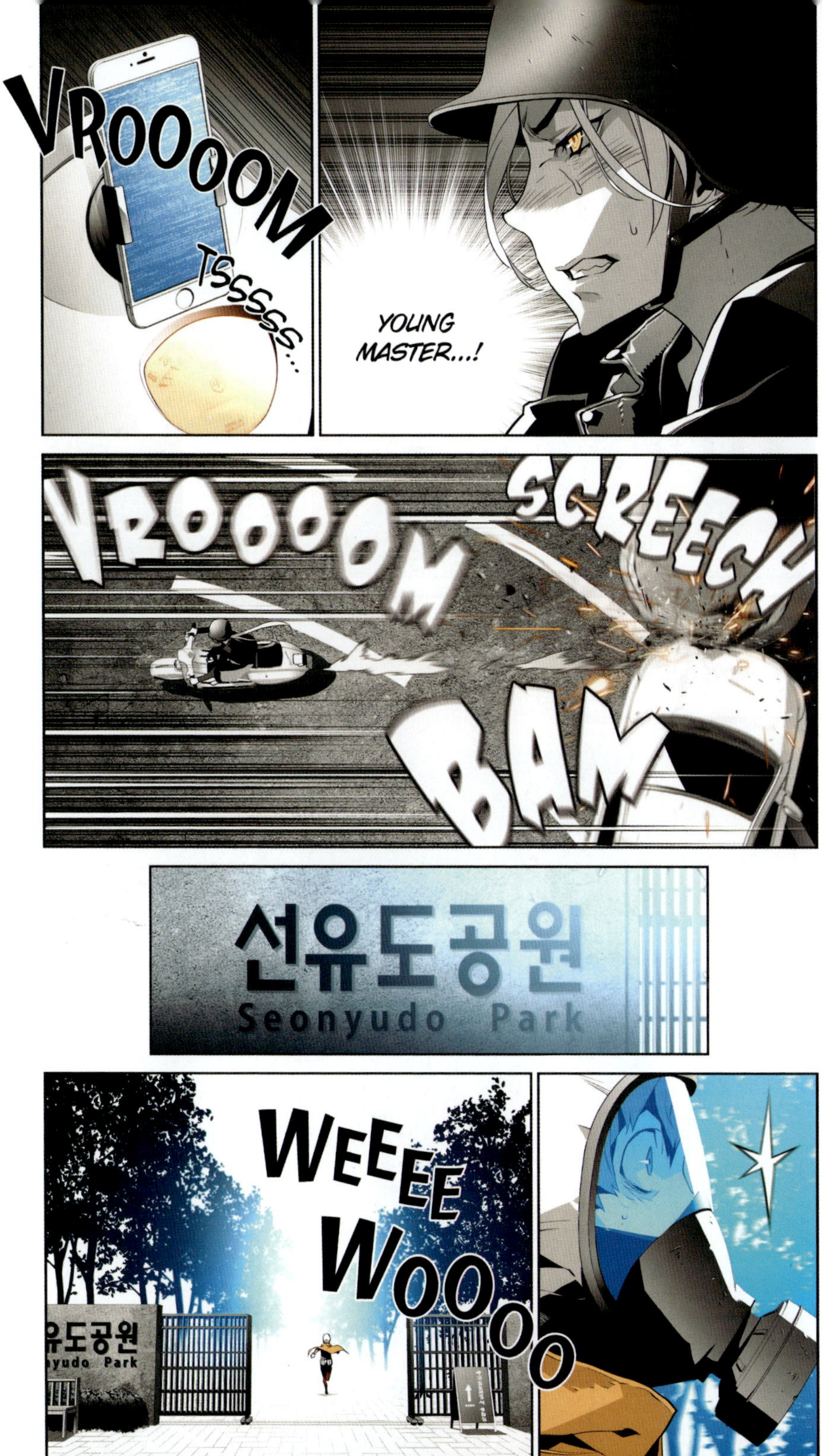
VROOOOM
TSSSSS...
YOUNG MASTER...!
VROOOOM
SCREECH
BAM
선유도공원
Seonyudo Park
WEEEE
WOOOO
유도공원
nyudo Park

WEEEE WOOOO

...!

THE POLICE...!!

I NEED TO MOVE QUICKLY!!

BZZT BZZT

WH-WHAT THE--?! WHAT'RE YA DOIN'?!

!

WAIT...!

AACK!

H-HELLO? IS SOMETHING WRONG?

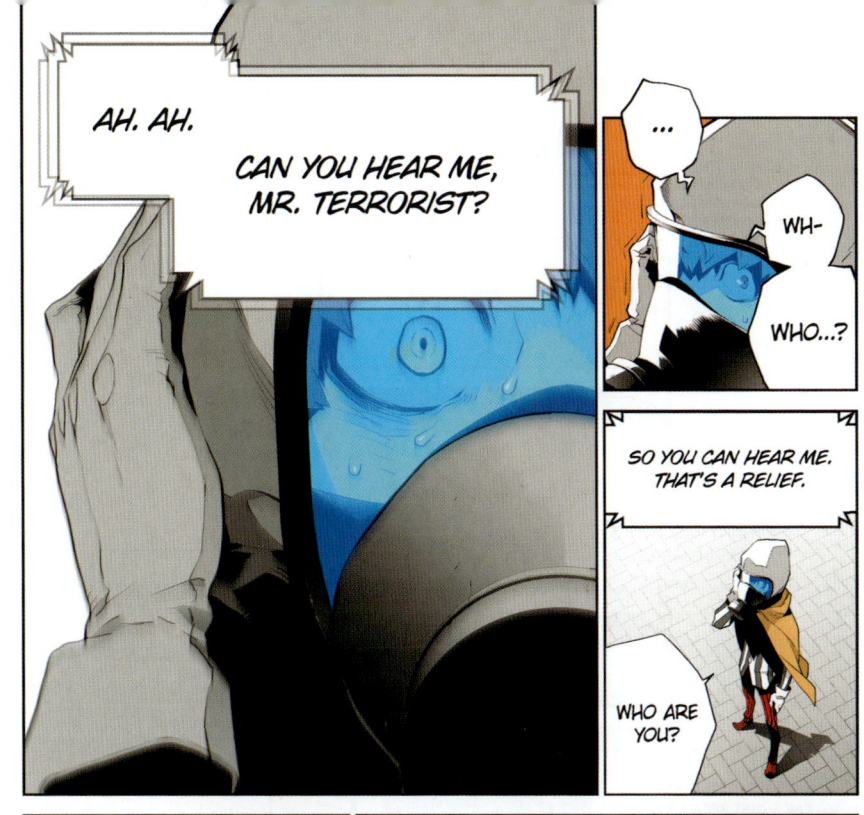

AH. AH.

CAN YOU HEAR ME, MR. TERRORIST?

...

WH- WHO...?

SO YOU CAN HEAR ME. THAT'S A RELIEF.

WHO ARE YOU?

I'M SURE YOU ALREADY HEARD THE POLICE COMING.

THERE'S NO TIME, SO LET'S MEET UP AND HAVE A TALK.

WEEE WOOO

...

I'M GOING TO TELL YOU SOMETHING BEFORE WE START WITH OUR TERROR ATTACK, YOUNG MASTER.

SEEING AS THE BOMBS HAVE BEEN INSTALLED IN PERFECT TIMING FROM THE BRIDGE'S ENTRANCE UP TO THE POINT OF THE ACCIDENT, IT IS HIGHLY POSSIBLE THAT THIS WAS AN INTENDED CRIME AND NOT JUST AN ACCIDENT.

A CRIME THAT AIMS TO HAVE AS MANY CASUALTIES AS POSSIBLE...

THE WORST TYPE OF CRIME.

AND IF THAT PLAN FAILS JUST BECAUSE OF ONE PERSON, WHICH IS YOU, YOUNG MASTER...

...THEY MIGHT NOT STAND DOWN.

THAT'S WHY... IF YOU END UP MEETING THE SUSPECT...

HUFF

HUFF

HUFF

HUFF...

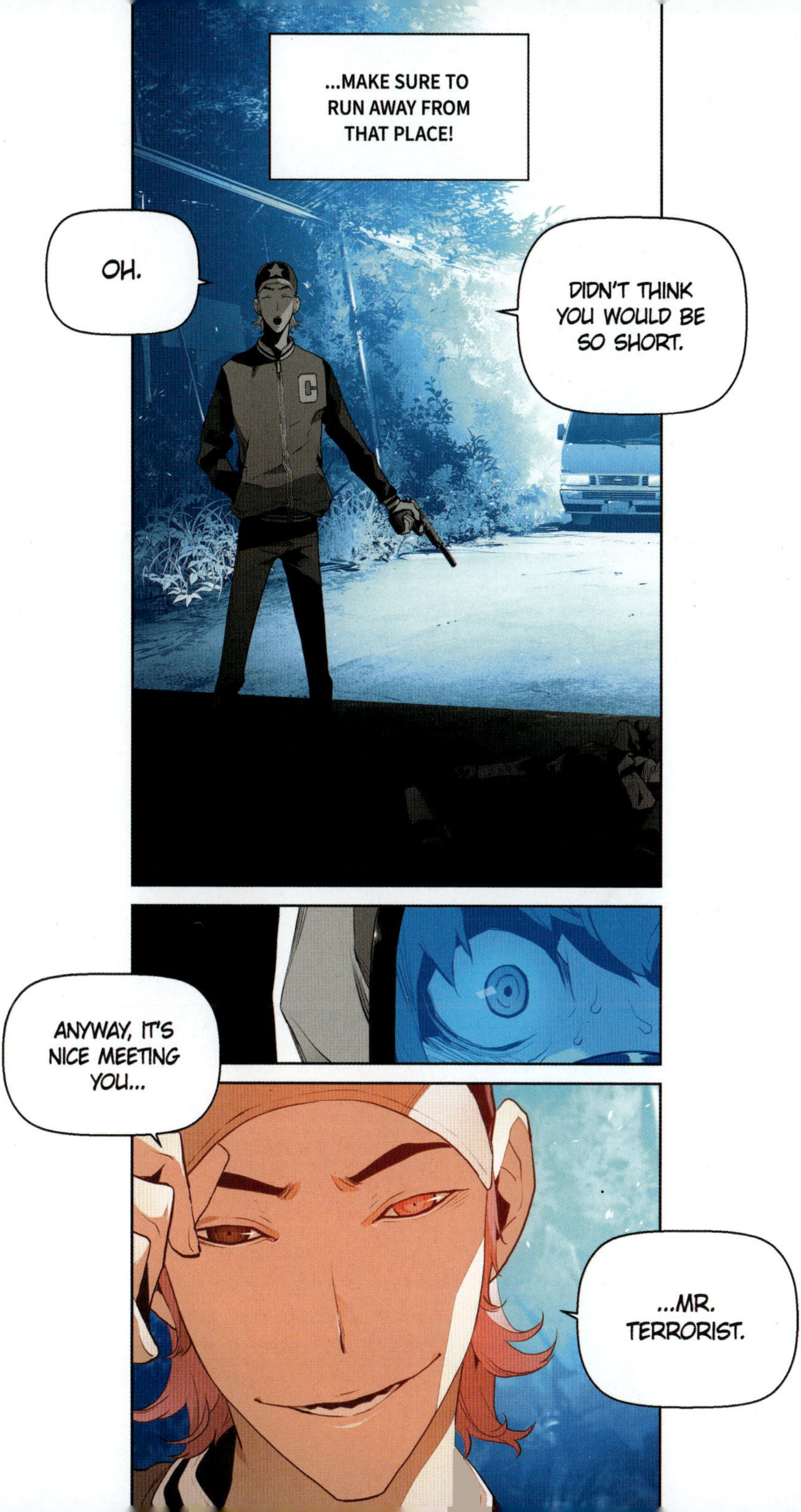
...MAKE SURE TO RUN AWAY FROM THAT PLACE!
OH.
DIDN'T THINK YOU WOULD BE SO SHORT.
ANYWAY, IT'S NICE MEETING YOU...
...MR. TERRORIST.

TERROR MAN

I'M SURE THAT THIS PERSON...

...WAS ON THE BRIDGE EARLIER.

WHY'S HE HERE NOW?

IT'S GONNA COLLAPSE...!

I DIDN'T THINK YOU'D ACTUALLY COME ALONE.

DID YOU REALLY PLAN ON LAUNCHING AN ATTACK ON THE BRIDGE?

STAY CALM... I NEED TO FIGURE OUT EXACTLY WHAT HAPPENED.

ON THE OTHER HAND... NOBODY GOT HURT BECAUSE I SHOWED UP.

IF THIS IS BECAUSE OF HIS ANGER OVER HIS PLAN GETTING RUINED, THEN HE HURT BONGCHUN TO LURE ME IN.

THIS PERSON DOESN'T PLAN ON HANDING ME OVER TO THE POLICE. IF HE DID, HE WOULD'VE DONE IT ALREADY.

THEN... THIS PERSON IS...

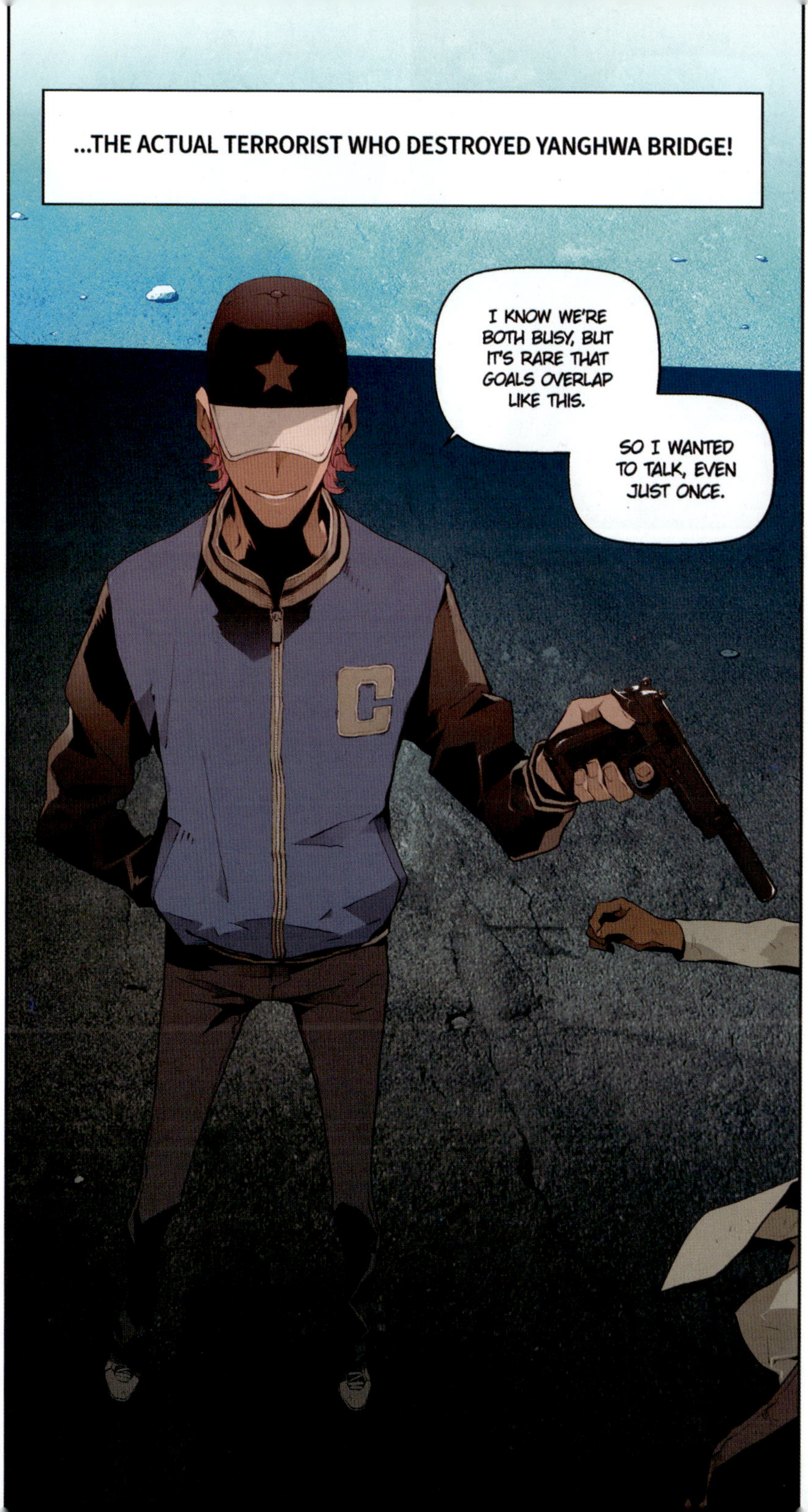
...THE ACTUAL TERRORIST WHO DESTROYED YANGHWA BRIDGE!
I KNOW WE'RE BOTH BUSY, BUT IT'S RARE THAT GOALS OVERLAP LIKE THIS.
SO I WANTED TO TALK, EVEN JUST ONCE.

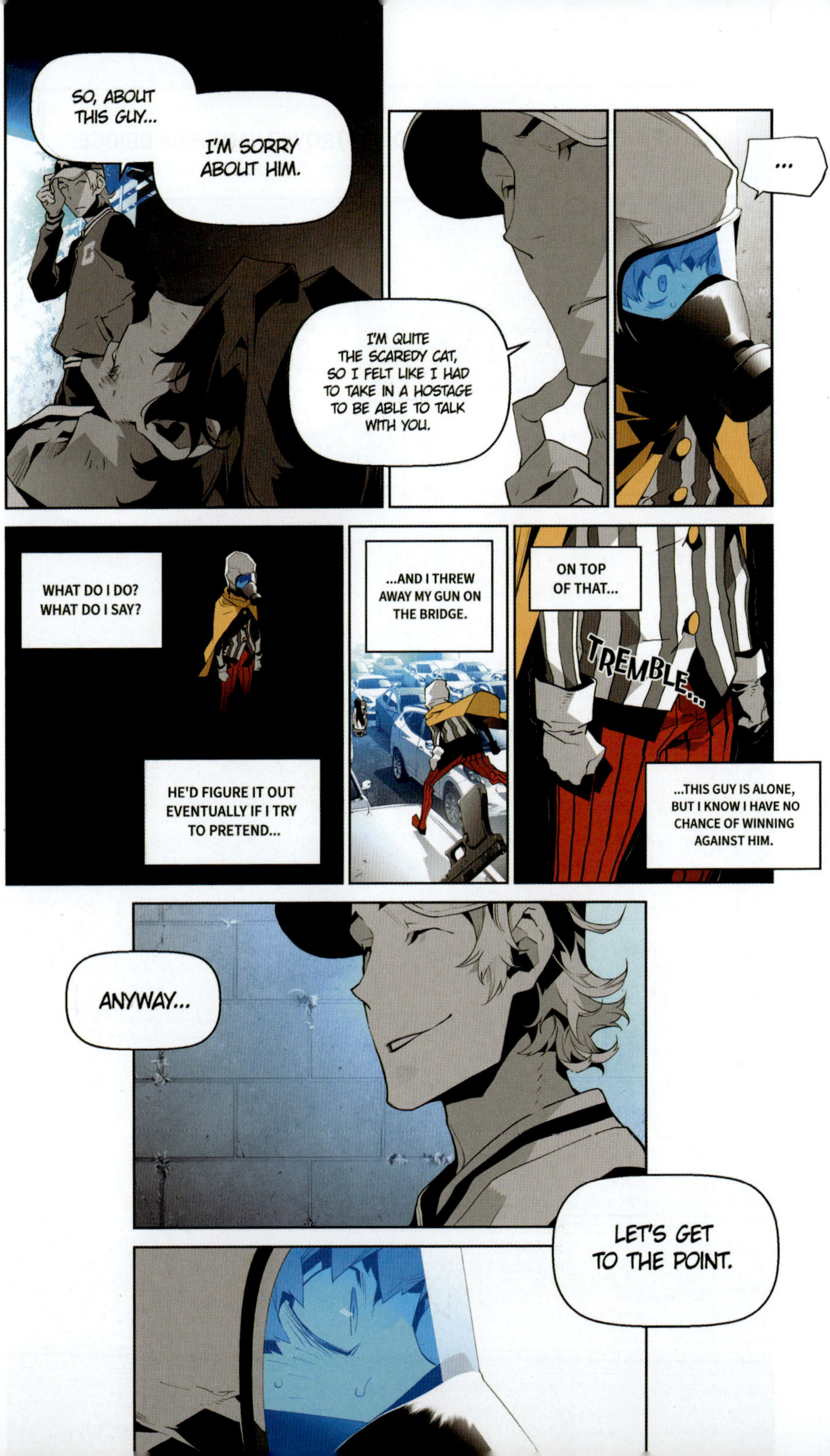

SO, ABOUT THIS GUY...
I'M SORRY ABOUT HIM.
I'M QUITE THE SCAREDY CAT, SO I FELT LIKE I HAD TO TAKE IN A HOSTAGE TO BE ABLE TO TALK WITH YOU.
...
WHAT DO I DO? WHAT DO I SAY?
HE'D FIGURE IT OUT EVENTUALLY IF I TRY TO PRETEND...
...AND I THREW AWAY MY GUN ON THE BRIDGE.
ON TOP OF THAT...
TREMBLE...
...THIS GUY IS ALONE, BUT I KNOW I HAVE NO CHANCE OF WINNING AGAINST HIM.
ANYWAY...
LET'S GET TO THE POINT.

DO YOU WANT TO WORK WITH ME?

WHAT...?

FIRST OF ALL, LET'S JUST SKIP ANY EMBARRASSING TALKS ABOUT IDEOLOGY OR BELIEFS.

JUST THINK ABOUT IT.

HOW MUCH MORE FUN WOULD IT BE IF THE PEOPLE WHO...

...DESTROYED A DEPARTMENT STORE AND A GREAT BRIDGE JOINED FORCES?

I DON'T THINK YOU'LL LOSE ANYTHING IF YOU ACCEPT MY OFFER.

ALTHOUGH, I DON'T KNOW WHAT YOUR GOAL IS.

BUT DOESN'T IT MAKE YOU FEEL BETTER WHEN YOU'RE ABLE TO KILL MORE?

FEEL BETTER?

WHAT NONSENSE IS THIS GUY SAYING? DID HE COMMIT THAT CRIME JUST FOR FUN?

WHAT... WHAT IF I DON'T WANT TO?

W-WE HAVE NO INTENTION OF COOPERATING WITH PEOPLE LIKE YOU...!

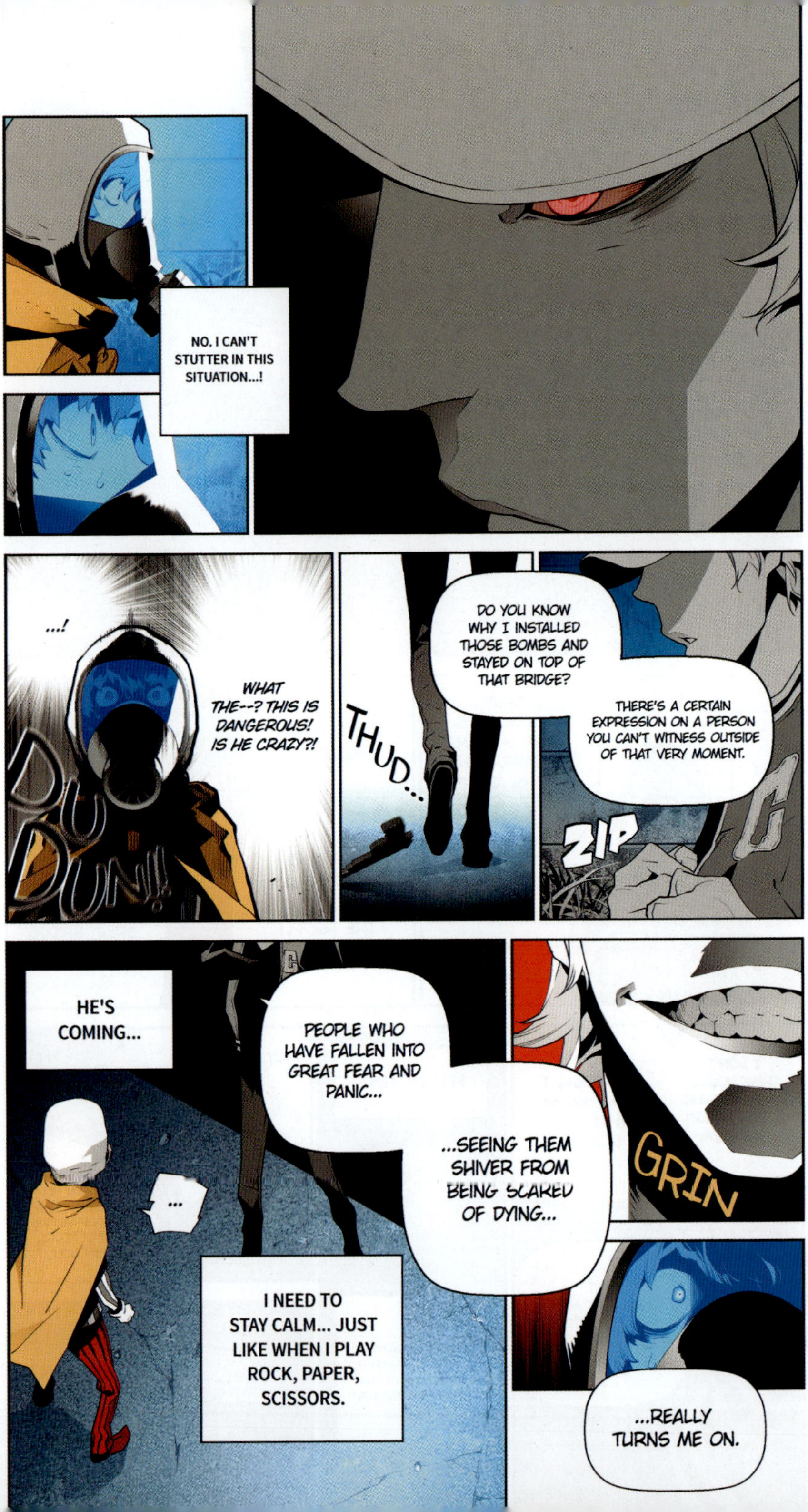
NO. I CAN'T STUTTER IN THIS SITUATION...!
...!
WHAT THE--? THIS IS DANGEROUS! IS HE CRAZY?!
DU DUN!
THUD...
DO YOU KNOW WHY I INSTALLED THOSE BOMBS AND STAYED ON TOP OF THAT BRIDGE?
THERE'S A CERTAIN EXPRESSION ON A PERSON YOU CAN'T WITNESS OUTSIDE OF THAT VERY MOMENT.
ZIP
HE'S COMING...
PEOPLE WHO HAVE FALLEN INTO GREAT FEAR AND PANIC...
...SEEING THEM SHIVER FROM BEING SCARED OF DYING...
GRIN
...
I NEED TO STAY CALM... JUST LIKE WHEN I PLAY ROCK, PAPER, SCISSORS.
...REALLY TURNS ME ON.

TING
TING
TING
SWISH
?!
OH.
...

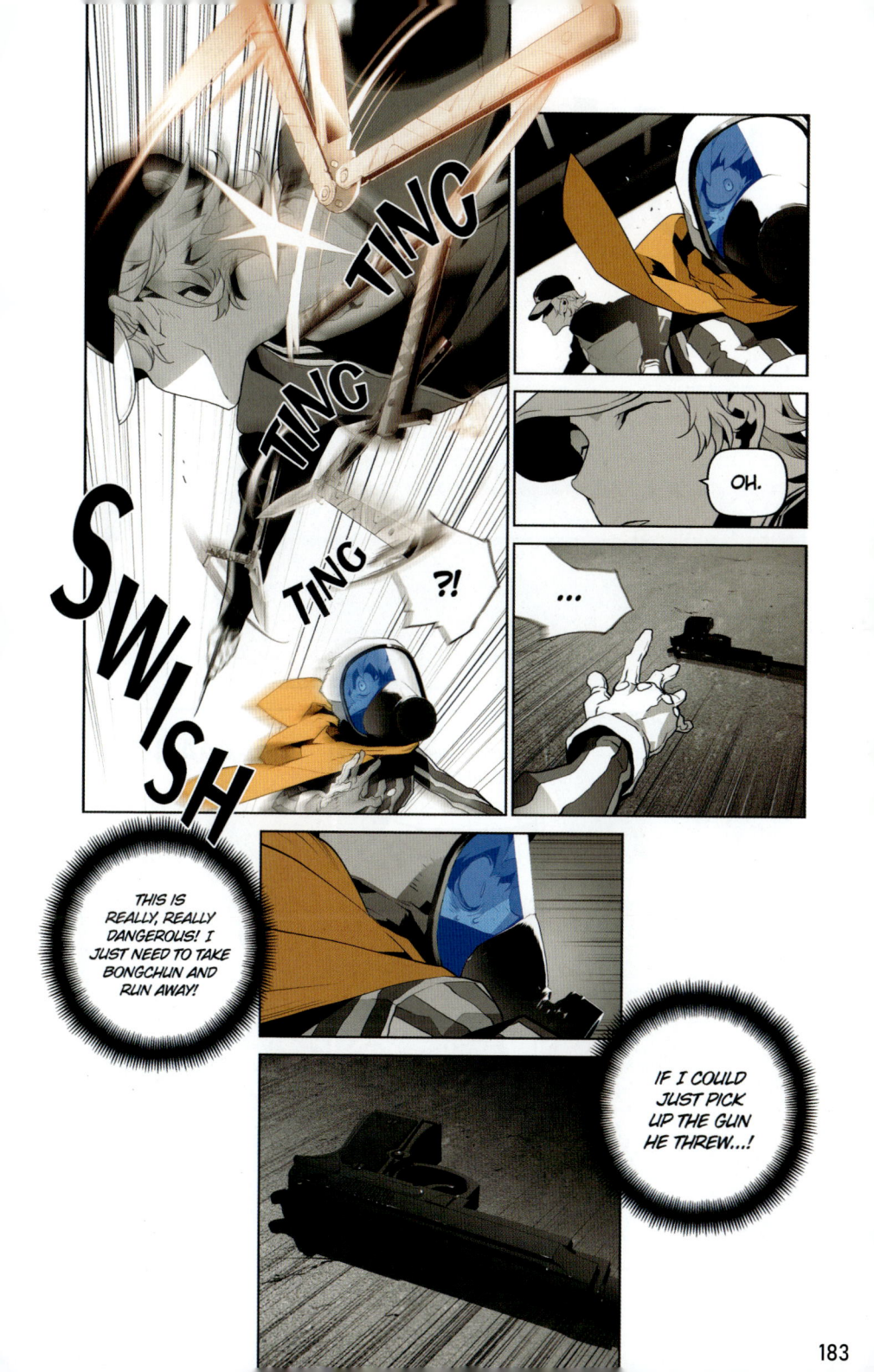

THIS IS REALLY, REALLY DANGEROUS! I JUST NEED TO TAKE BONGCHUN AND RUN AWAY!

IF I COULD JUST PICK UP THE GUN HE THREW...!

JUMP

BANG

WELL, THIS IS DISAPPOINTING.

AAAAAAAH!!

DROP

DIDN'T EXPECT YOU TO DROP FROM SOMETHING SO SHALLOW.

DON'T YOU THINK YOU'RE BEING TOO CLUMSY, MR. TERRORIST?

UGH...

EVEN YOUR VOICE EARLIER... HOW DO I SAY IT?

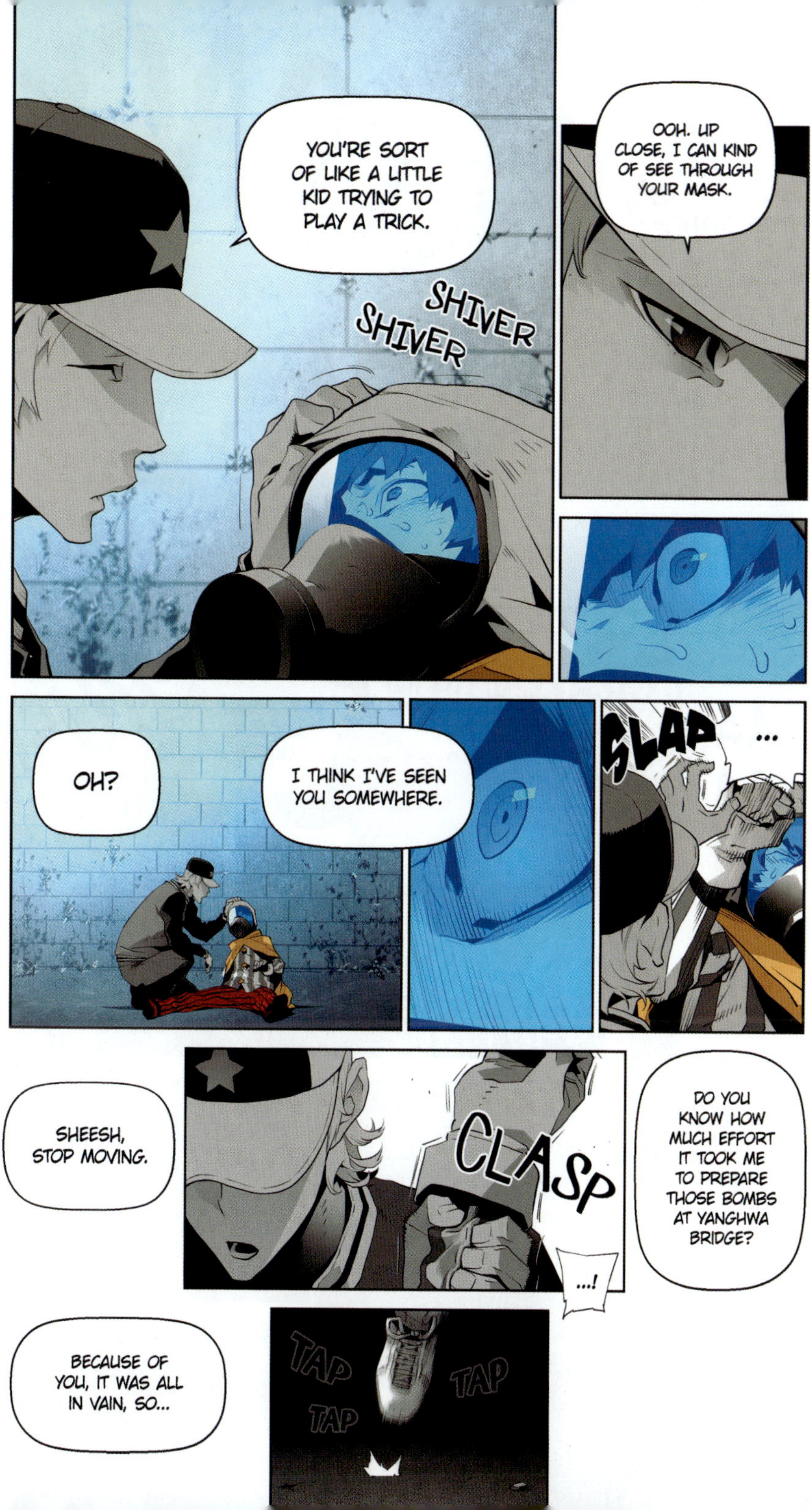
YOU'RE SORT OF LIKE A LITTLE KID TRYING TO PLAY A TRICK.
SHIVER
SHIVER
OOH. UP CLOSE, I CAN KIND OF SEE THROUGH YOUR MASK.
OH?
I THINK I'VE SEEN YOU SOMEWHERE.
SLAP
...
SHEESH, STOP MOVING.
CLASP
...!
DO YOU KNOW HOW MUCH EFFORT IT TOOK ME TO PREPARE THOSE BOMBS AT YANGHWA BRIDGE?
BECAUSE OF YOU, IT WAS ALL IN VAIN, SO...
TAP
TAP
TAP

YOU'RE PREPARED TO DIE, RIGHT?

CRACK

...!

AA AA AH HH !!!

CRACK
CRACK

HAHA! I LIKE THAT SOUND!!

SCREAM LOUDER! MORE!!

CLASP

CRUSH

THAT'S RIGHT... KILLING IS SO SIMPLE.

I NEED TO HEAR THOSE SCREAMS A BIT MORE.

VROOOOM

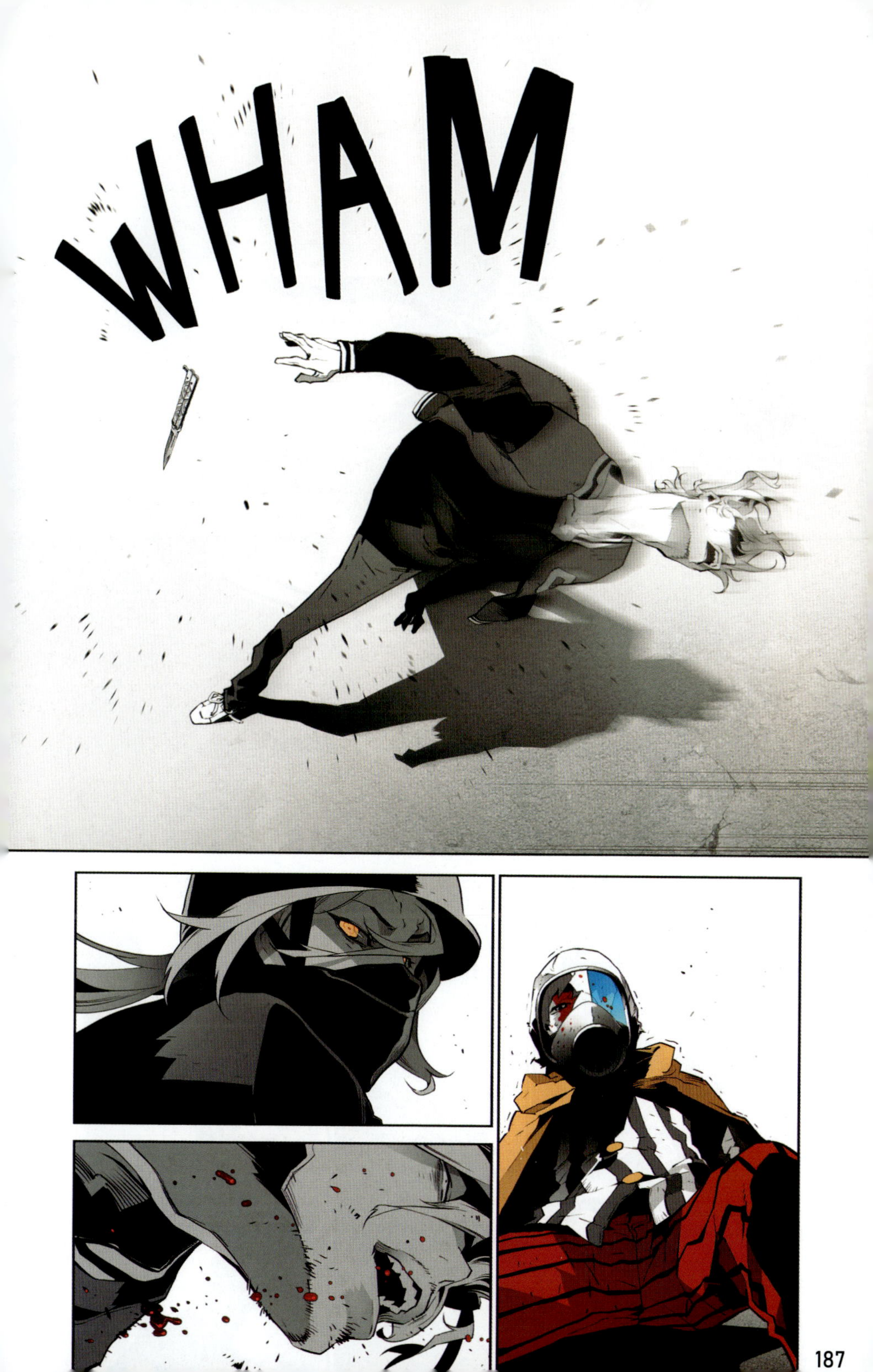
WHAM

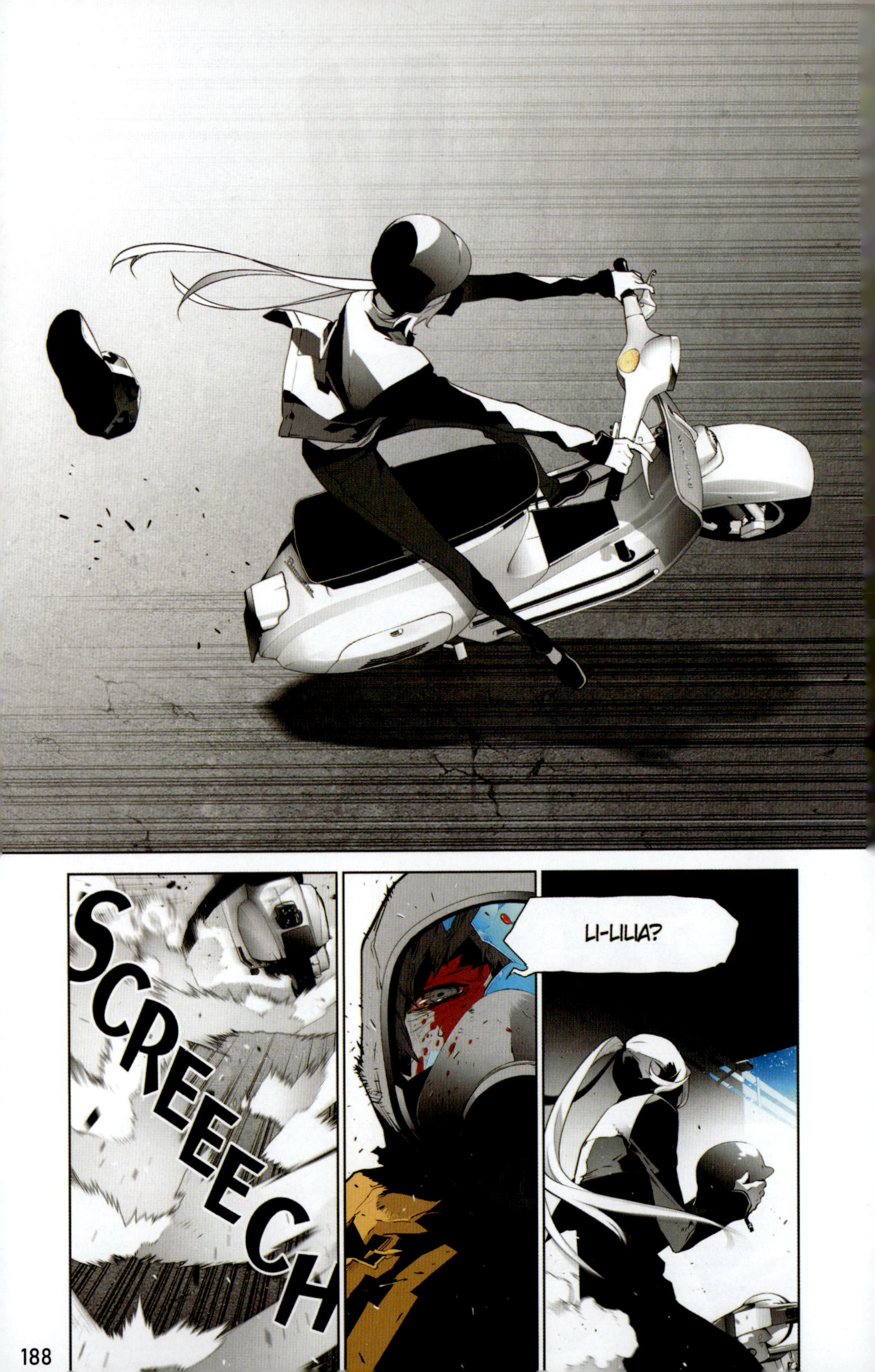
SCREEECH
LI-LILIA?

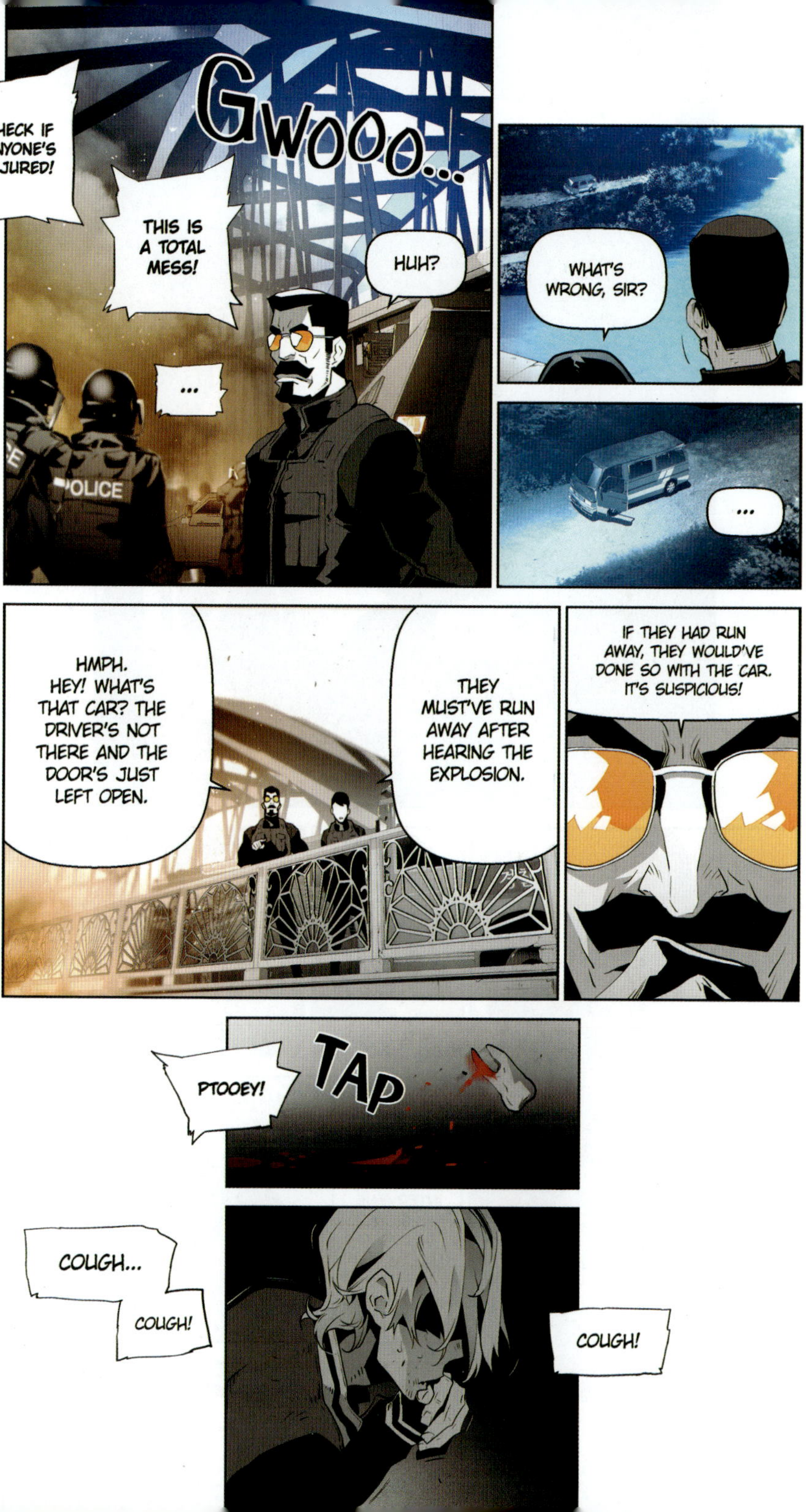
CHECK IF ANYONE'S INJURED!
GWOOO...
THIS IS A TOTAL MESS!
HUH?
...
POLICE
WHAT'S WRONG, SIR?
...
HMPH. HEY! WHAT'S THAT CAR? THE DRIVER'S NOT THERE AND THE DOOR'S JUST LEFT OPEN.
THEY MUST'VE RUN AWAY AFTER HEARING THE EXPLOSION.
IF THEY HAD RUN AWAY, THEY WOULD'VE DONE SO WITH THE CAR. IT'S SUSPICIOUS!
TAP
PTOOEY!
COUGH...
COUGH!
COUGH!

WHAT THE--?

THERE WAS SOMEONE ELSE?

SLOWLY...

NO...

RUN, LILIA...

HOW CRAZY OF YOU TO INTERVENE WITHOUT A SINGLE WEAPON!

CLICK

В этом мире...*
*IN THIS WORLD...

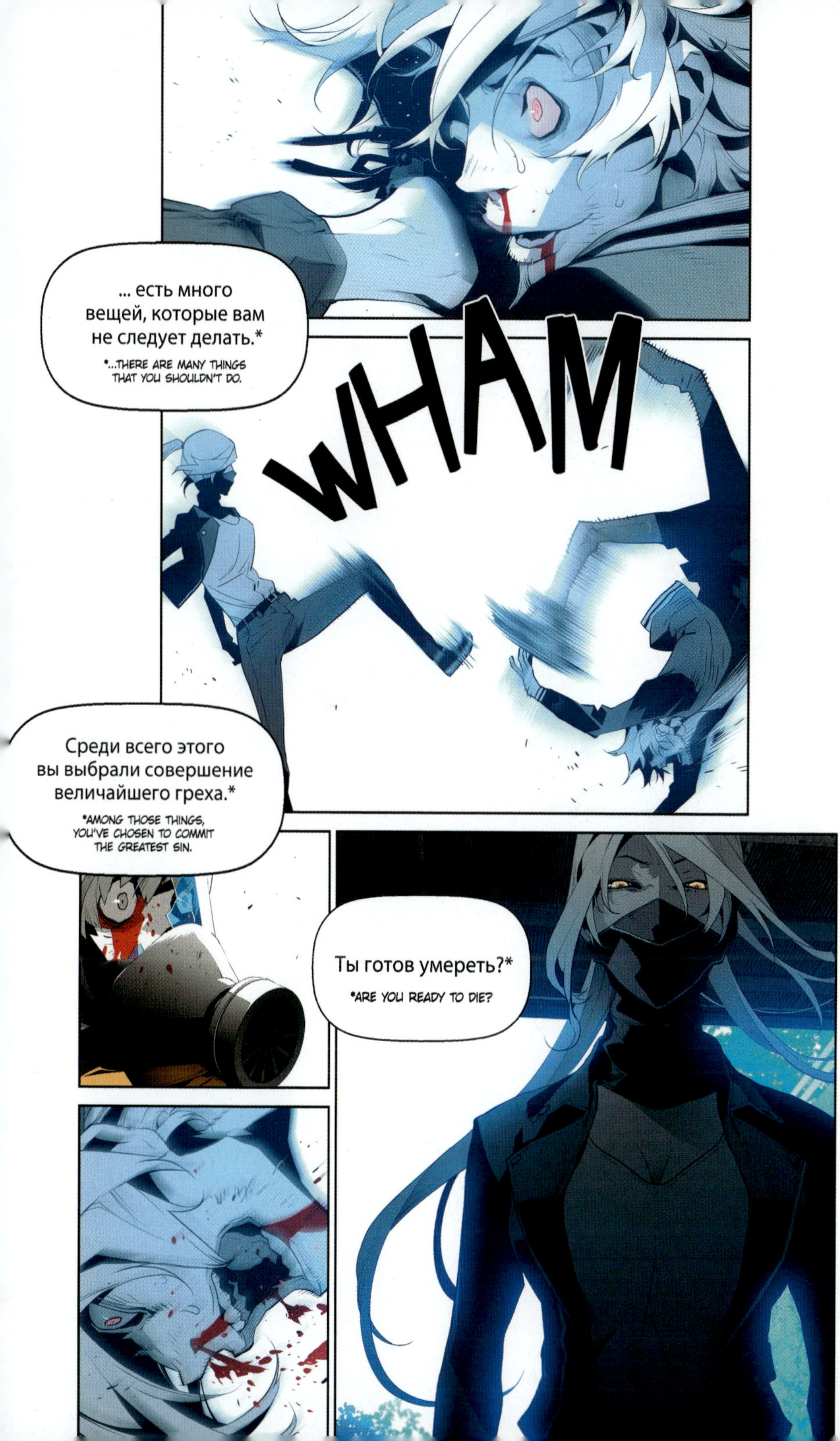

... есть много вещей, которые вам не следует делать.*
*...THERE ARE MANY THINGS THAT YOU SHOULDN'T DO.
WHAM
Среди всего этого вы выбрали совершение величайшего греха.*
*AMONG THOSE THINGS, YOU'VE CHOSEN TO COMMIT THE GREATEST SIN.
Ты готов умереть?*
*ARE YOU READY TO DIE?

TERROR MAN

THUD

UGH...!

YOU...

I SEE...

YOU'RE THE WOMAN THAT WORE THE DOLL MASK YESTERDAY AT THE DEPARTMENT STORE.

HOW AMAZING. I FEEL LIKE I'VE BEEN HIT BY A BRICK. YOU ARE A WOMAN, RIGHT?

THAT PUNK LYING ON THE GROUND... GUESS HE'S JUST YOUR LACKEY, HUH?

BUT SEEING AS YOU'RE TAKING SUCH WEAKLINGS WHO CAN'T EVEN ACT LIKE THUGS...

...YOU MUST BE SHORT ON PEOPLE, HUH?

HOW ABOUT GETTING RID OF THIS TRASH AND TEAMING UP WITH ME?

IF YOU WANT, I CAN BE SOMETHING ELSE AT NIGHT BESIDES BEING YOUR PARTNER IN CRIME.

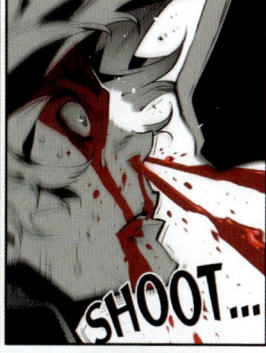

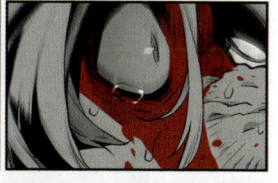

WHACK

SHOOT...

LIFT...

ARE YOUR EYES STILL INTACT?

A LONG TIME AGO, I WOULD'VE KILLED YOU AND SPILLED YOUR ORGANS OUT.

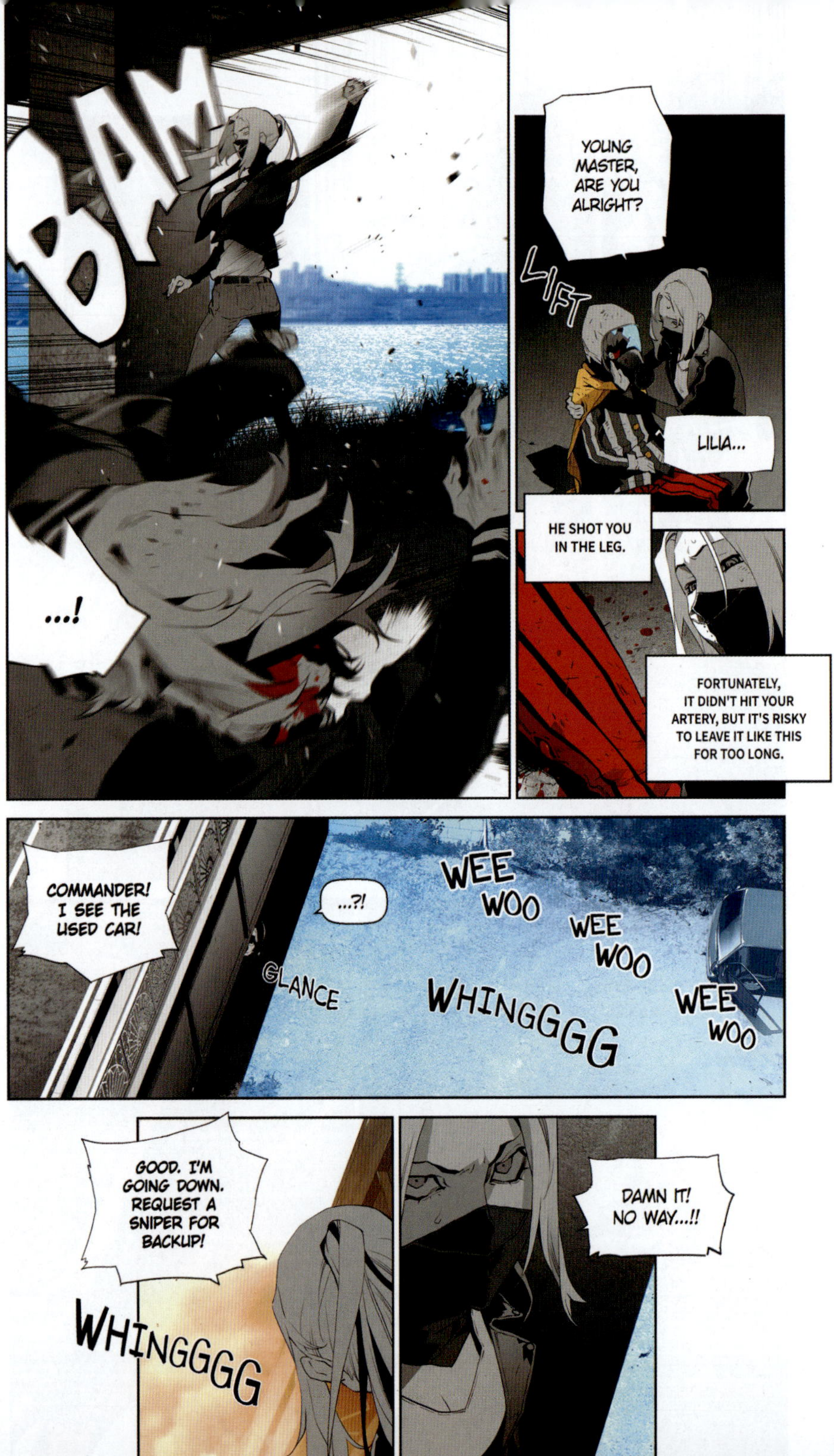
BAM
...!
YOUNG MASTER, ARE YOU ALRIGHT?
LIFT
LILIA...
HE SHOT YOU IN THE LEG.
FORTUNATELY, IT DIDN'T HIT YOUR ARTERY, BUT IT'S RISKY TO LEAVE IT LIKE THIS FOR TOO LONG.
COMMANDER! I SEE THE USED CAR!
...?!
GLANCE
WEE WOO
WEE WOO
WEE WOO
WHINGGGG
GOOD. I'M GOING DOWN. REQUEST A SNIPER FOR BACKUP!
DAMN IT! NO WAY...!!
WHINGGGG

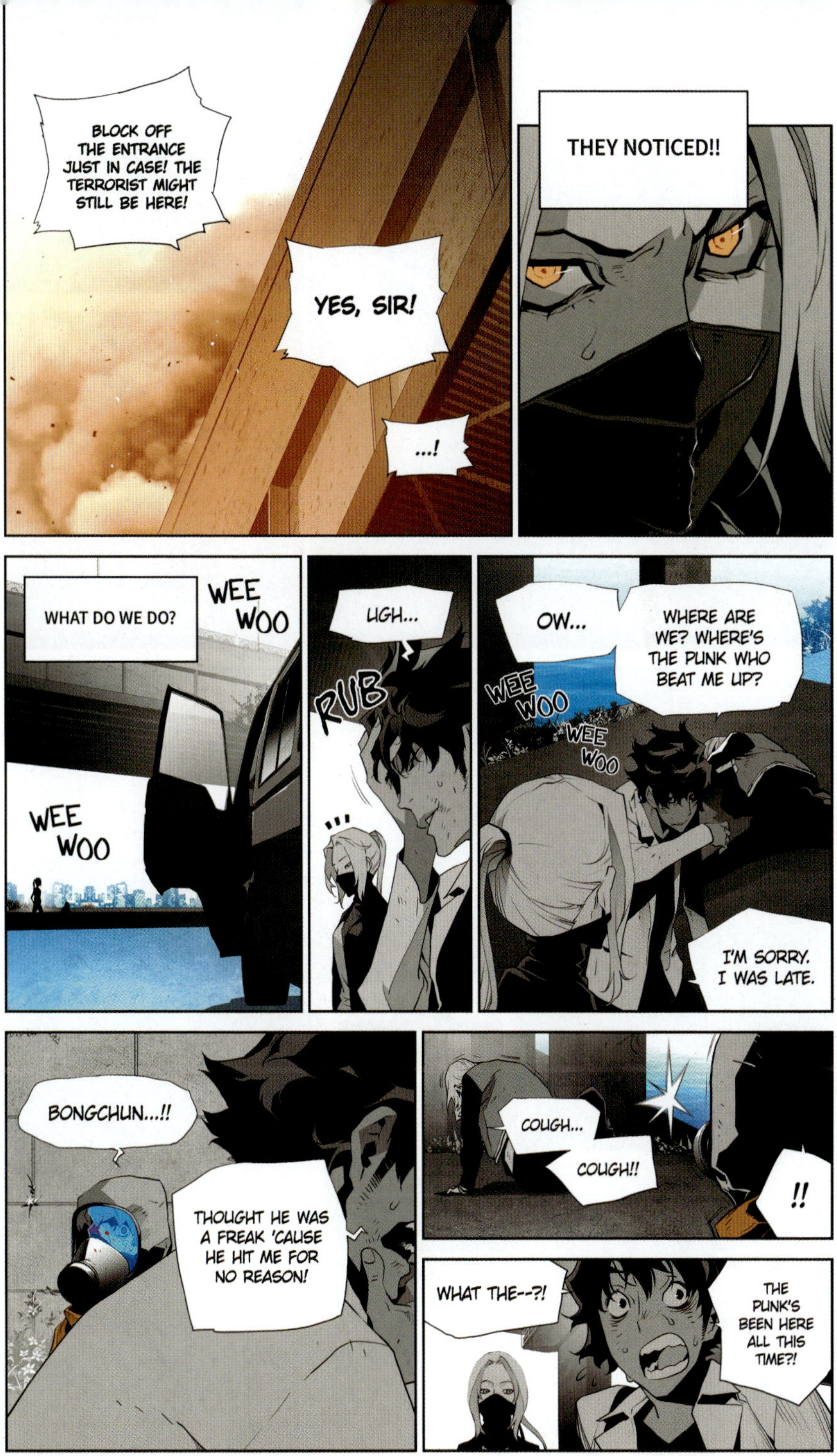
BLOCK OFF THE ENTRANCE JUST IN CASE! THE TERRORIST MIGHT STILL BE HERE!
YES, SIR!
...!
THEY NOTICED!!
WHAT DO WE DO?
WEE WOO
WEE WOO
UGH...
RUB
...
OW...
WHERE ARE WE? WHERE'S THE PUNK WHO BEAT ME UP?
WEE WOO
WEE WOO
I'M SORRY. I WAS LATE.
BONGCHUN...!!
THOUGHT HE WAS A FREAK 'CAUSE HE HIT ME FOR NO REASON!
COUGH...
COUGH!!
!!
WHAT THE--?!
THE PUNK'S BEEN HERE ALL THIS TIME?!

COUGH...

WEE WOO   WEE WOO

...!

THAT TATTOO...

MAY YOU REST IN PEACE.

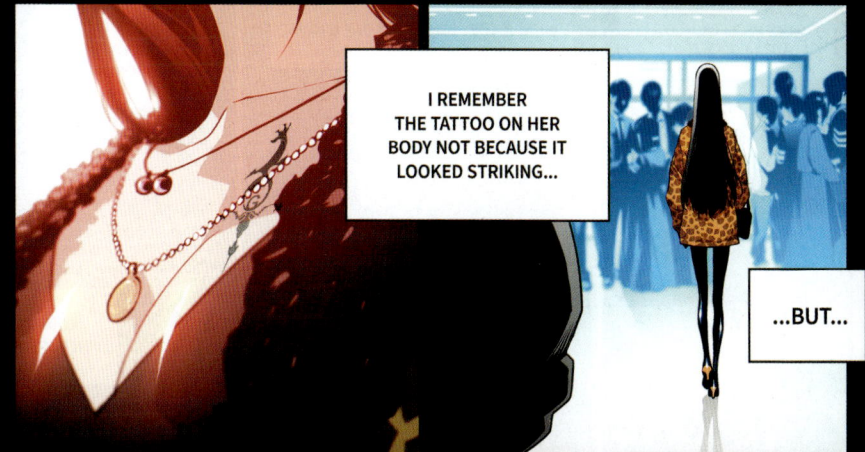

WHAT AN UNFORTUNATE INCIDENT.

TO LOSE THE CONNECTION AND THE MEMORY OF YOUR MOTHER IN AN INSTANT... WHAT AN AWFUL TRAGEDY THIS IS.

WHAT AN AWFUL GOD, THEN, DON'T YOU THINK?

COULD THIS BE FATE AS DECIDED BY GOD?

...!

I REMEMBER THE TATTOO ON HER BODY NOT BECAUSE IT LOOKED STRIKING...

...BUT...

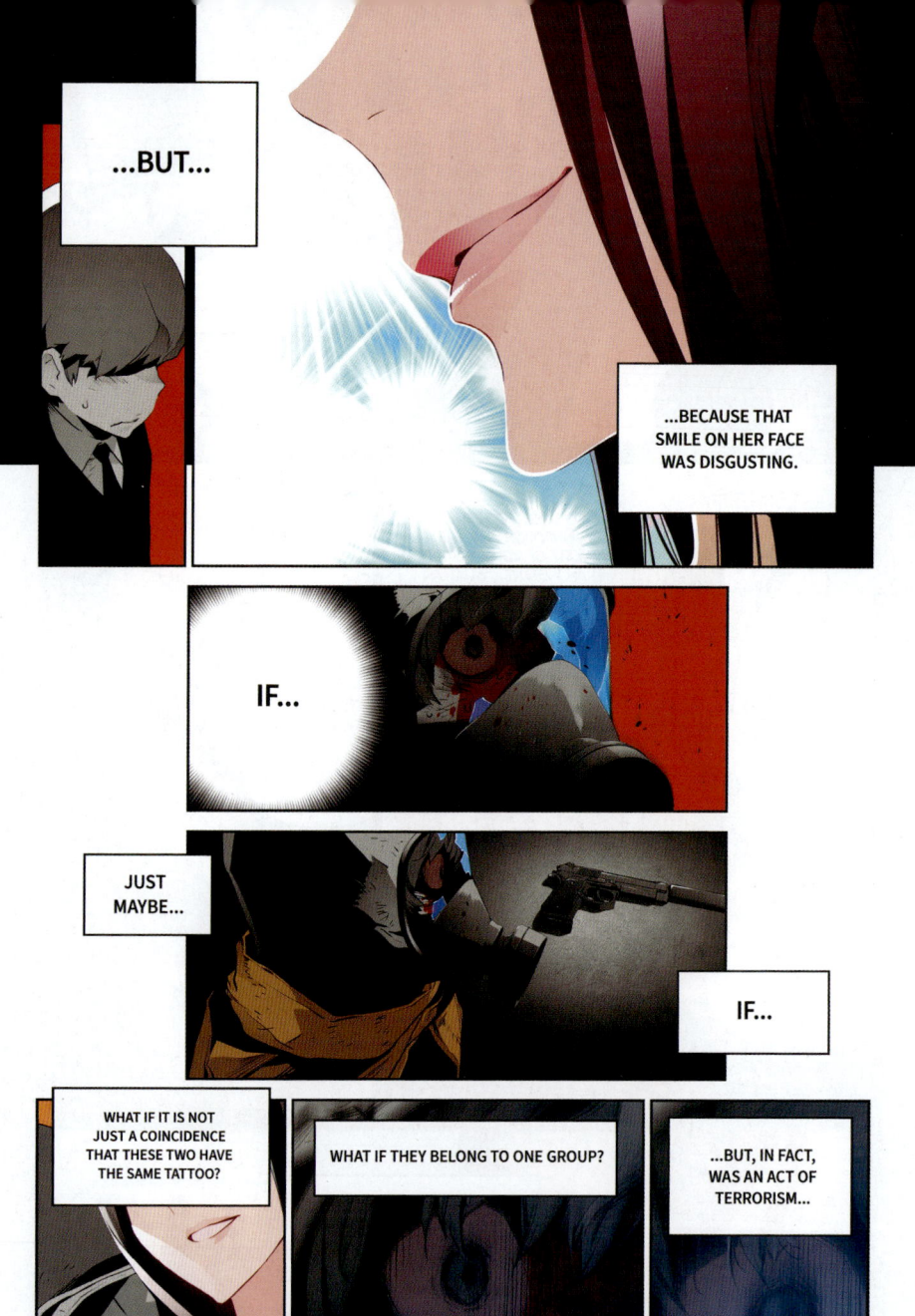

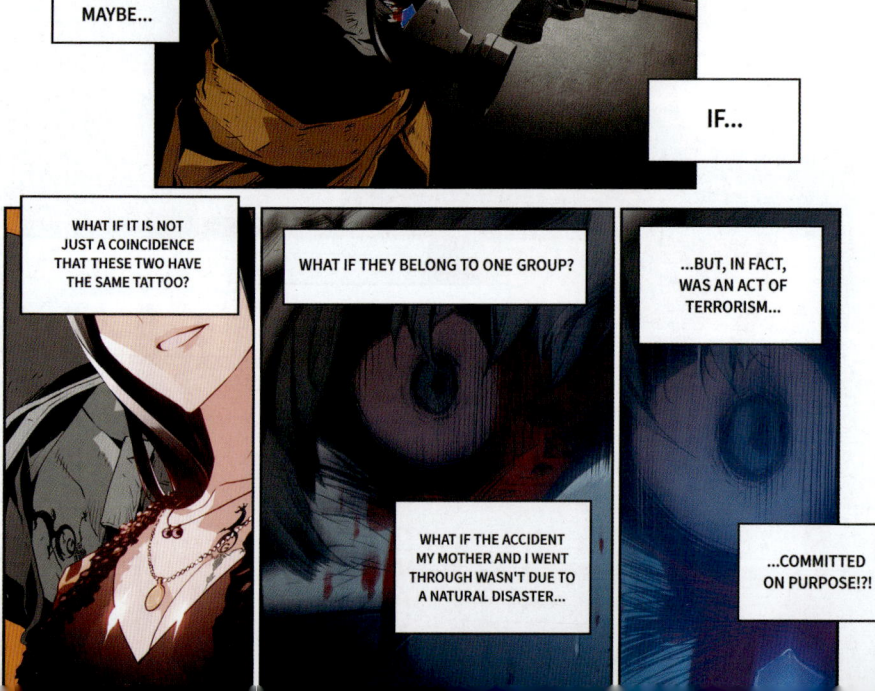

...BUT...

...BECAUSE THAT SMILE ON HER FACE WAS DISGUSTING.

IF...

JUST MAYBE...

IF...

WHAT IF IT IS NOT JUST A COINCIDENCE THAT THESE TWO HAVE THE SAME TATTOO?

WHAT IF THEY BELONG TO ONE GROUP?

...BUT, IN FACT, WAS AN ACT OF TERRORISM...

WHAT IF THE ACCIDENT MY MOTHER AND I WENT THROUGH WASN'T DUE TO A NATURAL DISASTER...

...COMMITTED ON PURPOSE!?!

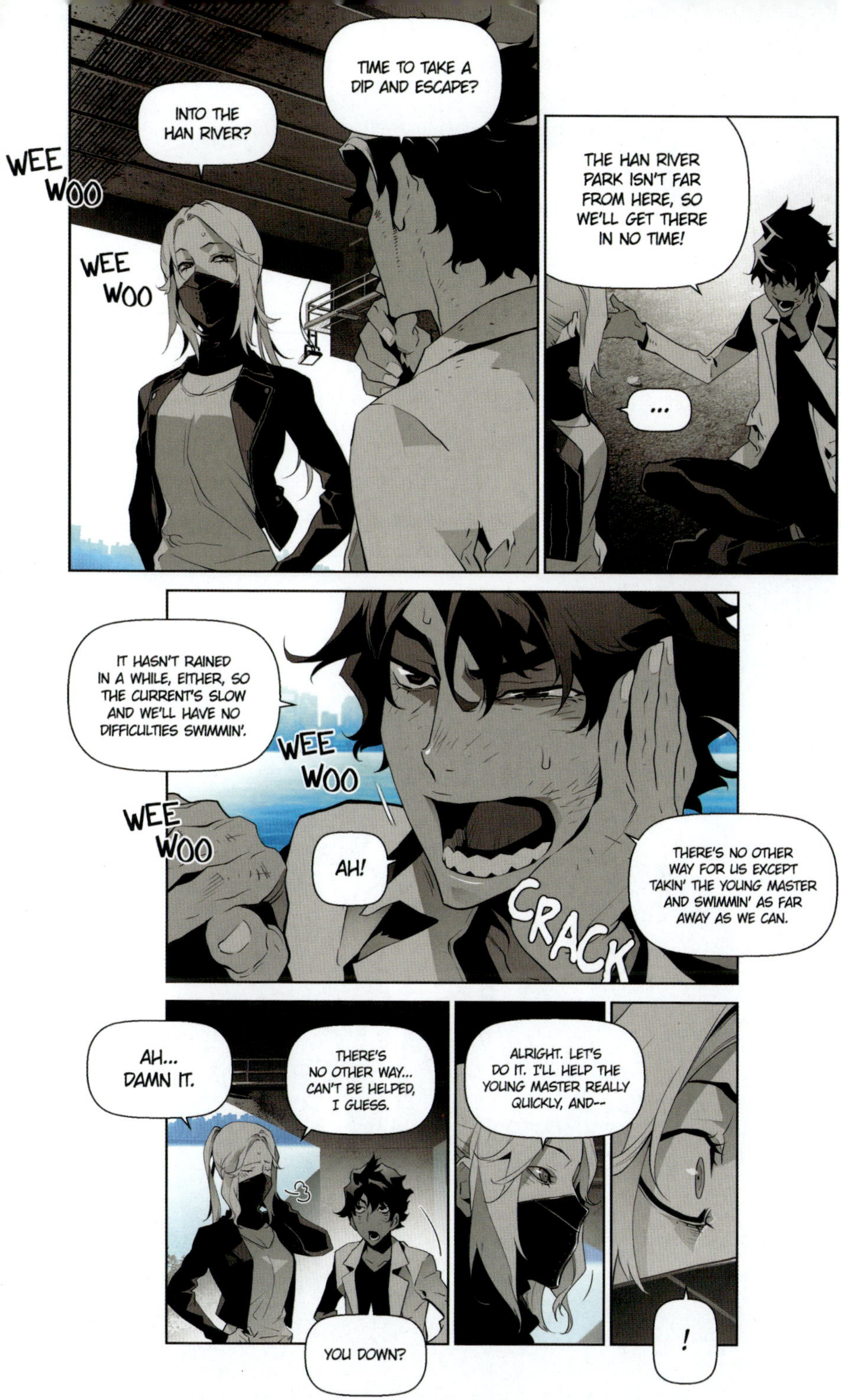
TIME TO TAKE A DIP AND ESCAPE?
INTO THE HAN RIVER?
WEE WOO
WEE WOO
THE HAN RIVER PARK ISN'T FAR FROM HERE, SO WE'LL GET THERE IN NO TIME!
...
IT HASN'T RAINED IN A WHILE, EITHER, SO THE CURRENT'S SLOW AND WE'LL HAVE NO DIFFICULTIES SWIMMIN'.
WEE WOO
WEE WOO
AH!
CRACK
THERE'S NO OTHER WAY FOR US EXCEPT TAKIN' THE YOUNG MASTER AND SWIMMIN' AS FAR AWAY AS WE CAN.
AH... DAMN IT.
THERE'S NO OTHER WAY... CAN'T BE HELPED, I GUESS.
YOU DOWN?
ALRIGHT. LET'S DO IT. I'LL HELP THE YOUNG MASTER REALLY QUICKLY, AND--
!

YOUNG...

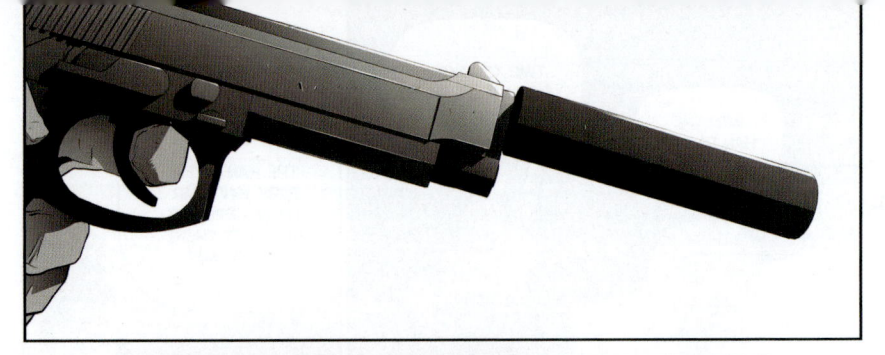

YOUNG MASTER...?

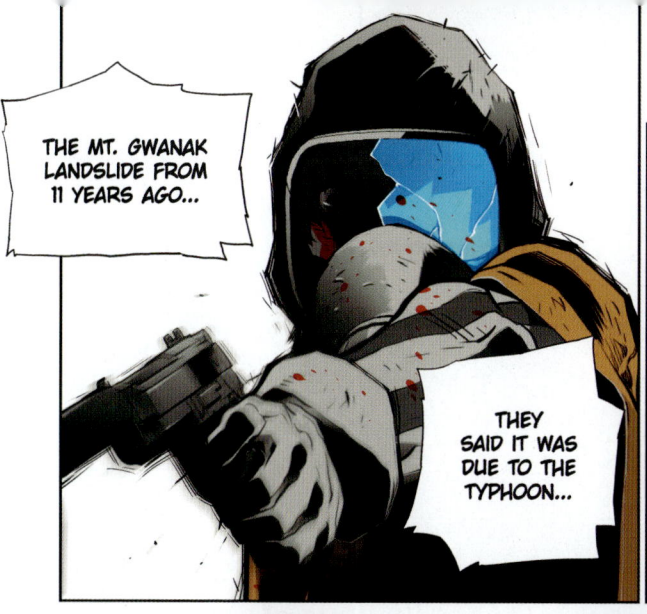

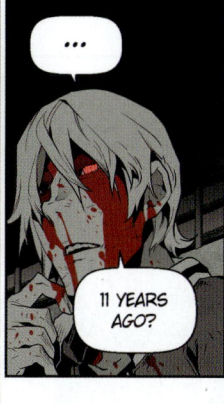

THE MT. GWANAK LANDSLIDE FROM 11 YEARS AGO...

...BUT NOW I GET IT. THAT WAS YOUR DOING, WASN'T IT?

THEY SAID IT WAS DUE TO THE TYPHOON...

YOUNG MASTER, WHAT ARE YOU SAYING ALL OF A SUDDEN?

D-DON'T YOU THINK WE NEED TO STOP HIM?

SAY IT!!

I'M ASKING IF THAT INCIDENT WAS ALSO YOUR DOING!!

TREMBLE

I'LL KILL YOU...

NO, IMPOSSIBLE.

DASH

CALM DOWN, YOUNG MASTER! THAT WAS 11 YEARS AGO! THAT DISASTER COULDN'T HAVE BEEN CAUSED BY THIS GUY!

...

11 YEARS AGO?

MT. GWANAK... LANDSLIDE?

AH!

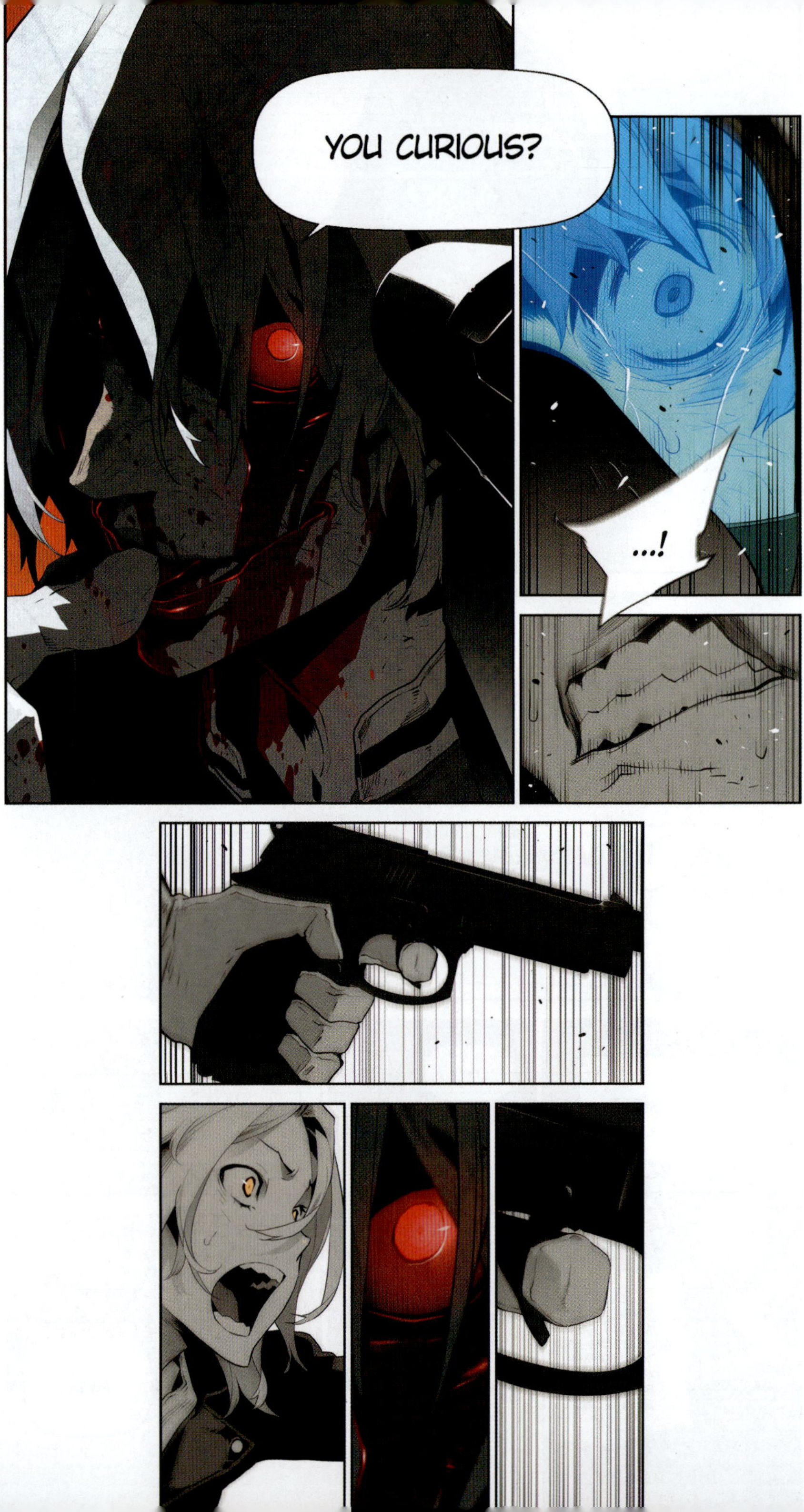
YOU CURIOUS?
...!

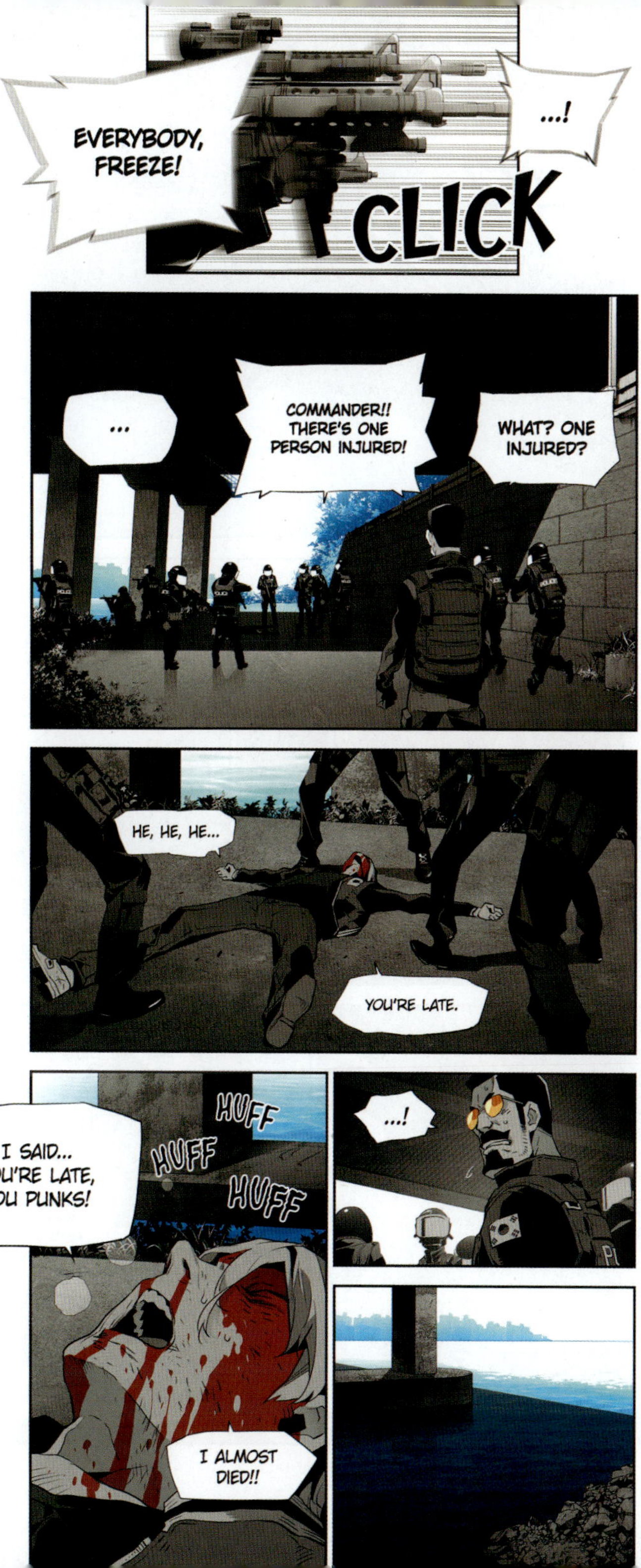
EVERYBODY, FREEZE!
...!
CLICK
...
COMMANDER!! THERE'S ONE PERSON INJURED!
WHAT? ONE INJURED?
HE, HE, HE...
YOU'RE LATE.
I SAID... YOU'RE LATE, YOU PUNKS!
HUFF
HUFF
HUFF
I ALMOST DIED!!
...!

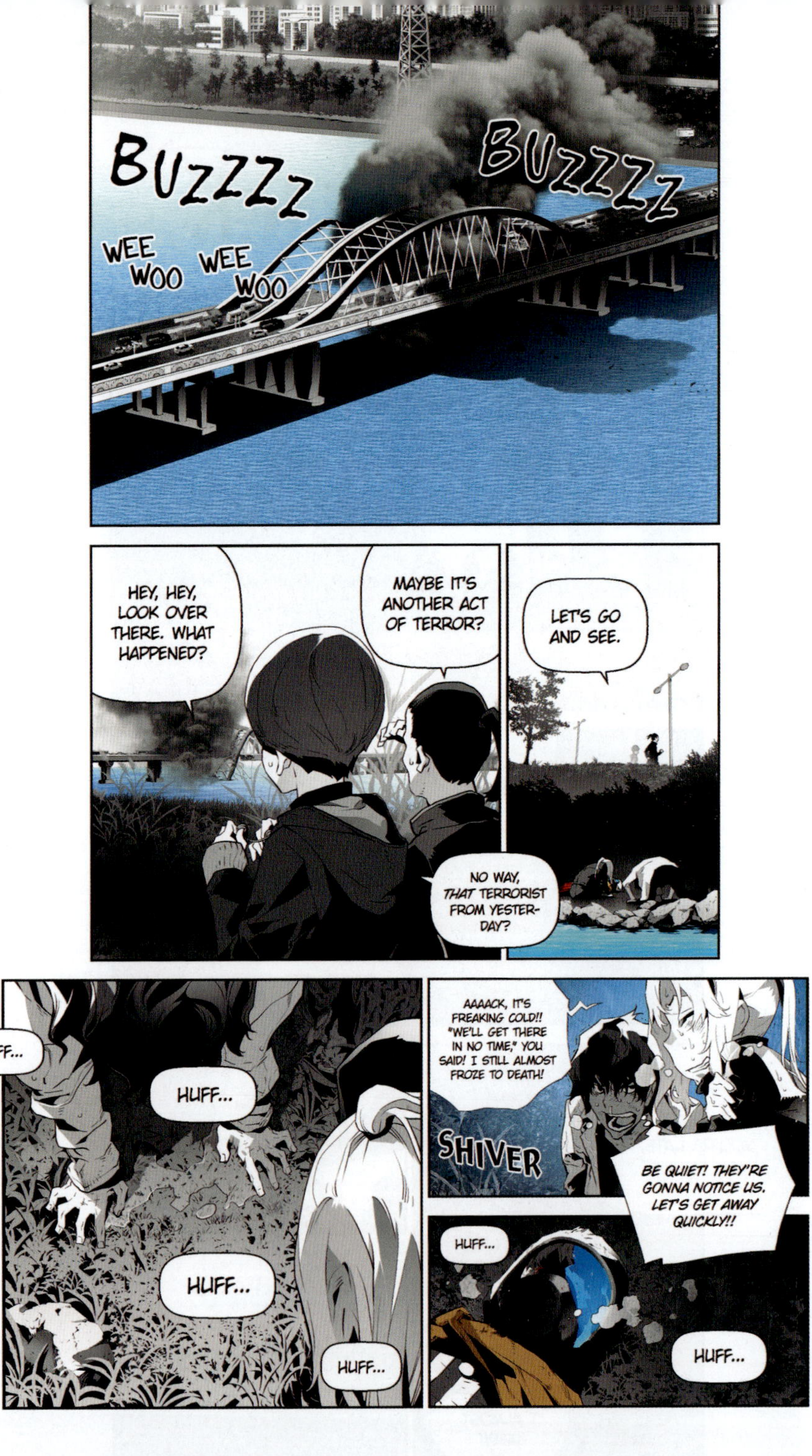
BUZZZZ
BUZZZZ
WEE WOO WEE WOO
HEY, HEY, LOOK OVER THERE. WHAT HAPPENED?
MAYBE IT'S ANOTHER ACT OF TERROR?
NO WAY, *THAT* TERRORIST FROM YESTER-DAY?
LET'S GO AND SEE.
HUFF...
HUFF...
HUFF...
HUFF...
AAAACK, IT'S FREAKING COLD!! "WE'LL GET THERE IN NO TIME," YOU SAID! I STILL ALMOST FROZE TO DEATH!
SHIVER
BE QUIET! THEY'RE GONNA NOTICE US. LET'S GET AWAY QUICKLY!!
HUFF...
HUFF...

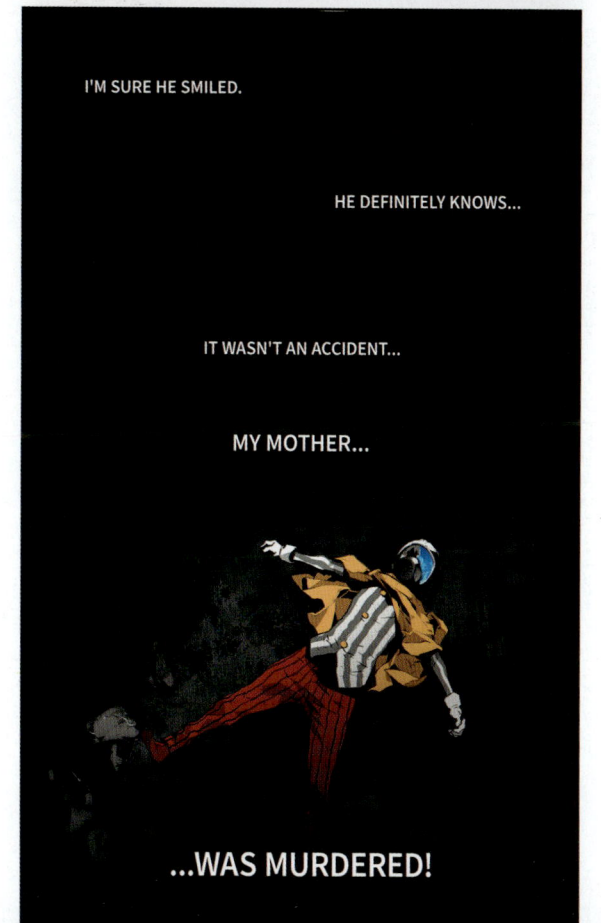

HE SMILED.

I'M SURE HE SMILED.

HE DEFINITELY KNOWS...

IT WASN'T AN ACCIDENT...

MY MOTHER...

...WAS MURDERED!

TERROR MAN

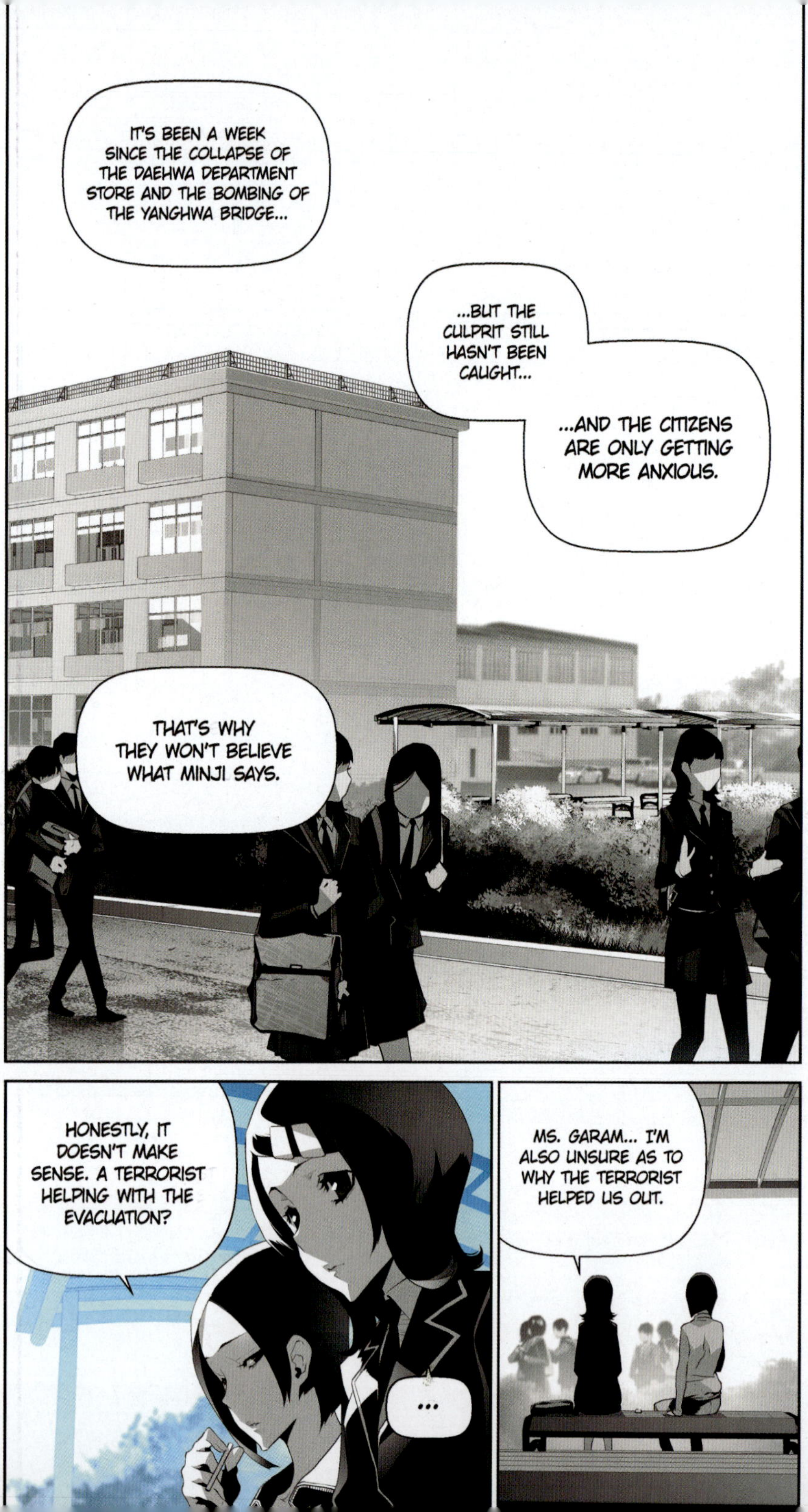
IT'S BEEN A WEEK SINCE THE COLLAPSE OF THE DAEHWA DEPARTMENT STORE AND THE BOMBING OF THE YANGHWA BRIDGE...
...BUT THE CULPRIT STILL HASN'T BEEN CAUGHT...
...AND THE CITIZENS ARE ONLY GETTING MORE ANXIOUS.
THAT'S WHY THEY WON'T BELIEVE WHAT MINJI SAYS.
HONESTLY, IT DOESN'T MAKE SENSE. A TERRORIST HELPING WITH THE EVACUATION?
...
MS. GARAM... I'M ALSO UNSURE AS TO WHY THE TERRORIST HELPED US OUT.

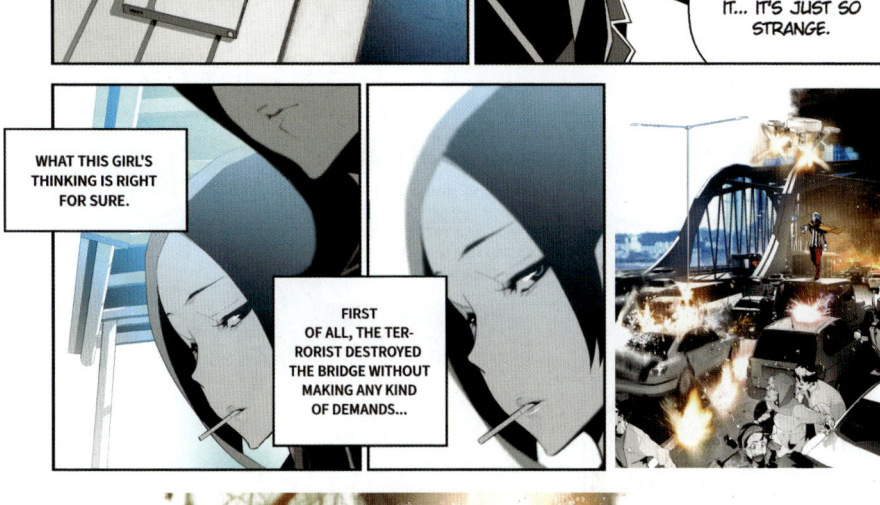

"TO BE HONEST, I EVEN THOUGHT OF REPORTING IT...

...BUT THE POLICE WOULD JUST TAKE IT AS NONSENSE. IT'D JUST BE A BOTHER.

NO MATTER HOW I THINK OF IT... IT'S JUST SO STRANGE."

WHAT THIS GIRL'S THINKING IS RIGHT FOR SURE.

FIRST OF ALL, THE TERRORIST DESTROYED THE BRIDGE WITHOUT MAKING ANY KIND OF DEMANDS...

...AS IF HE WANTED TO PURPOSEFULLY CHASE THE PEOPLE AWAY FROM IT!

...

EXCUSE ME FOR A MOMENT.

CLICK...

AH... OKAY.

ADD IN THE INCIDENT WITH THE DEPARTMENT STORE, AND THERE WERE NO CASUALTIES IN BOTH PLACES THE TERRORIST APPEARED.

HOO...

MAYBE... THE TERRORIST...

AH...

...

I THINK OF THIS EVERY TIME I SEE YOU, MISTER, BUT...

TAP

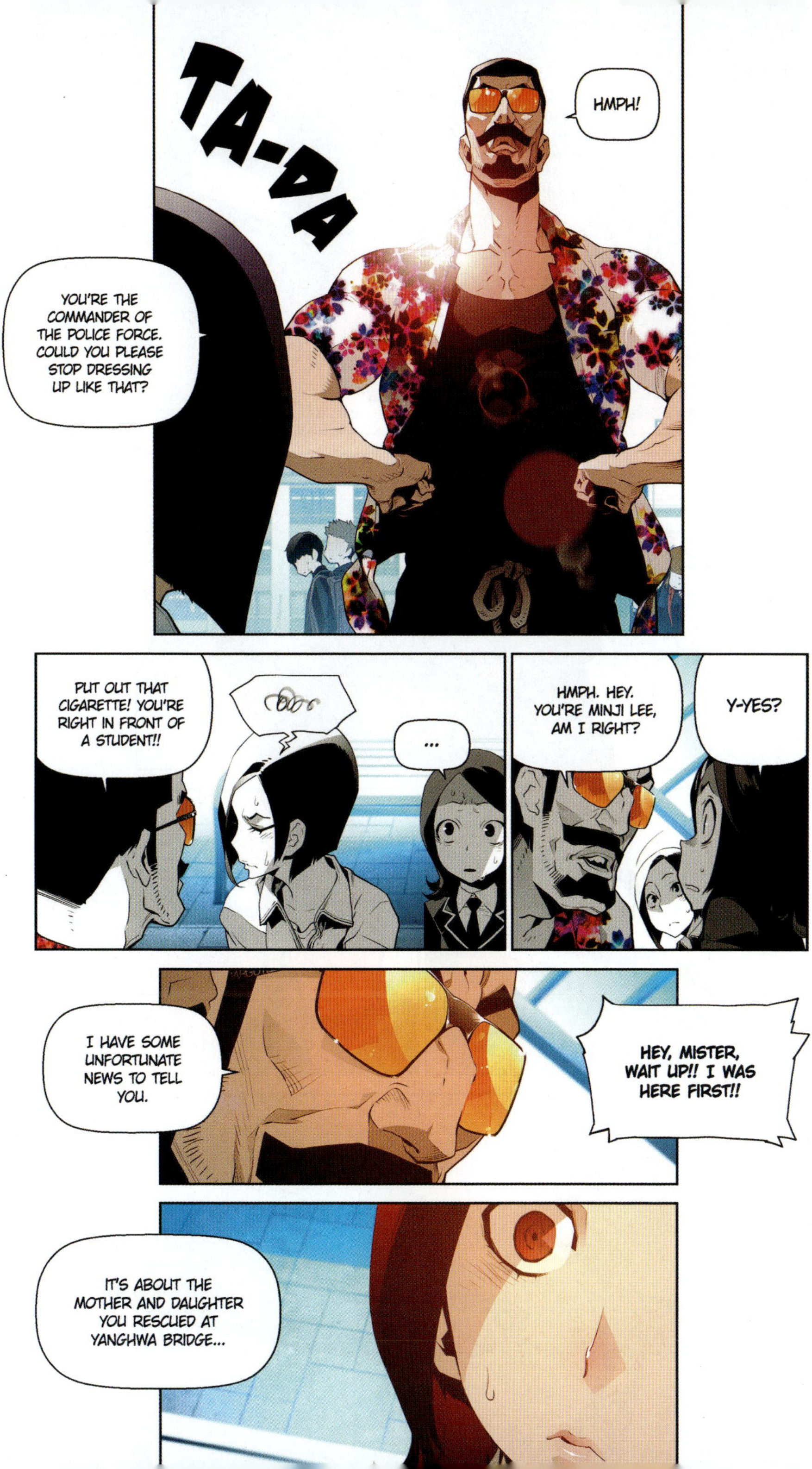
TA-DA
HMPH!
YOU'RE THE COMMANDER OF THE POLICE FORCE. COULD YOU PLEASE STOP DRESSING UP LIKE THAT?
PUT OUT THAT CIGARETTE! YOU'RE RIGHT IN FRONT OF A STUDENT!!
...
HMPH. HEY. YOU'RE MINJI LEE, AM I RIGHT?
Y-YES?
I HAVE SOME UNFORTUNATE NEWS TO TELL YOU.
HEY, MISTER, WAIT UP!! I WAS HERE FIRST!!
IT'S ABOUT THE MOTHER AND DAUGHTER YOU RESCUED AT YANGHWA BRIDGE...

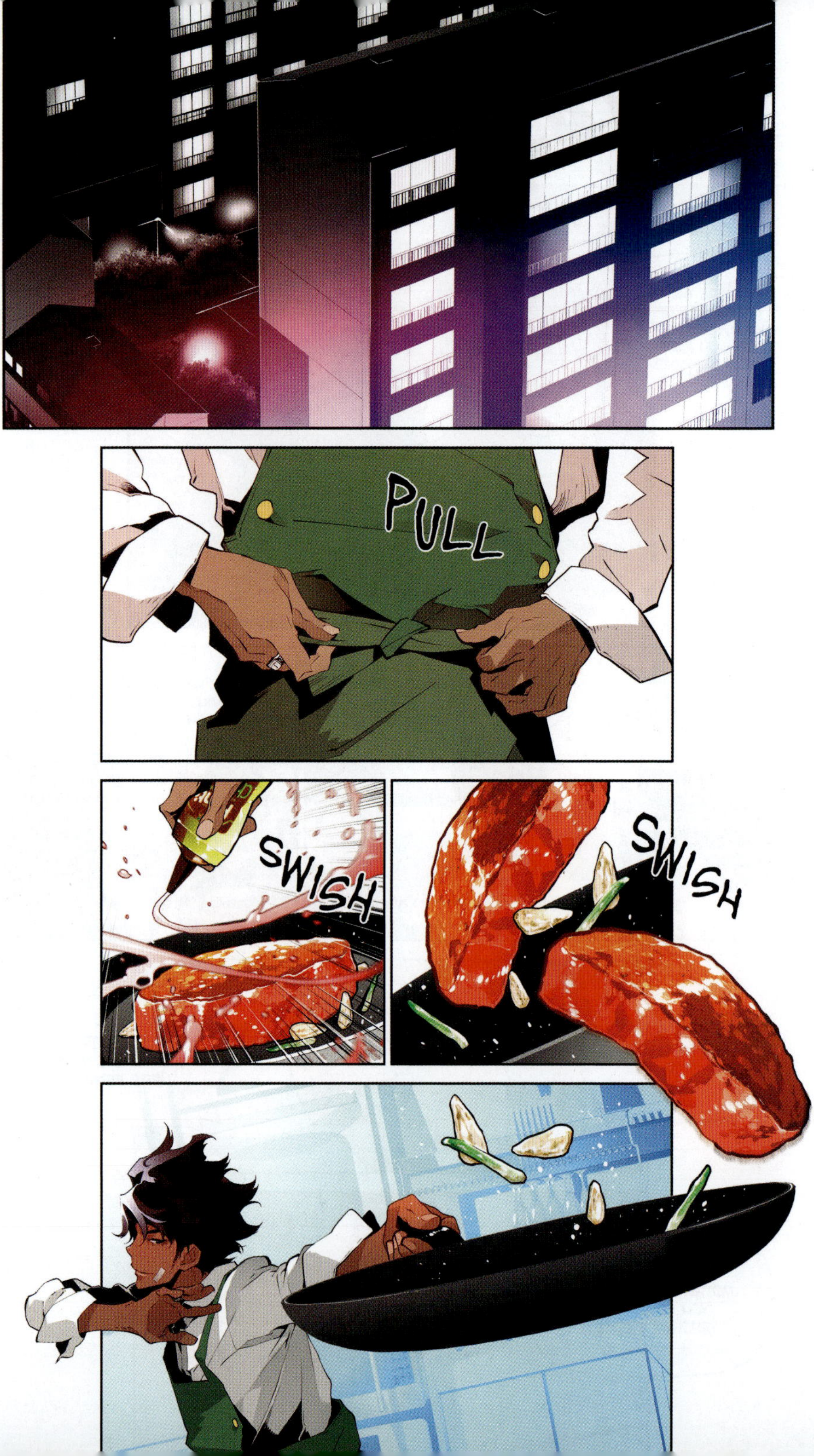
PULL
SWISH
SWISH

IT WASN'T WHAT I PLANNED, BUT THE STEAK FLEW FARTHER THAN EXPECTED, SO...

I REPLACED IT WITH ABALONE FROM THE CONVENIENCE STORE. IT'S STILL GOOD, SO DON'T WORRY.

SLIDE

...IT WAS INEDIBLE.

IT'S GON' BE GOOD.

AH... YES, THANK YOU.

GREAT, GREAT! THAT WAS SOME SHOW YOU PUT ON THERE IN THE KITCHEN!

YOU GOT A LOT TO SAY FOR A DISGUSTINGLY BAD COOK.

IF YA NEED SOMETHIN' ELSE, JUST CALL ME, YOUNG MASTER.

WILL IT BE ALRIGHT FOR BONGCHUN TO STAY HERE?

LEAVE HIM BE. HE SAYS OKAY TO ANYTHING AS LONG AS HE GETS PAID.

...

HEY!

ANYWAY, BACK TO WHAT WERE TALKING ABOUT EARLIER...

TO BE HONEST, I DON'T THINK THAT GUY'S INVOLVED IN THE ACCIDENT FROM 11 YEARS AGO.

YOU SAW HIM, TOO, YOUNG MASTER. IF IT WAS 11 YEARS AGO, WOULD HE HAVE BEEN OLD ENOUGH TO COMMIT SUCH A CRIME?

B-BUT...

HIS EXPRESSION DEFINITELY SAID HE KNOWS SOMETHING ABOUT THE MT. GWANAK LANDSLIDE...

...AND THAT MY MOTHER DIDN'T DIE FROM A NATURAL DISASTER.

YOUNG MASTER.

LET'S THINK REALISTICALLY NOW.

THAT PUNK LIED ON PURPOSE TO PLAY WITH YOU, YOUNG MASTER.

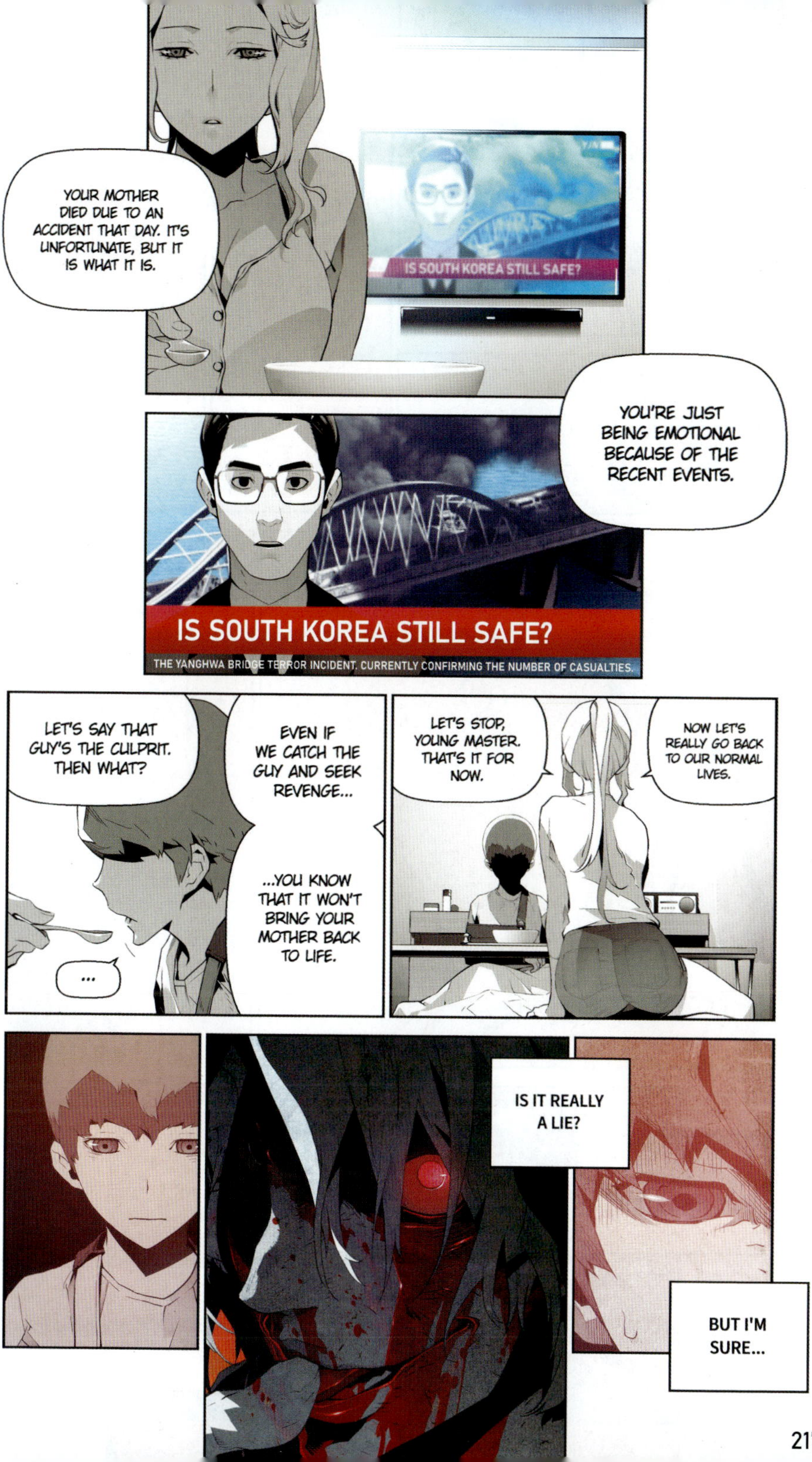
YOUR MOTHER DIED DUE TO AN ACCIDENT THAT DAY. IT'S UNFORTUNATE, BUT IT IS WHAT IT IS.
IS SOUTH KOREA STILL SAFE?
YOU'RE JUST BEING EMOTIONAL BECAUSE OF THE RECENT EVENTS.
IS SOUTH KOREA STILL SAFE?
THE YANGHWA BRIDGE TERROR INCIDENT. CURRENTLY CONFIRMING THE NUMBER OF CASUALTIES.
LET'S SAY THAT GUY'S THE CULPRIT. THEN WHAT?
EVEN IF WE CATCH THE GUY AND SEEK REVENGE...
...YOU KNOW THAT IT WON'T BRING YOUR MOTHER BACK TO LIFE.
...
LET'S STOP, YOUNG MASTER. THAT'S IT FOR NOW.
NOW LET'S REALLY GO BACK TO OUR NORMAL LIVES.
IS IT REALLY A LIE?
BUT I'M SURE...

LILIA, LISTEN.

I...

LILIA...?

...WILL BE PROVIDED AT THE HOSPITAL.

...!

AH... LET ME REPEAT.

SHOCKING NEWS.

YJN HD
YANGHWA BRIDGE TERROR CRIME

SIMSUNG SEOUL HOSPITAL

NEWS FLASH
THE YANGHWA BRIDGE TERROR INCIDENT.
CURRENTLY CONFIRMING THE NUMBER OF CASUALTIES

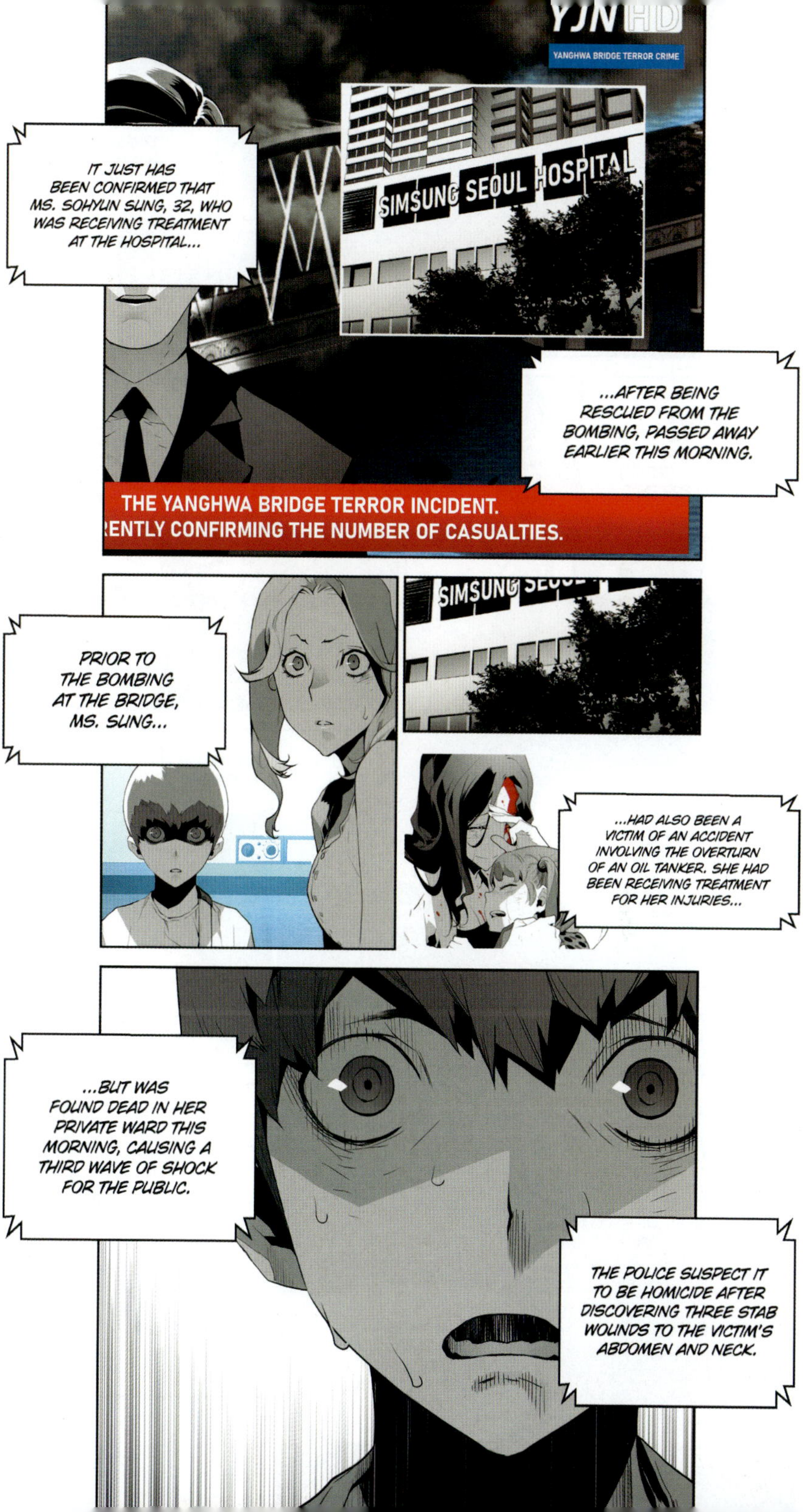
YJN HD
YANGHWA BRIDGE TERROR CRIME
IT JUST HAS BEEN CONFIRMED THAT MS. SOHYUN SUNG, 32, WHO WAS RECEIVING TREATMENT AT THE HOSPITAL...
SIMSUNG SEOUL HOSPITAL
...AFTER BEING RESCUED FROM THE BOMBING, PASSED AWAY EARLIER THIS MORNING.
THE YANGHWA BRIDGE TERROR INCIDENT.
RENTLY CONFIRMING THE NUMBER OF CASUALTIES.
PRIOR TO THE BOMBING AT THE BRIDGE, MS. SUNG...
SIMSUNG
...HAD ALSO BEEN A VICTIM OF AN ACCIDENT INVOLVING THE OVERTURN OF AN OIL TANKER. SHE HAD BEEN RECEIVING TREATMENT FOR HER INJURIES...
...BUT WAS FOUND DEAD IN HER PRIVATE WARD THIS MORNING, CAUSING A THIRD WAVE OF SHOCK FOR THE PUBLIC.
THE POLICE SUSPECT IT TO BE HOMICIDE AFTER DISCOVERING THREE STAB WOUNDS TO THE VICTIM'S ABDOMEN AND NECK.

YOU WENT TO THE HOSPITAL AND KILLED HER? WHY?

BECAUSE I KEEP GETTING MORE PISSED THE MORE I THINK ABOUT IT. I PREPARED SO HARD FOR THAT.

SO YOU RETALIATED? NO MATTER HOW MUCH YOU WERE HIT, DON'T YOU THINK YOU'RE BEING TOO PATHETIC?

BUT IT'S TRUE THAT OUR PLANS GOT RUINED BECAUSE OF THAT PUNK.

I GOT FUCKING MAD, SO I SHOULD AT LEAST BE ALLOWED TO LET IT OUT.

ANYWAY, WHAT DOES OUR SPONSOR THINK ABOUT THE SITUATION?

"GETTING IN OUR WAY?"

SERIOUSLY?

HASN'T IT BECOME KNOWN THAT THE BOMBING AT THE BRIDGE WAS CAUSED BY THAT TERRORIST? THEN THAT'S A WIN FOR YOU.

I THINK THOSE TERRORISTS ARE JUST GOING TO KEEP GETTING IN OUR WAY.

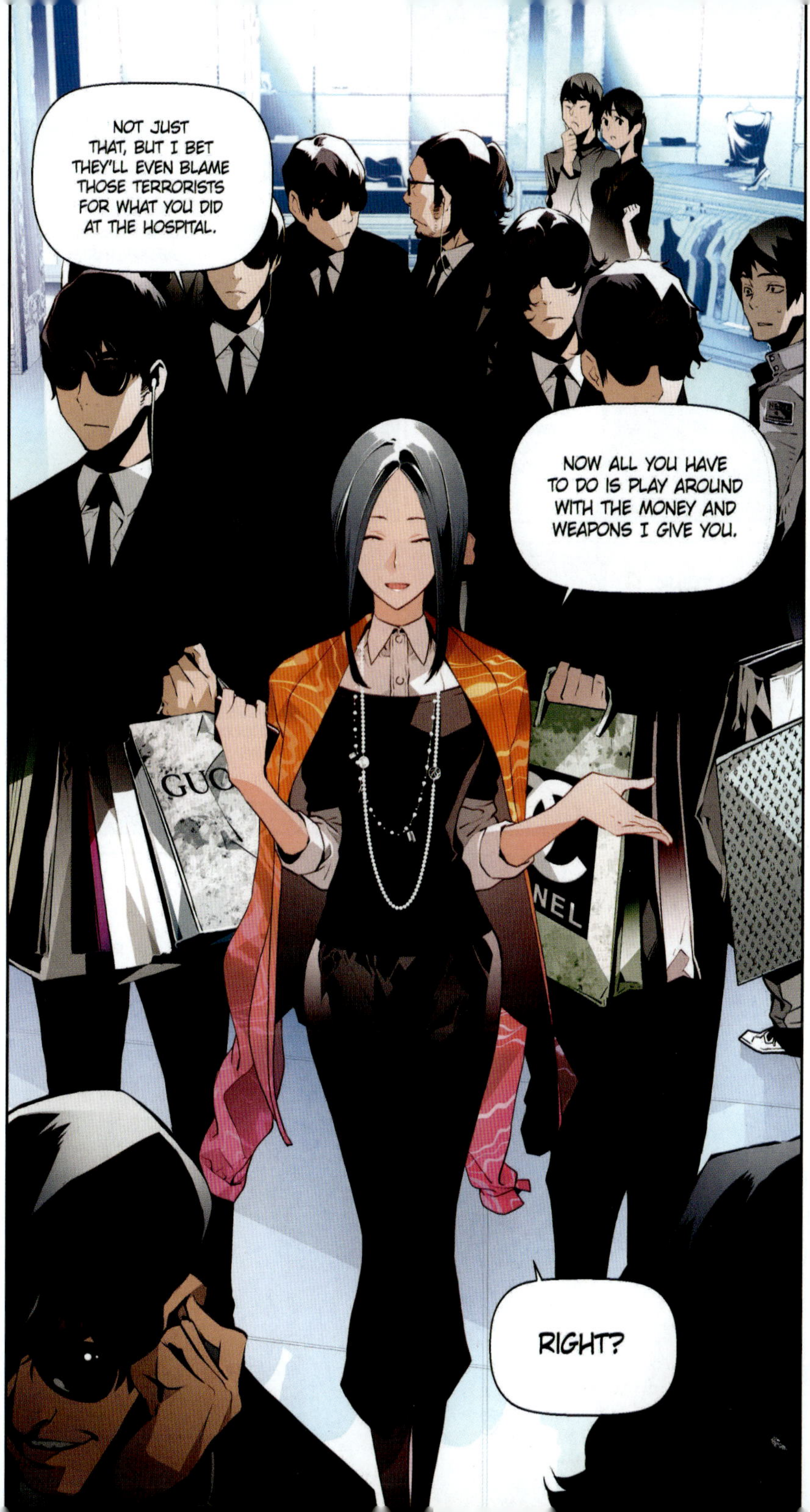
NOT JUST THAT, BUT I BET THEY'LL EVEN BLAME THOSE TERRORISTS FOR WHAT YOU DID AT THE HOSPITAL.
NOW ALL YOU HAVE TO DO IS PLAY AROUND WITH THE MONEY AND WEAPONS I GIVE YOU.
RIGHT?

...

BEEP...

THIS LADY SURE HAS SOME GUTS, TO CHATTER AWAY IN PUBLIC WITHOUT A CARE IN THE WORLD.

THEY'D GO AND LOOK FOR THOSE TERRORISTS IF YOU TOLD THEM ANY OF THE IDENTIFYING INFORMATION YOU KNOW.

WHY DIDN'T YOU SAY ANYTHING ABOUT THAT?

YOU THINK I'M CRAZY?

RUB

IF I TELL HER I GOT BEAT UP BY A WOMAN, THEN THERE'S NO WAY SHE WOULD STILL TRUST ME.

...

HEH

THAT RUSSIAN BITCH...

I'LL MAKE SURE TO FIND YOU AND GET MY REVENGE.

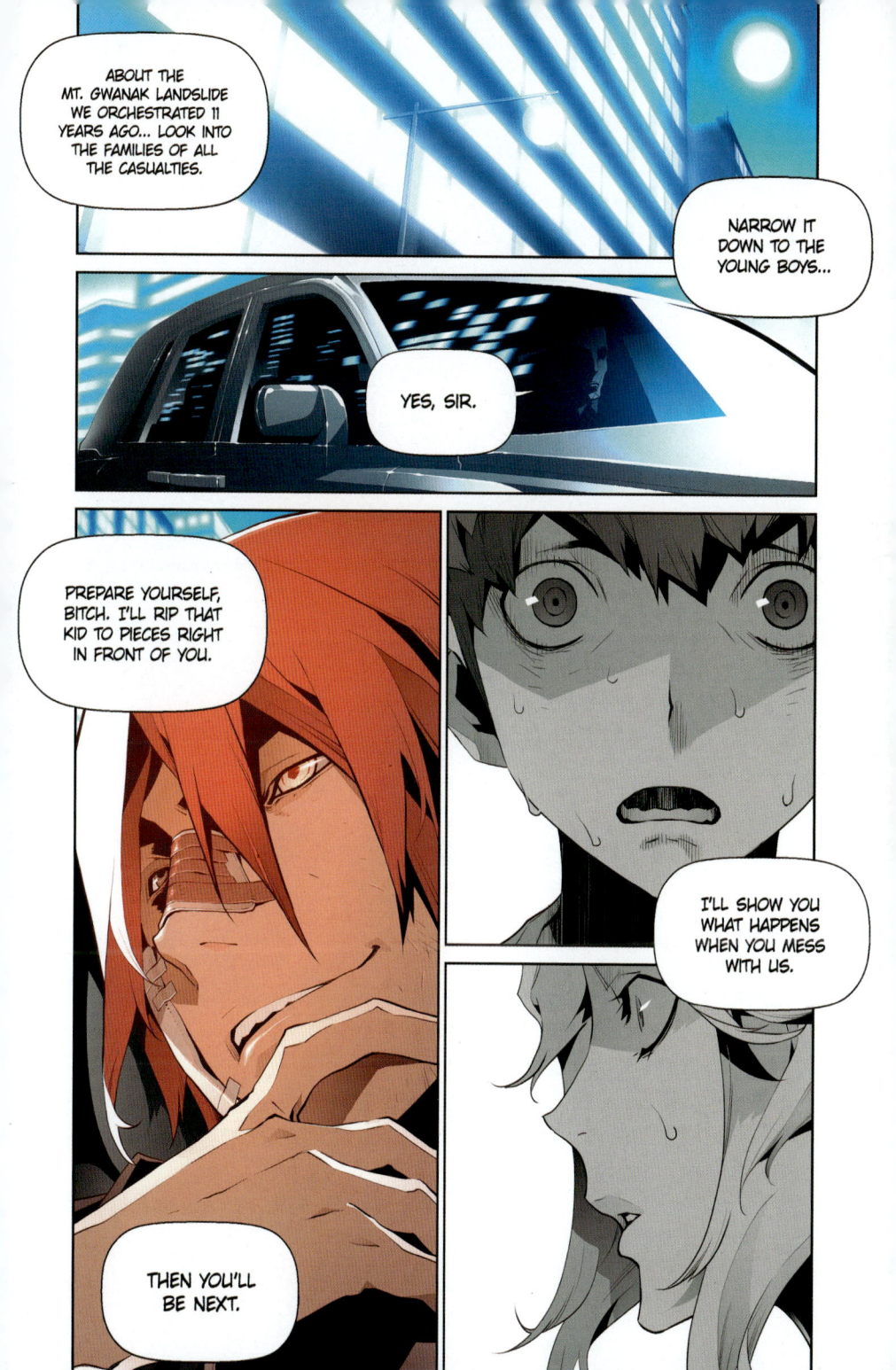

ABOUT THE MT. GWANAK LANDSLIDE WE ORCHESTRATED 11 YEARS AGO... LOOK INTO THE FAMILIES OF ALL THE CASUALTIES.

NARROW IT DOWN TO THE YOUNG BOYS...

YES, SIR.

PREPARE YOURSELF, BITCH. I'LL RIP THAT KID TO PIECES RIGHT IN FRONT OF YOU.

I'LL SHOW YOU WHAT HAPPENS WHEN YOU MESS WITH US.

THEN YOU'LL BE NEXT.

TERROR MAN

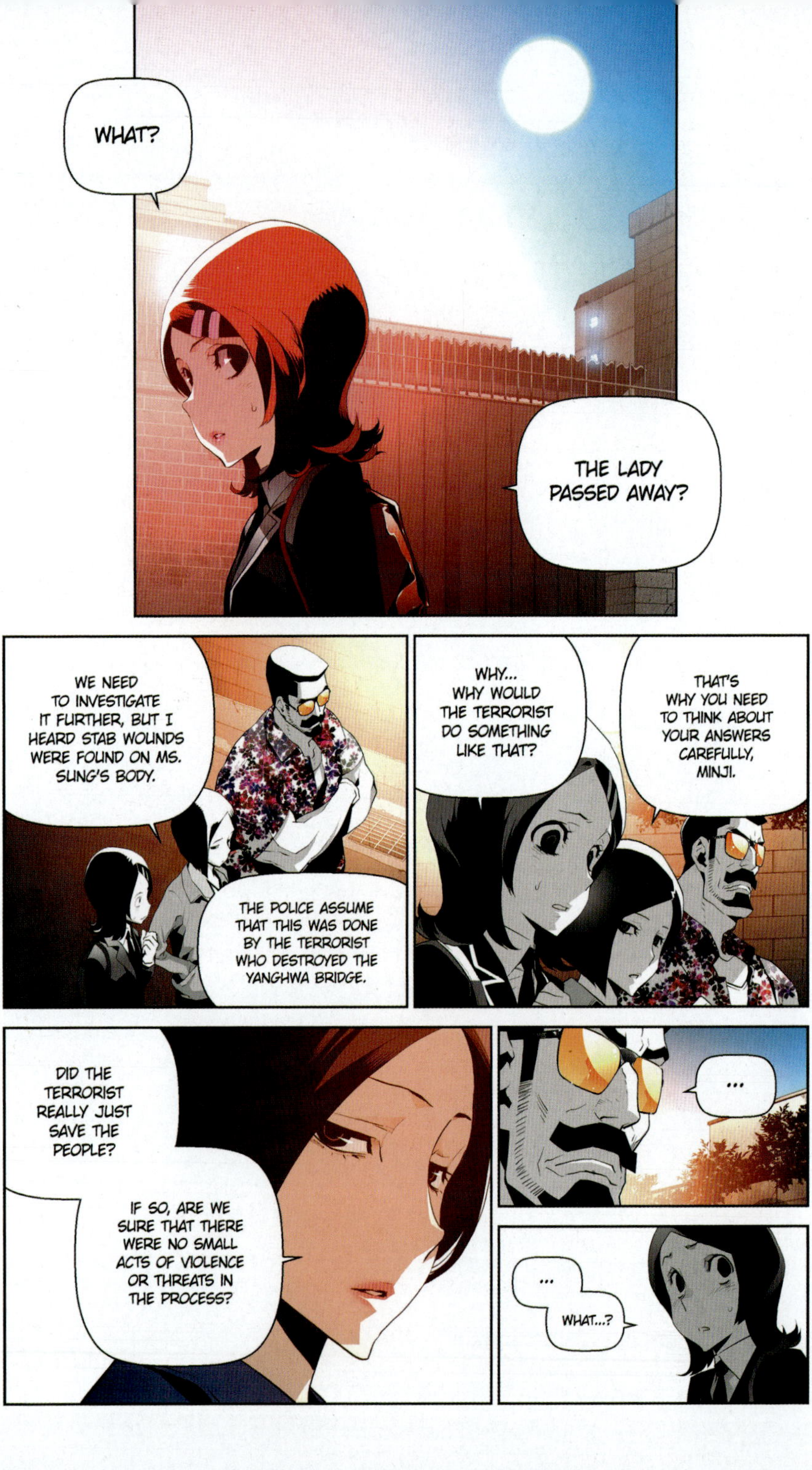
WHAT?
THE LADY PASSED AWAY?
WE NEED TO INVESTIGATE IT FURTHER, BUT I HEARD STAB WOUNDS WERE FOUND ON MS. SUNG'S BODY.
THE POLICE ASSUME THAT THIS WAS DONE BY THE TERRORIST WHO DESTROYED THE YANGHWA BRIDGE.
WHY... WHY WOULD THE TERRORIST DO SOMETHING LIKE THAT?
THAT'S WHY YOU NEED TO THINK ABOUT YOUR ANSWERS CAREFULLY, MINJI.
DID THE TERRORIST REALLY JUST SAVE THE PEOPLE?
IF SO, ARE WE SURE THAT THERE WERE NO SMALL ACTS OF VIOLENCE OR THREATS IN THE PROCESS?
...
...
WHAT...?

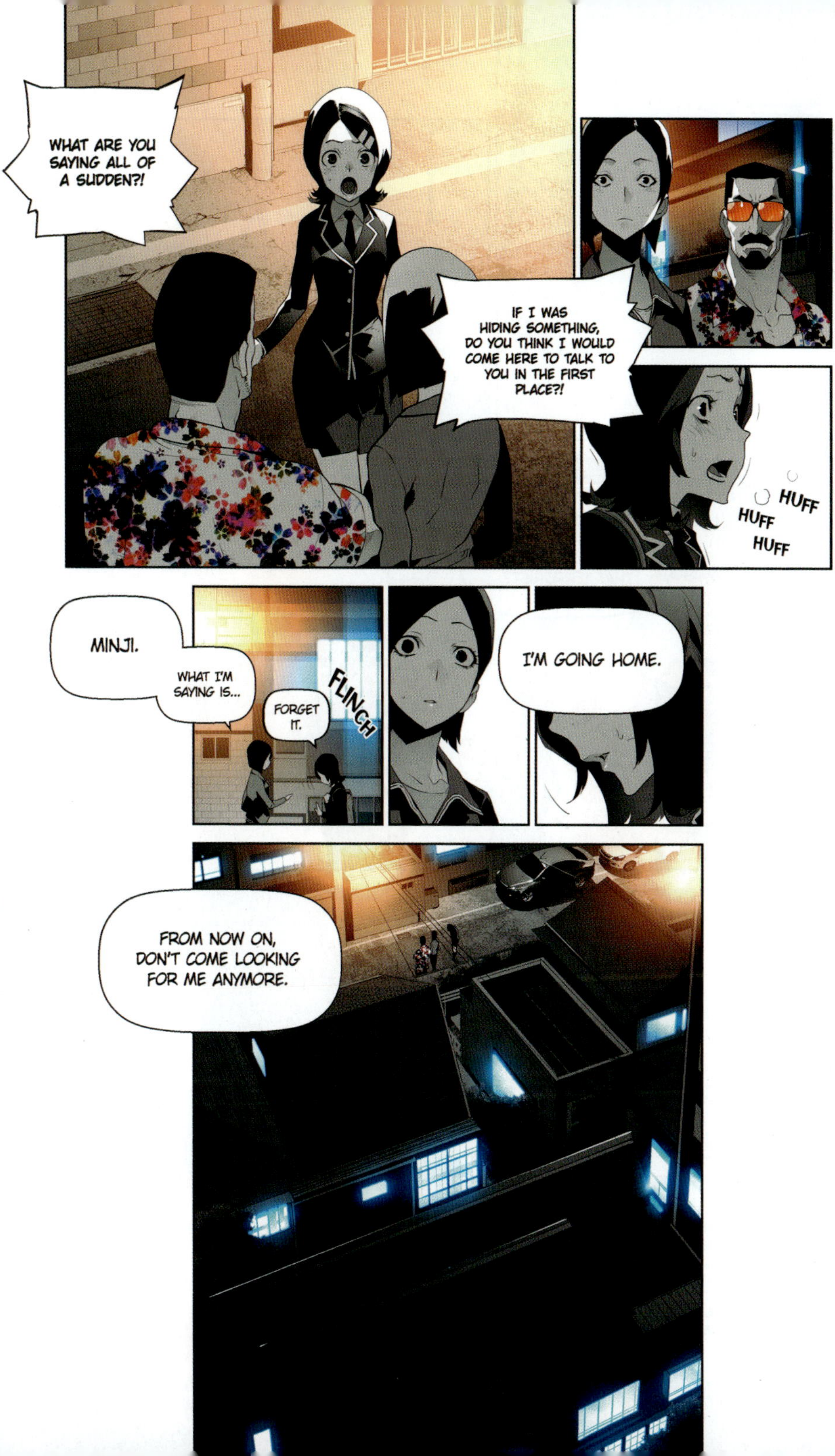
WHAT ARE YOU SAYING ALL OF A SUDDEN?!
IF I WAS HIDING SOMETHING, DO YOU THINK I WOULD COME HERE TO TALK TO YOU IN THE FIRST PLACE?!
HUFF HUFF HUFF
MINJI.
WHAT I'M SAYING IS...
FORGET IT.
FLINCH
I'M GOING HOME.
FROM NOW ON, DON'T COME LOOKING FOR ME ANYMORE.

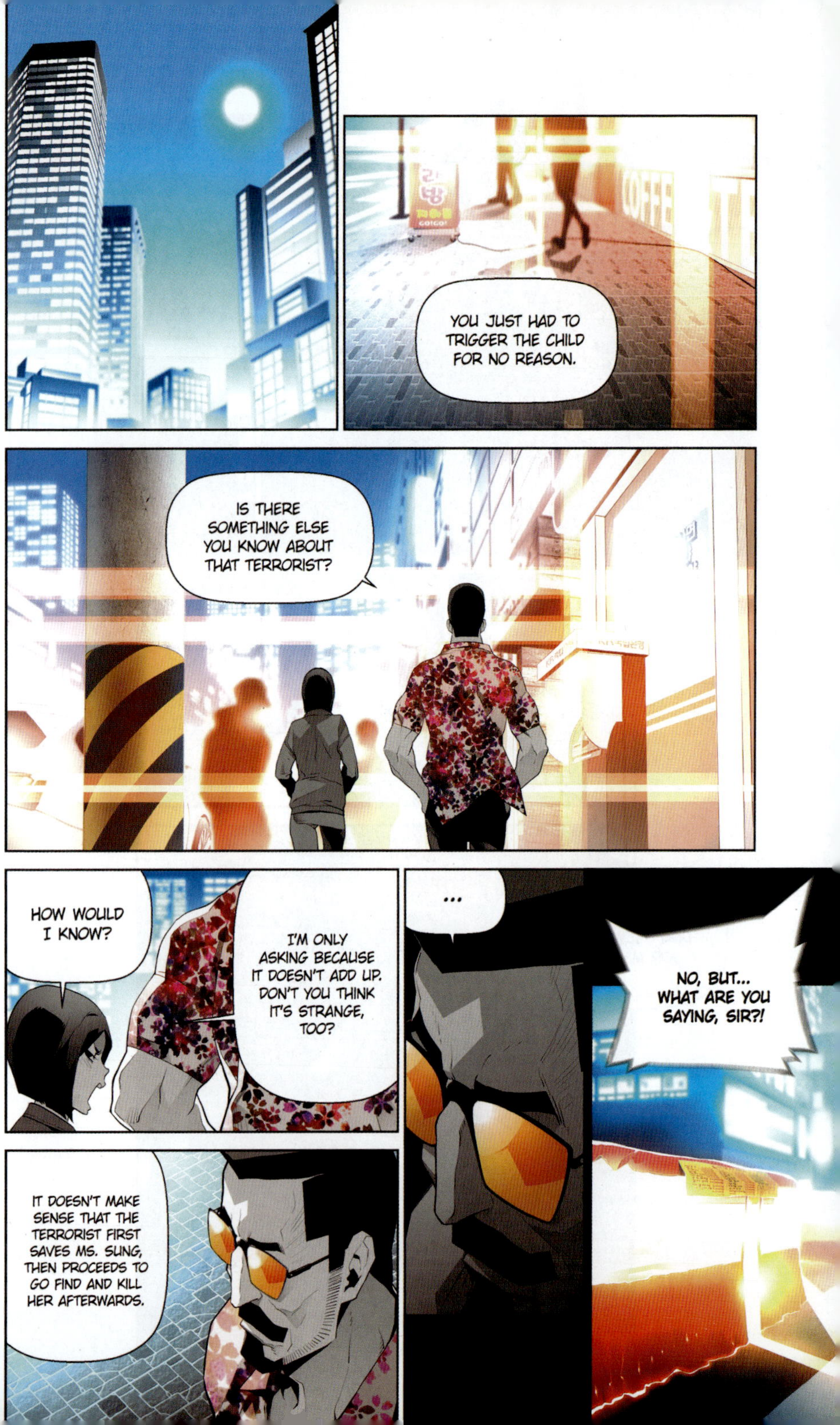
YOU JUST HAD TO TRIGGER THE CHILD FOR NO REASON.
COFFE
IS THERE SOMETHING ELSE YOU KNOW ABOUT THAT TERRORIST?
HOW WOULD I KNOW?
I'M ONLY ASKING BECAUSE IT DOESN'T ADD UP. DON'T YOU THINK IT'S STRANGE, TOO?
...
NO, BUT... WHAT ARE YOU SAYING, SIR?!
IT DOESN'T MAKE SENSE THAT THE TERRORIST FIRST SAVES MS. SUNG, THEN PROCEEDS TO GO FIND AND KILL HER AFTERWARDS.

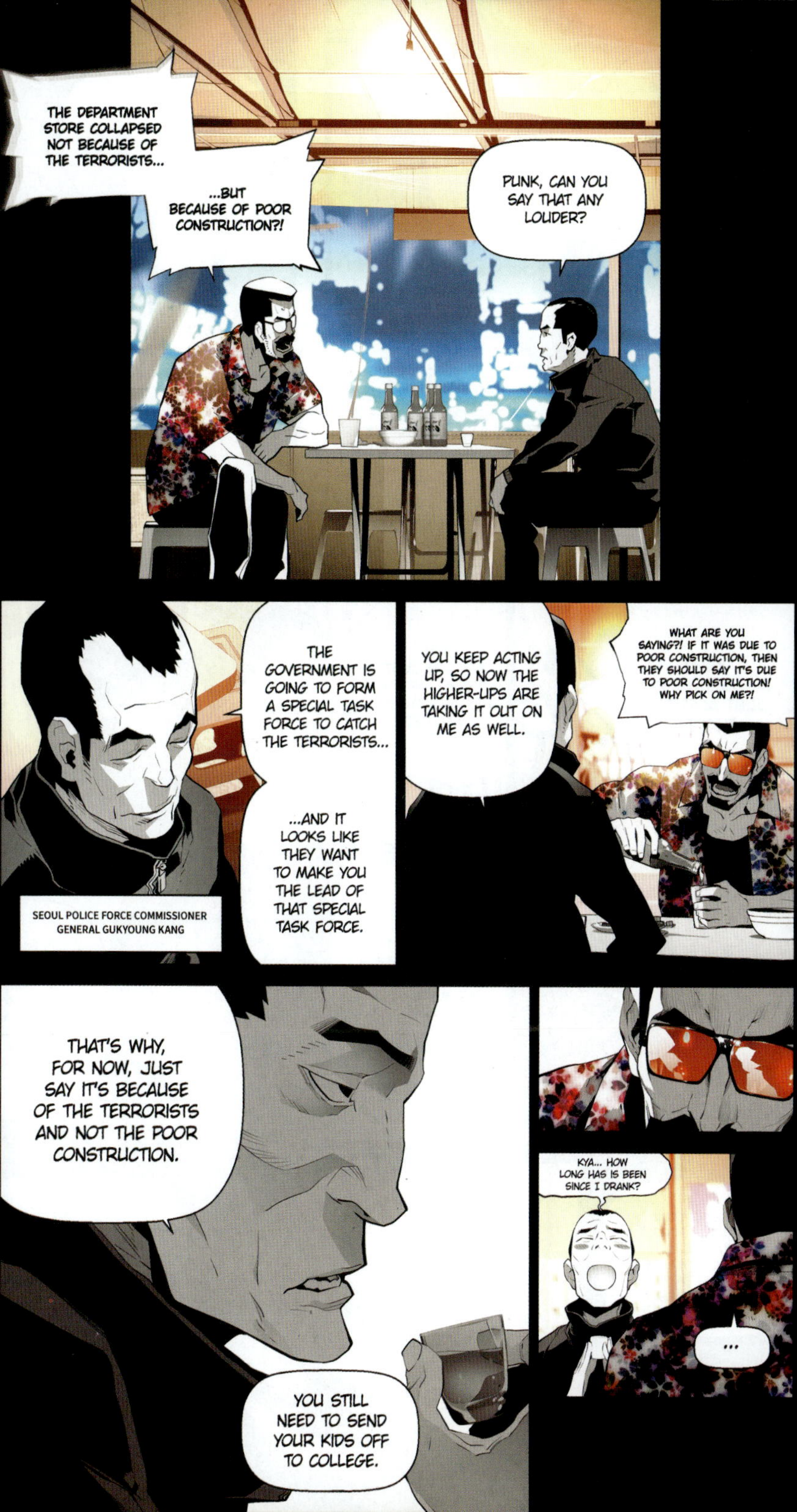
THE DEPARTMENT STORE COLLAPSED NOT BECAUSE OF THE TERRORISTS...
...BUT BECAUSE OF POOR CONSTRUCTION?!
PUNK, CAN YOU SAY THAT ANY LOUDER?
THE GOVERNMENT IS GOING TO FORM A SPECIAL TASK FORCE TO CATCH THE TERRORISTS...
...AND IT LOOKS LIKE THEY WANT TO MAKE YOU THE LEAD OF THAT SPECIAL TASK FORCE.
SEOUL POLICE FORCE COMMISSIONER GENERAL GUKYOUNG KANG
YOU KEEP ACTING UP, SO NOW THE HIGHER-UPS ARE TAKING IT OUT ON ME AS WELL.
WHAT ARE YOU SAYING?! IF IT WAS DUE TO POOR CONSTRUCTION, THEN THEY SHOULD SAY IT'S DUE TO POOR CONSTRUCTION! WHY PICK ON ME?!
THAT'S WHY, FOR NOW, JUST SAY IT'S BECAUSE OF THE TERRORISTS AND NOT THE POOR CONSTRUCTION.
YOU STILL NEED TO SEND YOUR KIDS OFF TO COLLEGE.
KYA... HOW LONG HAS IS BEEN SINCE I DRANK?
...

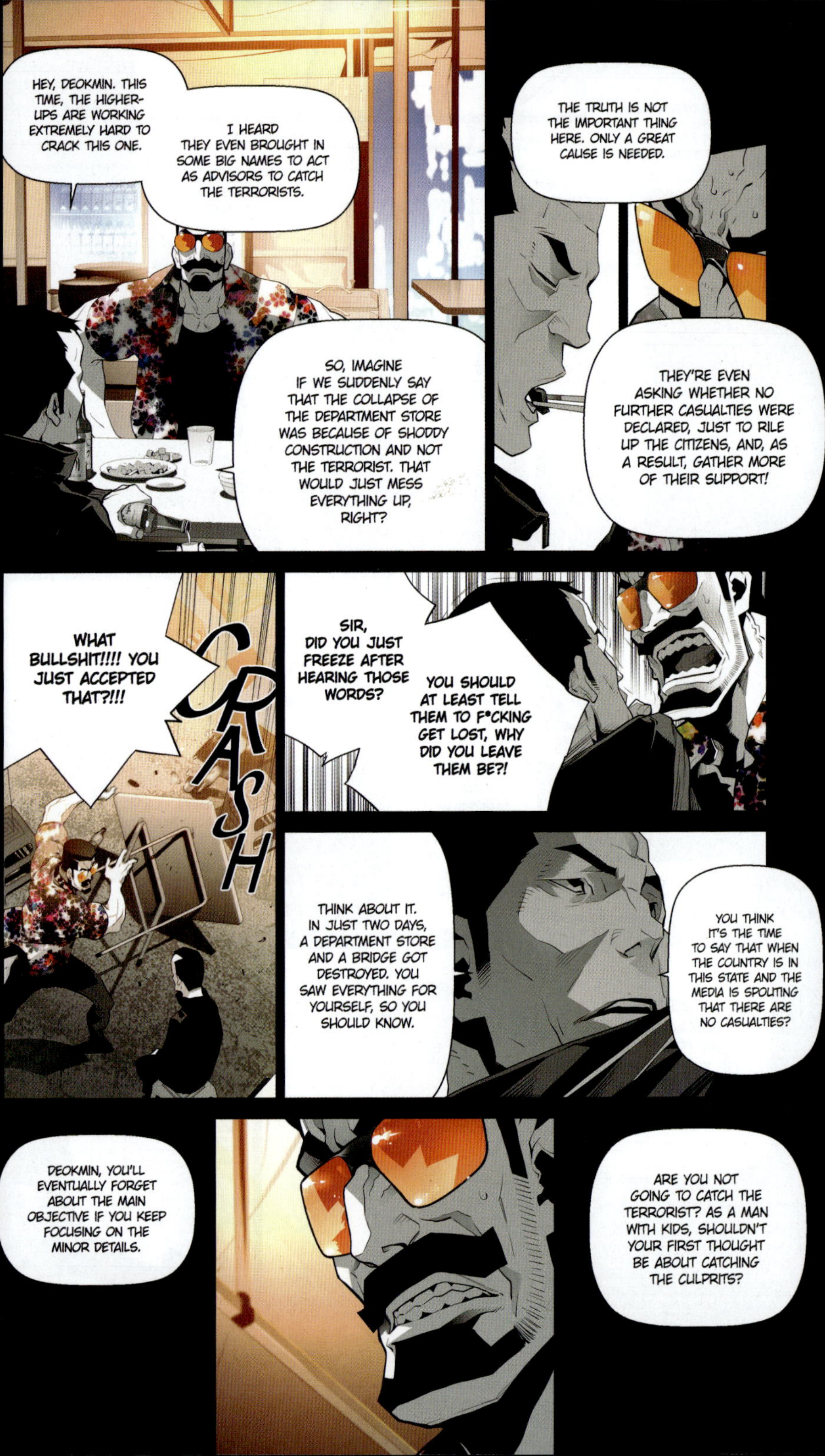

HEY, DEOKMIN. THIS TIME, THE HIGHER-UPS ARE WORKING EXTREMELY HARD TO CRACK THIS ONE.
I HEARD THEY EVEN BROUGHT IN SOME BIG NAMES TO ACT AS ADVISORS TO CATCH THE TERRORISTS.
SO, IMAGINE IF WE SUDDENLY SAY THAT THE COLLAPSE OF THE DEPARTMENT STORE WAS BECAUSE OF SHODDY CONSTRUCTION AND NOT THE TERRORIST. THAT WOULD JUST MESS EVERYTHING UP, RIGHT?
THE TRUTH IS NOT THE IMPORTANT THING HERE. ONLY A GREAT CAUSE IS NEEDED.
THEY'RE EVEN ASKING WHETHER NO FURTHER CASUALTIES WERE DECLARED, JUST TO RILE UP THE CITIZENS, AND, AS A RESULT, GATHER MORE OF THEIR SUPPORT!
WHAT BULLSHIT!!!! YOU JUST ACCEPTED THAT?!!!
CRASH
SIR, DID YOU JUST FREEZE AFTER HEARING THOSE WORDS?
YOU SHOULD AT LEAST TELL THEM TO F*CKING GET LOST, WHY DID YOU LEAVE THEM BE?!
THINK ABOUT IT. IN JUST TWO DAYS, A DEPARTMENT STORE AND A BRIDGE GOT DESTROYED. YOU SAW EVERYTHING FOR YOURSELF, SO YOU SHOULD KNOW.
YOU THINK IT'S THE TIME TO SAY THAT WHEN THE COUNTRY IS IN THIS STATE AND THE MEDIA IS SPOUTING THAT THERE ARE NO CASUALTIES?
DEOKMIN, YOU'LL EVENTUALLY FORGET ABOUT THE MAIN OBJECTIVE IF YOU KEEP FOCUSING ON THE MINOR DETAILS.
ARE YOU NOT GOING TO CATCH THE TERRORIST? AS A MAN WITH KIDS, SHOULDN'T YOUR FIRST THOUGHT BE ABOUT CATCHING THE CULPRITS?

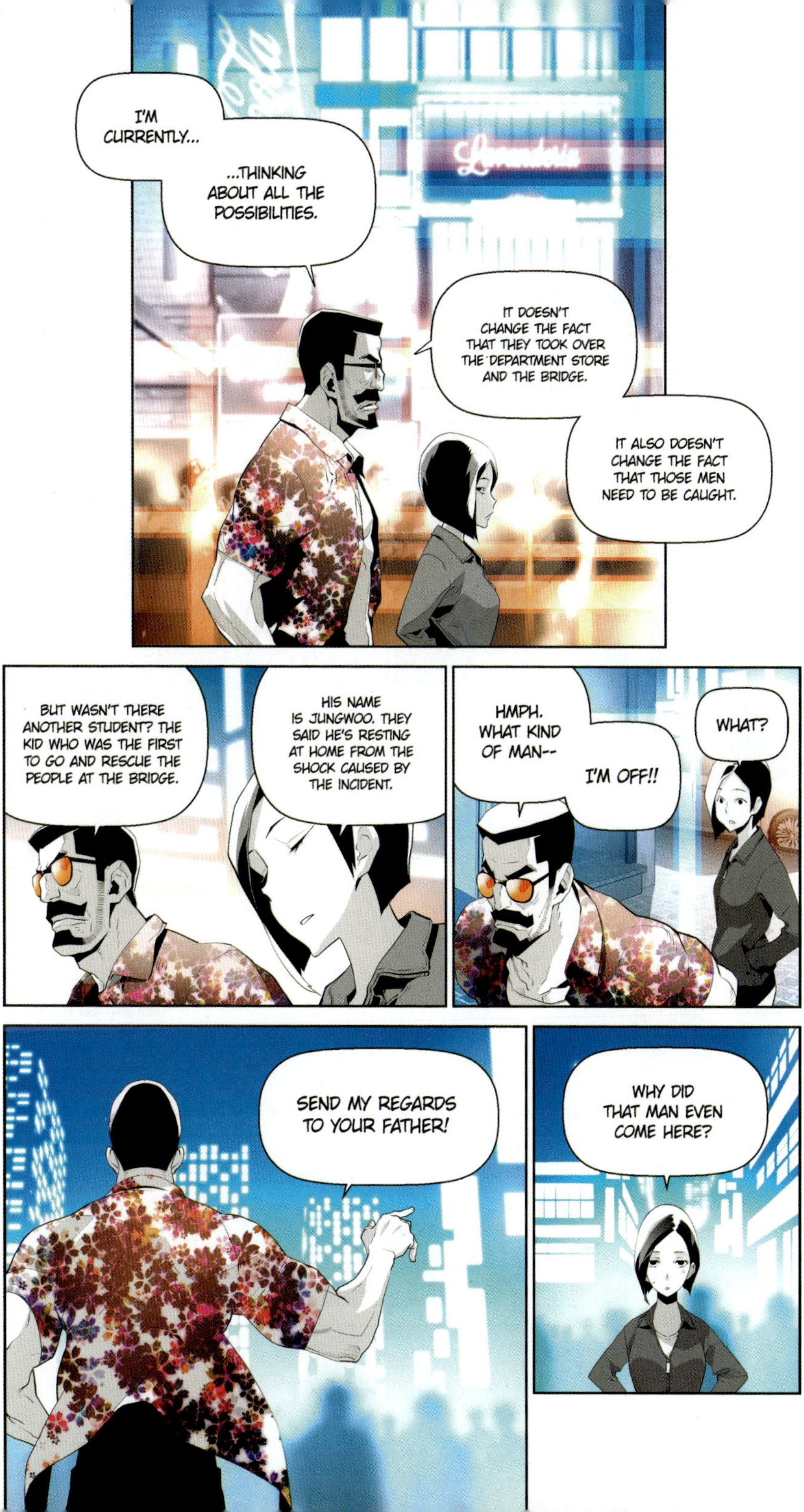
I'M CURRENTLY...
...THINKING ABOUT ALL THE POSSIBILITIES.
IT DOESN'T CHANGE THE FACT THAT THEY TOOK OVER THE DEPARTMENT STORE AND THE BRIDGE.
IT ALSO DOESN'T CHANGE THE FACT THAT THOSE MEN NEED TO BE CAUGHT.
BUT WASN'T THERE ANOTHER STUDENT? THE KID WHO WAS THE FIRST TO GO AND RESCUE THE PEOPLE AT THE BRIDGE.
HIS NAME IS JUNGWOO. THEY SAID HE'S RESTING AT HOME FROM THE SHOCK CAUSED BY THE INCIDENT.
HMPH. WHAT KIND OF MAN--
I'M OFF!!
WHAT?
SEND MY REGARDS TO YOUR FATHER!
WHY DID THAT MAN EVEN COME HERE?

I REALLY DID THE BEST THAT I COULD.

SAVING A PERSON FROM A FALLING CAR, EVACUATING PEOPLE FROM A COLLAPSING BRIDGE...

I ALREADY DID WHAT I CAN, SO NOW I CAN JUST SAY IT CAN'T BE HELPED.

BUT... LILIA.

DO YOU KNOW WHO I FIRST THOUGHT OF WHEN I HEARD ABOUT THAT LADY'S DEATH?

HER DAUGHTER...

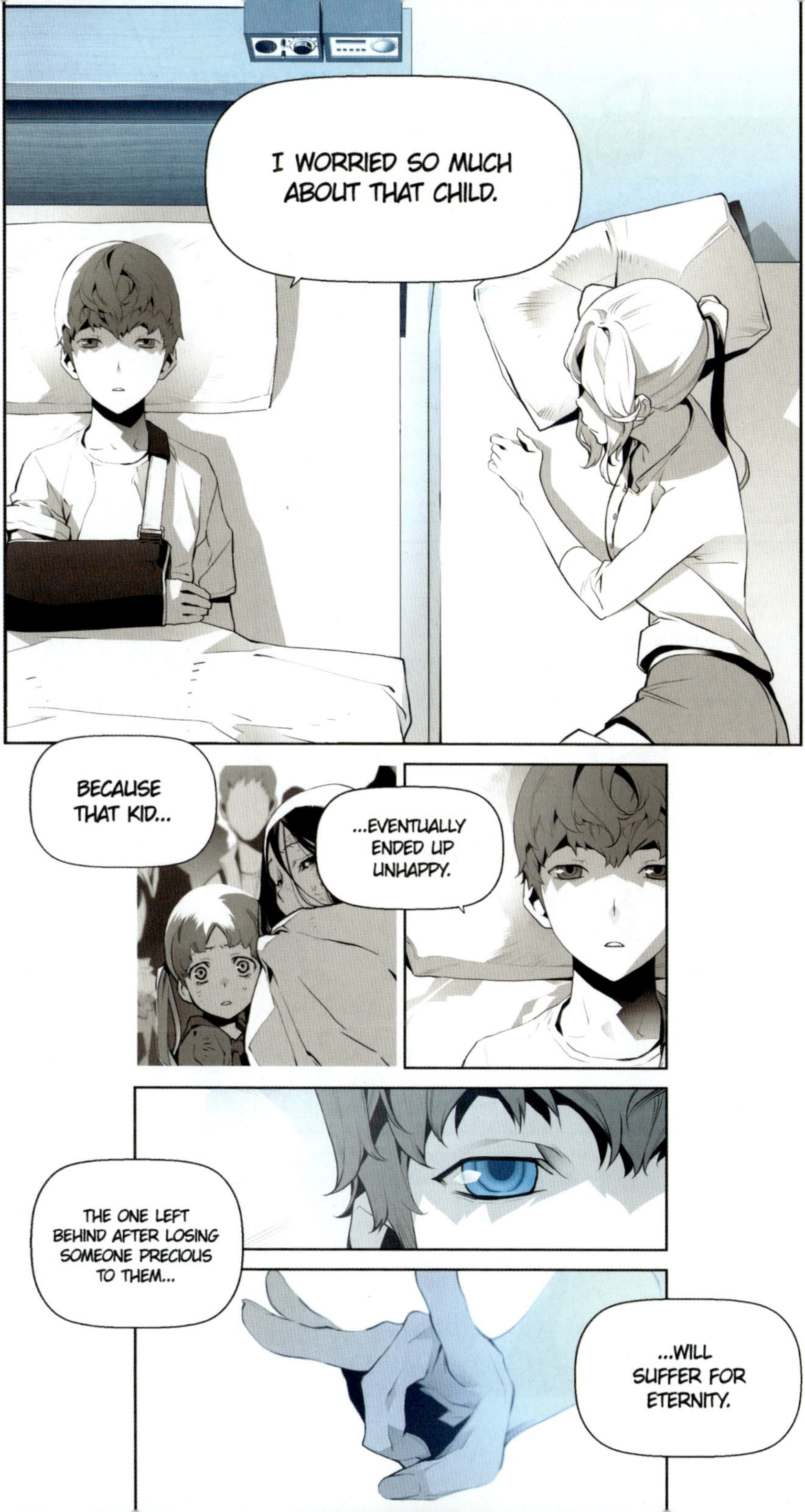
I WORRIED SO MUCH ABOUT THAT CHILD.
BECAUSE THAT KID...
...EVENTUALLY ENDED UP UNHAPPY.
THE ONE LEFT BEHIND AFTER LOSING SOMEONE PRECIOUS TO THEM...
...WILL SUFFER FOR ETERNITY.

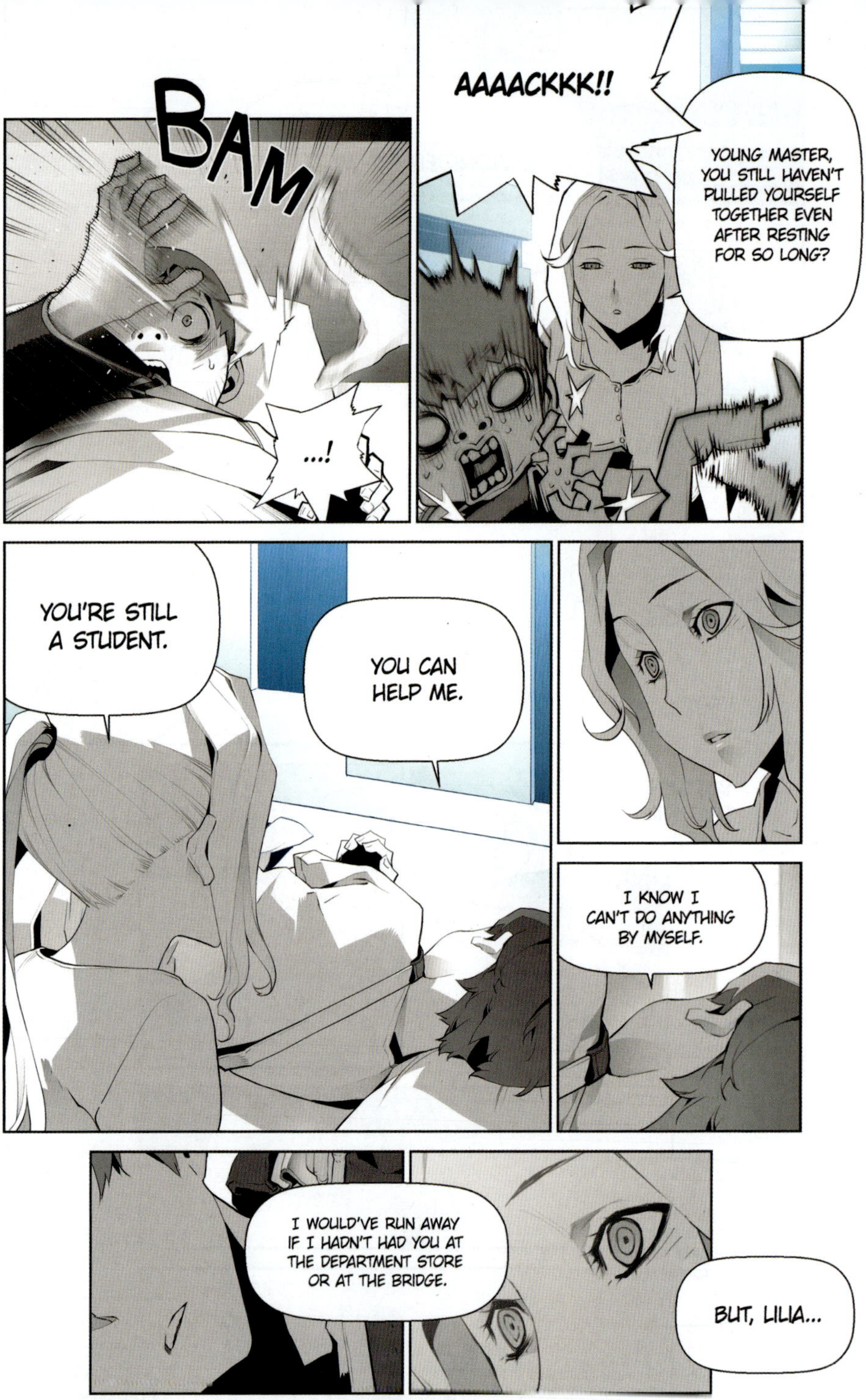
BAM
...!
AAAACKKK!!
YOUNG MASTER, YOU STILL HAVEN'T PULLED YOURSELF TOGETHER EVEN AFTER RESTING FOR SO LONG?
YOU'RE STILL A STUDENT.
YOU CAN HELP ME.
I KNOW I CAN'T DO ANYTHING BY MYSELF.
I WOULD'VE RUN AWAY IF I HADN'T HAD YOU AT THE DEPARTMENT STORE OR AT THE BRIDGE.
BUT, LILIA...

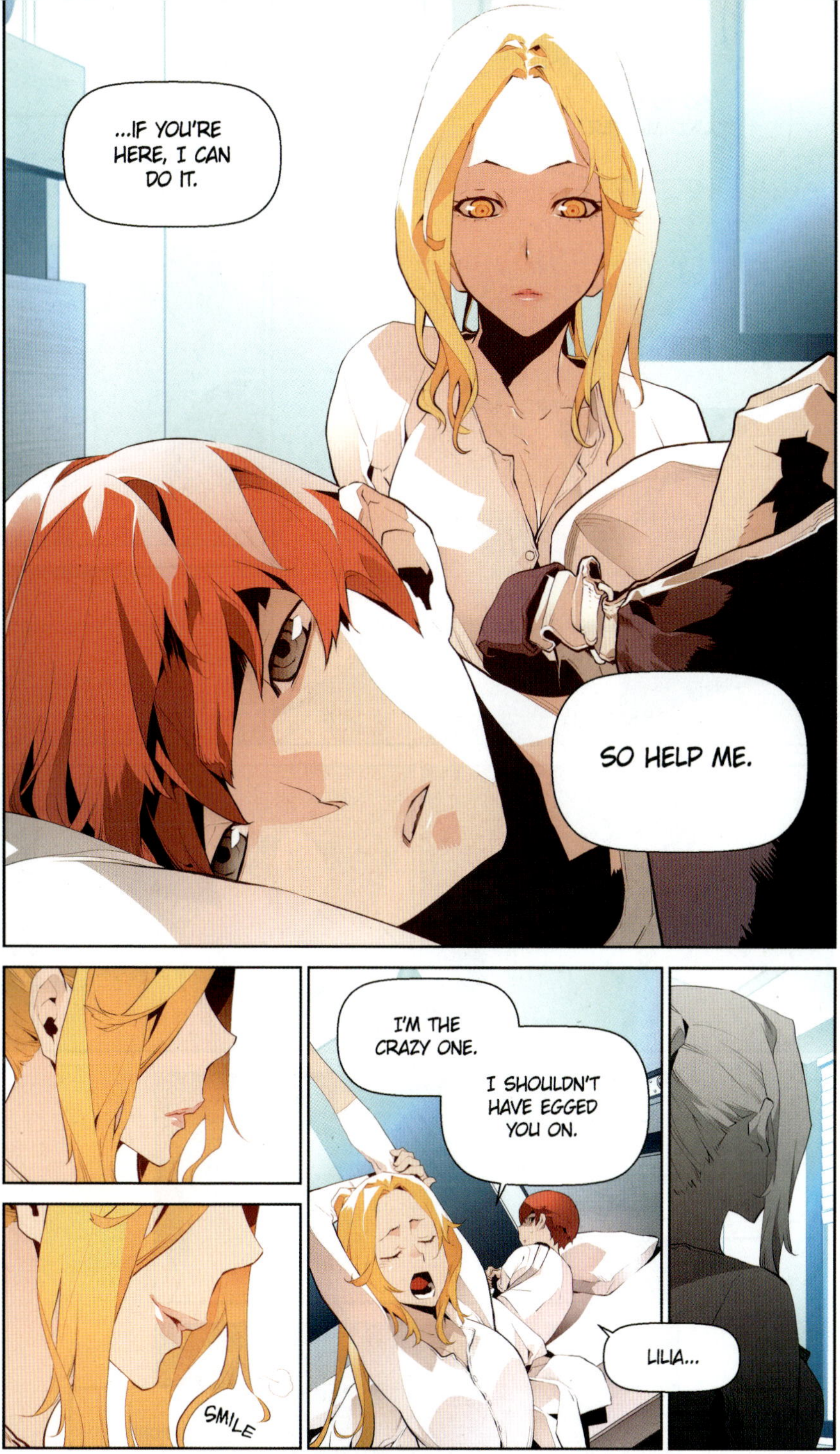

...IF YOU'RE HERE, I CAN DO IT.
SO HELP ME.
SMILE
I'M THE CRAZY ONE.
I SHOULDN'T HAVE EGGED YOU ON.
LILIA...

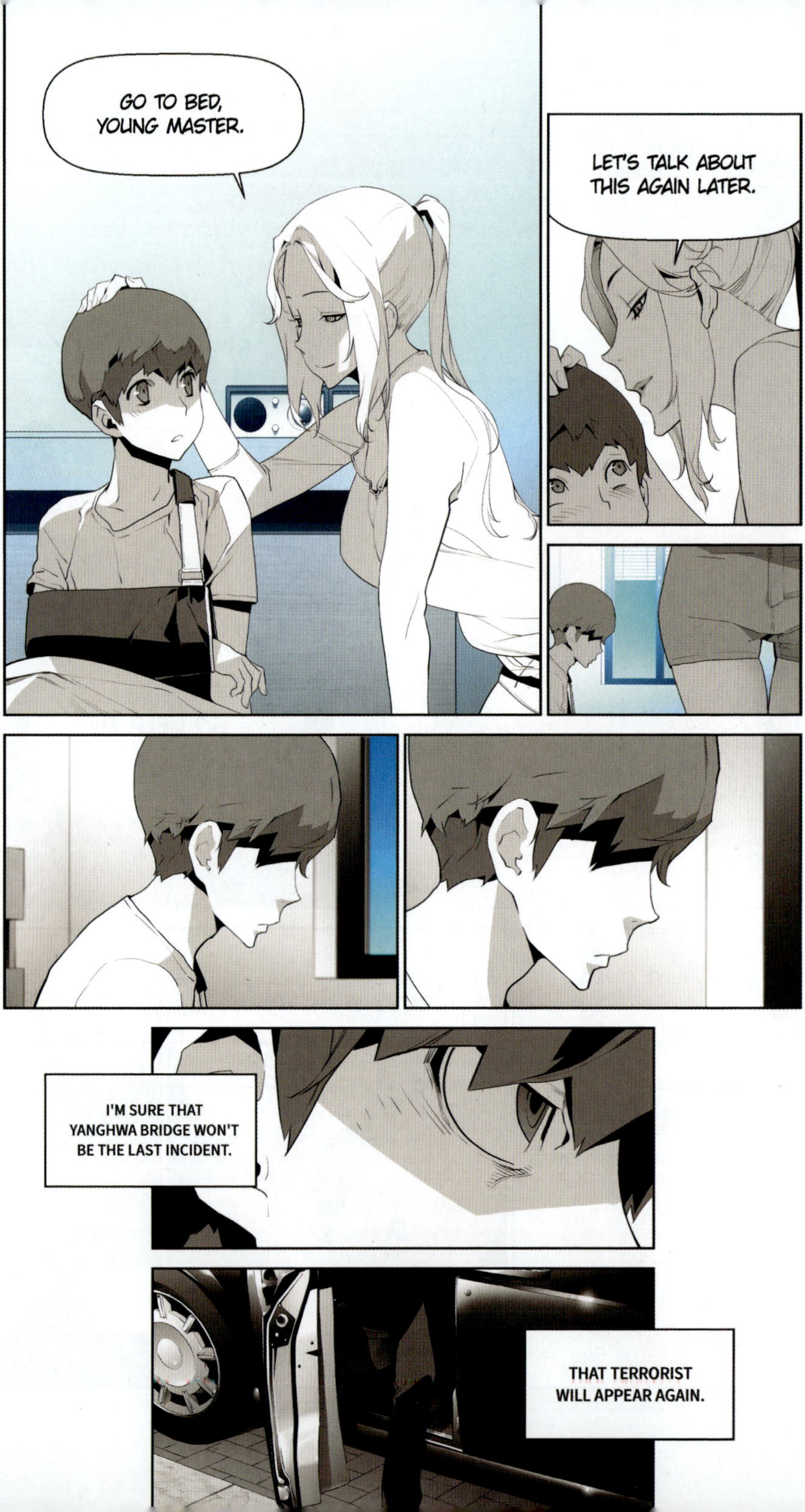
GO TO BED,
YOUNG MASTER.
LET'S TALK ABOUT
THIS AGAIN LATER.
I'M SURE THAT
YANGHWA BRIDGE WON'T
BE THE LAST INCIDENT.
THAT TERRORIST
WILL APPEAR AGAIN.

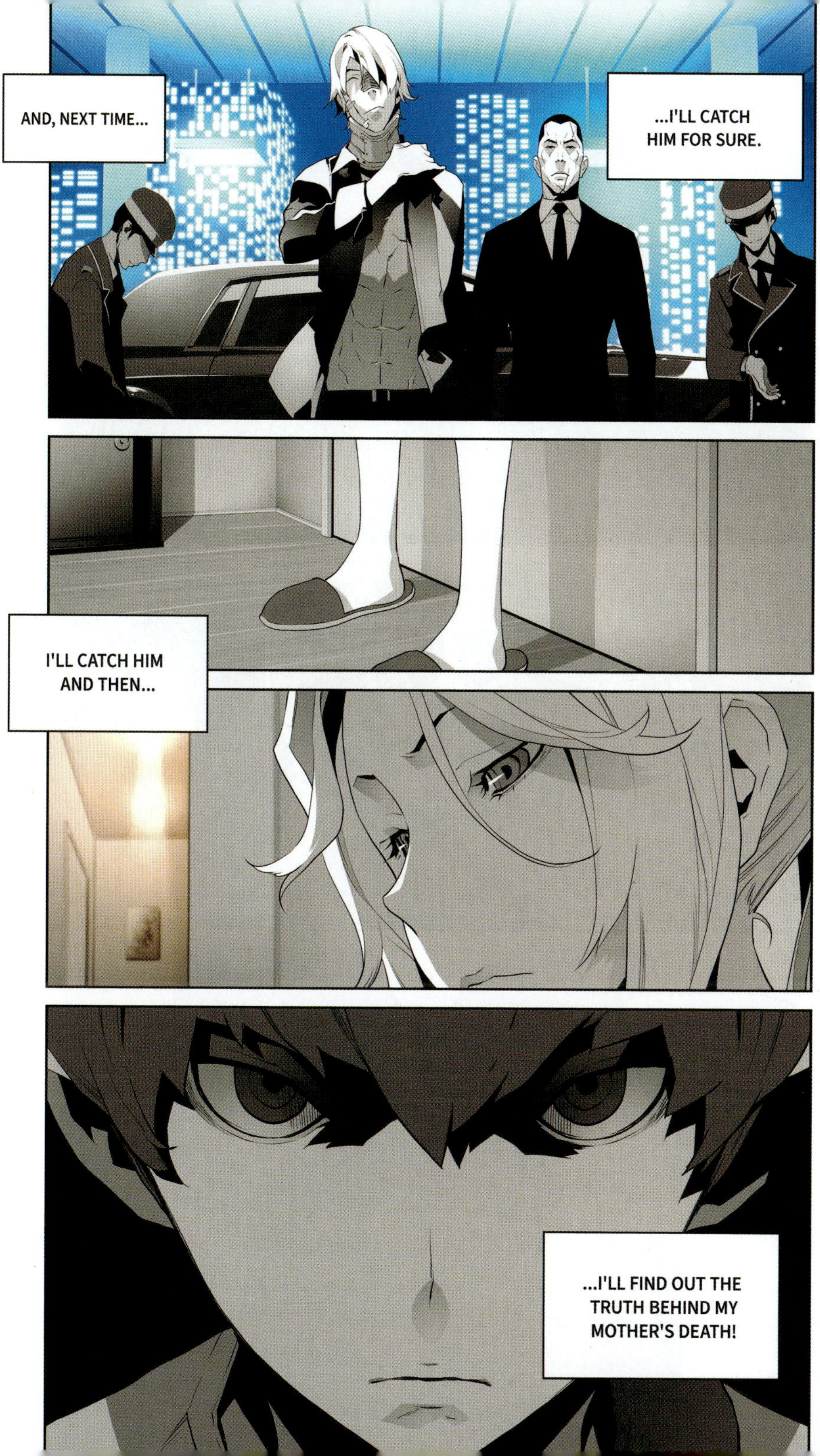
AND, NEXT TIME...
...I'LL CATCH HIM FOR SURE.
I'LL CATCH HIM AND THEN...
...I'LL FIND OUT THE TRUTH BEHIND MY MOTHER'S DEATH!

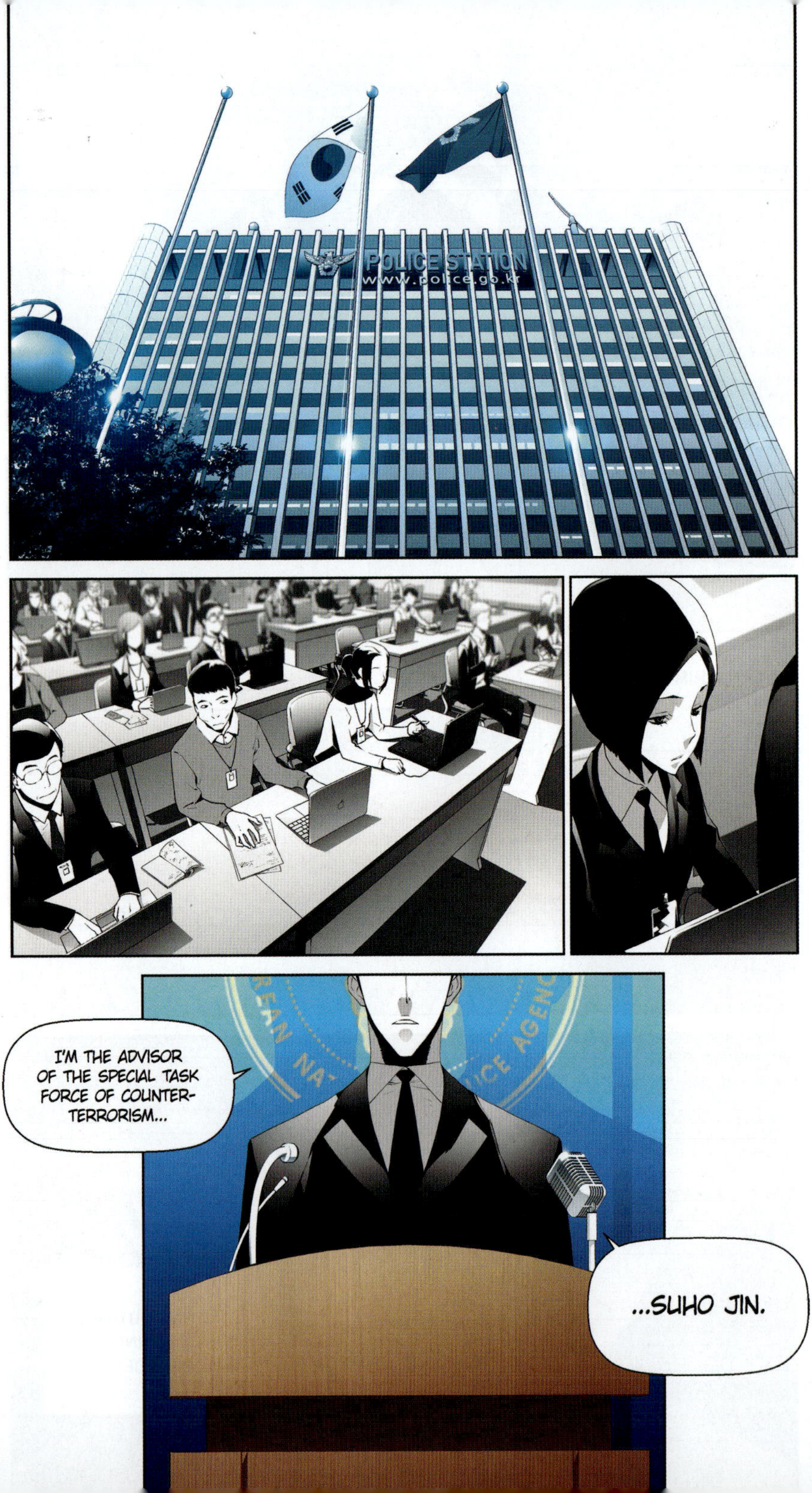
POLICE STATION
www.police.go.kr
I'M THE ADVISOR OF THE SPECIAL TASK FORCE OF COUNTER-TERRORISM...
...SUHO JIN.

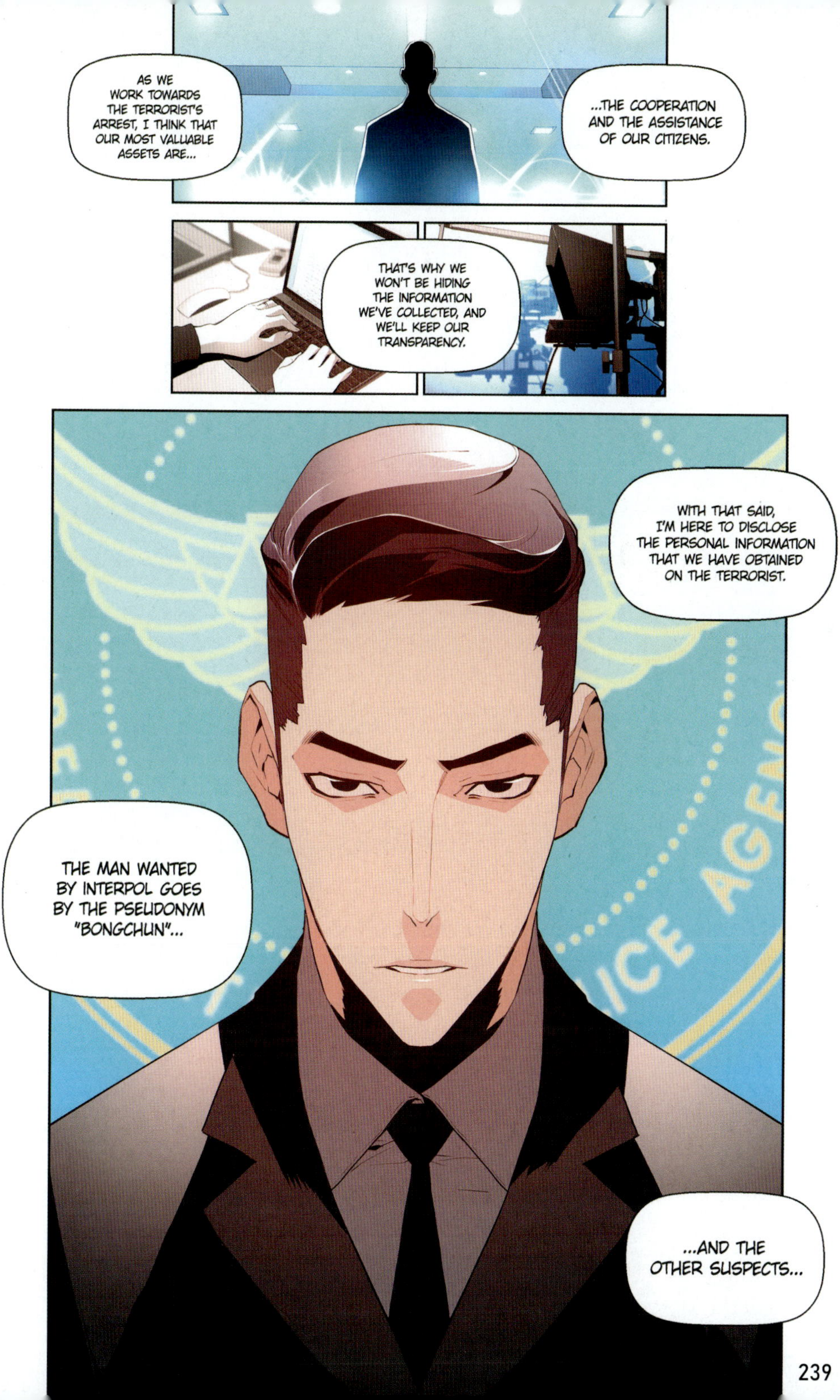
AS WE WORK TOWARDS THE TERRORIST'S ARREST, I THINK THAT OUR MOST VALUABLE ASSETS ARE...
...THE COOPERATION AND THE ASSISTANCE OF OUR CITIZENS.
THAT'S WHY WE WON'T BE HIDING THE INFORMATION WE'VE COLLECTED, AND WE'LL KEEP OUR TRANSPARENCY.
WITH THAT SAID, I'M HERE TO DISCLOSE THE PERSONAL INFORMATION THAT WE HAVE OBTAINED ON THE TERRORIST.
THE MAN WANTED BY INTERPOL GOES BY THE PSEUDONYM "BONGCHUN"...
...AND THE OTHER SUSPECTS...

TERROR MAN

YAAAWN...

WHAT ARE YOU DOING UP SO EARLY? GOING HOME?

YEAH, I NEED TO PACK UP AND GO. I'M SCARED I MIGHT GET INVOLVED WITH CERTAIN ACTIVITIES IF I STAY HERE, Y'KNOW.

TRUDGE TRUDGE

ARE YOU A COWARD? STOP ACTING LIKE THAT AND STAY FOR A LITTLE LONGER. I STILL HAVE A LOT OF FAVORS TO ASK OF YOU. I PAY YOU WELL ENOUGH, DON'T I?

THE MONEY'S NOT THE ISSUE HERE, WOMAN.

A SPECIAL TASK FORCE HAS BEEN FORMED TO CATCH THE TERRORISTS.

LOOK AT THE TV. THEY'RE EVEN HOLDIN' PRESS CONFERENCES AND ALL THAT STUFF.

PRESS

THIS IS THE ADVISOR OF THE SPECIAL TASK FORCE, SUHO JIN.

242

ALTHOUGH OUR SPECIAL TEAM IS FULL OF EXPERIENCED VETERANS...

THAT'S WHY WE WON'T KEEP INFORMATION WE HAVE COLLECTED TO OURSELVES AND WILL KEEP OUR TRANSPARENCY.

...I STILL BELIEVE THE COOPERATION OF OUR CITIZENS IS THE MOST IMPORTANT HELP.

FIRST OF ALL...

THOSE EYES ARE DISGUSTING.

WITH THAT, I AM HERE TO DISCLOSE THE PERSONAL INFORMATION THAT WE'VE OBTAINED ON THE TERRORISTS.

DU DUN

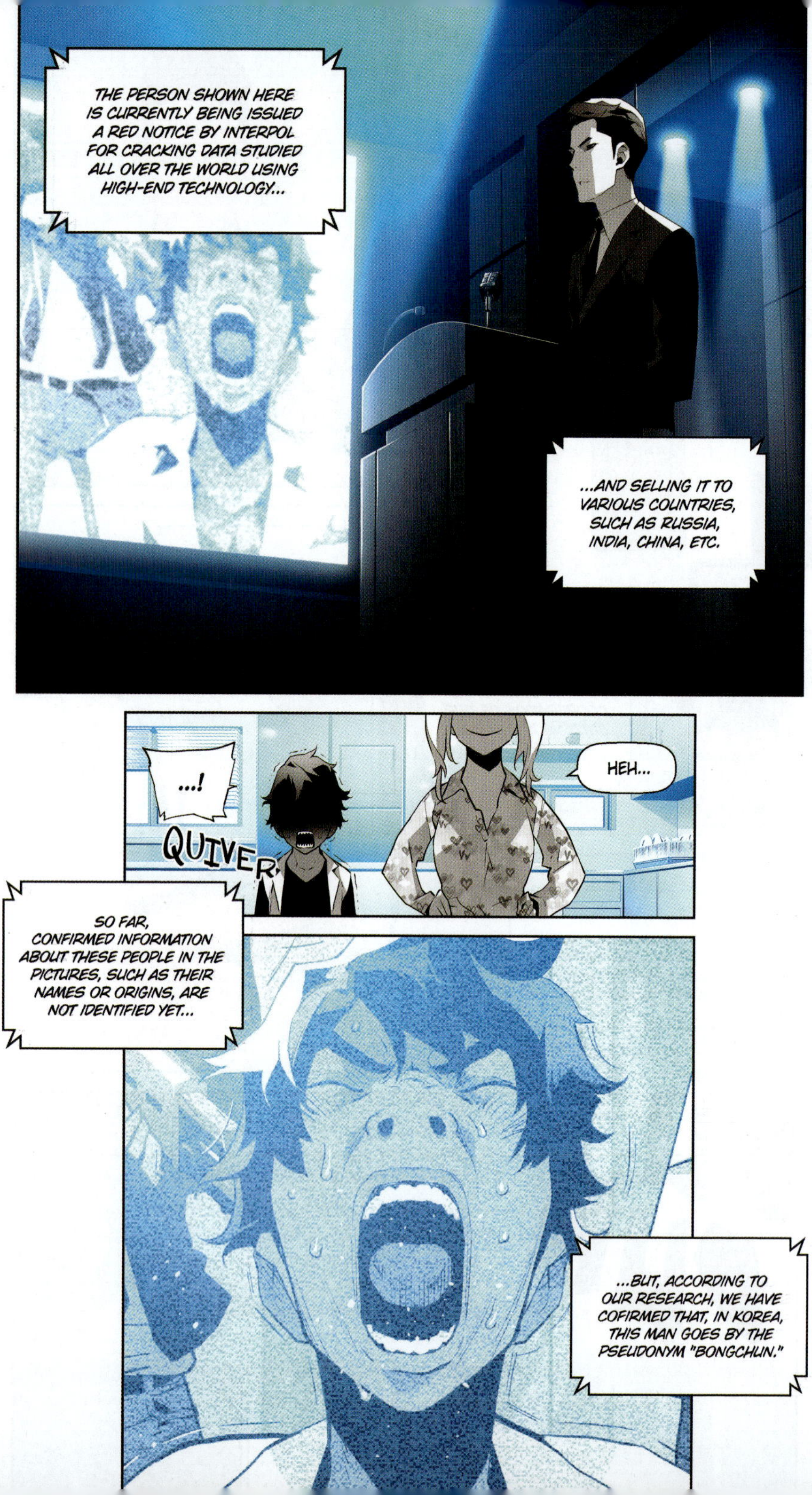
THE PERSON SHOWN HERE IS CURRENTLY BEING ISSUED A RED NOTICE BY INTERPOL FOR CRACKING DATA STUDIED ALL OVER THE WORLD USING HIGH-END TECHNOLOGY...
...AND SELLING IT TO VARIOUS COUNTRIES, SUCH AS RUSSIA, INDIA, CHINA, ETC.
...!
QUIVER
HEH...
SO FAR, CONFIRMED INFORMATION ABOUT THESE PEOPLE IN THE PICTURES, SUCH AS THEIR NAMES OR ORIGINS, ARE NOT IDENTIFIED YET...
...BUT, ACCORDING TO OUR RESEARCH, WE HAVE COFIRMED THAT, IN KOREA, THIS MAN GOES BY THE PSEUDONYM "BONGCHUN."

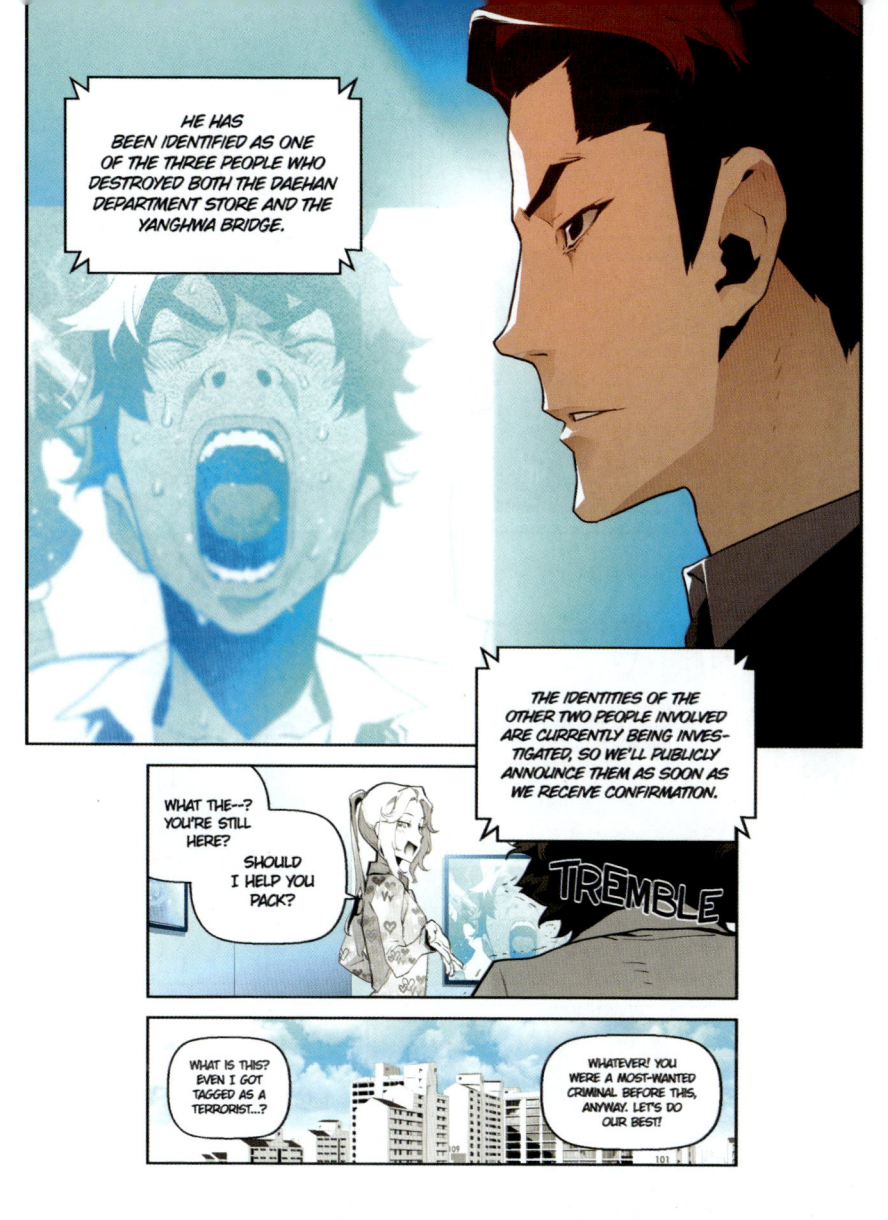

HE HAS BEEN IDENTIFIED AS ONE OF THE THREE PEOPLE WHO DESTROYED BOTH THE DAEHAN DEPARTMENT STORE AND THE YANGHWA BRIDGE.

THE IDENTITIES OF THE OTHER TWO PEOPLE INVOLVED ARE CURRENTLY BEING INVESTIGATED, SO WE'LL PUBLICLY ANNOUNCE THEM AS SOON AS WE RECEIVE CONFIRMATION.

WHAT THE--? YOU'RE STILL HERE?

SHOULD I HELP YOU PACK?

TREMBLE

WHAT IS THIS? EVEN I GOT TAGGED AS A TERRORIST...?

WHATEVER! YOU WERE A MOST-WANTED CRIMINAL BEFORE THIS, ANYWAY. LET'S DO OUR BEST!

HEY, MINHYUK.

?

245

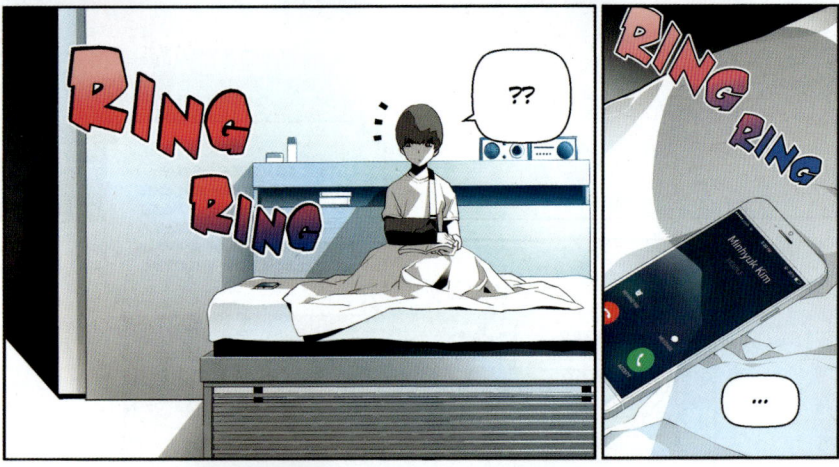

YOU SAID YOU'VE BEEN FRIENDS WITH JUNGWOO SINCE KINDERGARTEN, DIDN'T YOU? GIVE ME HIS NUMBER.

HOW MUCH ARE YOU PAYING FOR IT?

GIVE IT TO ME BEFORE YOU GET SMACKED.

ALRIGHT, JUST WAIT. HE SAID HE'S AT HOME RESTING, RIGHT?

GLARE

RING RING

??

RING RING

Minhyuk Kim

...

HELLO?

YOU'RE NOT COMING TO SCHOOL TODAY? WHEN ARE YOU COMING?

HERE.

YOU SURE YOU'RE FRIENDS? WHAT KIND OF CONVERSATION WAS THAT?

IN TWO TO THREE WEEKS? ALRIGHT, SEE YOU THEN.

TAKE CARE OF YOURSELF.

OH, RIGHT. MINJI WANTS TO TALK TO YOU.

MS. FYODOR AT THEIR HOME WILL FREAKING SCOLD ME IF WE TALK FOR TOO LONG.

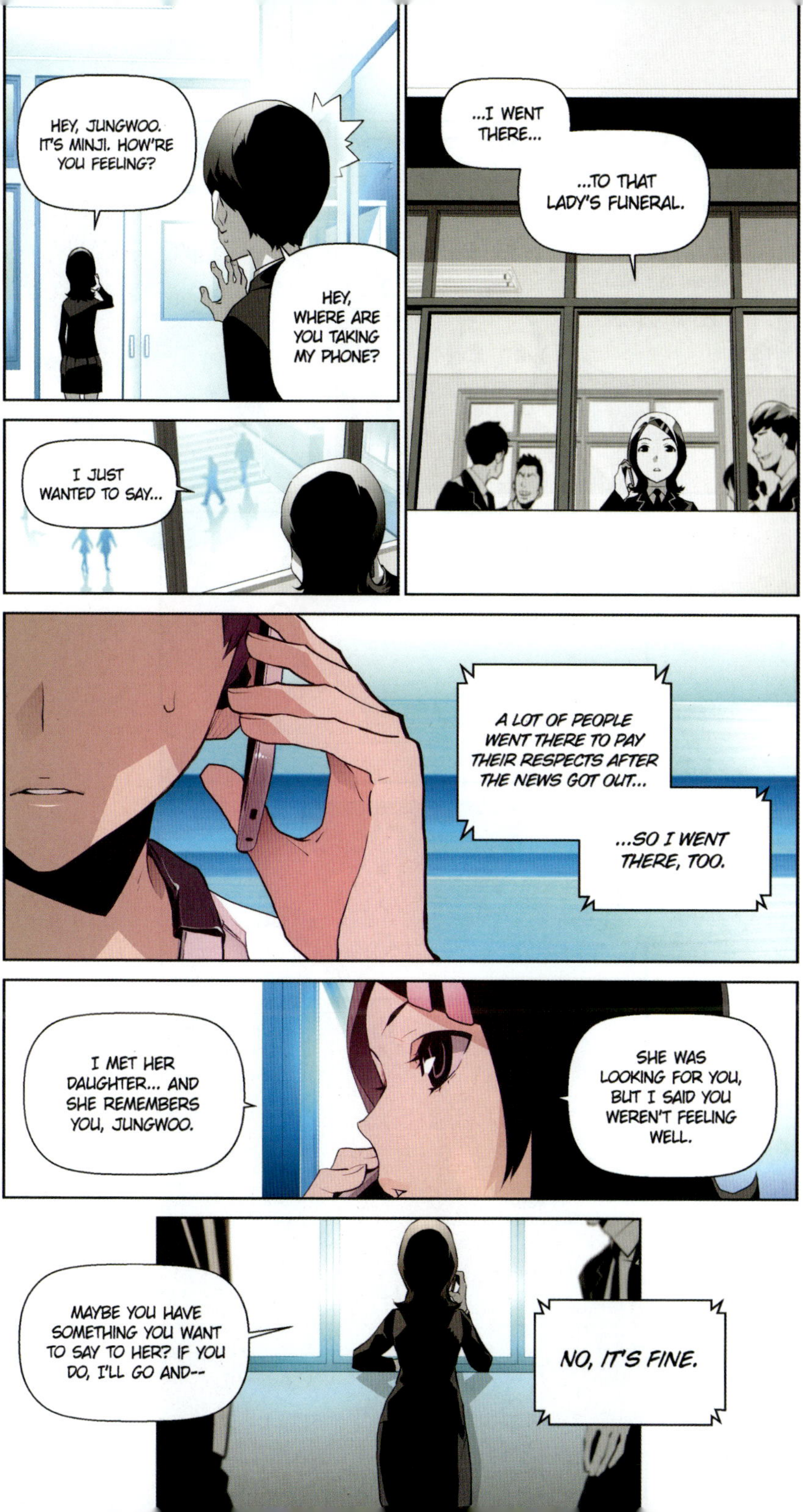
HEY, JUNGWOO. IT'S MINJI. HOW'RE YOU FEELING?
HEY, WHERE ARE YOU TAKING MY PHONE?
...I WENT THERE...
...TO THAT LADY'S FUNERAL.
I JUST WANTED TO SAY...
A LOT OF PEOPLE WENT THERE TO PAY THEIR RESPECTS AFTER THE NEWS GOT OUT...
...SO I WENT THERE, TOO.
I MET HER DAUGHTER... AND SHE REMEMBERS YOU, JUNGWOO.
SHE WAS LOOKING FOR YOU, BUT I SAID YOU WEREN'T FEELING WELL.
MAYBE YOU HAVE SOMETHING YOU WANT TO SAY TO HER? IF YOU DO, I'LL GO AND--
NO, IT'S FINE.

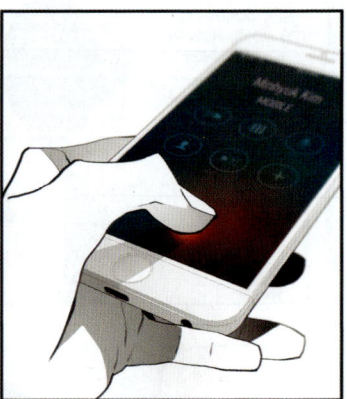

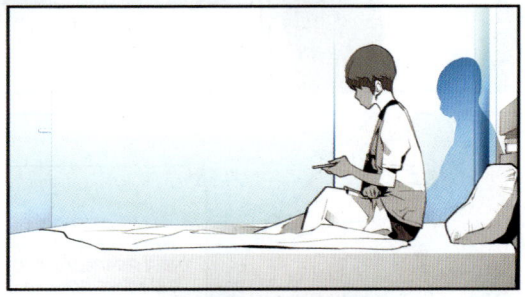

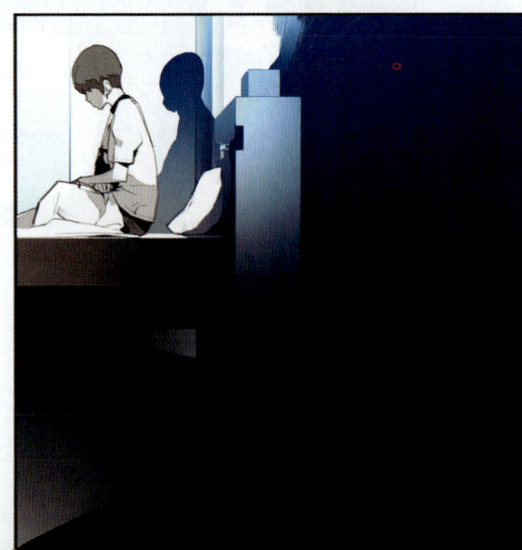

AH...
AH, REALLY?

OKAY.
THEN GET WELL SOON AND SEE YOU AT SCHOOL.

THANK YOU.
I'LL TAKE CARE OF MYSELF.

...

3 WEEKS LATER

YOUNG MASTER, ARE YOU SURE YOU'RE ALRIGHT NOW?

YES, I'M FINE NOW.

SCREECH

OH, HOW NICE IT IS TO BE YOUNG.

YOUR BONES HEAL FAST EVEN IF YOU BREAK THEM, AND YOU EASILY RECOVER EVEN AFTER BEING SHOT.

DON'T TREAT ME LIKE I'M SOME ROBOT...

...

WHERE ARE WE, LILIA?

SIHEUNG.

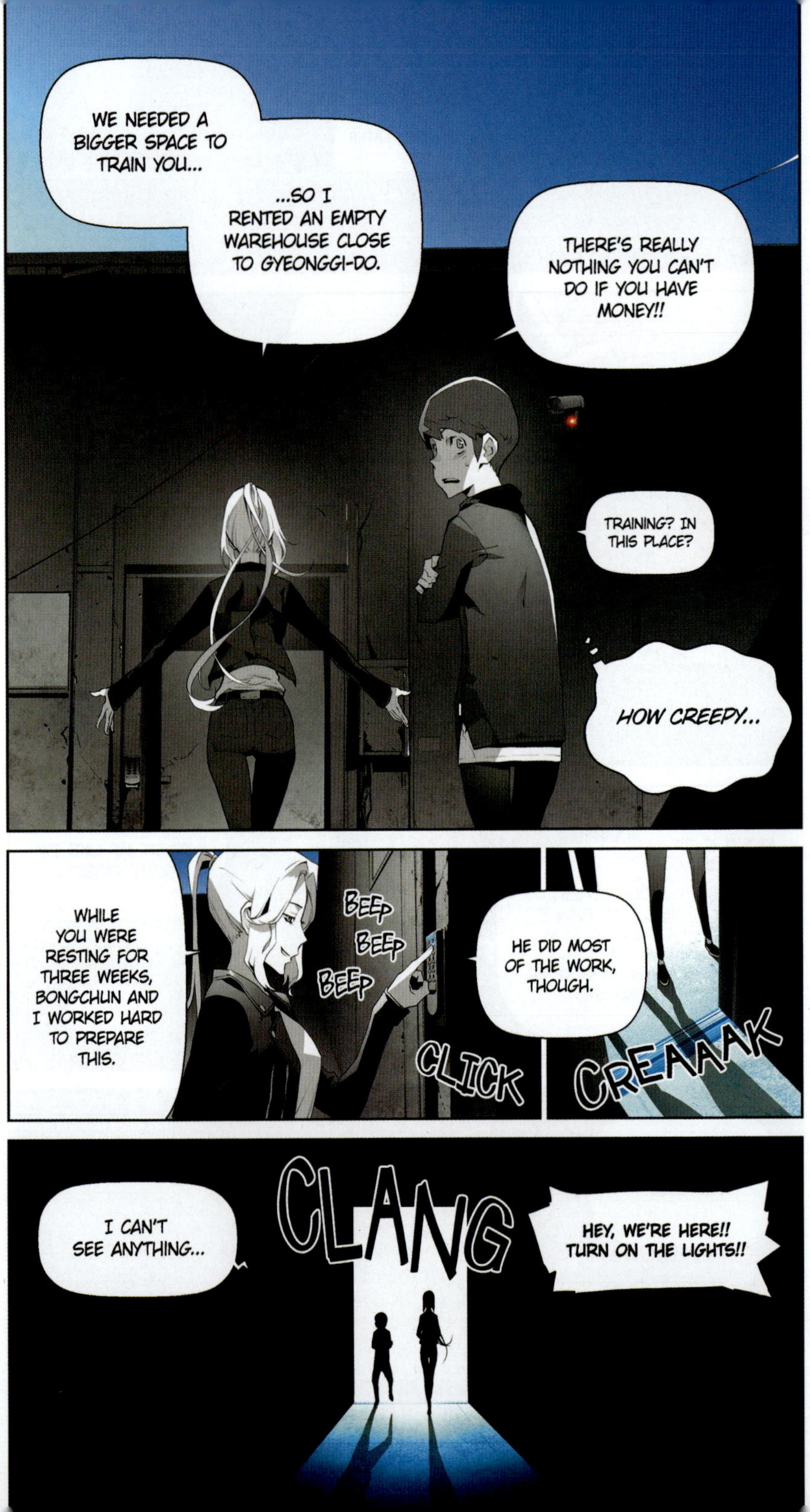

WE NEEDED A BIGGER SPACE TO TRAIN YOU...
...SO I RENTED AN EMPTY WAREHOUSE CLOSE TO GYEONGGI-DO.
THERE'S REALLY NOTHING YOU CAN'T DO IF YOU HAVE MONEY!!
TRAINING? IN THIS PLACE?
HOW CREEPY...
WHILE YOU WERE RESTING FOR THREE WEEKS, BONGCHUN AND I WORKED HARD TO PREPARE THIS.
BEEP
BEEP
BEEP
CLICK
HE DID MOST OF THE WORK, THOUGH.
CREAAAK
CLANG
I CAN'T SEE ANYTHING...
HEY, WE'RE HERE!! TURN ON THE LIGHTS!!

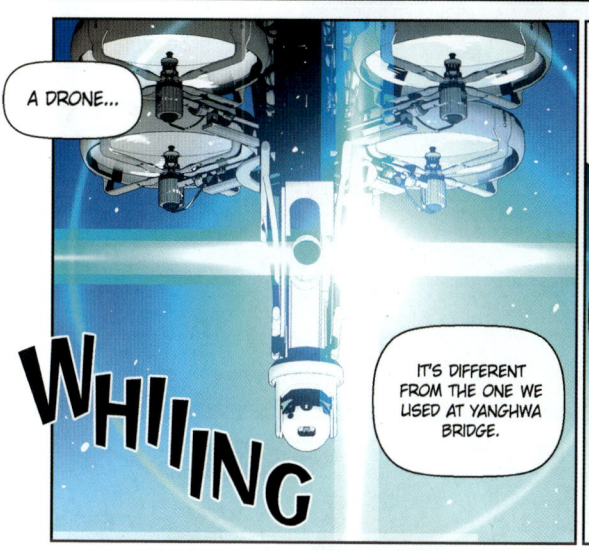

?!?!

TH-THIS...

A DRONE...

WE ORDERED JJAMPPONG AND THEN MADE THIS USING A PITCHING MACHINE.

IT'S DIFFERENT FROM THE ONE WE USED AT YANGHWA BRIDGE.

A PITCHING MACHINE? YOU MEAN... THE KIND THAT THROWS BASEBALLS?

HEY, STUPID!! I TOLD YOU TO TURN ON THE LIGHTS IN THE BUILDING, NOT THE DRONES' FLASHLIGHTS!!

THIS GIRL'S ATTITUDE... SERIOUSLY. TSK!

!!!

BEEP

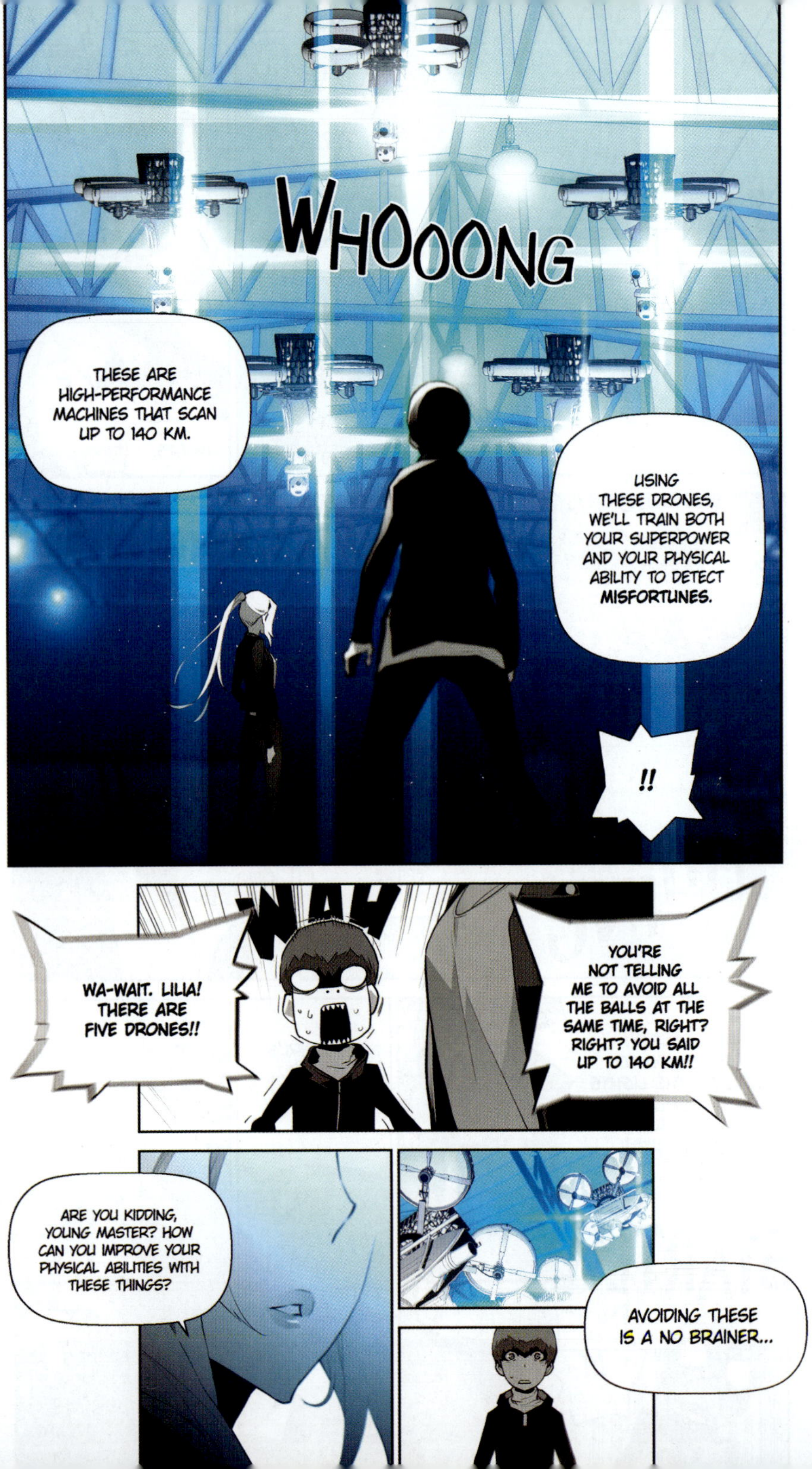
WHOOONG
THESE ARE HIGH-PERFORMANCE MACHINES THAT SCAN UP TO 140 KM.
USING THESE DRONES, WE'LL TRAIN BOTH YOUR SUPERPOWER AND YOUR PHYSICAL ABILITY TO DETECT MISFORTUNES.
!!
WAH
WA-WAIT. LILIA! THERE ARE FIVE DRONES!!
YOU'RE NOT TELLING ME TO AVOID ALL THE BALLS AT THE SAME TIME, RIGHT? RIGHT? YOU SAID UP TO 140 KM!!
ARE YOU KIDDING, YOUNG MASTER? HOW CAN YOU IMPROVE YOUR PHYSICAL ABILITIES WITH THESE THINGS?
AVOIDING THESE IS A NO BRAINER...

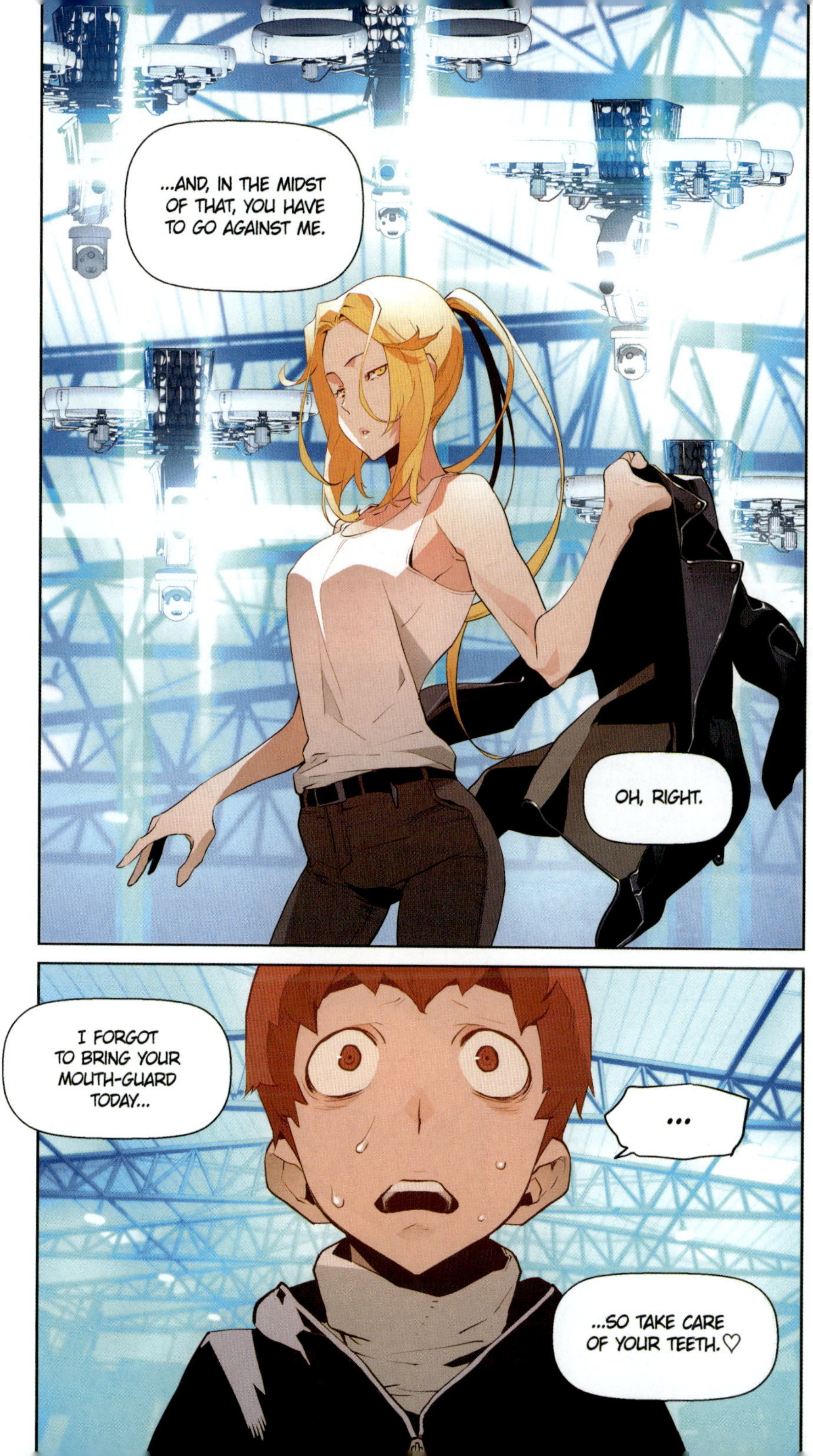
...AND, IN THE MIDST OF THAT, YOU HAVE TO GO AGAINST ME.
OH, RIGHT.
I FORGOT TO BRING YOUR MOUTH-GUARD TODAY...
...
...SO TAKE CARE OF YOUR TEETH.♡

WOW, LOOK AT ALL THIS SPACE THAT IS BLOCKED OFF.

THE SOUTH KOREAN POLICE SURE ARE WORKING HARD.

IT HASN'T BEEN LONG SINCE A HUGE INCIDENT HAPPENED, YET HERE THEY ARE, JUST LETTING A CIVILIAN WALK IN AND OUT LIKE THIS.

WELL, TO BE EXACT... IT'S A CRIMINAL AND NOT A CIVILIAN.

NOT ONLY THE POLICE, BUT EVEN THE MILITARY...

...ARE ACTING TOO RELAXED.

I CAN'T EVEN FEEL AN OUNCE OF ANXIETY.

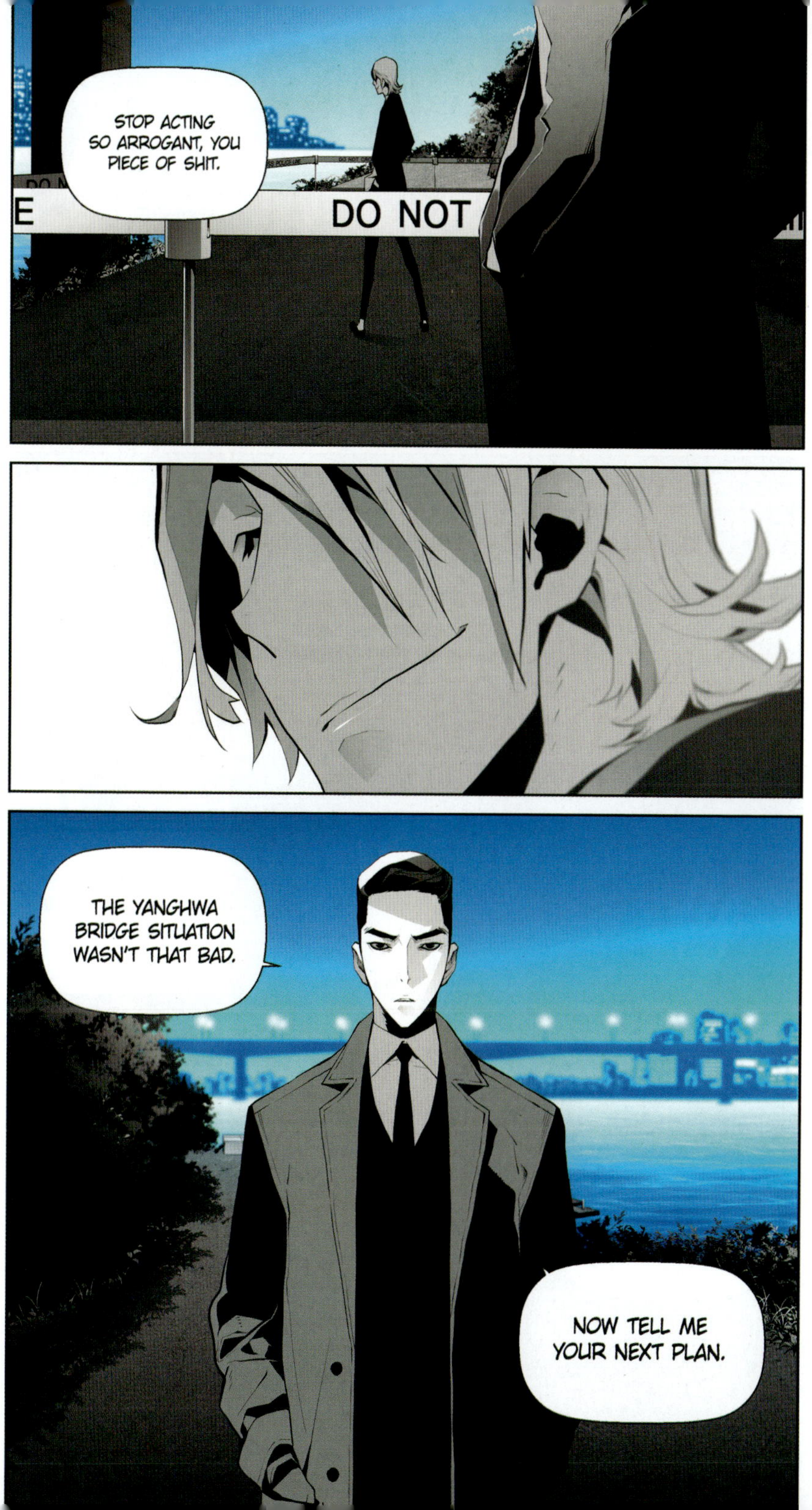

STOP ACTING SO ARROGANT, YOU PIECE OF SHIT.
DO NOT
THE YANGHWA BRIDGE SITUATION WASN'T THAT BAD.
NOW TELL ME YOUR NEXT PLAN.

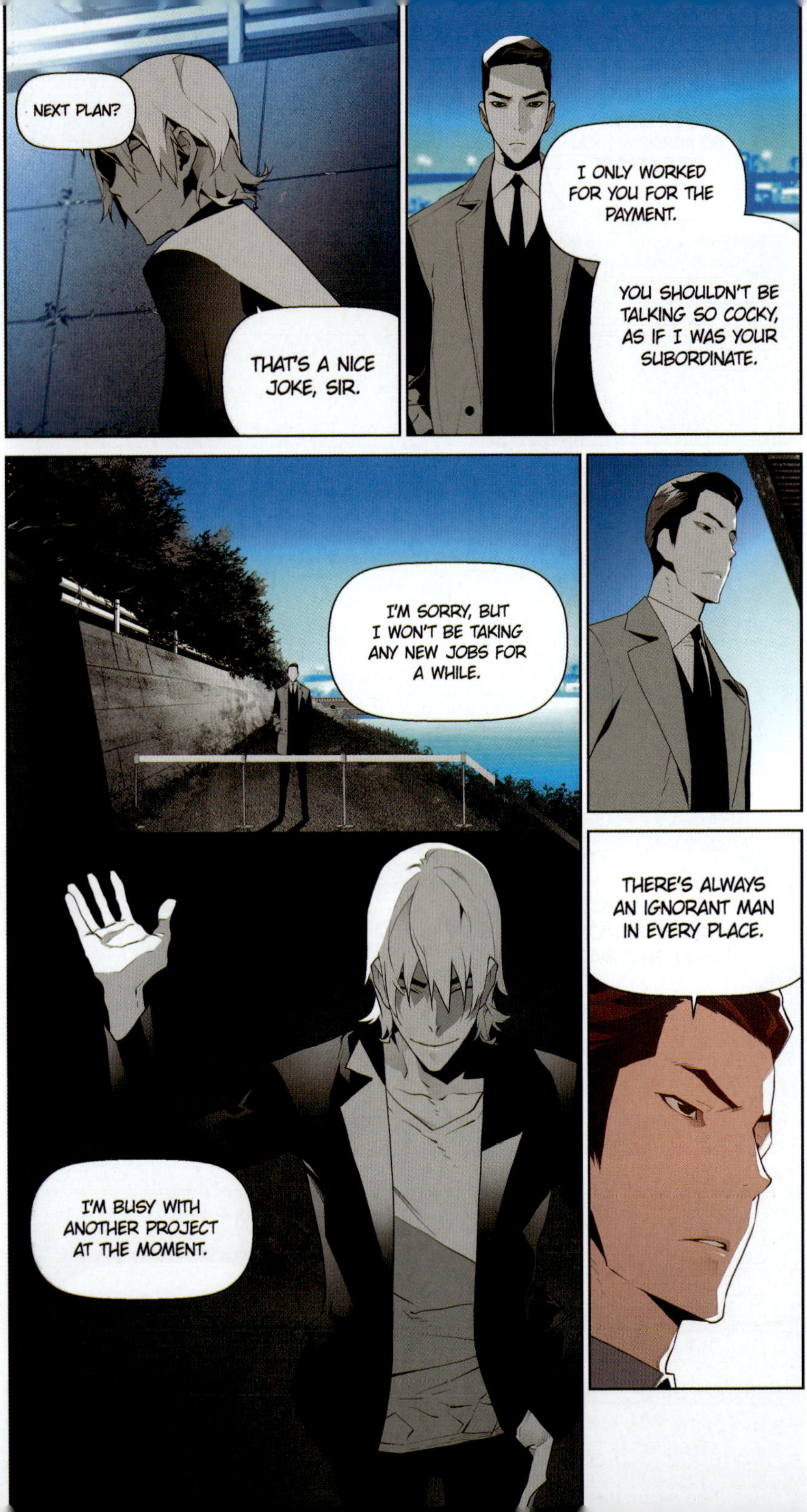
NEXT PLAN?
THAT'S A NICE JOKE, SIR.
I ONLY WORKED FOR YOU FOR THE PAYMENT.
YOU SHOULDN'T BE TALKING SO COCKY, AS IF I WAS YOUR SUBORDINATE.
I'M SORRY, BUT I WON'T BE TAKING ANY NEW JOBS FOR A WHILE.
I'M BUSY WITH ANOTHER PROJECT AT THE MOMENT.
THERE'S ALWAYS AN IGNORANT MAN IN EVERY PLACE.

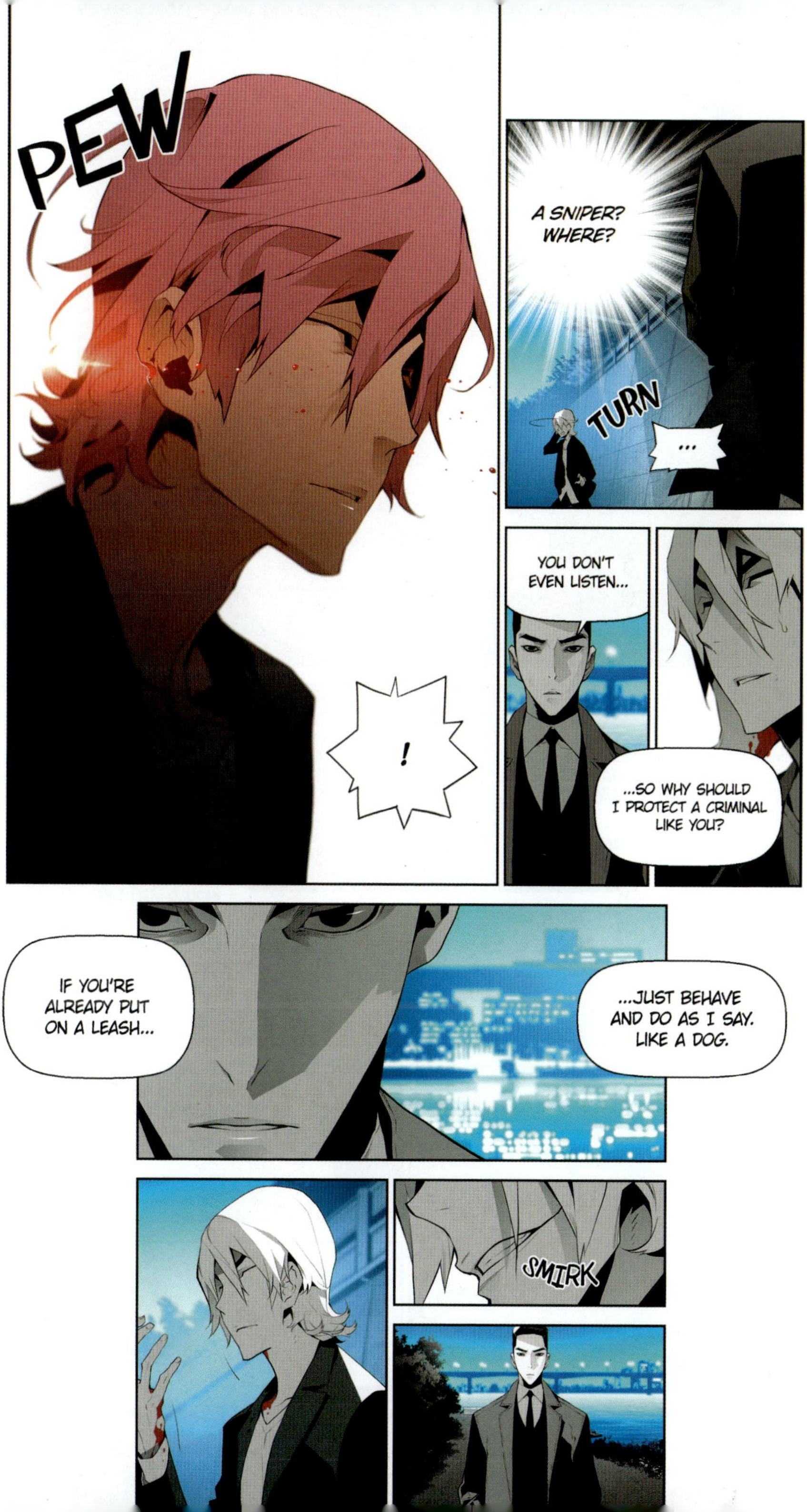
PEW
!
A SNIPER? WHERE?
TURN
...
YOU DON'T EVEN LISTEN...
...SO WHY SHOULD I PROTECT A CRIMINAL LIKE YOU?
IF YOU'RE ALREADY PUT ON A LEASH...
...JUST BEHAVE AND DO AS I SAY. LIKE A DOG.
SMIRK

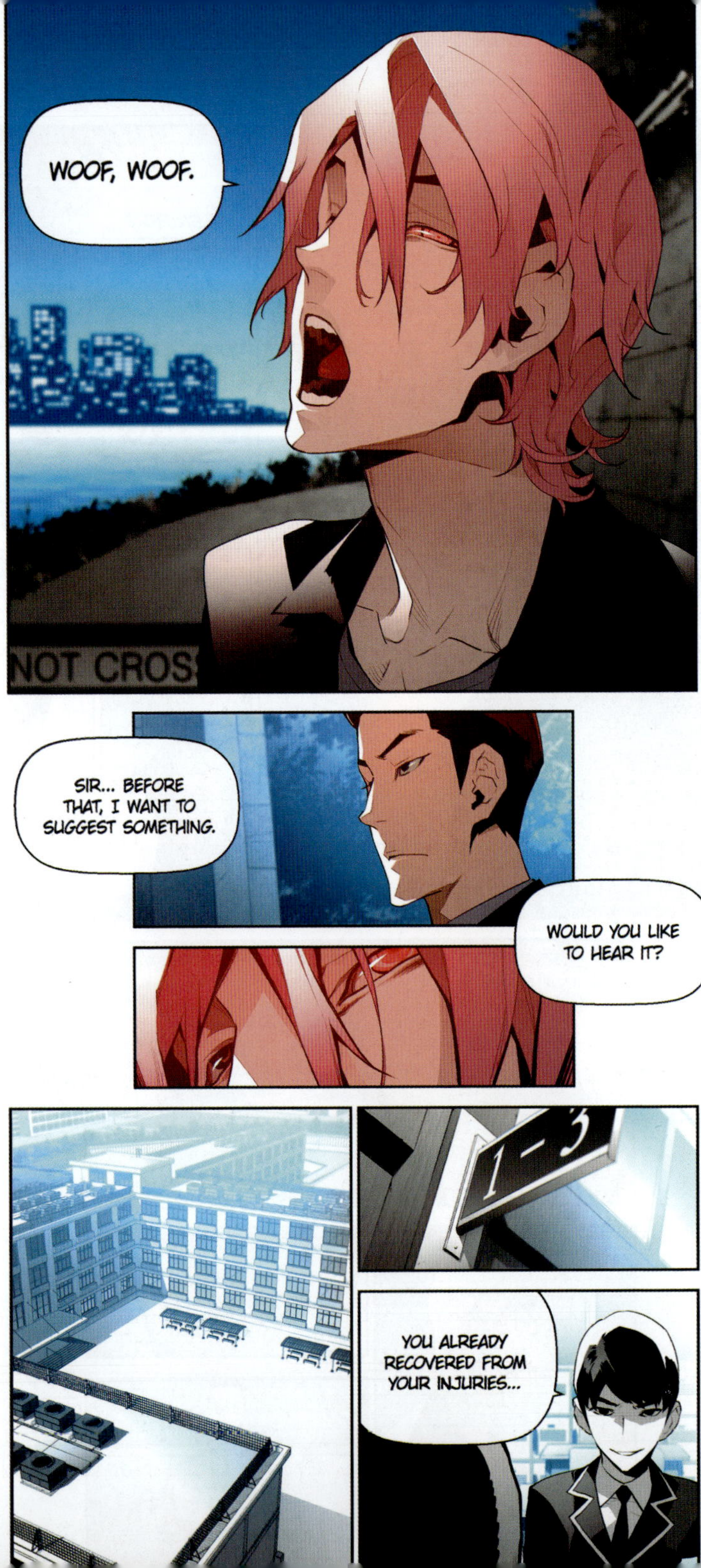
WOOF, WOOF.
NOT CROS
SIR... BEFORE THAT, I WANT TO SUGGEST SOMETHING.
WOULD YOU LIKE TO HEAR IT?
1-3
YOU ALREADY RECOVERED FROM YOUR INJURIES...

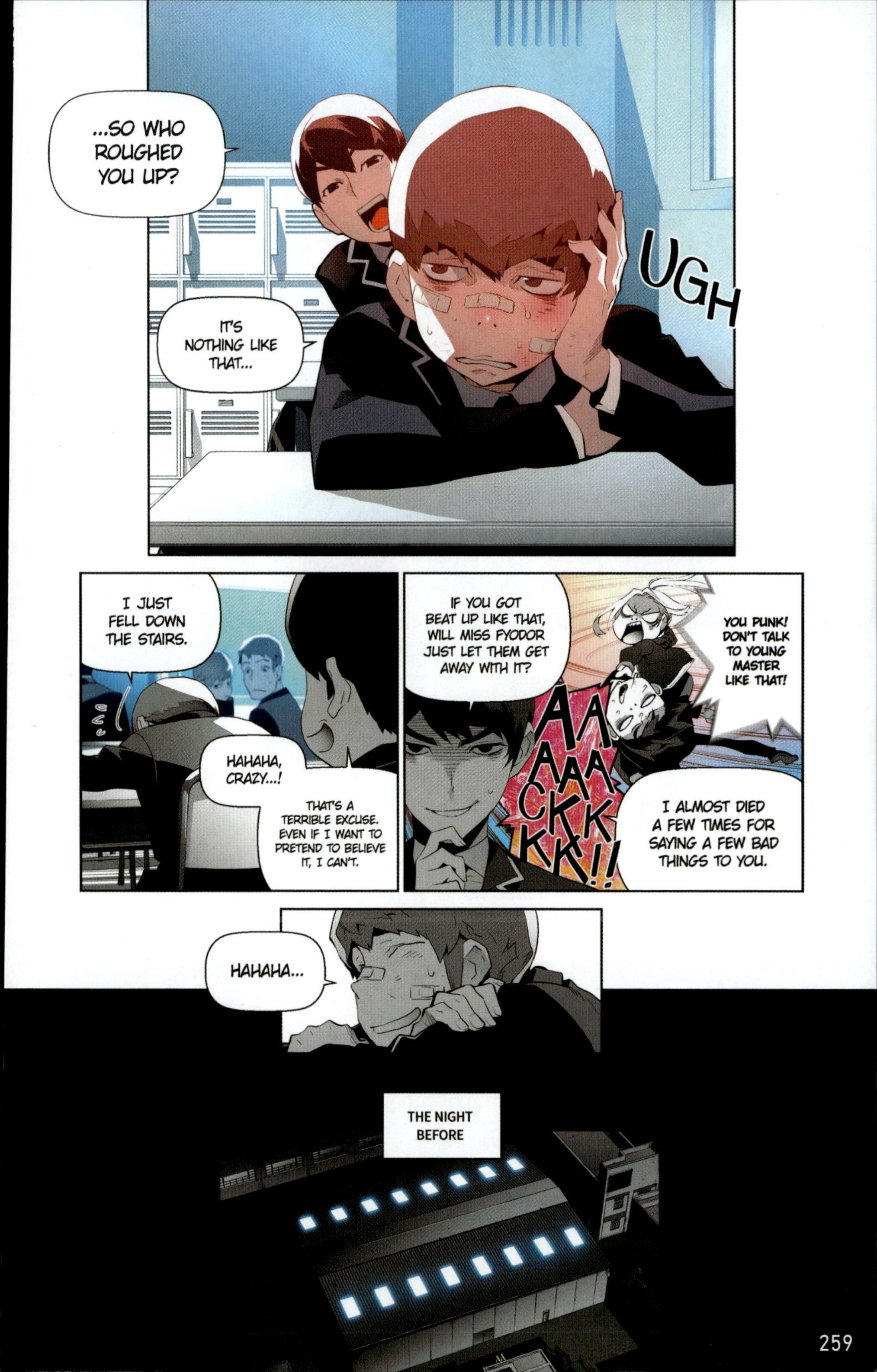

...SO WHO ROUGHED YOU UP?

IT'S NOTHING LIKE THAT...

UGH

I JUST FELL DOWN THE STAIRS.

HAHAHA, CRAZY...!

THAT'S A TERRIBLE EXCUSE. EVEN IF I WANT TO PRETEND TO BELIEVE IT, I CAN'T.

IF YOU GOT BEAT UP LIKE THAT, WILL MISS FYODOR JUST LET THEM GET AWAY WITH IT?

YOU PUNK! DON'T TALK TO YOUNG MASTER LIKE THAT!

AAAACKKKK!!

I ALMOST DIED A FEW TIMES FOR SAYING A FEW BAD THINGS TO YOU.

HAHAHA...

THE NIGHT BEFORE

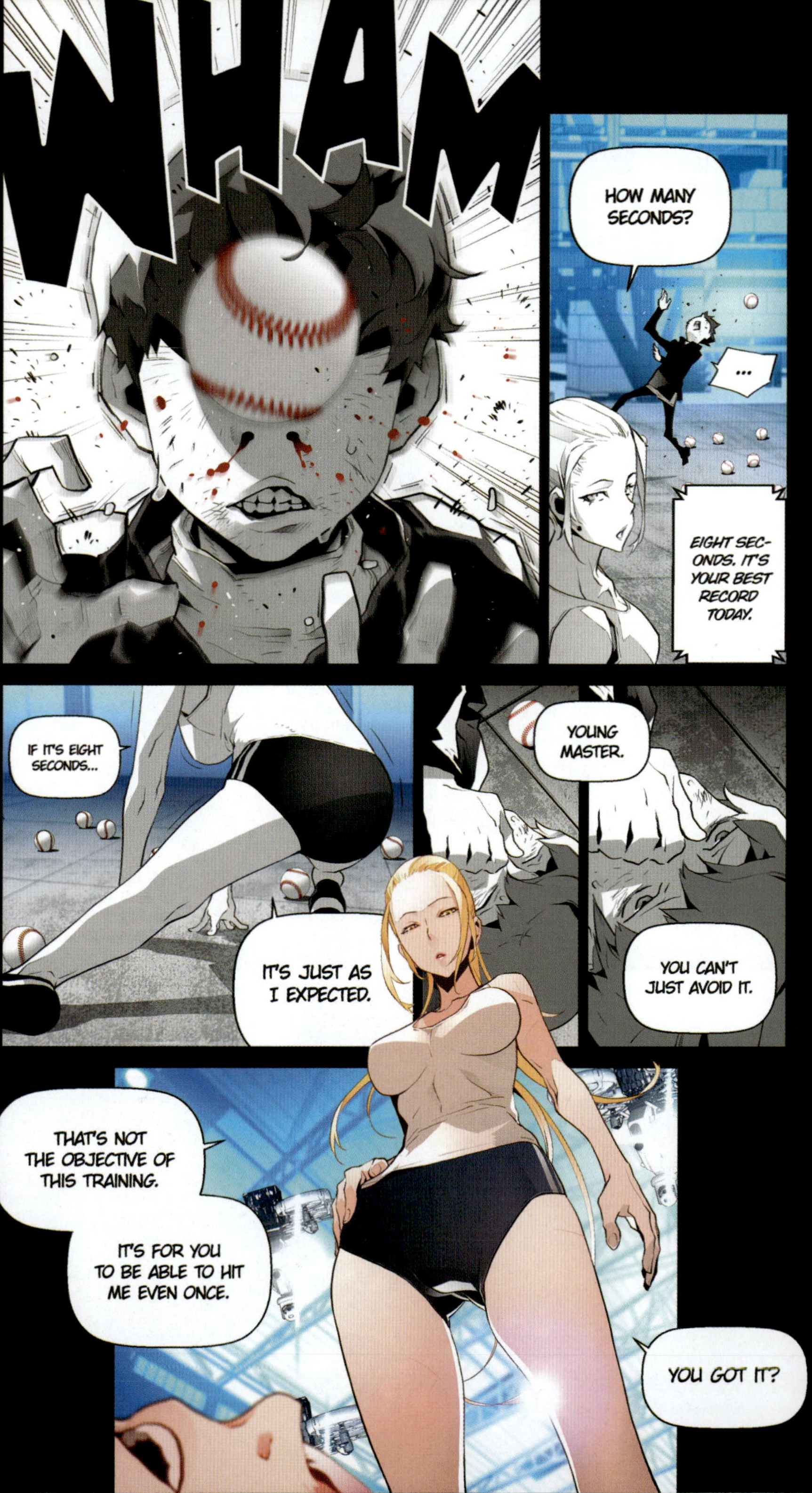
WHAM
HOW MANY SECONDS?
...
EIGHT SECONDS. IT'S YOUR BEST RECORD TODAY.
IF IT'S EIGHT SECONDS...
IT'S JUST AS I EXPECTED.
YOUNG MASTER.
YOU CAN'T JUST AVOID IT.
THAT'S NOT THE OBJECTIVE OF THIS TRAINING.
IT'S FOR YOU TO BE ABLE TO HIT ME EVEN ONCE.
YOU GOT IT?

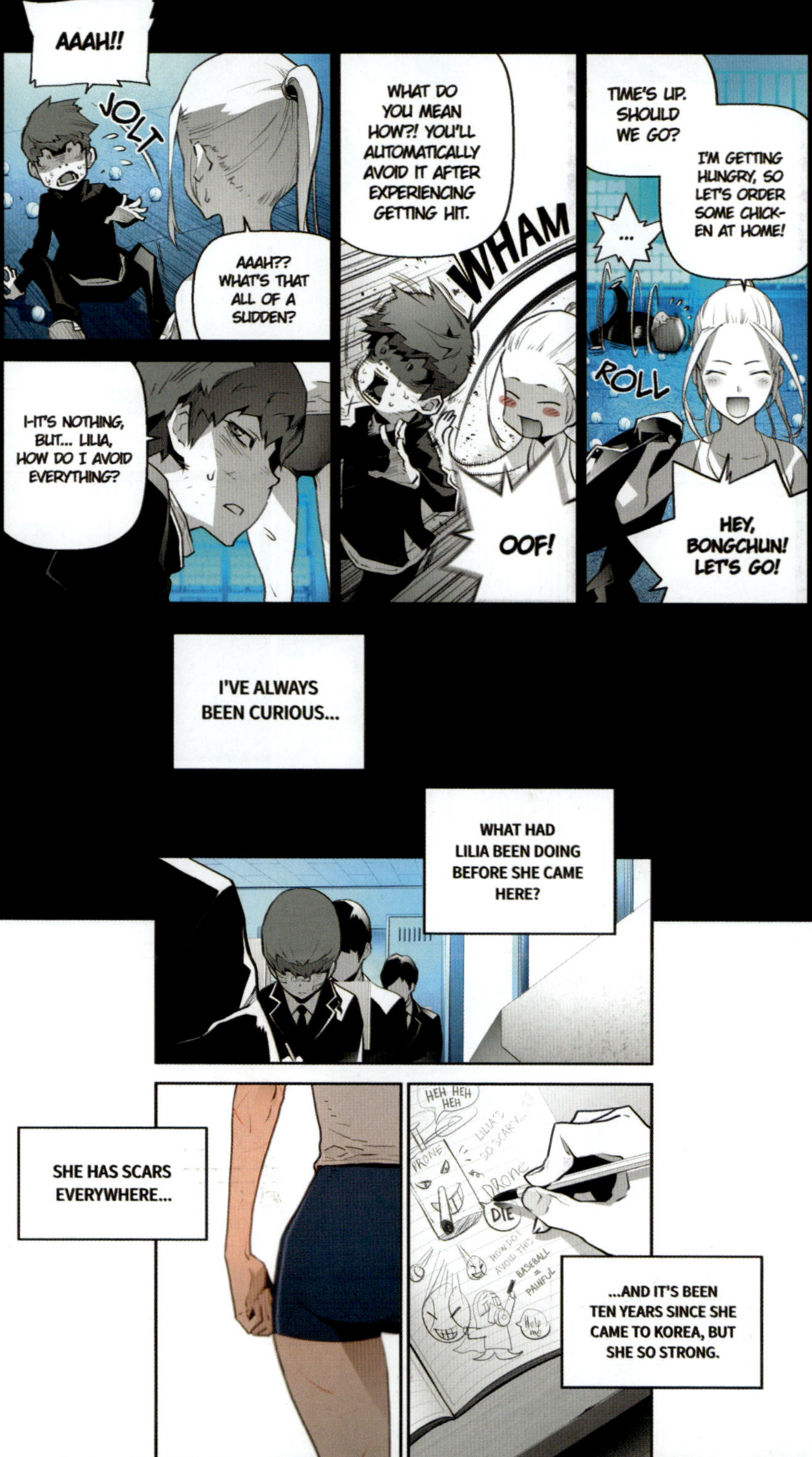
AAAH!!
JOLT
AAAH?? WHAT'S THAT ALL OF A SUDDEN?
I-IT'S NOTHING, BUT... LILIA, HOW DO I AVOID EVERYTHING?
WHAT DO YOU MEAN HOW?! YOU'LL AUTOMATICALLY AVOID IT AFTER EXPERIENCING GETTING HIT.
WHAM
OOF!
TIME'S UP. SHOULD WE GO?
I'M GETTING HUNGRY, SO LET'S ORDER SOME CHICK-EN AT HOME!
...
ROLL
HEY, BONGCHUN! LET'S GO!
I'VE ALWAYS BEEN CURIOUS...
WHAT HAD LILIA BEEN DOING BEFORE SHE CAME HERE?
SHE HAS SCARS EVERYWHERE...
HEH HEH HEH
DRONE
DIE
BASEBALL = PAINFUL
Help me
...AND IT'S BEEN TEN YEARS SINCE SHE CAME TO KOREA, BUT SHE SO STRONG.

...

IT WOULD TAKE ME YEARS TO BECOME AS GOOD AS HER, RIGHT?

GETTING STRONG IS IMPORTANT...

...BUT, RIGHT NOW, I NEED TO UTILIZE MY ABILITY TO WIN AGAINST LILIA.

THAT PITCHING MACHINE DRONE... IT TAKES AROUND THREE SECONDS TO RELOAD AFTER THROWING A BALL.

IF I CAN JUST MAKE GOOD USE OF THIS INFORMATION...

IN SHORT, THE DRONE WON'T BE ABLE TO THROW ANOTHER BALL FOR THREE SECONDS AFTER THROWING ONE...

HEY, PUNK!!

STARTLED

LOOK AT YOU DOZING OFF JUST BECAUSE I LET YOU. DO YOU WANT ME TO GIVE YOU A BLANKET? HUH?

NO MATTER HOW MUCH YOU HIDE IN THE BACK...

...I CAN SEE YOU ALL THE WAY FROM THE FRONT, ALRIGHT?

HIDE... THEN SLEEP...

...

HUH?

262

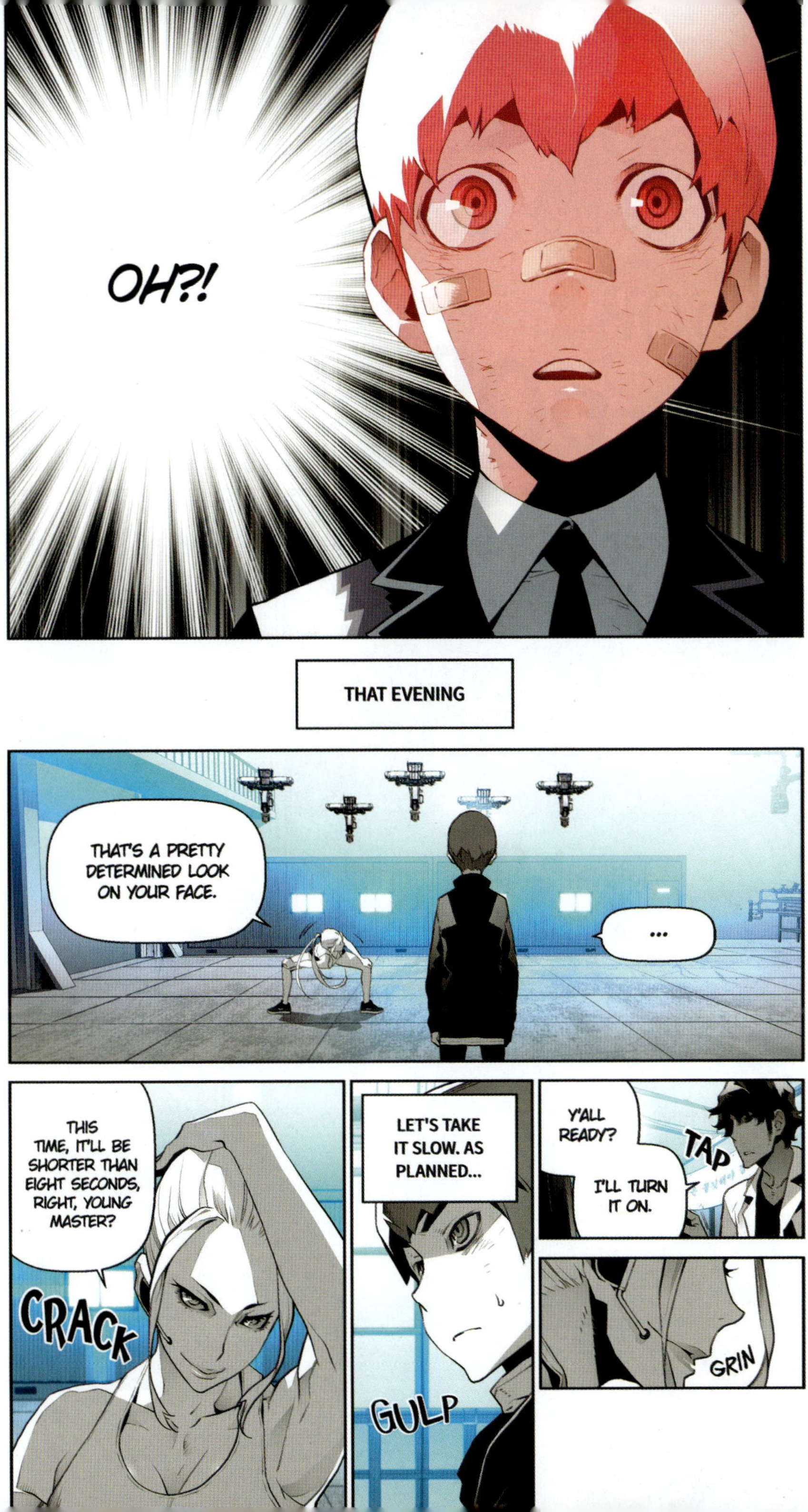
OH?!
THAT EVENING
THAT'S A PRETTY DETERMINED LOOK ON YOUR FACE.
...
THIS TIME, IT'LL BE SHORTER THAN EIGHT SECONDS, RIGHT, YOUNG MASTER?
CRACK
LET'S TAKE IT SLOW. AS PLANNED...
GULP
Y'ALL READY?
TAP
I'LL TURN IT ON.
GRIN

POP POP POP POP POP

START!!

PA PA PANG

!!

DID HE COME UP WITH A STRATEGY AFTER ONE DAY?

DASH

I'M TURNING IN JUST ONE DIRECTION ON PURPOSE...

...BUT IT LOOKS LIKE HE'S AIMING FOR SOMETHING SPECIFIC.

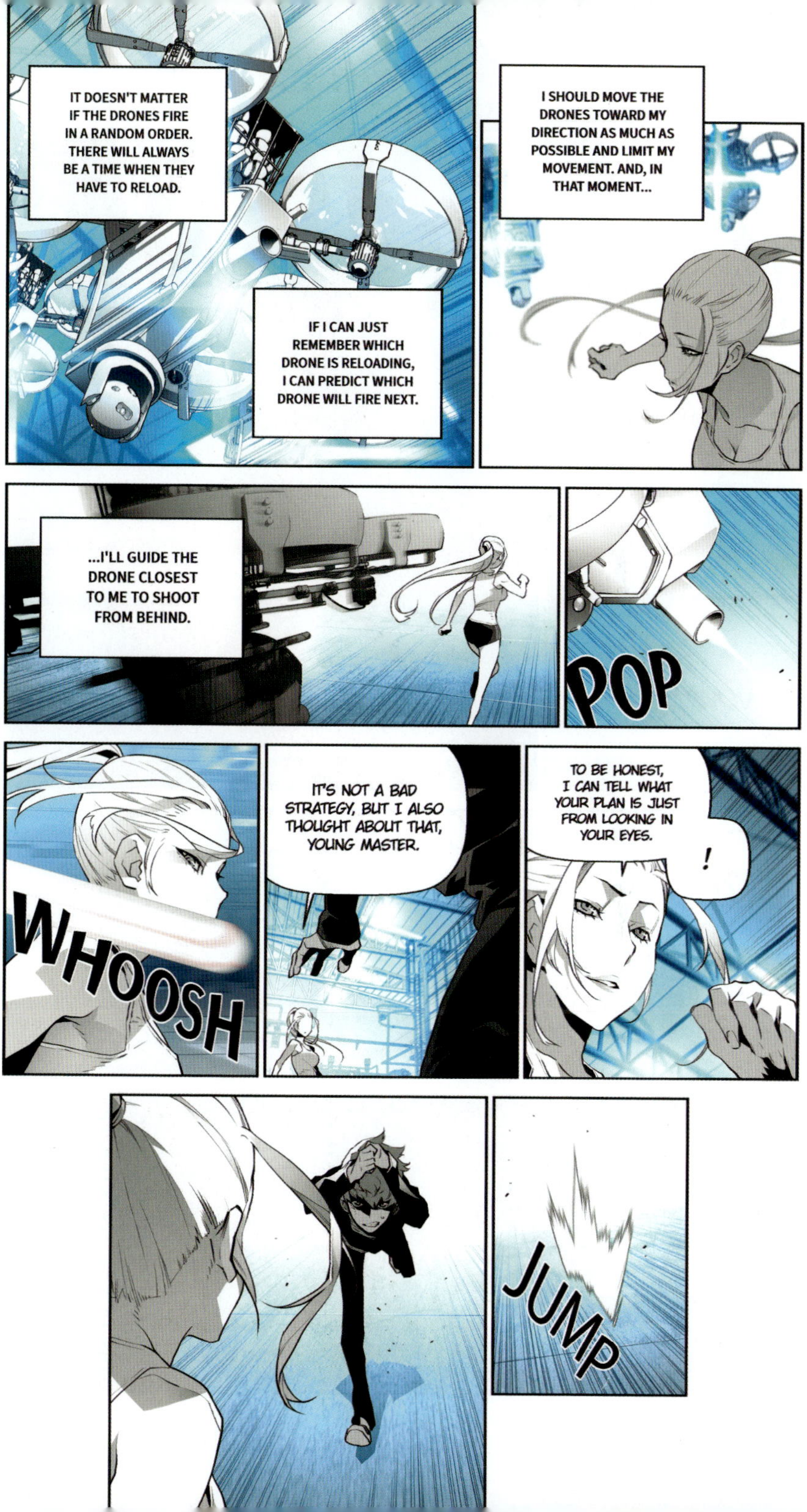
IT DOESN'T MATTER IF THE DRONES FIRE IN A RANDOM ORDER. THERE WILL ALWAYS BE A TIME WHEN THEY HAVE TO RELOAD.
IF I CAN JUST REMEMBER WHICH DRONE IS RELOADING, I CAN PREDICT WHICH DRONE WILL FIRE NEXT.
I SHOULD MOVE THE DRONES TOWARD MY DIRECTION AS MUCH AS POSSIBLE AND LIMIT MY MOVEMENT. AND, IN THAT MOMENT...
...I'LL GUIDE THE DRONE CLOSEST TO ME TO SHOOT FROM BEHIND.
POP
WHOOSH
IT'S NOT A BAD STRATEGY, BUT I ALSO THOUGHT ABOUT THAT, YOUNG MASTER.
TO BE HONEST, I CAN TELL WHAT YOUR PLAN IS JUST FROM LOOKING IN YOUR EYES.
!
JUMP

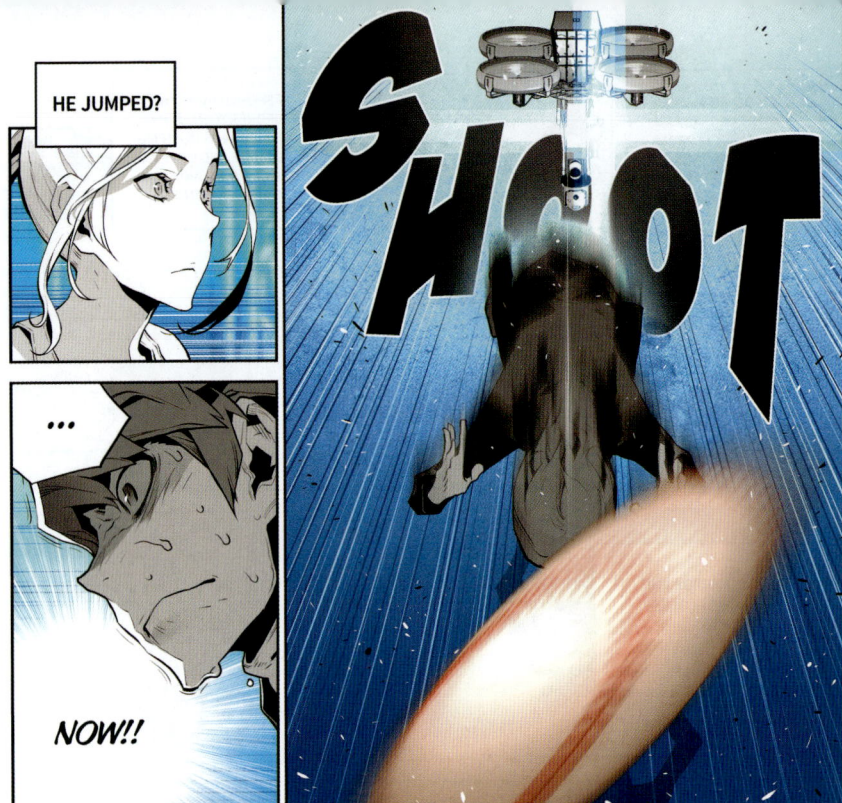

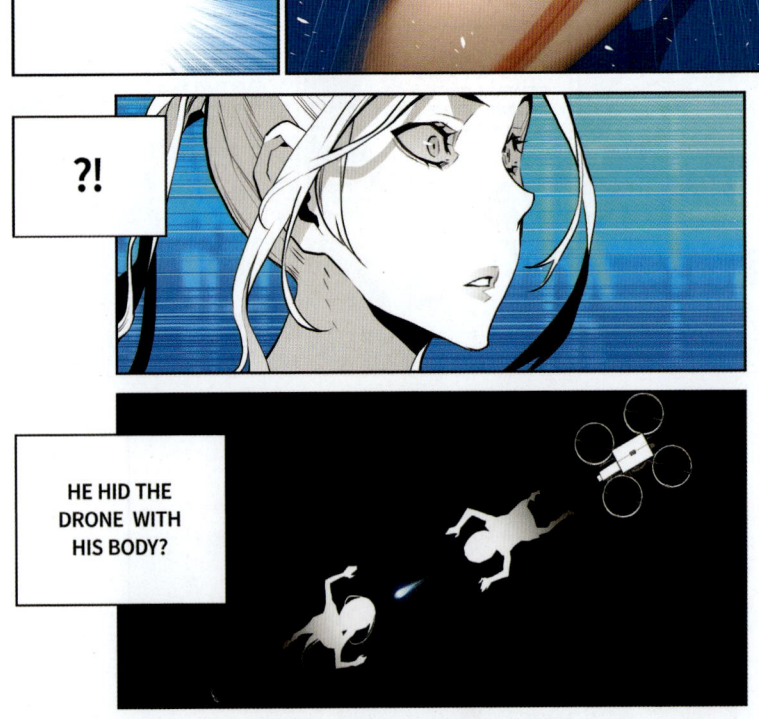

| HE JUMPED?

...

NOW!!

SH**OO**T

?!

HE HID THE DRONE WITH HIS BODY?

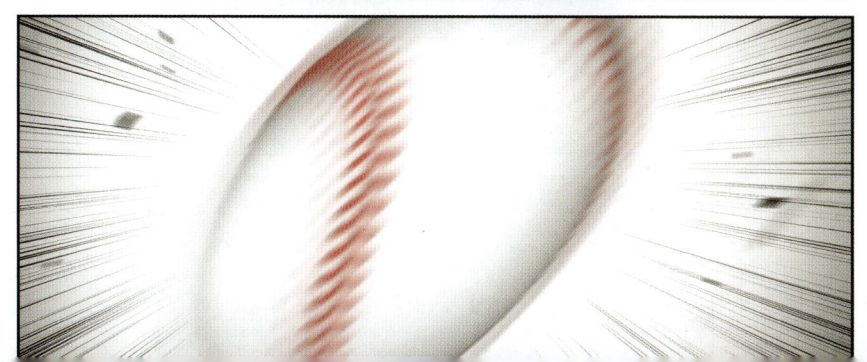

HE TRIED TO HAVE THE DRONE FIRE FROM A DISTANCE TOO CLOSE TO REACT TO.

GOOD!

WHAM

HAVE EIGHT SECONDS PASSED?

...

YOU'RE DOING QUITE WELL FOR A BEGINNER.

CRACK

Y-YOU SHATTERED IT WITH YOUR FIST...

IS THAT POSSIBLE?

I GUESS SO. I JUST DID IT, RIGHT?

GET UP. WE NEED TO KEEP GOING.

...

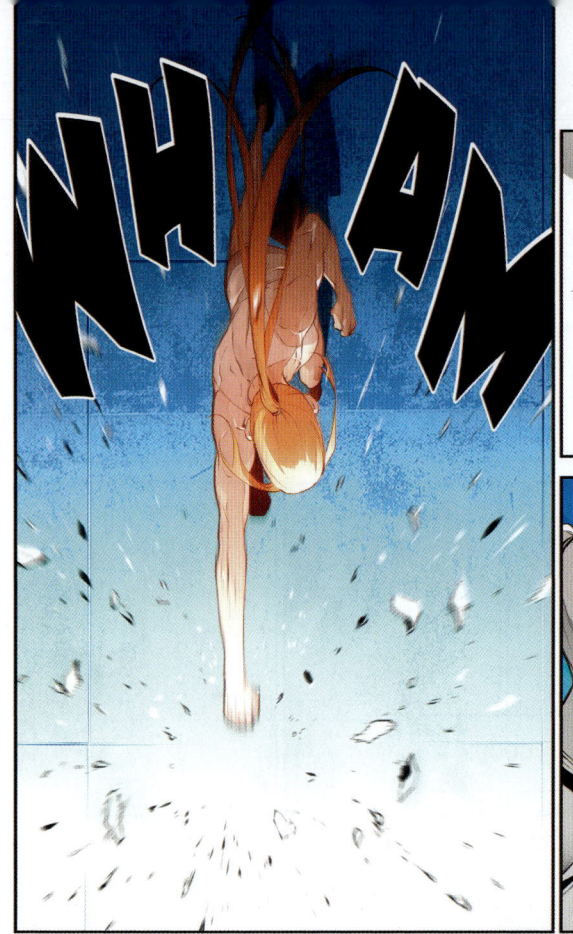

AS EXPECTED, YA CAN'T USE YER BRAIN AGAINST THAT GIRL.

MAY I...

...SUGGEST A TEST DRIVE TO THE YOUNG MASTER?

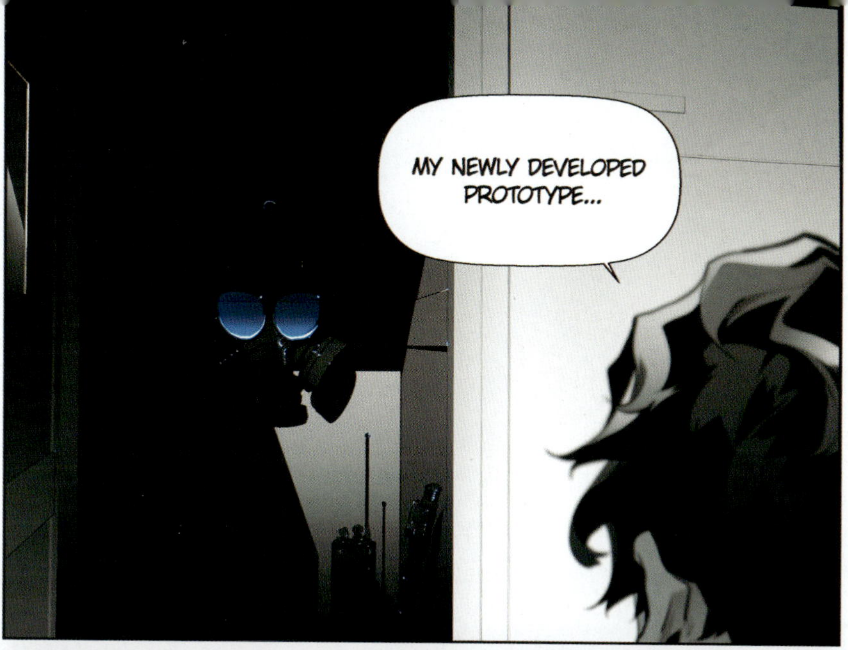
MY NEWLY DEVELOPED PROTOTYPE...

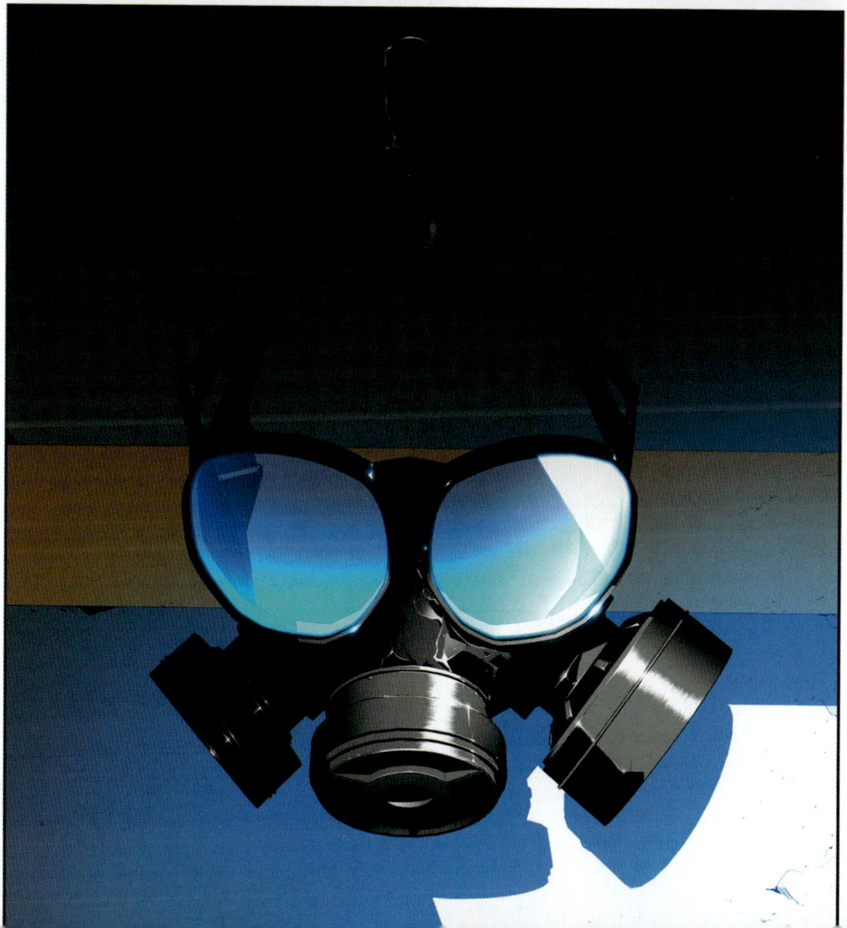

TERROR MAN

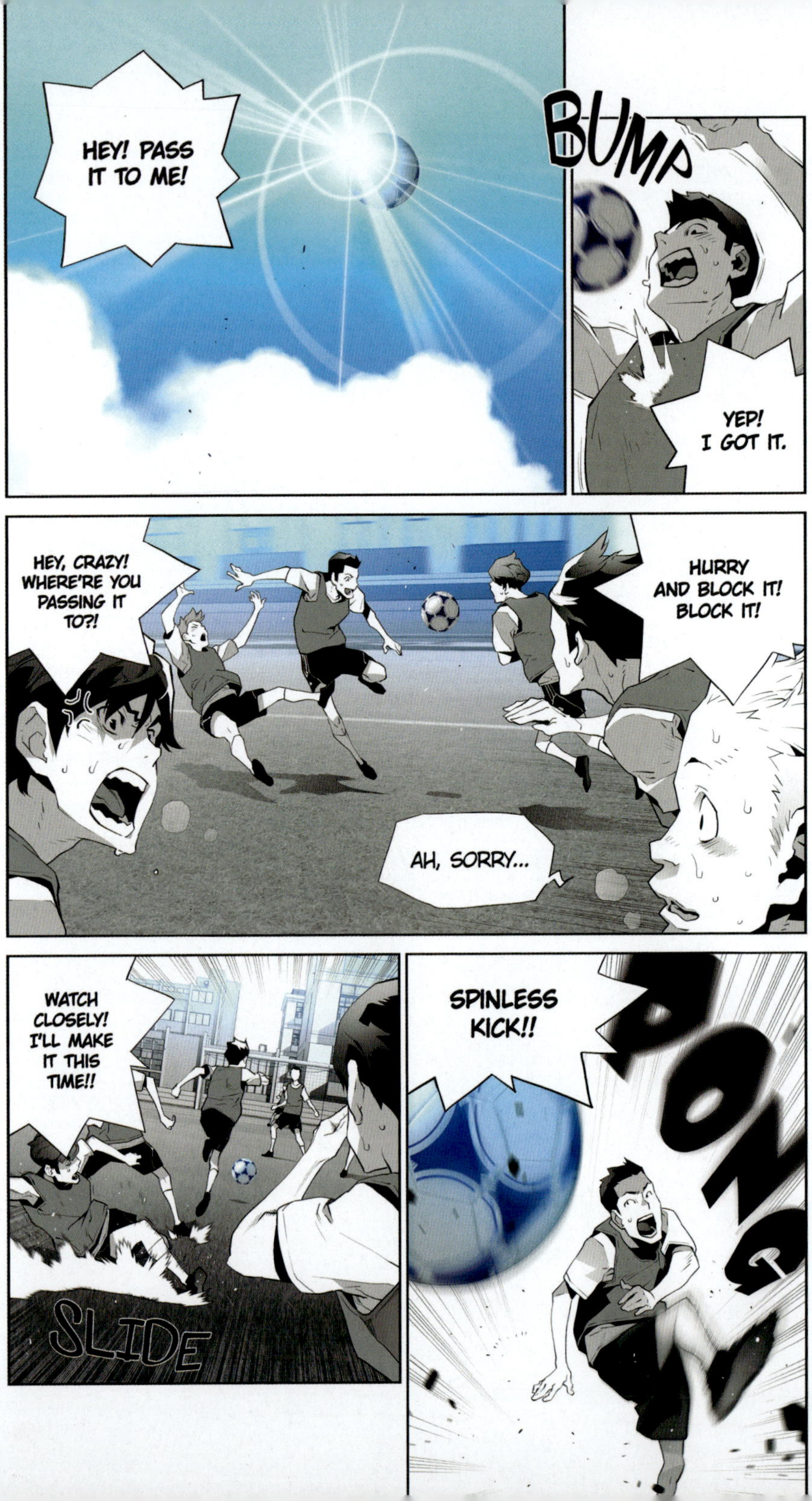
HEY! PASS IT TO ME!
BUMP
YEP! I GOT IT.
HEY, CRAZY! WHERE'RE YOU PASSING IT TO?!
HURRY AND BLOCK IT! BLOCK IT!
AH, SORRY...
WATCH CLOSELY! I'LL MAKE IT THIS TIME!!
SLIDE
SPINLESS KICK!!
DONG

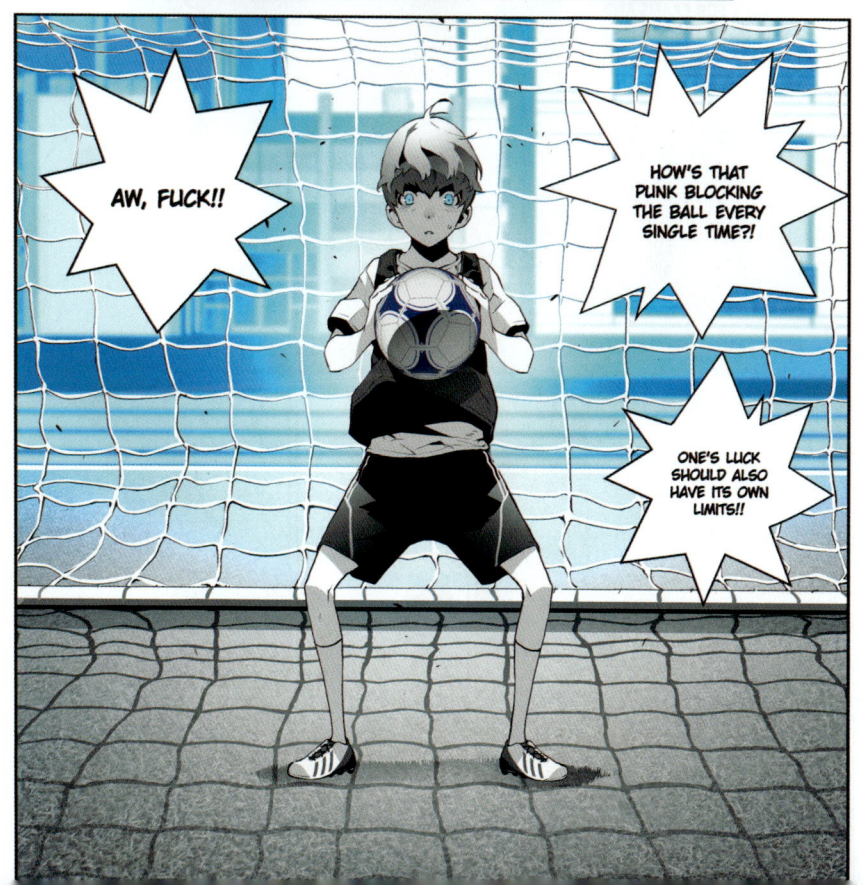

?!

BAM

WHAT THE--?!

...!

HE BLOCKED IT AGAIN?

AW, FUCK!!

HOW'S THAT PUNK BLOCKING THE BALL EVERY SINGLE TIME?!

ONE'S LUCK SHOULD ALSO HAVE ITS OWN LIMITS!!

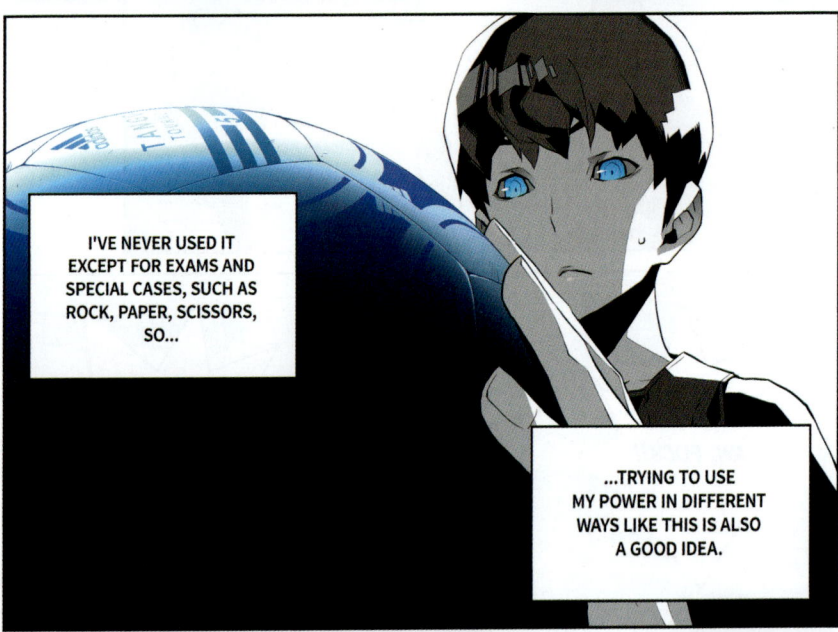

HEY, HE'S FREAKING GOOD AT BLOCKING.

WAAAHHH

I CAN'T BELIEVE WE HAD TO NAG HIM TO BE THE GOALKEEPER. WHERE DID HE TRAIN?

...

SO I CAN UTILIZE IT WHEN PLAYING SOCCER, TOO.

I'VE NEVER USED IT EXCEPT FOR EXAMS AND SPECIAL CASES, SUCH AS ROCK, PAPER, SCISSORS, SO...

...TRYING TO USE MY POWER IN DIFFERENT WAYS LIKE THIS IS ALSO A GOOD IDEA.

I MIGHT EVEN GET TO UPGRADE MY POWER LIKE THIS, JUST LIKE IN WEBTOONS.

TAP

WHAT'RE YOU DOING? KICK IT!

I NEED TO PRACTICE, LITTLE BY LITTLE!

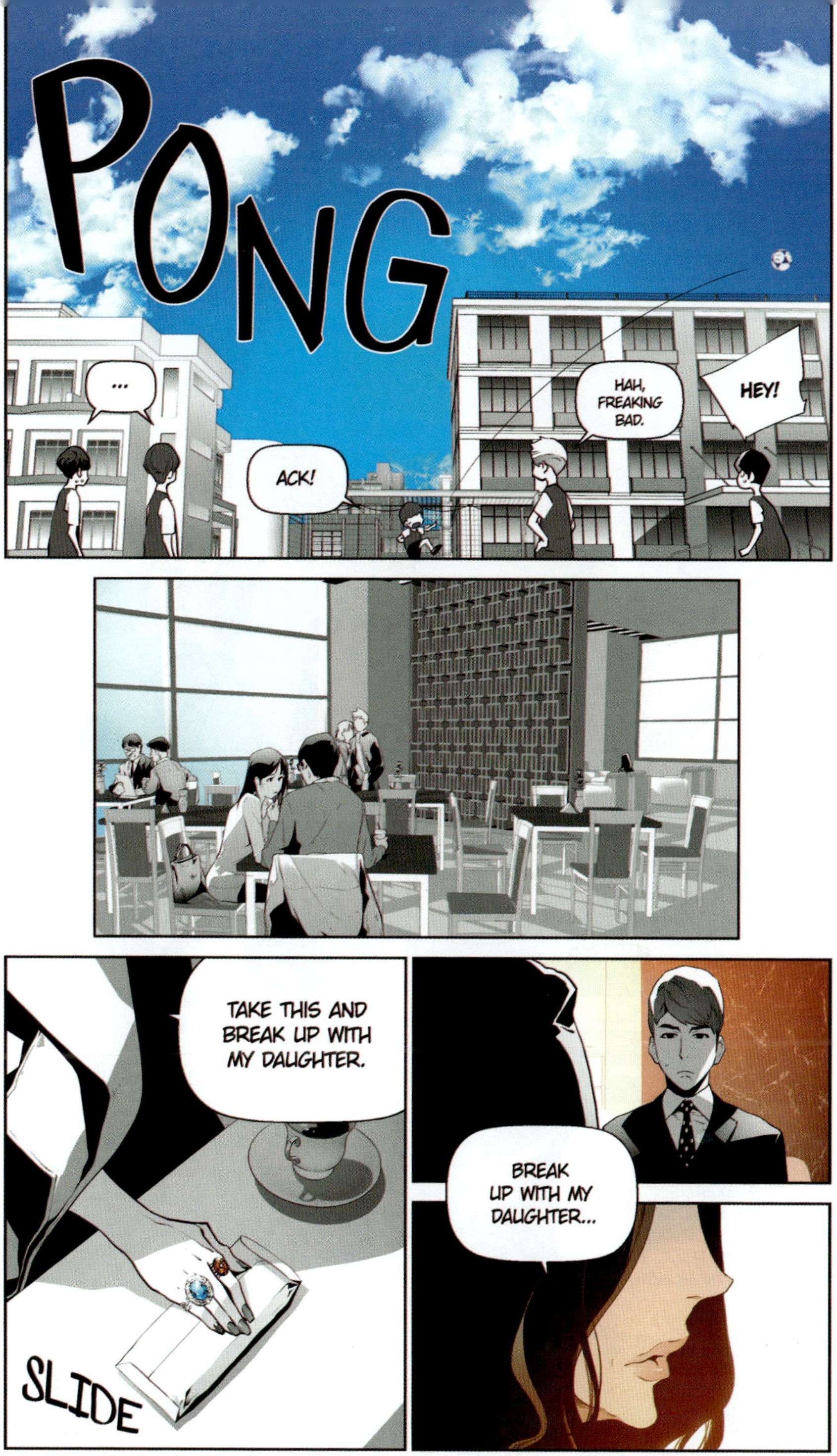
PONG
...
ACK!
HAH, FREAKING BAD.
HEY!
TAKE THIS AND BREAK UP WITH MY DAUGHTER.
SLIDE
BREAK UP WITH MY DAUGHTER...

...AND GO OUT WITH ME. HOW'S THAT?!

...

THUMP THUMP

WHAT AN EXCITING DRAMA. WHY'D I WAIT SO LONG TO WATCH IT?

WHAT AN AWFUL STORYLINE. SWITCH CHANNELS!!

MIND YER OWN BUSINESS!

YOU'VE ALREADY BEEN EXERCISIN' FOR HOURS WITHOUT EATIN' A MEAL. STOP AND LET'S ORDER PIZZA. I'M FREAKIN' HUNGRY.

I'M FINE. GO EAT BY YOURSELF.

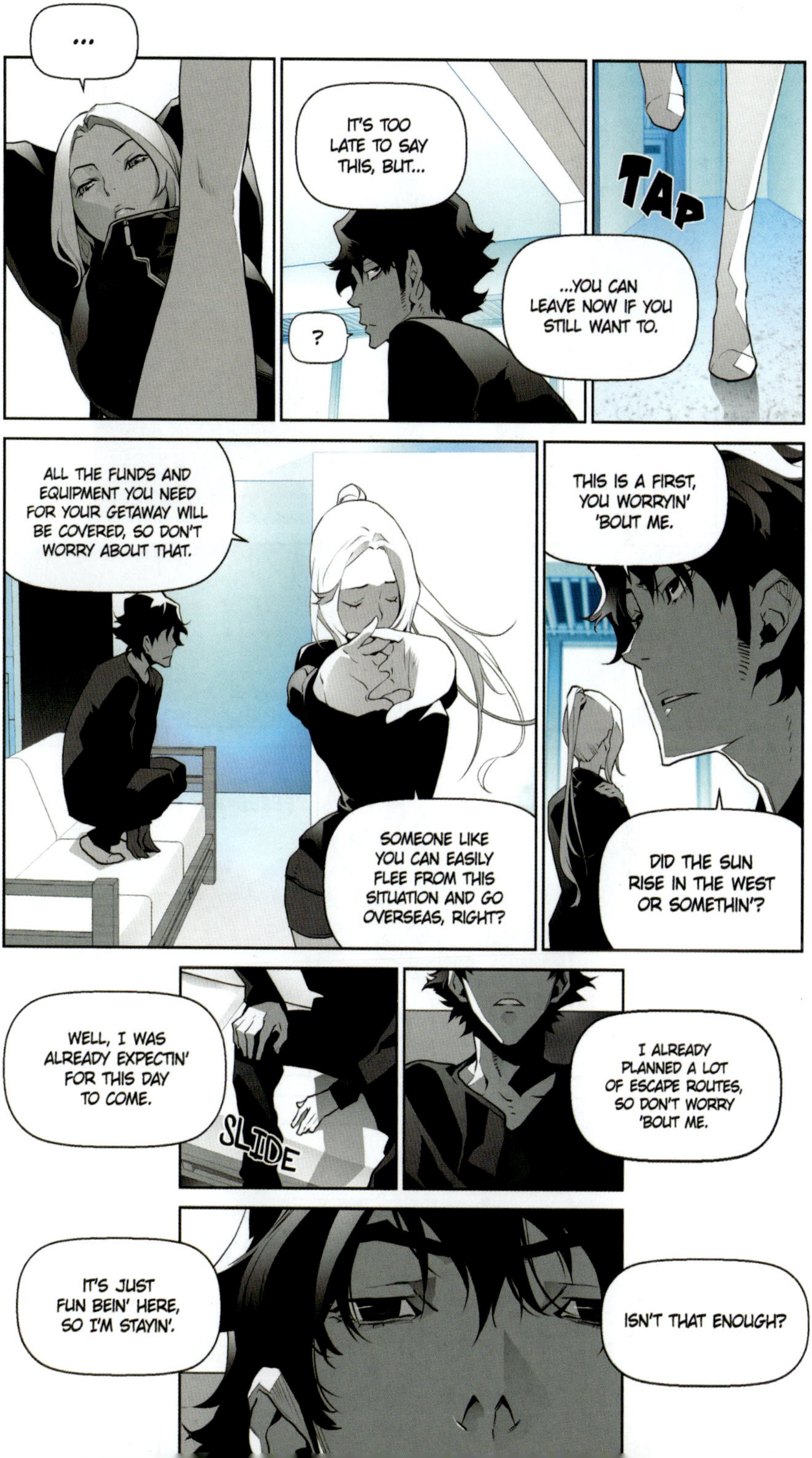
...
IT'S TOO LATE TO SAY THIS, BUT...
?
TAP
...YOU CAN LEAVE NOW IF YOU STILL WANT TO.
ALL THE FUNDS AND EQUIPMENT YOU NEED FOR YOUR GETAWAY WILL BE COVERED, SO DON'T WORRY ABOUT THAT.
SOMEONE LIKE YOU CAN EASILY FLEE FROM THIS SITUATION AND GO OVERSEAS, RIGHT?
THIS IS A FIRST, YOU WORRYIN' 'BOUT ME.
DID THE SUN RISE IN THE WEST OR SOMETHIN'?
WELL, I WAS ALREADY EXPECTIN' FOR THIS DAY TO COME.
SLIDE
I ALREADY PLANNED A LOT OF ESCAPE ROUTES, SO DON'T WORRY 'BOUT ME.
IT'S JUST FUN BEIN' HERE, SO I'M STAYIN'.
ISN'T THAT ENOUGH?

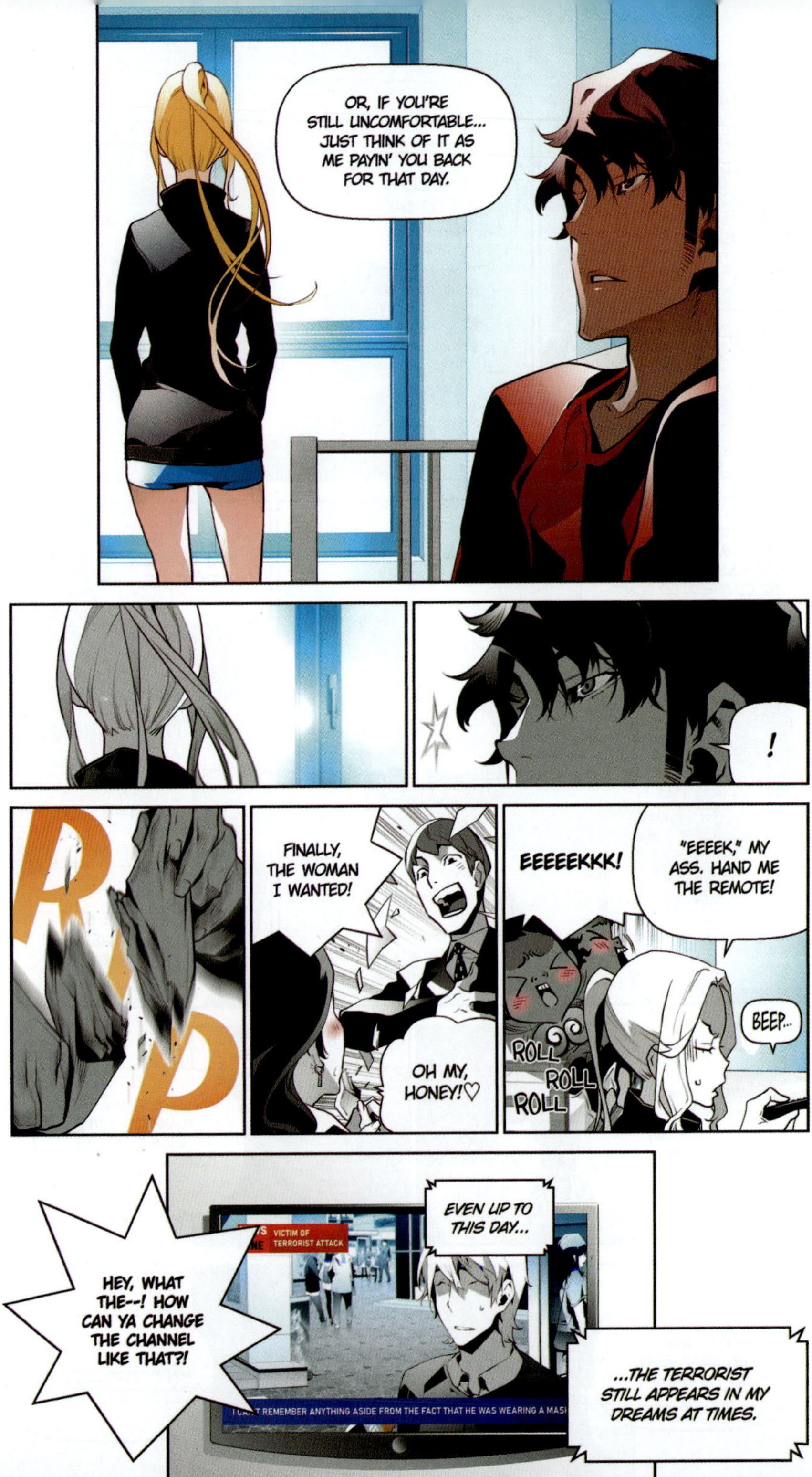

OR, IF YOU'RE STILL UNCOMFORTABLE... JUST THINK OF IT AS ME PAYIN' YOU BACK FOR THAT DAY.
!
RIP
FINALLY, THE WOMAN I WANTED!
OH MY, HONEY!♡
EEEEEKKK!
"EEEEK," MY ASS. HAND ME THE REMOTE!
ROLL ROLL ROLL
BEEP...
VICTIM OF TERRORIST ATTACK
EVEN UP TO THIS DAY...
HEY, WHAT THE--! HOW CAN YA CHANGE THE CHANNEL LIKE THAT?!
REMEMBER ANYTHING ASIDE FROM THE FACT THAT HE WAS WEARING A
...THE TERRORIST STILL APPEARS IN MY DREAMS AT TIMES.

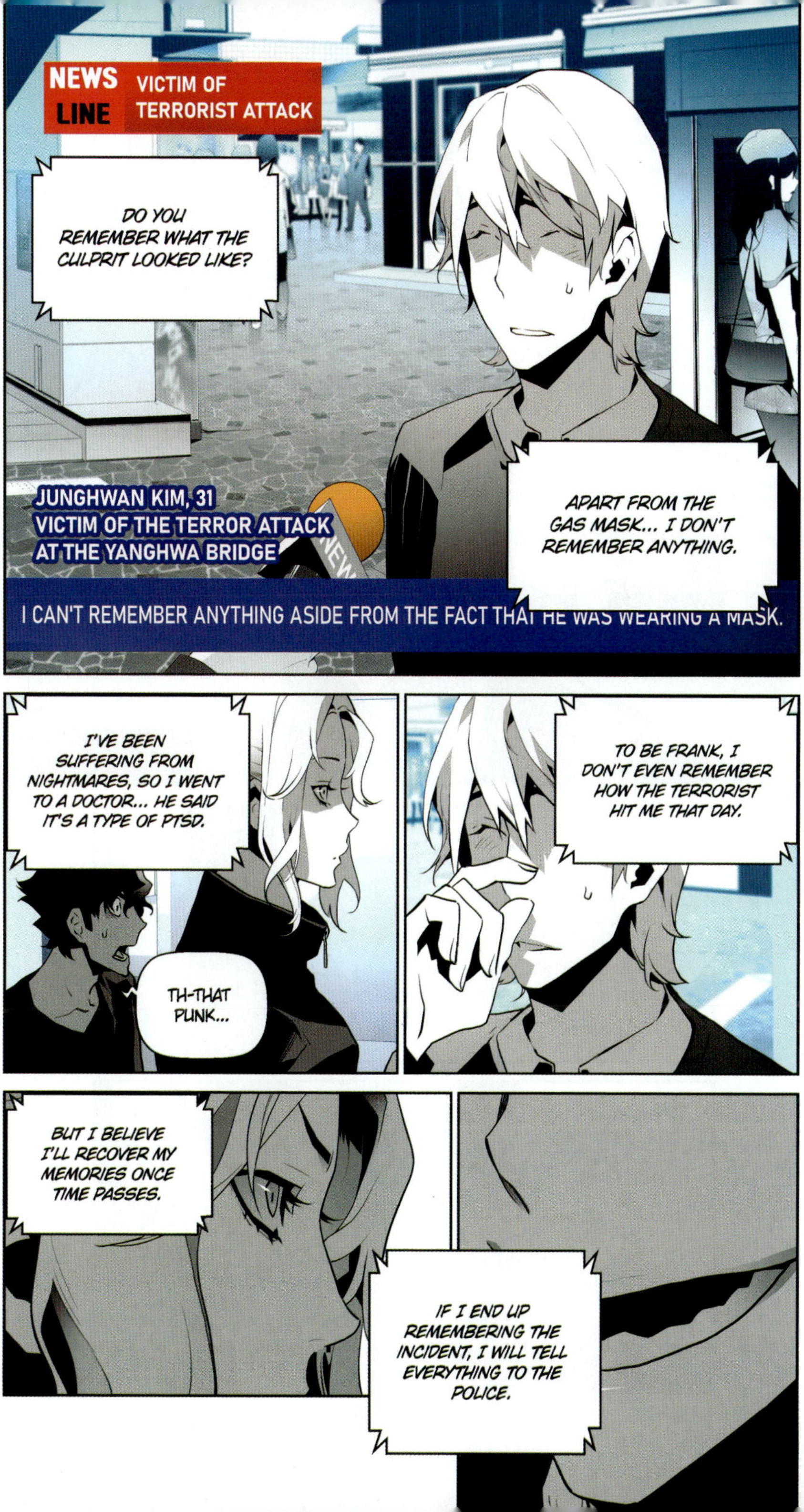
NEWS LINE
VICTIM OF TERRORIST ATTACK
DO YOU REMEMBER WHAT THE CULPRIT LOOKED LIKE?
JUNGHWAN KIM, 31
VICTIM OF THE TERROR ATTACK AT THE YANGHWA BRIDGE
APART FROM THE GAS MASK... I DON'T REMEMBER ANYTHING.
I CAN'T REMEMBER ANYTHING ASIDE FROM THE FACT THAT HE WAS WEARING A MASK.
I'VE BEEN SUFFERING FROM NIGHTMARES, SO I WENT TO A DOCTOR... HE SAID IT'S A TYPE OF PTSD.
TH-THAT PUNK...
TO BE FRANK, I DON'T EVEN REMEMBER HOW THE TERRORIST HIT ME THAT DAY.
BUT I BELIEVE I'LL RECOVER MY MEMORIES ONCE TIME PASSES.
IF I END UP REMEMBERING THE INCIDENT, I WILL TELL EVERYTHING TO THE POLICE.

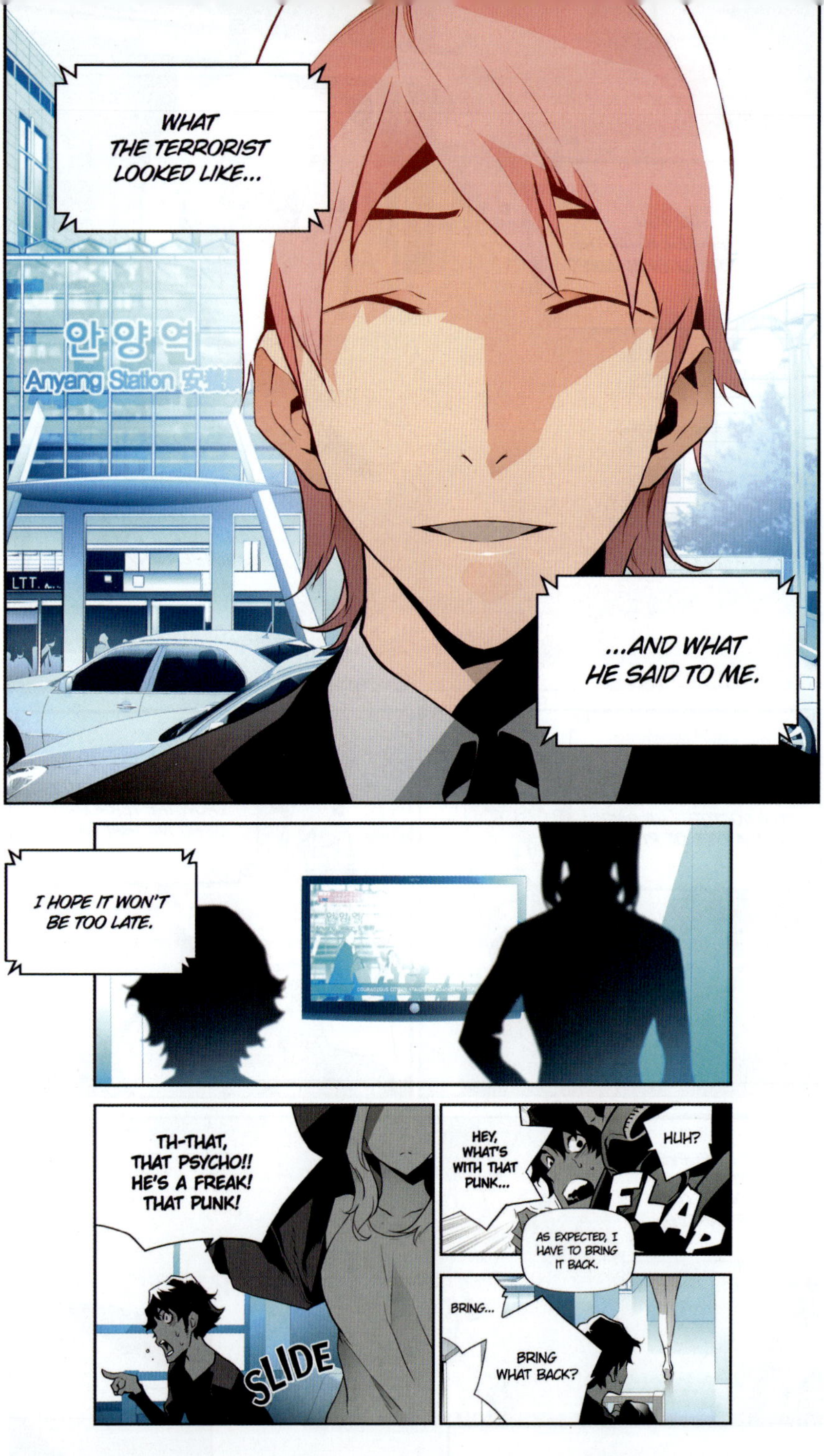
WHAT THE TERRORIST LOOKED LIKE...
안양역
Anyang Station
...AND WHAT HE SAID TO ME.
I HOPE IT WON'T BE TOO LATE.
TH-THAT, THAT PSYCHO!! HE'S A FREAK! THAT PUNK!
SLIDE
HEY, WHAT'S WITH THAT PUNK...
HUH?
FLAP
AS EXPECTED, I HAVE TO BRING IT BACK.
BRING...
BRING WHAT BACK?

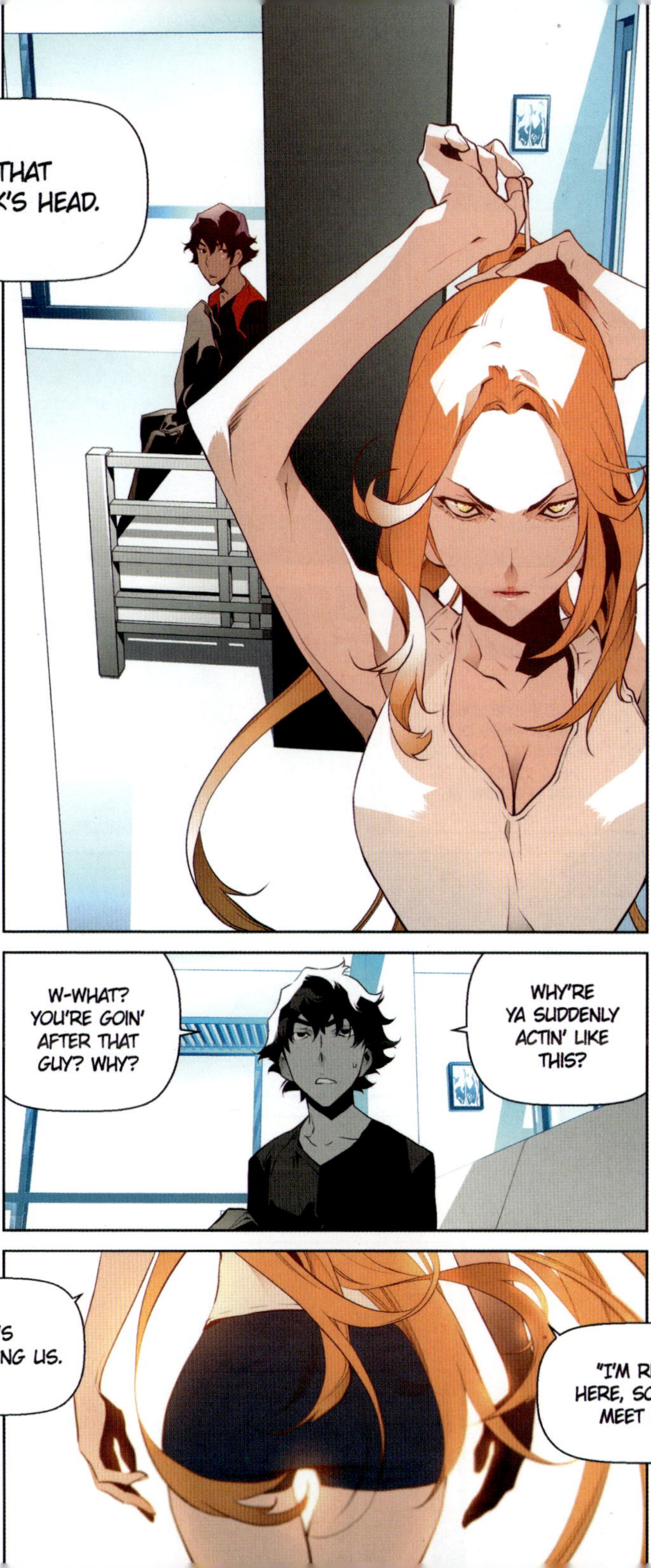
THAT PUNK'S HEAD.
W-WHAT? YOU'RE GOIN' AFTER THAT GUY? WHY?
WHY'RE YA SUDDENLY ACTIN' LIKE THIS?
HE'S PROVOKING US.
"I'M RIGHT HERE, SO LET'S MEET UP."

US? WHY?	SAY IT!!
...	I'M ASKING IF THAT INCIDENT WAS ALSO YOUR DOING!!

BECAUSE OF THAT?

BUT IF THE YOUNG MASTER FINDS OUT YA WENT AFTER THAT GUY, HE'LL THROW A FIT AND FOLLOW YA.

JUST STOP HIM FROM GOING FOR TODAY.

PLEASE.

SQUEAK

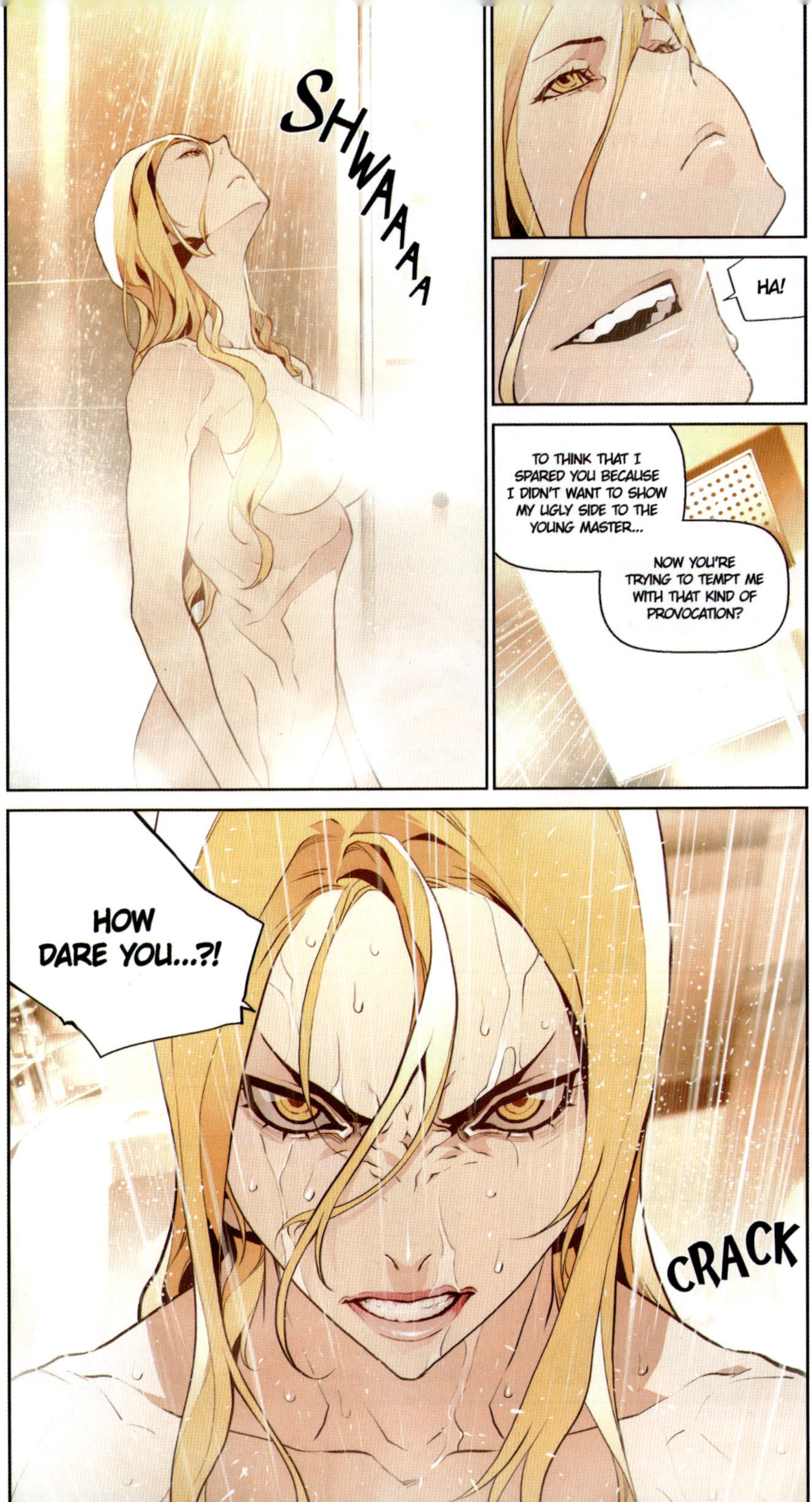
SHWAAAA
HA!
TO THINK THAT I SPARED YOU BECAUSE I DIDN'T WANT TO SHOW MY UGLY SIDE TO THE YOUNG MASTER...
NOW YOU'RE TRYING TO TEMPT ME WITH THAT KIND OF PROVOCATION?
HOW DARE YOU...?!
CRACK

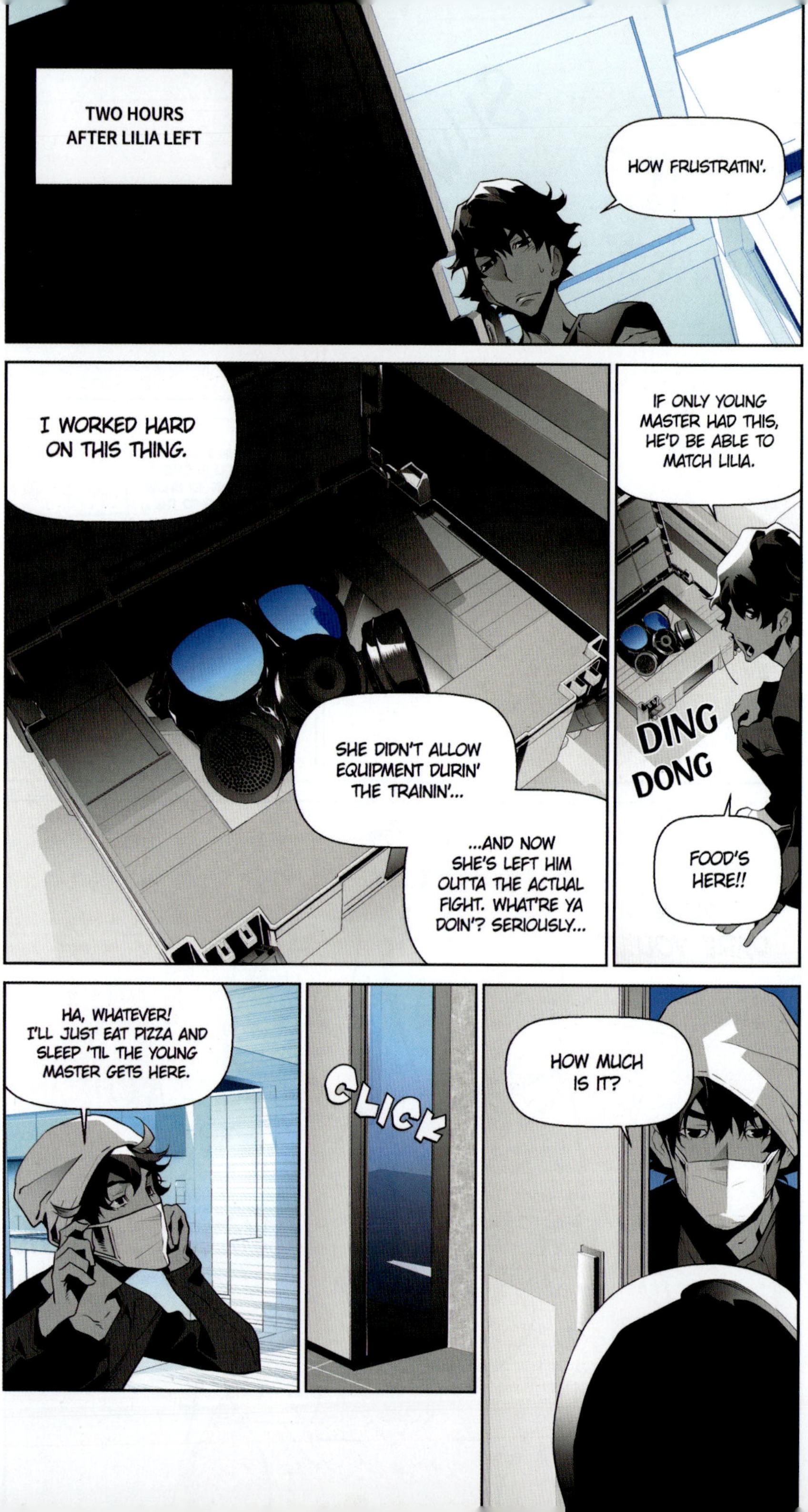
TWO HOURS
AFTER LILIA LEFT
HOW FRUSTRATIN'.
I WORKED HARD ON THIS THING.
SHE DIDN'T ALLOW EQUIPMENT DURIN' THE TRAININ'...
...AND NOW SHE'S LEFT HIM OUTTA THE ACTUAL FIGHT. WHAT'RE YA DOIN'? SERIOUSLY...
IF ONLY YOUNG MASTER HAD THIS, HE'D BE ABLE TO MATCH LILIA.
DING DONG
FOOD'S HERE!!
HA, WHATEVER! I'LL JUST EAT PIZZA AND SLEEP 'TIL THE YOUNG MASTER GETS HERE.
CLICK
HOW MUCH IS IT?

H-HELLO, I'M REPORTER GARAM HAN FROM CHO KOOK DAILY.

IS JUNGWOO MIN TH-- OH?

REPORTER?!

...

HUH?

IS... THIS NOT JUNGWOO MIN'S HOUSE?

IS HE A FOREIGNER? I THINK I'VE SEEN HIM SOMEWHERE.

SLAM

IS THAT GUY... THE ONE FROM THE WANTED LIST?

THUD THUD THUD

WAIT A SECOND! PLEASE OPEN THE DOOR!!

EXCUSE ME!!

HELLO? I'M TALKING TO THE POLICE, RIGHT?!

TERROR MAN

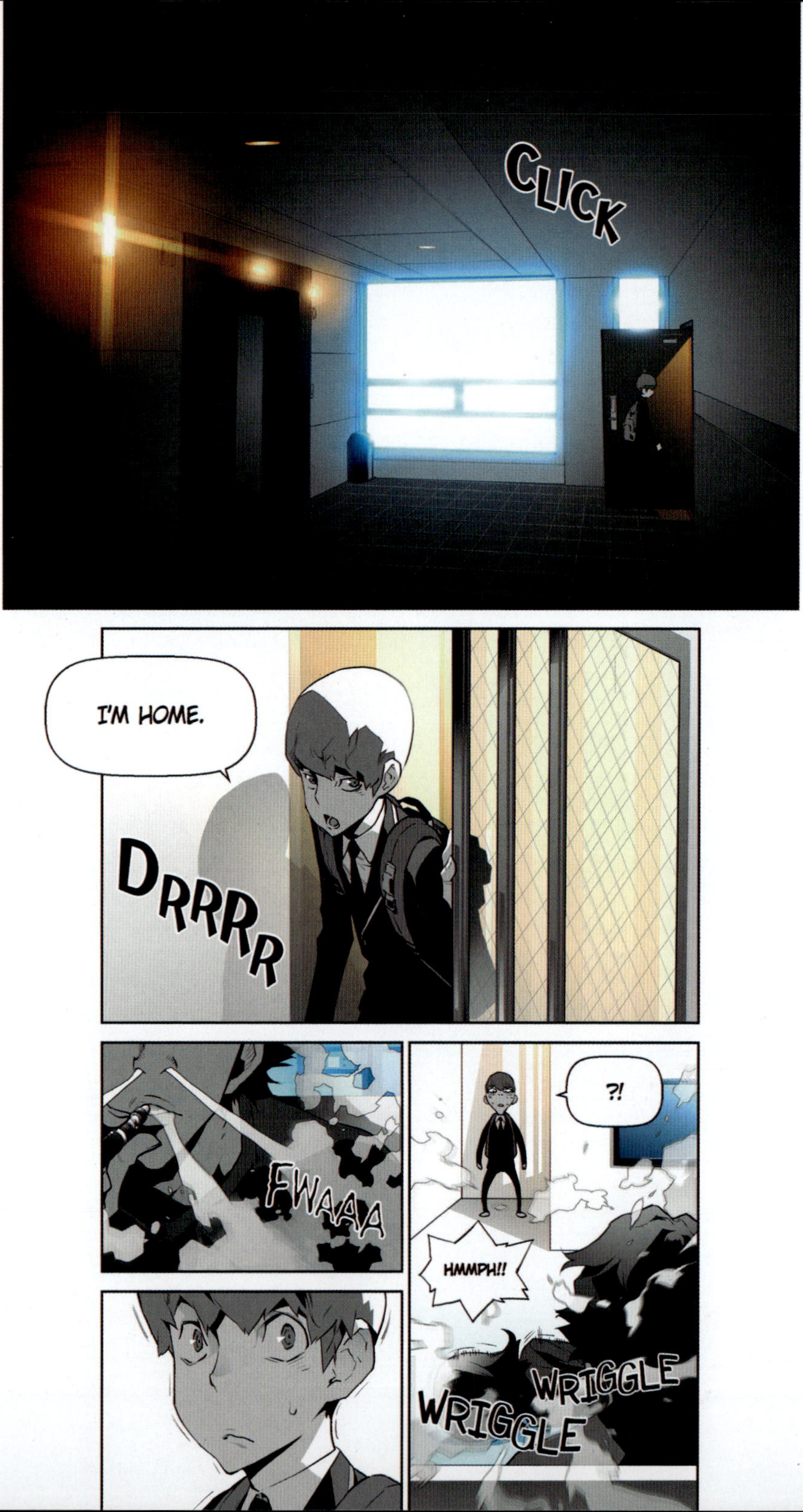
CLICK
I'M HOME.
DRRRRR
FWAAAA
?!
HMMPH!!
WRIGGLE
WRIGGLE

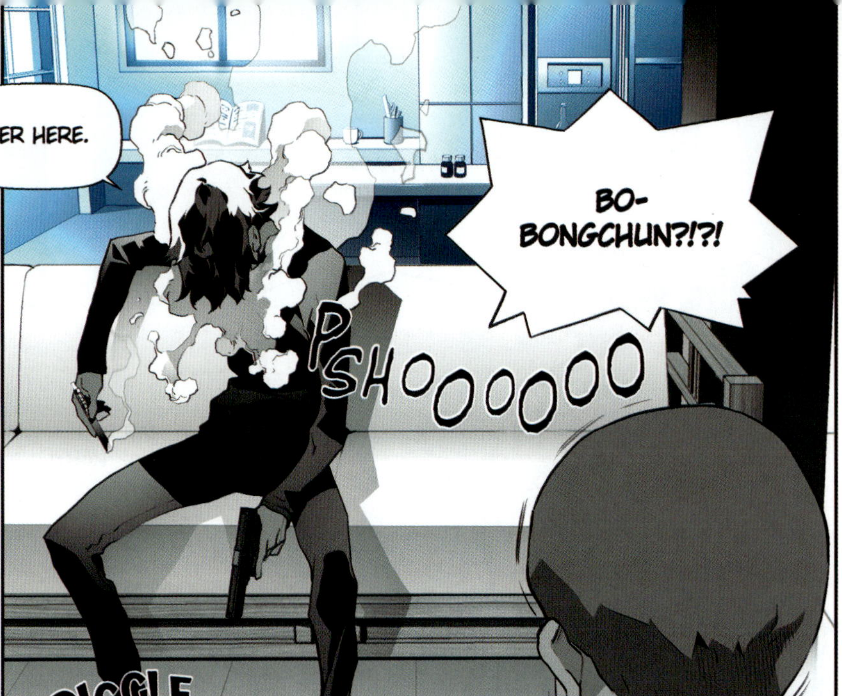
YER HERE.
BO-
BONGCHUN?!?!
PSHOOOOOOO
WRIGGLE
WRIGGLE
HUP!
HUP!
HUP!
HUP!
HUPP!

TERROR MAN

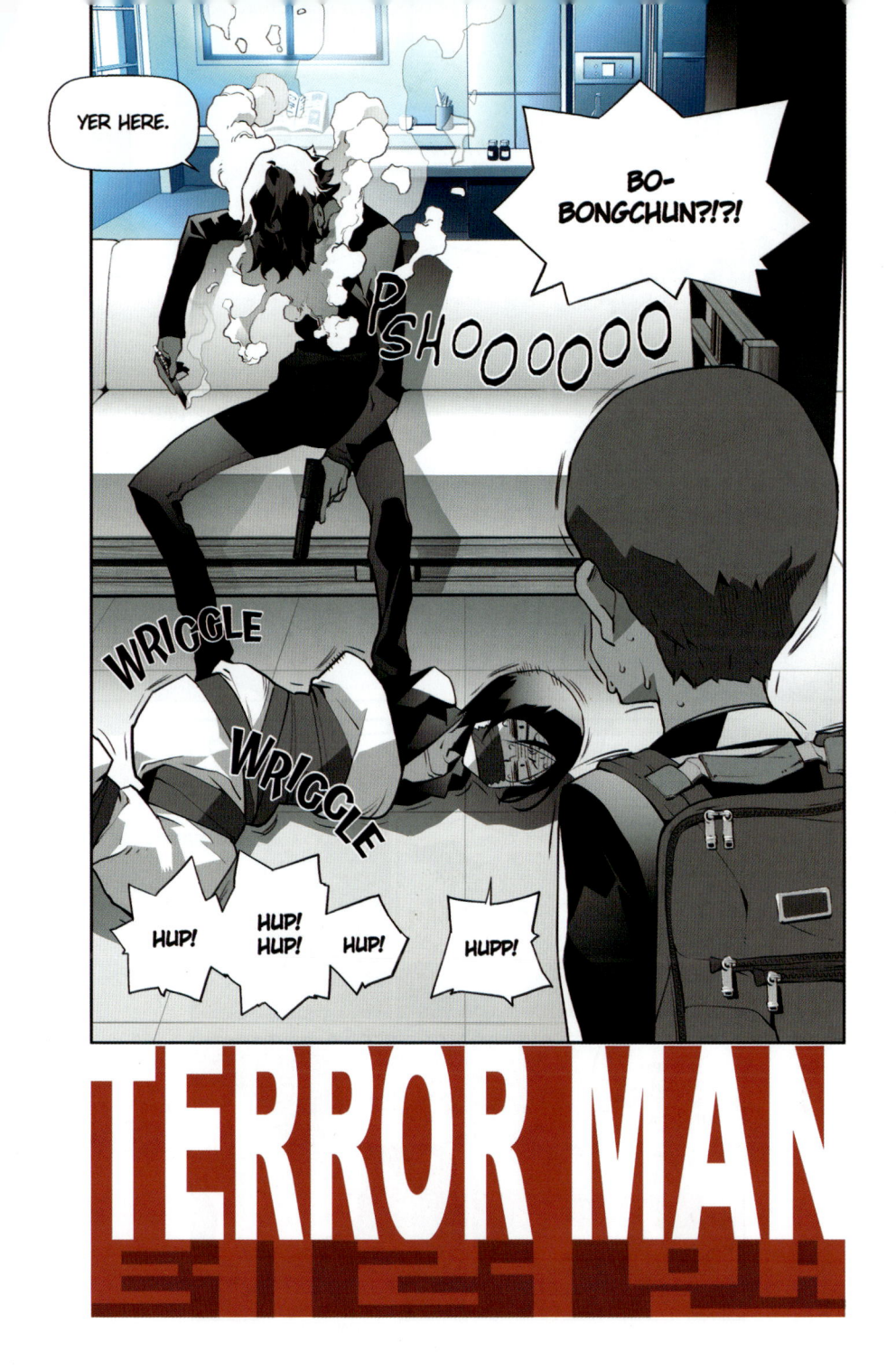

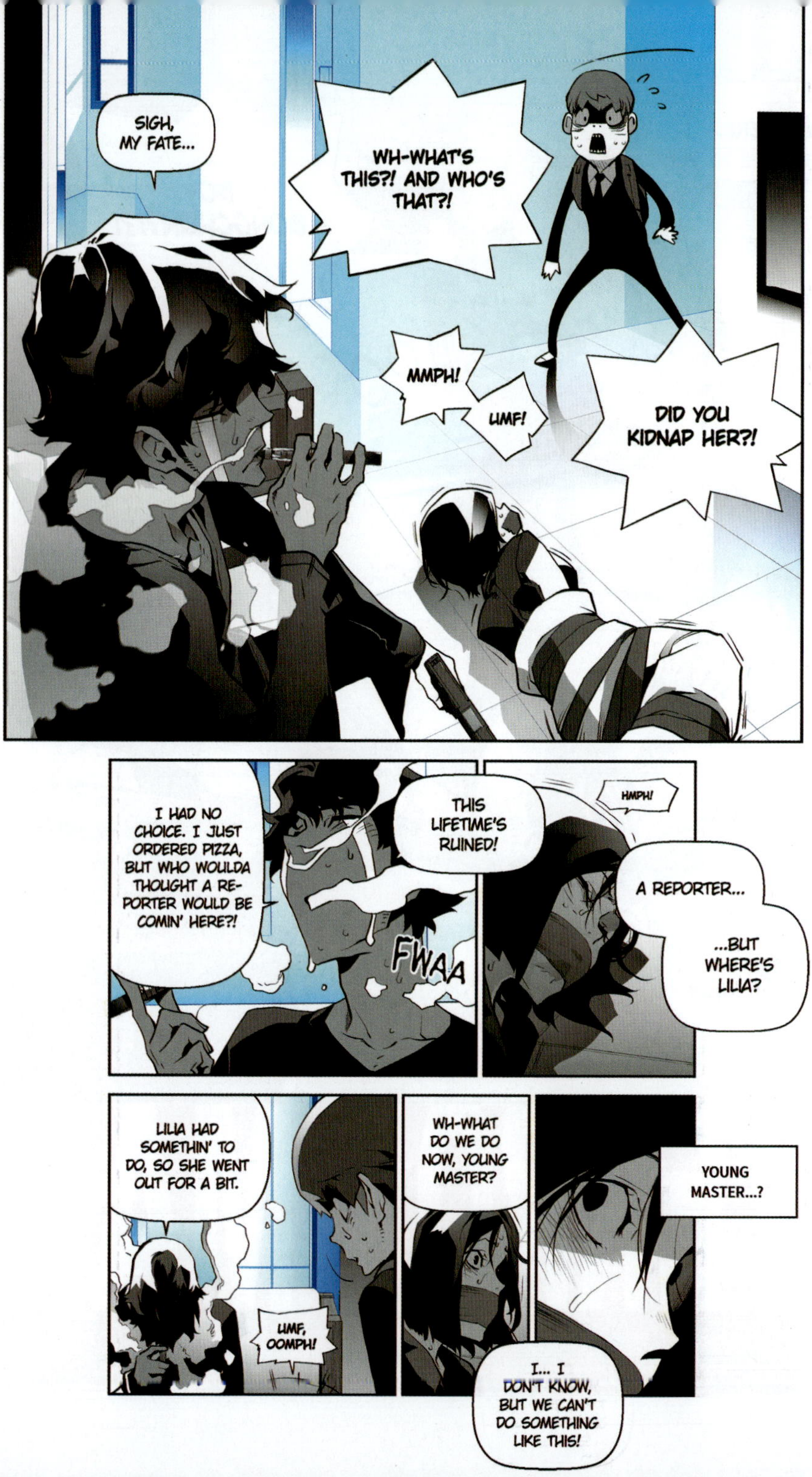
SIGH, MY FATE...
WH-WHAT'S THIS?! AND WHO'S THAT?!
MMPH!
UMF!
DID YOU KIDNAP HER?!
I HAD NO CHOICE. I JUST ORDERED PIZZA, BUT WHO WOULDA THOUGHT A RE-PORTER WOULD BE COMIN' HERE?!
THIS LIFETIME'S RUINED!
FWAA
HMPH!
A REPORTER...
...BUT WHERE'S LILIA?
LILIA HAD SOMETHIN' TO DO, SO SHE WENT OUT FOR A BIT.
UMF, OOMPH!
WH-WHAT DO WE DO NOW, YOUNG MASTER?
YOUNG MASTER...?
I... I DON'T KNOW, BUT WE CAN'T DO SOMETHING LIKE THIS!

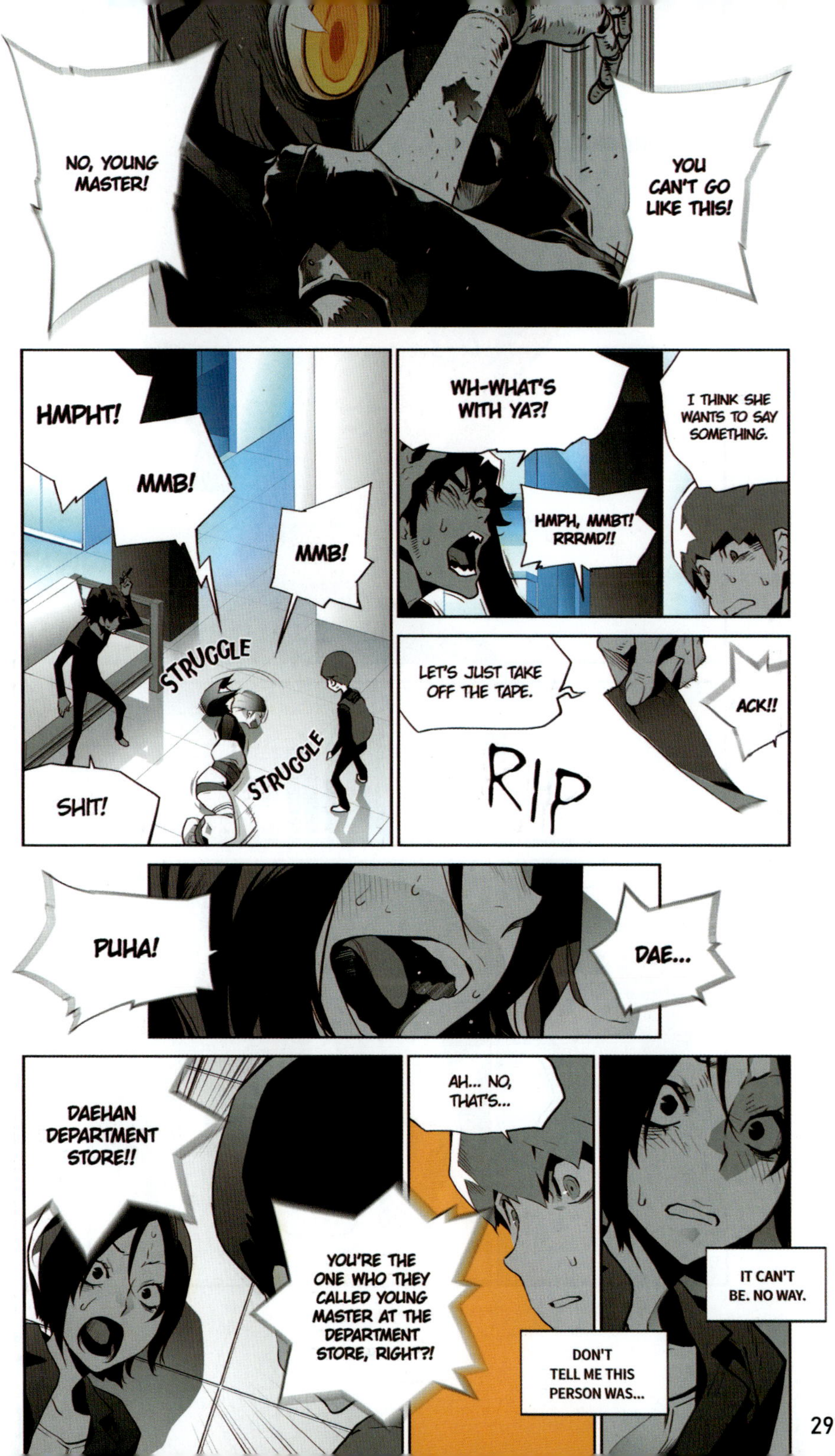
NO, YOUNG MASTER!
YOU CAN'T GO LIKE THIS!
HMPHT!
MMB!
MMB!
STRUGGLE
STRUGGLE
SHIT!
WH-WHAT'S WITH YA?!
HMPH, MMBT! RRRMD!!
I THINK SHE WANTS TO SAY SOMETHING.
LET'S JUST TAKE OFF THE TAPE.
ACK!!
RIP
PUHA!
DAE...
DAEHAN DEPARTMENT STORE!!
YOU'RE THE ONE WHO THEY CALLED YOUNG MASTER AT THE DEPARTMENT STORE, RIGHT?!
AH... NO, THAT'S...
DON'T TELL ME THIS PERSON WAS...
IT CAN'T BE. NO WAY.

THE TERRORIST...

...IS A STUDENT?

...

SO...

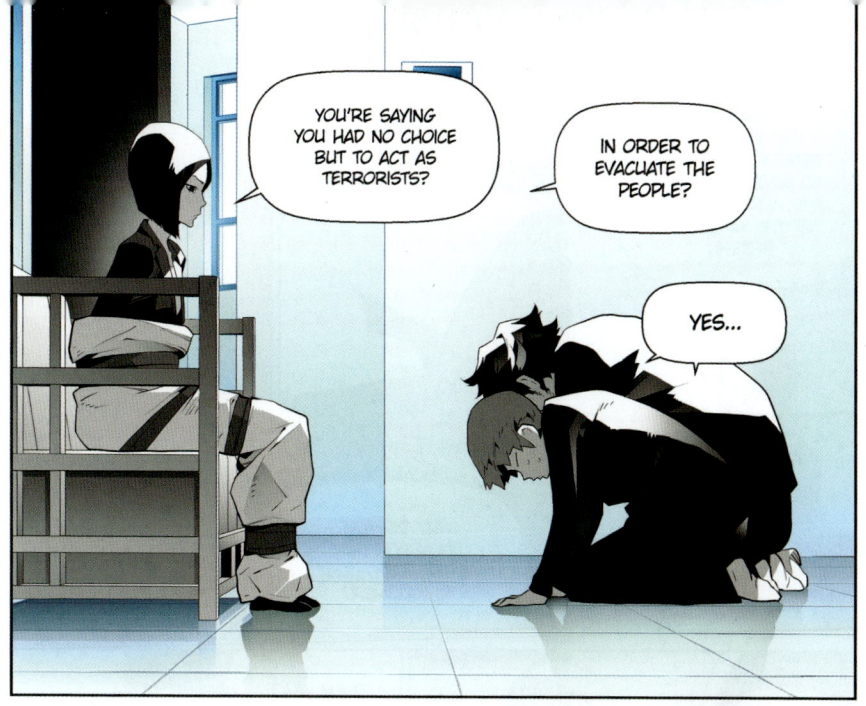

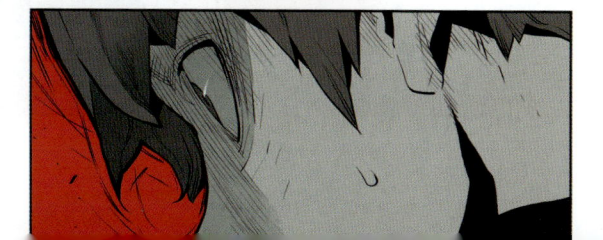

"YOU'RE SAYING YOU HAD NO CHOICE BUT TO ACT AS TERRORISTS?"

"IN ORDER TO EVACUATE THE PEOPLE?"

"YES..."

"YOU MIGHT NOT BELIEVE US, BUT THIS FRIEND OF OURS RIGHT HERE HAS SOME SUPERPOWER THAT LETS HIM SEE FUTURE ACCIDENTS."

"SO HE KNEW THAT THE DEPARTMENT STORE AND THE BRIDGE WERE GONNA COLLAPSE, BUT THERE WAS NO WAY TO EVACUATE THE PEOPLE."

"WHAT ARE YOU SAYING ALL OF A SUDDEN?"

"A SUPERPOWER...? WHAT?"

"WHAT IN THE WORLD...? FORGET IT. LET'S TALK ABOUT THAT LATER."

"THEN..."

"...WHY DID YOU KILL MS. SUNG?"

293

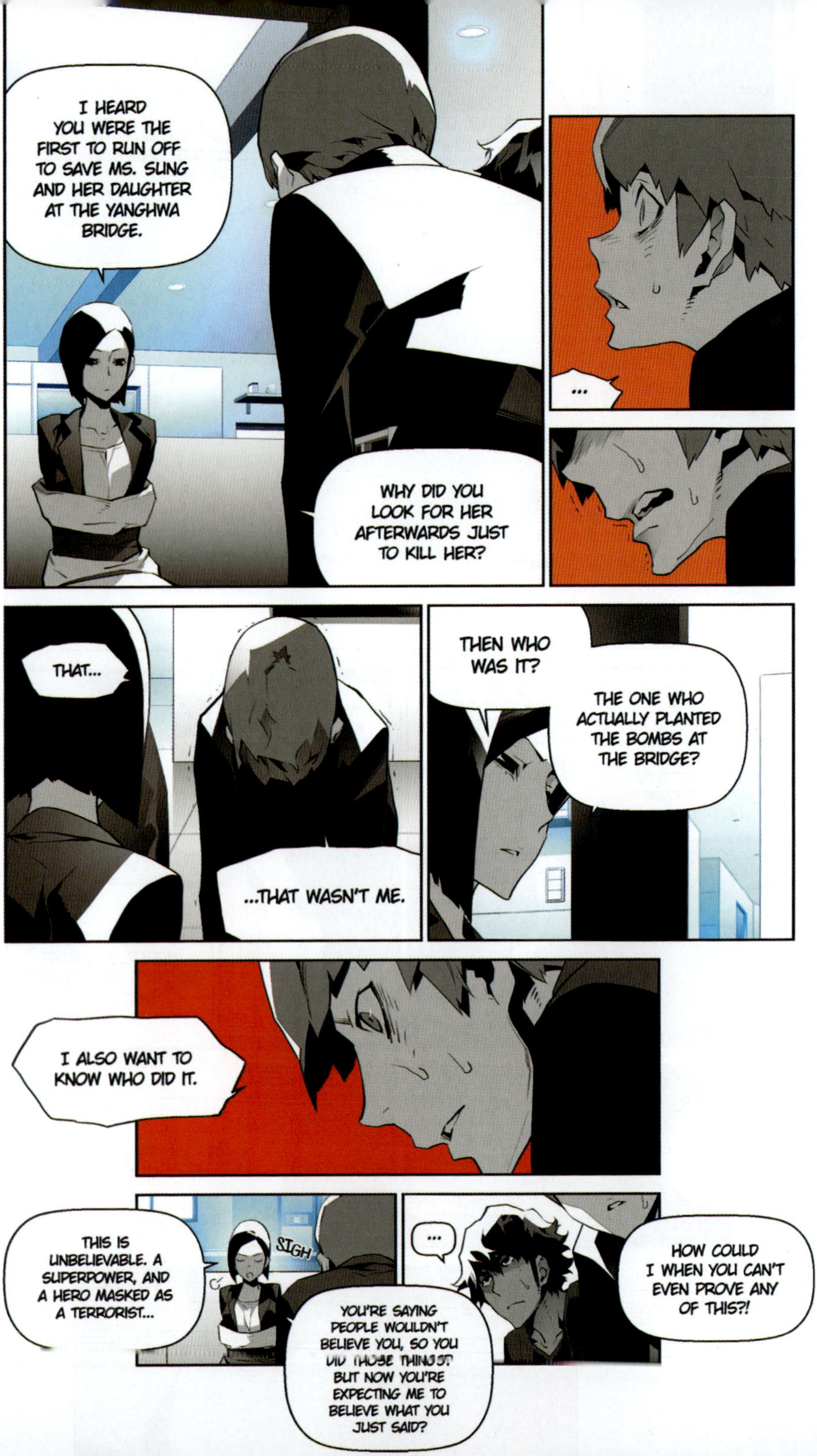
I HEARD YOU WERE THE FIRST TO RUN OFF TO SAVE MS. SUNG AND HER DAUGHTER AT THE YANGHWA BRIDGE.
WHY DID YOU LOOK FOR HER AFTERWARDS JUST TO KILL HER?
...
THAT...
...THAT WASN'T ME.
THEN WHO WAS IT?
THE ONE WHO ACTUALLY PLANTED THE BOMBS AT THE BRIDGE?
I ALSO WANT TO KNOW WHO DID IT.
THIS IS UNBELIEVABLE. A SUPERPOWER, AND A HERO MASKED AS A TERRORIST...
SIGH
YOU'RE SAYING PEOPLE WOULDN'T BELIEVE YOU, SO YOU DID THOSE THINGS? BUT NOW YOU'RE EXPECTING ME TO BELIEVE WHAT YOU JUST SAID?
...
HOW COULD I WHEN YOU CAN'T EVEN PROVE ANY OF THIS?!

THE REAL CULPRIT...

THERE'S NO OTHER WAY. ALTHOUGH I FEEL BAD FOR LILIA...

...IS AT ANYANG.

LILIA'S ALSO IN THAT AREA.

WHAT?! WHAT DO YOU MEAN?!

THINK ABOUT IT. IF WE WERE THE REAL CRIMINALS, YA THINK WE'D BE HERE EXPLAININ' THIS TO YA?

WE'RE GONNA SHOW YA WE'RE NOT THE REAL CULPRITS, SO COME WITH US.

...

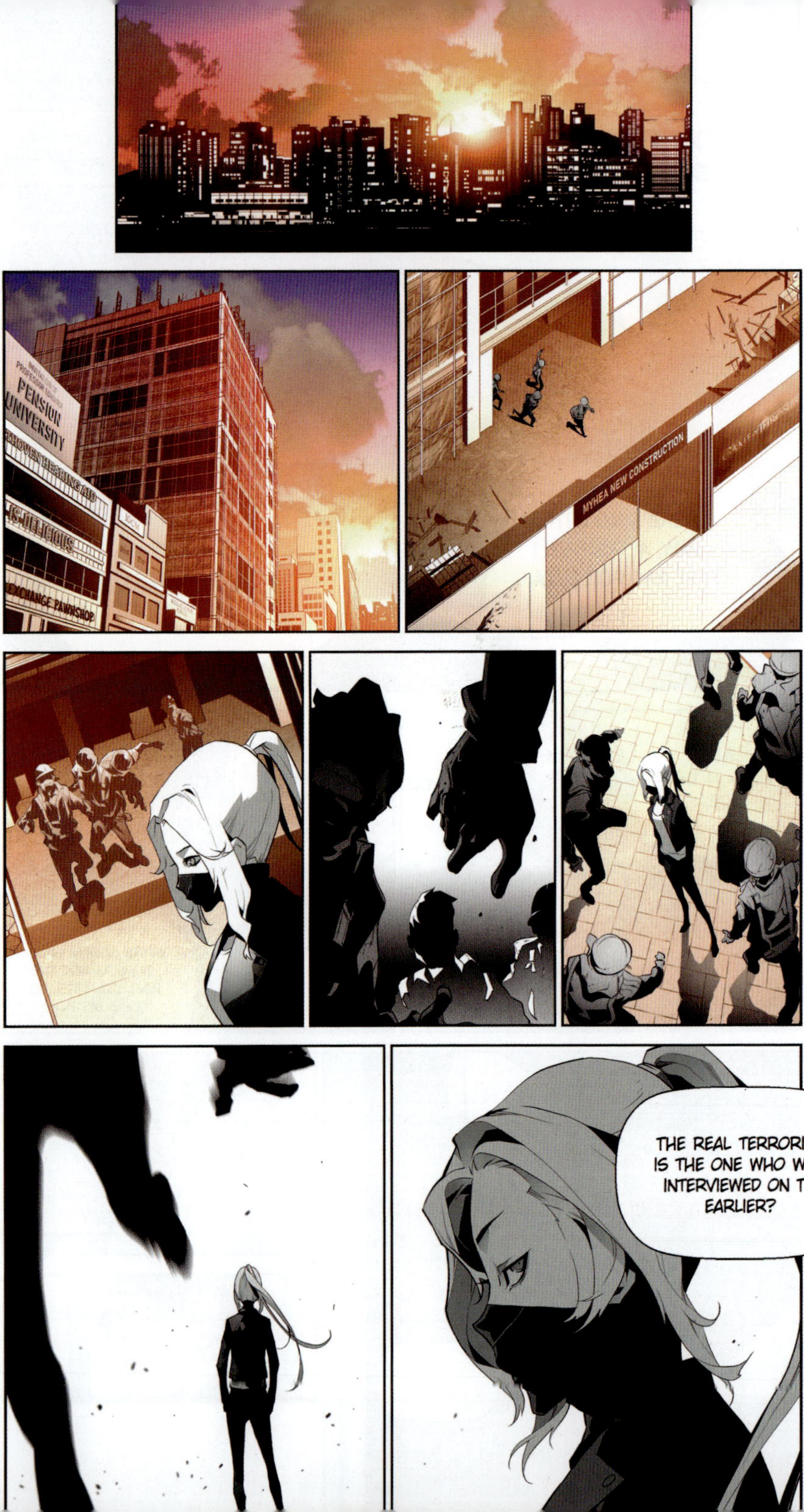
PENSION UNIVERSITY
EXCHANGE PAWNSHOP
MYHEA NEW CONSTRUCTION
THE REAL TERRORIST IS THE ONE WHO WAS INTERVIEWED ON TV EARLIER?

THAT'S RIGHT. IF YA THINK ABOUT IT, WE'RE ALSO VICTIMS HERE. I EVEN GOT BEAT NEAR TO DEATH BY THAT PUNK.

THIS IS WHY I HATE SEOUL. LOOK AT THIS TRAFFIC.

EVERYONE'S GETTIN' OFF WORK. OF COURSE THERE'D BE TRAFFIC.

IT'S ALL HARD TO BELIEVE.

EVEN LILIA WENT WITHOUT A WORD... WHY...?

AH... THANK YOU... FOR BELIEVING US.

WHAT ARE YOU SAYING?

I CAN'T BELIEVE WHAT YOU'RE SAYING. THAT'S WHY I'M COMING ALONG WITH YOU.

...

FIRST OF ALL, THAT SUPERPOWER... IS IT EVEN REAL?

CAN YOU SHOW ME?

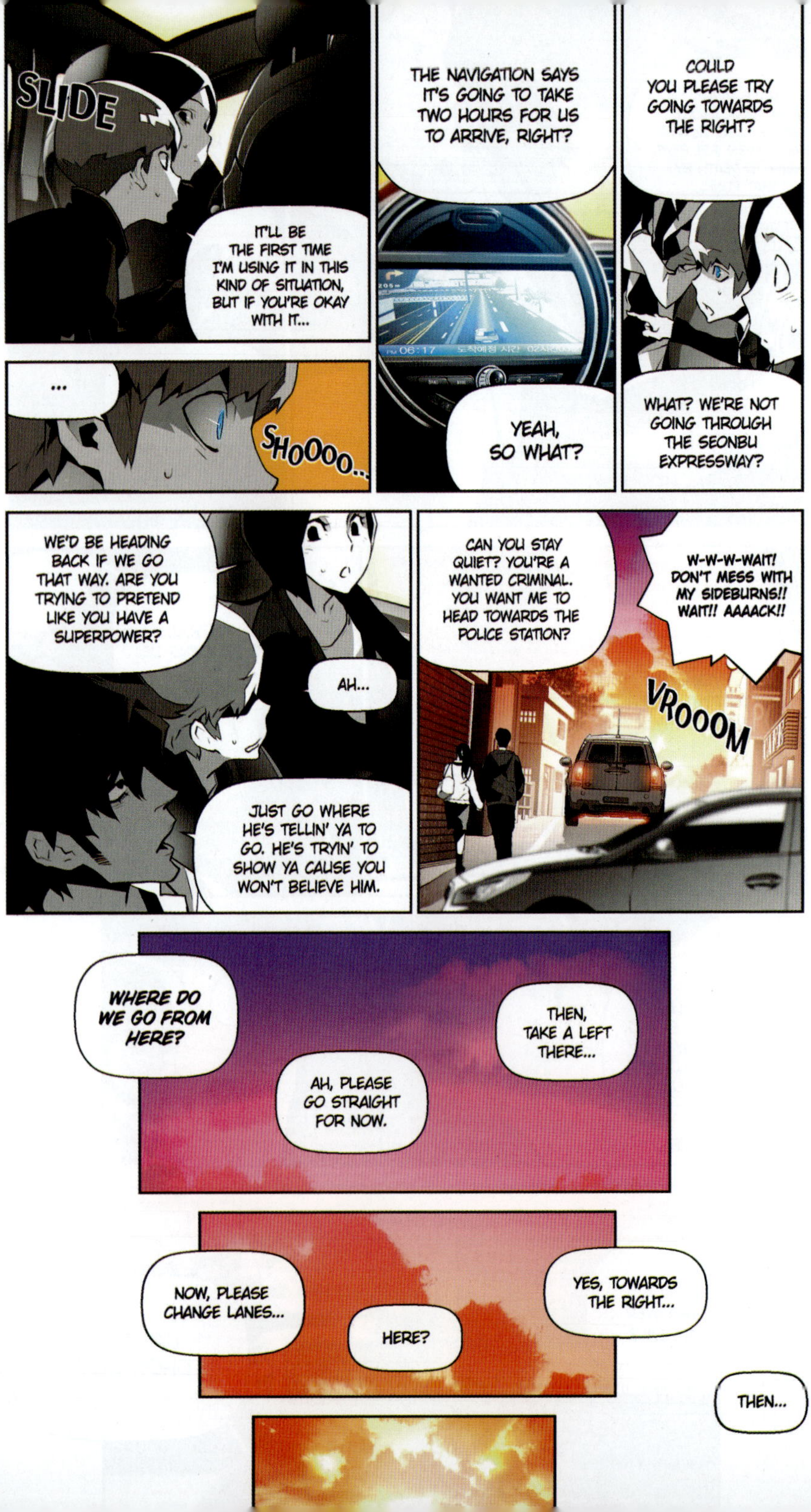
SLIDE
IT'LL BE THE FIRST TIME I'M USING IT IN THIS KIND OF SITUATION, BUT IF YOU'RE OKAY WITH IT...
THE NAVIGATION SAYS IT'S GOING TO TAKE TWO HOURS FOR US TO ARRIVE, RIGHT?
COULD YOU PLEASE TRY GOING TOWARDS THE RIGHT?
...
SHOOOO...
YEAH, SO WHAT?
WHAT? WE'RE NOT GOING THROUGH THE SEONBU EXPRESSWAY?
WE'D BE HEADING BACK IF WE GO THAT WAY. ARE YOU TRYING TO PRETEND LIKE YOU HAVE A SUPERPOWER?
AH...
JUST GO WHERE HE'S TELLIN' YA TO GO. HE'S TRYIN' TO SHOW YA CAUSE YOU WON'T BELIEVE HIM.
CAN YOU STAY QUIET? YOU'RE A WANTED CRIMINAL. YOU WANT ME TO HEAD TOWARDS THE POLICE STATION?
W-W-W-WAIT! DON'T MESS WITH MY SIDEBURNS!! WAIT!! AAAACK!!
VROOOM
WHERE DO WE GO FROM HERE?
AH, PLEASE GO STRAIGHT FOR NOW.
THEN, TAKE A LEFT THERE...
NOW, PLEASE CHANGE LANES...
HERE?
YES, TOWARDS THE RIGHT...
THEN...

SCREECH

WE GOT HERE IN AN HOUR?! DOES HE REALLY HAVE A SUPERPOWER?!

...

GOOD JOB.

PHEW...

HERE.

??

SLIDE

IF WE ACTUALLY RUN INTO THE REAL TERRORIST, MAKE SURE TO RECORD EVERYTHING.

I'LL BE FOLLOWING YOU QUIETLY FROM BEHIND...	...SO, IF YOU'RE REALLY INNOCENT, DON'T EVEN THINK OF SECRETLY RUNNING AWAY.

W-WHAT ABOUT ME?!

YOUR FACE HAS ALREADY BEEN REVEALED. YOU'RE NOT GOING OUT THERE.

...

AH, SERIOUSLY?! YOUNG MASTER...!!

CLICK

THIS IS MY NEWLY DEVELOPED GAS MASK. IF NEEDED, USE IT IMMEDIATELY.

THANK YOU.

IT'S PRETTY GOOD. YER GONNA BE SHOCKED ONCE YA TRY IT OUT.

THERE'S ALSO A COMMUNICATION FEATURE INSTALLED...

...SO I'LL TELL YA ALL ABOUT ITS NEW FEATURES WHEN YA PUT IT ON.

NEW FEATURES?

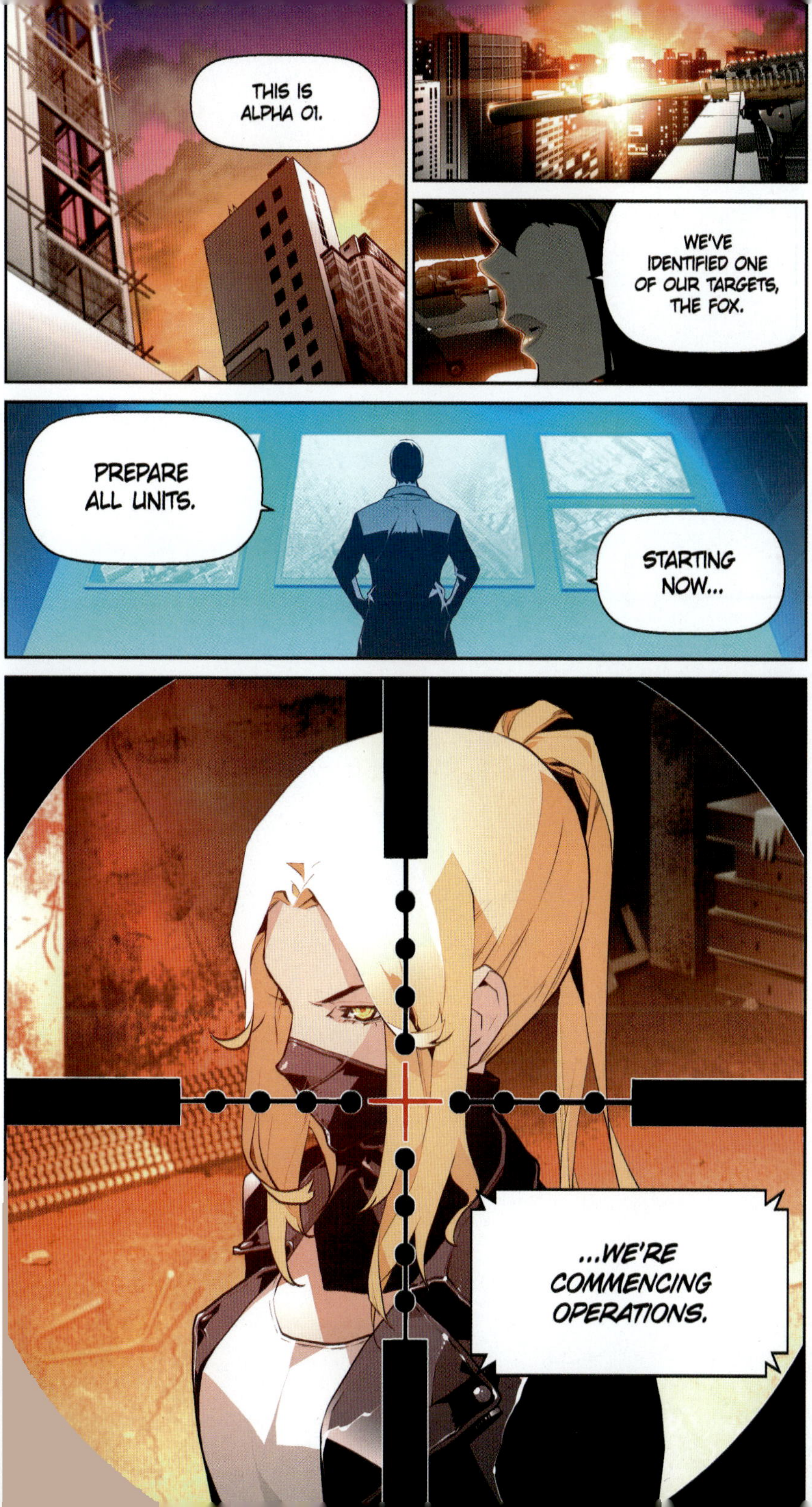
THIS IS ALPHA 01.
WE'VE IDENTIFIED ONE OF OUR TARGETS, THE FOX.
PREPARE ALL UNITS.
STARTING NOW...
...WE'RE COMMENCING OPERATIONS.

TERROR MAN

TERROR MAN

TERROR MAN VOLUME 1

author DONGWOO HAN
illustration JINHO KO
planning YLAB CO. LTD.
SEJONG OH, SOYEON KIM, HANNA PARK,
YOONHA JUNG, SOWON JUNG, JUN LEE, SEONWOO YOON
design INNO WAVE | innowave-design.com

FOR ABLAZE

managing editor RICH YOUNG
editor KEVIN KETNER
associate editor AMY JACKSON
designers JULIA STEZOVSKY & RODOLFO MURAGUCHI

TERROR MAN Vol. 1 Published by Ablaze Publishing, 11222 SE Main St. #22906 Portland, OR 97269. TERROR MAN Vol 1© 2016 Dongwoo Han and Jinho Ko, YLAB. All rights reserved. Original Korean webtoon edition published by YLAB Corporation. English translation rights arranged by YLAB Corporation through Topaz Agency. ABLAZE TM & © 2023 ABLAZE LLC. All rights reserved. All name, characters, events, and locales in this publication are entirely fictional. Any resemblance to actual persons (living or dead), events or places, without satiric intent is coincidental. No portion of this book may be reproduced by any means (digital or print) without the written permission of Ablaze Publishing except for review purposes. Printed in China. This book may be purchased for educational, business, or promotional use in bulk. For sales information, advertising opportunities or licensing, email: info@ablazepublishing.com

Publisher's Cataloging-in-Publication data

Names: Dongwoo Han, author. | Jinho Ko, artist.
Title: Terror man , vol. 1 / written by Dongwoo Han; art by Jinho Ko.
Description: Portland, OR: Ablaze, 2023.
Identifiers: ISBN: 978-1-68497-131-2
Subjects: LCSH Psychics--Comic books, strips, etc. | Korean fiction--Translations into English. | Psychological fiction. | Graphic novels. | BISAC COMICS & GRAPHIC NOVELS / Manga / Supernatural
Classification: LCC PN6790.K63 .W66 T47 v.1 2022 | DDC 741.5--dc23

/ablazepub   @AblazePub   @AblazePub

www.ABLAZE.net

To find a comics shop in your area go to:
www.comicshoplocator.com

TERROR MAN

WRITTEN BY **DONGWOO HAN**
ILLUSTRATED BY **JINHO KO**

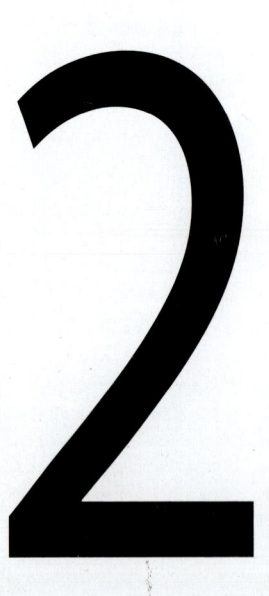

2

ABLAZE MANGA

YLAB

COMING SOON...